D1348431

90710 000 391 261

Praise for *The Fire Starters*

'Shot through this gripping tangle of events is real insight. Carson explores our complexities with her tremendously keen eye.'
AIMEE BENDER

'Spectacular . . . Dark, beautiful, at once grittily real and wildly magical. Insanely alluring.'
DONAL RYAN

'Jan Carson seems to have invented a new Belfast in this gripping, surprising, exhilarating novel.'
RODDY DOYLE

'With her idiosyncratic blend of warm intelligence, dark humour, and magic realism, Jan Carson brings us a singular portrait of a city and its people struggling with questions of guilt, responsibility, and the limits of love.'
CARYS DAVIES

'Gripping, affecting, surprising. I inhaled it.'
LISA McINERNEY

'Shimmering with wit, simmering with an incandescent rage, shot through with a seam of wild magic, *The Fire Starters* is a powerful, disturbing portrait of East Belfast and its people and its hope for the future . . . I won't be the only reader to proclaim that, in the best way possible, Jan Carson is on fire.'
LUCY CALDWELL

'Irresistible, vivid and gripping.'
CAOILINN HUGHES

'A brilliant, wry novel, fizzing with energy.'
BARNEY NORRIS

'Both a fiercely gripping thriller and a beautifully twisted fable, *The Fire Starters* is an electrifying blast of Belfast Gothic: a luminous, furious vision of a city at war with itself.'
MICHAEL HUGHES

Also by Jan Carson

Malcolm Orange Disappears

STORIES
Children's Children
Postcard Stories

The Fire Starters

Jan Carson

doubleday

TRANSWORLD IRELAND
Penguin Random House Ireland,
Morrison Chambers, 32 Nassau Street, Dublin 2, Ireland
www.transworldireland.ie

Transworld Ireland is part of the Penguin Random House group of companies
whose addresses can be found at global.penguinrandomhouse.com

First published in the UK and Ireland in 2019
by Doubleday Ireland
an imprint of Transworld Publishers

Copyright © Jan Carson 2019

Jan Carson has asserted her right under the Copyright,
Designs and Patents Act 1988 to be identified as the author of this work.

This book is a work of fiction and, except in the case of historical fact,
any resemblance to actual persons, living or dead, is purely coincidental.

Every effort has been made to obtain the necessary permissions with
reference to copyright material, both illustrative and quoted. We apologize
for any omissions in this respect and will be pleased to make the
appropriate acknowledgements in any future edition.

A CIP catalogue record for this book
is available from the British Library.

ISBNs 9780857525741 (hb)
9781781620465 (tpb)

Typeset in 11.25/14.5 pt Adobe Garamond by Jouve (UK), Milton Keynes
Printed and bound in Great Britain by Clays Ltd, Elcograf S.p.A.

Penguin Random House is committed to a sustainable
future for our business, our readers and our planet. This book
is made from Forest Stewardship Council® certified paper.

1 3 5 7 9 10 8 6 4 2

For my parents, with love and thanks.

London Borough of Richmond Upon Thames	
RTES DISCARDED	
90710 000 391 261	
Askews & Holts	
AF	£14.99
	9780857525741

siren

ˈsʌɪr(ə)n/

noun

noun: **siren**; plural noun: **sirens**; noun: **greater siren**; plural noun: **greater sirens**

1. a device that makes a loud prolonged signal or warning sound.

2. GREEK MYTHOLOGY each of a number of women or winged creatures whose singing lured unwary sailors on to rocks.

In old days there were angels who came and took men by the hand and led them away from the city of destruction. We see no white-winged angels now. But yet men are led away from threatening destruction: a hand is put into theirs, which leads them forth gently towards a calm and bright land, so that they look no more backward; and the hand may be a little child's.

George Eliot, *Silas Marner*

JUNE

Jonathan

YOUR EARS ARE not the same as mine.
It has taken me three months to notice this. I am sorry. I am not really sorry. I have been preoccupied. There are so many things to worry about now there are two of us. You were not here. Then you were. You didn't send word to say you were coming. You didn't call ahead. How could you have? All the same it was a shock. One morning I was I. The next, I was we. There was not enough time to prepare; not enough time to run away.

Before you, I was already afraid. My fears were spread across different rooms and all the doors were firmly closed. Coming sharply from one room into another, I could pretend not to see the accumulating clutter. After you arrived there were no longer lines keeping one fear from the next. My individual fears spread into each other, like puddles pooling wildly until I had a lake on my hands. I couldn't see the bottom of it. I couldn't see the sides. I was a drowning man.

I have made a list of the fears that did not exist before you: the fear of people and the fear of lacking people, the fear of money, telephones and time. The fear of silence and the fear of sounds. The fear of dropping you on your head and your head being split in two, like an egg, with all the wet parts leaking out. I thought this list might be a kind of ladder, something I could climb upwards out of myself. But one fear fed the next and there wasn't enough paper for all my fearful thinking. I did not write down this list for fear it might be found and held against me. This was another fear to add to my list.

Between you, and the worry of you, everything else has begun to peel away. I have not had the time to notice your ears. But this morning, when I lifted you out of the bath, I was not thinking about my job or your breakfast. I was not thinking about all the ways this house is falling down around us in strips. It was the weekend. I was giving myself a little space to sit down and breathe.

It has been many weeks since I last sat down and did not immediately stand up. Time is the biggest thing you have taken from me: time and the permission to leave. This morning I took the time to stare at you. I even turned on the long light over the bathroom mirror. I think you enjoyed being looked at. You smiled at me. It was the first time you had smiled at me. I'm sure of this. I've been watching your mouth as if it is a clock. Your mouth is a kind of clock and there is nothing I can do to slow it down.

You were pink from the bath. The type of pink that is actually white speckled with thousands of tiny red dots, like a painting. Your fingernails were sharp. They required cutting or biting. I have read on the internet that biting is recommended in the early months. Maybe I will do this tonight. Your hair was running in wet threads over your head. Your hair is like contour lines hilling on a map. Usually you are covered with curls. The curls are a kind of shield, shadowing the edges of your face, as if you're trying to keep yourself a secret. I liked seeing the shape of your head with no hair. It made me think of baby birds before

4

their feathers have fluffed out, or very old men. I held you up to the bathroom window, turned you this way and that in the watery light. For the first time I particularly noticed your ears.

It's not that I've been disregarding your ears. I've always suspected they were there. I've known your ears in the same way I knew you possessed fingers, toes, eyes and the possibility of teeth; all your organs, present and quietly ticking. This was not just professionalism on my part. With you, I actually wanted to keep note. When observing bodies the obvious miracles are easy to take for granted. I'm speaking of the details common to all human beings. I include smiling, sleeping and certain motor responses among the general specifics. Your freckles I paid particular attention to, and your hair. Both are uncommon and quite striking. I do not know if these will turn out to be beautiful or ugly in the eyes of your peers. It isn't my place to say.

Your hair is so black it appears damp even when dry. This is not a good sign. This is not the worst sign. Plenty of women have shiny hair. I keep telling myself this, but it's hard to hook into the truth of it. It is much easier to believe the worst.

Your hair, if I'm honest, is why I put you in a hat. Your mouth, the reason I'm considering a balaclava. I am afraid for us both every time I see your damp black hair. I do not even want to believe you have a mouth. I know mouths are necessary, for breathing and such, but I cannot look at yours directly. The red of it is like an ambulance siren saying a terrible thing is already happening, and soon I will see it for myself. I want to place my hand across your mouth and make it disappear.

And now, this morning, another fear to add to my list. I have noticed that your ears are different from mine.

This is not a good sign. This is two for your mother and only your eyes for me. I have been holding on to your eyes for anchors. They are exactly the same nut-brown colour as mine. I like to look at your eyes and see the reflection of myself, mirroring in the black. I like to think, There you are, Little One. Just as much mine as hers.

Your mother had ocean-blue eyes. Any other colour would have been an insult. But yours are brown, like land, like soil, like tree trunks and autumn leaves mulching into winter. You are a ground baby, and on good days I believe that you are mine. 'To Hell with your ears and your hair,' I say to myself. Your mother can have them. They are secondary concerns. Your eyes are mine, and do they not say that the eyes are almost as holy as the heart? Windows to the soul, they say, and other such reassuring sentiments. Eyes are greater than hair and ears combined. I am also hopeful for your hands, which form fists like my fists when you're sleeping, your little sausage feet, and the way you may carry yourself, bent slightly forwards, when walking across a room.

I will do my best to teach myself into you. 'Carry your back like this,' I will say, 'and your legs as if they don't hold the memory of water.' I will remind you, over and over again, that people cannot swim. I will shield you from pictures of swimming pools and swimmers on the television. I will say, 'Water is for drinking, and washing, that's all.' I will say, 'Fold your hands, Little One, you belong to me.'

I will hope your ears can hear but they may already be ringing with your mother's songs.

I will wait and I will watch your mouth.

Your mouth is where the world will begin or end. I cannot bear to look at it. I am watching it, like a clock, even now. I am waiting to see what will come out of it; to see if you are hers or mine.

1

This Is Belfast

THIS IS BELFAST. This is not Belfast.

Better to avoid calling anything a spade in this city. Better to avoid names and places, dates and second names. In this city names are like points on a map or words worked in ink. They are trying too hard to pass for truth. In this city truth is a circle from one side and a square from the other. It is possible to go blind staring at the shape of it. Even now, sixteen years after the Troubles, it is much safer to stand back and say with conviction, 'It all looks the same to me.'

The Troubles are over now. They told us so in the newspapers and on the television. Here, we're very great with religion. We need to believe everything for ourselves. (We're all about sticking the finger in and having a good hoke around.) We did not believe it in the newspapers or on the television. We did not believe it in our bones. After so many years of sitting one way, our spines had set. We will take centuries to unfold.

The Troubles have only just begun. This is hardly true either. It depends upon who you're talking to, how they're standing, and which particular day you've chosen for the chat. Those who are ignorant of our situation can look it up on Wikipedia and find there a three-thousand-word overview. Further articles can be read online and in academic journals. Alternatively, a kind of history may be acquired from talking to the locals. Piecing this together will be a painstaking process, similar to forging one jigsaw puzzle from two, or perhaps twenty.

The Troubles is too less a word for all of this. It is a word for minor inconveniences, such as overdrawn bank accounts, slow punctures, a woman's time of the month. It is not a violent word. Surely we have earnt ourselves a violent word, something as blunt and brutal as 'apartheid'. Instead, we have a word like 'scissors', which can only be said in the plural. The Troubles is/was one monster thing. The Troubles is/are many individual evils caught up together. (Other similar words include 'trousers' and 'pliers'.) The Troubles is always written with a capital T as if it were an event, as the Battle of Hastings is an event with a fixed beginning and end, a point on the calendar year. History will no doubt prove it is actually a verb; an action that can be done to people over and over again, like stealing.

And so we draw no lines. We say this is not Belfast but rather a city similar to Belfast, with two sides and a muck-brown river soldering one to the other. Roads, other roads, train tracks, chimneys. All those things common to a functional city are present here in limited measure. Shopping centres. Schools. Parks, and the unspoken possibility of green acres glooming in the spring. Three hospitals. A zoo, from which animals occasionally escape. To the east of the city, a pair of yellow cranes stride across the horizon, like bow-legged gentlemen. To the west, a hill, hardly a mountain by Alpine standards, trips over itself as it tumbles into the bay. Strung along the coastline there are very many buildings. They are perched like coy bathers, dipping their toes in the greeny sea. There are boats: big boats, smaller boats and that sunken boat, which holds the whole city captive from the ocean floor. There are no future boats.

Instead, there are glass and gunmetal structures stapled across the skyline. These are like stairs ascending towards the tooth-white heights once occupied by God. These are office blocks and hotels for visiting strangers: Americans mostly, and people from other earnest places. We have scant respect for these people and the photographs they will take. They believe themselves brave for coming to this city or, at the very least, open-minded. We wish to say to them, 'Are you mad? Why have you come here? Don't you know there are other proper cities just one hour away by budget airline? There is even Dublin.' We are not supposed to say this. We have already begun to lean on their money.

We put the visitors in black beetle taxis and drive them round and round the ring road, up the tiny streets and down, until they, too, are dizzy, seeing this city from so many angles. We feed them fried eggs and bacon on almost-white plates and say, 'There you go, a taste of local cuisine. That'll set you up for the day.' We dance for them and their foreign money. We are also prepared to cry if this is expected. We wonder what our grandparents would say to all this clamour, all this proving talk.

In this city we have a great love of the talking. The talking can be practised on buses and park benches, from pulpits and other high places. It is occasionally expressed in poems, more frequently on gable walls. It swells in the presence of an audience, though a second party is not strictly required. There is never enough silence to contain all our talking. We have talked ourselves sideways on subjects such as politics and religion, history, rain and the godless way these elements are bound together, like some bastard version of the water cycle. We continue to believe that across the sea, Europe (and also the world) is holding its breath for the next chapter in our sad story. The world is not waiting for us. There are louder voices around the table now. African. Russian. Refugee. They say terrible things in words that require translation. We are wet paper in comparison.

This city continues to talk. It tells anyone inclined to listen that it is a European city, twinned with other European cities. Who is this city kidding? It has no piazza, no marble fountains, no art to speak of. It crouches on the edge of the Continent, like a car park for mainland Europe. The people, when they speak, have a homely sound off them, like boiled potatoes dripping butter. There is no sun to speak of and no one sits outside at café tables. Even when there is a sun it is only a kind of cloud for the rain to hide behind. This is not a city as Barcelona is a city, or Paris, or even Amsterdam. This is a city like a word that was once bad and needs redeeming, 'queer' being the first that comes to mind.

Which is not to say this place is without charm. Despite its best attempts to disappoint, people do not leave and those who do keep coming back. They say, 'It's the people,' and 'You'd go a long way before you found a better breed of person.' They say, 'It's certainly not the weather we came for.' There is truth in every version of this.

Sammy Agnew has known this city his entire life. The map of its little streets and rivers is stamped into him, like a second set of fingerprints. When he opens his mouth, it is this city's sharp and stringy words that come nosing out. He cannot bear the sound of his own voice played back. Sammy can't stand this place, can't quite curse it either. He'd give anything to scrape himself clean of it. To flit and start again, some place warmer like Florida or Benidorm. Some place less like a goldfish bowl. He has tried. God only knows how hard he's tried. But this place is like a magnet: coaxing, dragging, reeling him back in. No matter how far he goes, by plane or boat, or in his everyday thinking – which is the hardest place to achieve distance – he'll still be a son of this city; a disloyal son but, none the less, linked.

Sammy keeps himself to the edge of things now, toeing the line where the nicer neighbourhoods fold into the not so nice. He knows he isn't above any of it. The stink of a backstreet beginning cannot be washed off with soap or careful distance.

He is this place, as his children are this place. This is not necessarily a good thing to carry, though, these days, there's a sort of mumbling hope rising off the city, swelling mostly in the young. There are even individuals proud to raise their heads and say, 'I'm from here and I will not apologize for it.' Sammy thinks these folks are fools. He fears for his children, his son in particular. There's a hardness in the boy, peculiar to this place. Hardness is not the worst way to hold yourself in a city so marked by disappointment. Yet Sammy knows that hardness left to simmer breeds rage, and rage is next to cruelty, and this is what he sees every time he looks at Mark: this city, fouling his boy up, just like it once ruined him.

Jonathan Murray was born here, too, just five minutes up the road from Sammy, though the distance between them is continental. It isn't just money that keeps one man from mixing with the other. It's education and reputation, and something harder to pin down; a whole different way of carrying yourself through life. Jonathan couldn't say he knows this city like Sammy knows it, for knowing implies familiarity and he's been holding himself at a distance for as long as he can remember. It isn't home to him. It doesn't even feel close. He drives its pressing streets daily and doesn't take time to look. He couldn't say with any confidence that this is not the place it was ten years ago, or point to any marked difference from the shooting days of the seventies and eighties. It could be any such city to him: mid-sized, industrial, sea-skimmed. Cardiff. Liverpool. Glasgow. Hull. One damp metropolis looks much the same as the next. Jonathan has no real sense of where he is or where he belongs; what it means to have a home.

This is Belfast. This is not Belfast. This is the city that won't let either man go.

*

It is summer in the city now. Not yet high summer, but hot enough to leave the local lads bare-chested, their backs, bellies and shoulders already pinking to the colour of cooked-ham slices. It is a World Cup summer. The people here are particularly fond of football because it is a game of two sides and involves kicking. The sound of televised crowds can be heard grumbling through the open windows of every other house in the East. Drink has been taken. More drink will be taken. In the morning the smell of it will be like a damp cloth in a closed room. Overhead a helicopter hovers. It is a sort of insect, humming. Its blades turn the hot air this way and that. It is barely moving.

The women, who are mostly indifferent to sport, have dragged dining-room chairs into the street. They sit in front of their houses, like fat Buddhas, watching the traffic idle. Sometimes they call to each other across the road. 'Good to see the weather back,' or 'I hear it's to turn at the weekend.' Sometimes they duck into their little kitchens, returning with fizzy drinks in glasses and tins. Before drinking they press the coldness against their foreheads for a minute and sigh. Afterwards the flesh is pink, as if it has been burnt. The deep V of their breasts is also pink and turning red. By ten o'clock it will smart like nettle stings but they do not, for a minute, consider sun cream. Sun cream is only for holidays abroad. The local sun is weaker. It is less inclined to provoke cancer than the continental sun. Every woman on the street is determined to be brown by September. They wear their skirts hoicked up above the knee, revealing splayed thighs and varicose veins, winter fur and occasionally the fine-laced ghost of a petticoat hem. They are their mothers and their grandmothers before them. They have been guarding these streets in similar fashion since the shipyards demanded houses, a hundred terraced streets rose in response, and this became known as the glorious East.

The children who belong to these women are watching the football or kicking their own footballs between cars. They are wavering up and down the street on hand-me-down bikes, their arms raised high above the handlebars, as if caught in the act of charismatic worship. It is two full months till school. All of July. All of August. When they think about the end of the holidays it is like thinking about the distance between solar systems. This is eternity, and the children are giddy on the wideness of it.

The air is hot in the East. Someone has lit a barbecue. The smell of cooking meat catches in the noses of the women, making their throats run. If the weather holds they will get the barbecue out at the weekend. If the weather holds longer, they may take a run up the coast: north to Portrush, where there are friends with static caravans, or down to Newcastle for the water park. The weans love the water park and the long, sanded beach.

There is nothing like a beach in the East, nothing for the weans but the street and, at the end of the street, the shop. There is not even a garden or a decent-sized patch of grass. People think the East is red, white and blue but these women know differently. The colour of the East is grey, forty shades, each one firmer than the last. This is a perfect complement to the rain and only a problem when the sun comes out. There is nowhere to plant a barbecue here. When the street is your garden to back and front, there is nowhere for a deckchair to sit. In the summer the rest of the city stinks of cut grass and hedges. There's no grass in the East to cut. The summer here smells of melting tar and bins, traffic exhaling on the Newtownards Road. On the warmest days the sea can still be smelt, curdling in the basin of the Connswater, like the egg and brine stench of a public toilet.

It is almost five now. The match is over. They have won, which means, on the other side of the city, they have lost. There are two sides to everything here, especially football. Everyone is obliged to pick a side and stick.

The men are rising from the sofa and flicking the television to mute. 'What's for tea?' they are asking the women.

'What's for tea, yourself?' the women are replying.

They are saying this with sauce, one hand hipped and shoulders cocked to the left, like young girls in heels. In the East a stand-off precedes every meal. Nothing is for certain until the first mouthful is taken. The contents of the fridge are dissected, curated, found either wanting or worthy. A meal is fashioned from the shrapnel. If there is not enough eating for a full meal, a child is dispatched to the shop for something to add bulk.

Tonight, as they eat their shepherd's pie, their potato waffles and boil-in-the-bag rice, the people of the East smell barbecued meat wafting over their plates. The scent leaves them disappointed with their own dinner. Nothing they eat today will taste as good as the barbecue they are shovelling inside their head. Behind the barbecue there is another burnt smell, like the dry heat of a hairdryer left on too long. Somewhere in the East something is on fire. It is not the first fire of the season. It will not be the last.

Parts of the city are alight. A single fire here, another there, each one planned and planted by a different hand. And these are not the usual Eleventh Night bonfires which, every year, herald the beginning of another Twelfth. They're neither traditional nor expected. The women pulling their uPVC windows shut against the smoke catch a whiff of burnt air and tut softly. They enjoy a good bonfire as much as the next one, but they don't approve of fires lit before their appointed time. It's not even July yet. Parade season's barely begun.

At night, from Black Mountain and Craigantlet, these fires appear as birthday candles or amber blossoms dotted across the cityscape. They are surprisingly beautiful. From this distance there is no heat off them. There is no pattern apparent either. The only thing binding one fire to the next is its height – at least thirty feet off the ground – and its intent, which is, as the politicians like to put it, the desire to cause as much disruption as possible.

Across the political spectrum the new fires are widely condemned. 'The time for this sort of thing is over,' the politicians say. On television they look glass-eyed. This comes from years of staring straight down the barrel of a camera and lying. 'We've moved on,' they say. 'This kind of behaviour will not be tolerated.' No arrests are made. The fires continue. The city migraines with the constant shriek of sirens speeding from one incident to the next. The police are bricked and bottled attending the fires. They come now, in riot gear, expecting trouble. The fire brigade is overworked. They are considering help from across the water: extra men, extra engines, a fresh perspective on the same grim problem. Water for hoses and paddling pools may be banned.

None of this is without precedent. The summer is always strained in this city. There are always sirens and bonfires and angry people protesting in groups. Those who can afford to avoid the worst of it are always leaving for the Continent and coming back when it's blown over. It's been like this for decades. But this summer is different. This summer will become known as the Summer of the Tall Fires. It will be written with a capital S, because of its association with the Troubles.

It is only June now and the summer has not yet grown into its name, but everywhere in the city people are clutching for the correct way to say it, for a collective noun they might use in conversation. Something both wide and specific is required; a word that will set this year apart from the bonfire seasons, which bookend every ordinary summer. A baptism of fire? That is not quite right, for a baptism is a holy thing and there's nothing holy about this season. It is more like the Blitz. At times it seems as if the whole city is on fire, one building burning into the next. The oldest residents can still recall the warm nights in 1941 when the whole city flamed red with German spite and all but the richest took to the hills, clutching pillows and blankets. Though, from a distance, these nights look similar, they are very different. The Tall Fires have not been started by a faraway enemy. This is the kind of violence a group of people will do to themselves.

It is impossible to tell who calls it first: a journalist, a news anchor, a small child, perhaps, for it has the ring of something a wean might say. By the end of June it has stopped being called 'sporadic fires' and 'arson attacks'. It is only ever referred to as the 'Tall Fires'. Talk of it is not just in the local newspapers now. It is in the mainland papers and on the proper BBC. The politicians fear it will make America: potential visitors will remember it is not safe to visit the city. This is to be avoided at all costs.

In the East, people are torn. It is part of their culture to burn things, yet they cannot possibly condone burning without order. The right and wrong of this is dragged backwards and forwards across the little streets. Strangers pressing their ears against the thin walls that separate one house from the next may well hear shreds of the argument leaking through the wallpaper. 'It's our tradition'; 'Why should we listen to the politicians?'; 'It's only a matter of time before somebody gets hurt.' Yes, the people of the East are torn. They have a peculiar angle on the whole situation.

There have always been bonfires in this part of the city. Not these haphazard pyres. Traditional bonfires, limited to a single night of burning. Each July on the Eleventh Night the whole city will flame and afterwards cool and, though it's hellish in the moment, at least it happens only once a year. There is a history behind this practice. Something about King Billy picking his way through a darkened city, and the bonfires marking his way. Something about setting everyone up for the Orange parades on the Twelfth. Most people cannot remember the story in any detail but the memory of fire is hard to forget. These are no bonfires as outsiders might picture bonfires, with sticks and logs and perhaps an effigy of Guy Fawkes flaming on top. These are mountains of molten wood, two months or more in the construction.

Everyone is involved in the building, especially the children. They go from door to door begging wood and furniture. They pile it high on wheelbarrows and skateboards, dragging it through the streets to the place where the bonfire will be built. They sleep in shifts beside their wood, guarding against theft and those outside elements who would instigate fire before its proper time. The older lads do the building. They've learnt this skill from their fathers and profligate uncles, who also taught them drinking and pissing in the street. There is architecture in arranging the tyres and wooden pallets that hold these high temples together, collecting and connecting all the elements until the bonfire's tip soars high above the surrounding chimney pots.

When the bonfires burn, the flames leap a hundred feet into the air. The entire city is shrouded in a blanket fog. The heat is an angry god. Nearby windows buckle. Satellite dishes droop, like week-old flowers wilting in the vase. People cannot remain inside their homes for fear of being cooked. Children scream, in fear and thin delight, and sometimes the whole structure slides loose. The fire comes swimming down the street as if it is a burst volcano. This is a glorious thing to look upon, from the periphery, with a cold can in hand. There is always music playing loudly. If you close your eyes, it sounds like Christmas come early.

The other side is not quite so festive. Injuries occur. Children fall from great heights. They break bones or die. Sparks spitting from the dry wood catch on synthetic tracksuits, and the fire, sinking its teeth into an arm or leg, will claim its pound of flesh.

Bystanders drink, and drink too much, and by midnight are throwing punches at their neighbours' sons. They appear in silhouette with the bonfire helling behind them. These are the kind of photographs the newspapers really go for. Afterwards the asphalt will bubble for almost a week. Streets are permanently damaged. They cost public money to fix. Those people not raised on bonfires question the wisdom of lighting large fires in residential areas and why it is permitted to burn flags and even effigies of people still alive. But there have always been bonfires in the East. No one has succeeded in putting them out and there have never been restrictions before.

'It's like this,' the politicians have now said, paraphrasing themselves for the press. 'Tradition is one thing, but these enormous bonfires are in breach of health and safety. It's only a matter of time before someone gets killed.'

People have already been injured, but it has not stopped the advance of the bonfires. All over the East and in certain parts of the West they have been inching ever upwards, like burning Babels: one foot, two foot, ten foot closer to Heaven with every passing year. The tallest are seventy or even eighty feet high now. This is approximately twenty-five metres in metric or, for those given to visualization, the equivalent of stacking three average-sized houses one on top of another. This is not even counting the flags shimmering from the topmost point of the pyre.

'Enough is enough,' the politicians have finally decided. They've been charged with the responsibility of moving things forward and most people in this city no longer want bonfires. 'You can have your traditional bonfires,' they've said, 'but they can't be any higher than thirty feet.' Thirty feet still sounds ludicrous to them. But the politicians here know how quickly things will kick off if they chance an outright ban. Best to do away with the practice gradually. Best to wear the bonfires down. Inch by inch, if necessary. Most people think thirty feet is quite a reasonable compromise, or that bonfires should be banned outright, or, if they are particularly innovative, suggest one enormous bonfire on the city's edge, where no damage can be done.

In the East almost everyone thinks the restrictions are a terrible idea. They are only just beginning to scratch the surface of possibility when it comes to height and fire. Why should they stop now? Why not push for a hundred feet, or two? A flaming statement that might be seen from space or, more importantly, Dublin. They are talking about the injustice of it all in every pub and corner shop. The women tanning themselves on the pavement are thick with it. Even the children are pissed: half a bonfire means half the scavenging, and what will they do with the rest of the month? There is talk of disregarding the politicians and building the bonfires as high as they bloody well want. For the most part it's only talk. The football and the heat have drained the fight right out of the men. They are only good for cold beer and jawing.

But now, weeks before the bonfire season begins in earnest, there has been a spate of very different fires. Tall Fires, each one planted as close to the thirty-foot mark as possible. The first in the lingerie department of Marks & Spencer's Royal Avenue store, stuffed beneath a rack of silk pyjamas, the second in the disabled toilet at the Linenhall Library. Then the City Hospital, the Royal Hospital and the education suite of the Ulster Museum, where the ancient Bengal tiger, stuffed inside his glass case, took the worst of it. It is only after the fifth fire that the police begin to notice patterns: the height, the time, the perpetrators in blue jeans and tracksuit hoods drawn over their heads so they may be anyone at all scuttling across the CCTV footage.

These fires have been planned meticulously. They start in

pre-prepared rucksacks packed with a careful mix of petrol, paper and firelighter. They are always left in a particularly flammable situation. No one has been hurt yet. The fires are set to go off when there are few people around: first thing in the morning, or just before closing. This is a small mercy, the police say, in their official statements, but it is only a matter of time before an injury occurs. This is fire, after all. No one can predict its sly inclinations.

Once the fires are officially linked, it seems they are everywhere. At first they are only planted in high-profile spots. Half of the city's listed buildings are suffering from scorch marks and water damage. The cost is astronomical, the possibility of losing one of Belfast's signature buildings too painful to contemplate. Stormont and the City Hall are on high alert, bordered by a ring of police officers with bulletproof vests and fire extinguishers. Now, having caught the media's eye, the fire starters have moved on to less obvious targets: bridges, warehouses, derelict buildings and social housing, the abandoned carcass of Maysfield Leisure Centre. The whole city is alight. But this is not anarchy. This is carefully orchestrated chaos. There are rules to the game: do not harm civilians, do not be seen and, most importantly, the thirty-foot rule, this being the central tenet of the Tall Fires.

In the last few days a video has appeared on the internet. People are re-posting it on Facebook and YouTube and, on the local news, there is a grainy snippet, repeating morning, afternoon and night. The video features a person who calls himself the Fire Starter. It is impossible to tell who he is. It may even be a woman. It wears a Guy Fawkes mask and a black hooded sweatshirt drawn high over the head. It does not speak but, given the message, it is easy to imagine a thin East Belfast accent, all nose and high up in the throat. It holds cardboard signs to the camera.

'Do not harm civilians.'

'Do not be seen.'

'Start your fire thirty feet off the ground.'

'I'm the Fire Starter.'

In the background, the music playing, loud as a pneumatic drill, is the Prodigy's 'Firestarter'. It is easy to imagine devil horns concealed beneath the hood.

Once all the cardboard signs have been revealed, a black screen appears, with five words printed in white capital letters: 'LEAVE OUR CIVIL LIBERTIES ALONE.' This is the sole demand of the person orchestrating all the Tall Fires. He or she is one person with a hundred arms, all of whom are willing to set their own protest fires. The city will burn until the politicians agree to lift their restrictions, for it is all but impossible to stop a fire moving in so many directions at once.

No one knows who the Fire Starter is, no one except Sammy Agnew, and he's not quite ready to admit this yet. He's recognized something familiar in the slope of the Fire Starter's shoulders, the way he moves his hands and holds his head at a cocky angle, like he's looking for a slap. At first it was only a suspicion. Sammy couldn't be sure. Didn't want to believe it. But he's watched the video so many times now. Over and over on his laptop, keeping the sound down so his wife can't hear. His first instinct is always to protect her. Sammy's tried not to see it. He would do almost anything to be wrong. But, he knows who's behind that mask. He's almost certain. Still, he could be wrong, couldn't he?

It is five o'clock now in the East. The fire brigade has gathered in the car park of Connswater shopping centre. They're doing their best to control a small fire on the second level of the multi-storey. Having been lit beneath a Vauxhall Corsa, the fire has already caused one small explosion and spread to the cars on either side. The heat is building itself into a wall. Beneath their masks and fireproof jumpsuits the firemen are slick with smoke-sweat. A group of teenagers have gathered by the trolley park. Soon they will be lobbing things at the firemen and paramedics. They won't be sure why they're doing this but will feel the itch of necessity in their elbow joints, a kind of violence inherited from the previous generation. When the bricks are pressed into their hands, they'll draw their arms back and pitch like professionals.

Half a mile away in Orangefield, Jonathan Murray catches the acrid stench of burning car in the back of his nose. He coughs on the choke of it. His eyes begin to run. Despite the heat he closes his window. He hasn't watched the news in months, or read a paper. During this period he's left the house for ten minutes at most, dashing to the little Tesco at the top of the road and back. Lately, his world's been reduced to a three-bed semi off the Castlereagh Road, and he's pretty much tied to it. He doesn't know about the Tall Fires or the ban on bonfires over thirty feet. He doesn't even know this is a World Cup year, though he's vaguely aware that it is warm outside and must therefore be summer. He has not thought about anything but his daughter for six weeks now.

It has taken him a long time to call her a name. This name is Sophie and he has not yet settled on it. The fear of her is the first thing he thinks about each morning. He carries the weight of her presence to bed each night. Under different circumstances he might have loved her but he won't allow himself to love her now. He will not be cruel to her either.

He closes the curtains over the window but the smell of smoke is still in the room. Jonathan's grown up in the East and this smell is not unfamiliar. It must be bonfire season. Where have the weeks gone? It's a year already since Sophie's mother.

She's sleeping on her belly tonight, the white hump of her nappy lumping under the blanket. Because of the heat, he has not dressed her in three days. It's nice to get a break from the laundry. Who knew how many outfits a baby could go through in a day, or how many times they'd need feeding? There have been so many things to learn.

Jonathan stands over Sophie's cot and watches the breath come in and out of her. She's not so dreadful when she's sleeping but it's hard to trust her. He bends down and peers at her face through the cot's bars. Her lips lift slightly at the edges. This is no longer wind. She's beginning to smile. Other stages will come soon and, before he can stop it, there will be words.

Sophie must not speak for there is no way of being sure what she will say. Jonathan is thinking about cutting her tongue out. He'll do a good job of this because he's a doctor. He has trained for seven years to cut bits off and sew them back on. This evening isn't the first time he's stood over his daughter's cot and pictured himself slicing through flesh and curled muscle. He has considered the blood and the way he will stem it, the anaesthetic required and, afterwards, the painkillers. He is hoping it will not come to this, but if it does, he won't allow himself a choice.

Jonathan closes the window in Sophie's room. It's terribly hot tonight. There's an atmosphere in the East like steam building inside a pipe.

2

Belfast Is For Lovers

I HAVE ALWAYS been Jonathan. Never John. John is my father's name. It is already taken. I am certainly not Jonny, though sometimes I call myself this at home and swagger from one room to the next, chin cocked like a wide boy. Jonny Murray is the name of a rugby player, or a young fella you'd meet in the toilets of a Cookstown nightclub, chatting away as he rinses his hands under the cold tap. Jonny Murray is easy in his own skin. He drives his car loosely with one hand and wears slogan T-shirts, a different one each day: 'Loser', 'Harvard', 'Hello Ladies'. Jonny talks to women as if they are, all of them, speaking the same language. He is not afraid to dance or be looked at thoroughly, this being the root cause of all my fears.

I think I'd like to have been Jonny, or maybe someone else entirely.

But I'm Jonathan, only, ever, all three syllables. This wasn't my choice. First I had parents, like pinched nerves, telling me, and then I was a doctor. There was no room for turning in between. I've thought about changing my name but it's too late at thirty, and my patients wouldn't trust a doctor named Jonny.

In the past I've tried to shorten my name. Particularly at university when I was still trying with girls. 'Hi,' I'd say, extending my hand across the table to take the hand of a girl I didn't know – any decent-looking one would do. 'Jonny Murray, nice to meet you.' But Jonny has always been a clumsy fit for Murray; too many Ys knocking against each other. My own name would catch on the back of my teeth, like dry spit. So many girls turned away from me, purposefully leaning into other conversations, I never even caught their names. Eventually I gave up. Then I was Jonathan again or, more often than not, silent.

In the health centre I'm Dr Murray to patients and colleagues alike. I wonder, with my colleagues, if this is distance or just good practice between professionals. I listen outside the staff-room to hear if the other doctors are on first-name terms. It is impossible to tell from listening. They only say things like 'Pass us a teaspoon,' and 'Is there any milk in the fridge?' They rarely have the need for names of any sort. Still, I feel as if I'm on the edge of the outside of a circle. I'm almost certain the other doctors go by Chris and Sarah and Martin/Marty when I'm not around. I suspect that everyone is going to the pub after work and no one is inviting me. I try to tell myself that I'm not particularly bothered one way or the other and, in the evening, watch them leave the car park through a thin slip in my office blinds. They leave in separate cars, but this proves nothing.

Lately, I've developed a kind of fantasy where the lady receptionists call me 'Doc'. Their voices saying my name are like warm milk in a mug. I know this is a ridiculous thing to imagine, and impractical, for there are four doctors in the practice, each one equally entitled to the name Doc. Better to invent myself a personal nickname. 'Minty', perhaps, after the boiled sweets that share my second name. But I know the lady receptionists haven't an A level between them. They are kindly creatures who type and answer phones. By themselves, they wouldn't come up with something as sharp as 'Minty'. I have abandoned my fantasy now. I am, at all times, a pragmatist, even when daydreaming about the lady receptionists and the things they wear beneath their blouses.

I don't have a middle name. This was my parents' doing. They had not planned on children. If pressed, they might have expressed a preference for dogs or garden ornaments over miniature versions of themselves. I was, and continue to be, an 'accident', though in truth I believe this word is an inaccurate term for the act of planting a child seed inside your wife's belly. Accidents are occurrences without intent, such as broken crockery or crashed cars. Often alcohol is involved. Yet, 'accident' is how my conception has always been referred to in the Murray household. 'Disappointing ending' may be a better description, or 'unfortunate repercussion', for I've been told the act itself was carefully planned and even featured candles.

After the initial 'accident' my parents enjoyed nine whole months of their own company. This should have been more than enough time to get used to the idea of children. They did not become used to the idea of children and, instead, spent those months drinking, dining out and holidaying with friends on the French Riviera, disguising their ever-growing problem beneath smocks and gathered sundresses. My father has told me that the discovery of Mother's belly, blooming into its third trimester, came as a fresh shock every time she undressed for bed. He was unable to look at it directly and instead looked down the side of his wife with unfocused eyes, as one might both watch and not watch a particularly harrowing scene on the television. 'What shall we do about this?' Mother would ask, pointing towards the place where her trousers no longer met, and Father would shrug and say, 'Let's talk about it tomorrow.' Wine would be poured, usually red, and the next evening the same scene would play itself out, like a last-season sitcom. When the baby arrived my mother was still saying, 'What shall we do about this?' but the answer couldn't be put off any longer.

This, it should be noted, was the sort of thing that passed for a bedtime story when I was a child. Perhaps it's little wonder I turned out the way I did.

Neither party had wished to own a child. The option of giving it to someone else was not to be considered either. My parents were professionals: she a lawyer, he working with money, not an accountant exactly but something similar. They did not move in the kind of circles where babies could be given away. Their friends and acquaintances would think them terribly common to have acquired a child without particularly wanting one. This was the sort of thing people did in housing estates. If word got out, they would no longer be invited to dinner parties. They'd be stared at, with whispers, in the dining rooms of Belfast's better hotels. My parents could not see themselves as outcasts, so they kept the baby and called it Jonathan.

Their imagination, much like their enthusiasm, was a creature of limited means. It could not stretch to a second name. Then they christened me and I could not get away from it. Without a middle name I was indistinguishable from all the thousands of other Jonathan Murrays populating the Western world, solid men, no doubt, with jobs in engineering, wives and family cars they kept for three years and traded up. There is no point in googling my own name for kicks. There are at least ten other Jonathan Murrays in Belfast alone, a hundred if I widen the search to include the rest of Ireland.

I took my name as an excuse to grow into an unremarkable child. My parents did nothing to convince me otherwise. They were not the sort of cruel that is done with sticks or even words. I was never short of food or necessary gadgets, for my mother approached parenting as a competitive sport. She couldn't bear to be seen falling behind her peers. Neither were my parents particularly engaged. It was not uncommon for them to pay the babysitter to attend my school concerts with a camcorder. They did not watch these videos afterwards but kept them on a shelf in the study in case evidence of their interest was ever required. On more than one occasion they forgot my birthday, presenting me with gifts several days before or after the actual date. They did not touch me kindly or unkindly. As soon as I turned sixteen they emigrated to New Zealand, claiming this was for work.

I did not go with my parents to New Zealand. I was finishing my GCSEs. Two years after there would be A levels and then I'd go to Queen's University to study medicine. My father had explained this to me at least two hundred times beginning on the day I turned twelve. It was written down for the lawyer and, like my name, could not be changed. There was money for a private boarding school, money for fees and also a car, should I want one when I was old enough to drive. All I had to do was let my parents leave me behind. It had taken sixteen years for them to manage this without appearing dreadful in the eyes of their friends.

'It would be cruel to move you to New Zealand, Jonathan,' my mother explained. (She'd organized a dinner party so the neighbours could hear her say this like a sensible parent.) 'All your little friends are here in Belfast,' she continued. 'We wouldn't want to take you away from them.' Under pressure, I couldn't think of a single person I'd call friend . . . maybe the kid who sat next to me in science and had once lent me a pen. I wasn't even certain of this boy's name. Timothy or Nicholas, I thought. Something prissy. But, I could see the hooks in Mother's eyes. She was desperate, as was my father, folding and unfolding his hands urgently beneath the tablecloth. It would be good to be shot of them both. The weight of their disinterest was something I lugged around constantly, like a dead leg. So I said, 'Of course, Mother. It's best if I stay here.' I wasn't particularly bothered either way.

After this, I was mostly by myself. The length of this time was approximately fourteen years.

It would be unfair to say that I didn't try to make friends during this period. For a while, during university, I was part of a group of medical students. The collective noun for such a gathering is 'class'; the alternative, 'a lethargy'. Neither fitted the group well for they were the kind of keen achievers who did not require a classroom to suck the lesson out of life. They were not, on paper, compatible and certainly did not look like friends you'd photograph and keep. They understood themselves linked together by circumstance as much as choice. They knew not to speak of the odd way they looked when grouped around a table. Or the long silences. Theirs was a fragile kind of dependence, easily frayed.

I was never quite sure if this was friendship. But it was better than the vast nothing of my previous years. I was often in the same place with these people at the same time: hospital canteens, lecture theatres, student pubs, cinemas . . . We talked to and about each other and sometimes arranged structured activities such as ten-pin bowling. At Christmas there was a Secret Santa and I both gave and received a pair of gift-wrapped novelty socks. It was a relief to open my own present and realize I had not failed by giving socks. On my birthday there was a shop-bought cake, and everyone sang 'Happy birthday to you, dear Jonathan,' awkwardly, in a restaurant. That was nice but I never, for a moment, felt particularly dear to any of them. I was one of seven: three girls and four boys. I understood it was only my white coat and stethoscope that bound me to the other six.

During this period I would occasionally sit back in my chair, distancing myself from the table chatter, to look at the familiar faces sitting around me. 'Are these people my friends?' I'd ask myself. I didn't really like them or enjoy their company, but perhaps friendship required something more than ease. Yes, I eventually concluded, having weighed up the evidence before me (Christmas socks, birthday cake, and the evening a rather drunk Nuala had kissed me up against a parked Clio), these were indeed my friends. This was what it felt like to have a friend and be a friend. It was a decidedly disappointing sensation.

As a child, I'd ruined myself on the idea of friends. TV was to blame for this, which is to say my parents were actually to blame. They'd raised me lonely with a television set in every room. I did not trust friendship unless it was perfect and singing, and singing, or even dancing, on television, as it was in the movies. When I pictured myself with friends it was always a sunny, blond kind of friendship I longed for, like the clean hunger I had for swimming pools every time I smelt chlorine. This was an indefinable American sentiment, all white teeth and laughter and beautiful people curled around each other, like children rather than sex. This sat ugly in East Belfast where the rain washed the lightness out of everything it touched. It did not take into account the real arms and weary smiles of those people who'd offered me a home for Christmas or study time in the library. Those people were not beautiful enough. They were not beautiful at all.

I held my friends up against the television and understood them as pale fish in comparison. I'd hoped for remarkable friends and lovers. I had, by the final year of university, acquired neither. Still, all was not lost. There were things that could be done. We could try harder at being young. We could do better haircuts, and sex, and swimming in places where swimming was not generally permitted. We could be louder in conversation. This might be enough to redeem us. However, I did not know how to say this without leaving marks. Instead I said nothing and quietly shrank. I lost touch with every one of those people as soon as I graduated.

Sometimes, in the run-up to my thirtieth, I would dwell on my teens and early twenties and tear up with the sort of disappointment that is like being sad for another person, even though that person is actually yourself. There had been no costume parties for me, no crazy road trips or summer romances. I wouldn't have my youth back now or the chance to be reckless. This was a sadness I couldn't share with anyone else. I had never once been in love with anyone. I couldn't imagine myself loose enough. I blamed my mother and father for this. Occasionally, after two drinks, I'd set aside my parents, and admit that the disappointment was my own doing. My fault for holding myself like a closed cupboard, for being too tight to dance or risk my arm around a stranger's waist. Knowing this didn't help. By the time I turned thirty I'd settled into myself. I was a forgotten kind of person. I struggled to see how time or circumstance might change this. I wasn't brave enough to try.

At night I watched television as if it were another person in the room. I sometimes talked back to the screen. I paid my bills before they were due and went every day to a job I neither liked nor particularly disliked. Every week I ate the same meals on the same days and never drank more than two glasses straight, for fear of becoming a man who drinks alone. For exercise I ran three miles each morning on a treadmill in the spare room. It would have been pleasant to run outside with the cyclists and the early-day dog-walkers but I couldn't bear the thought of being looked at and judged ridiculous. I didn't allow myself room for self-pity. This, once admitted, would be the end. The end did not always sound like the most terrible thing. Sometimes it sounded like a very sensible option.

Two years previously, while navigating the no man's land between Christmas and New Year, I'd brought home from work a small brown cylinder of a prescription drug. It sat on my bedside table for a week, glowing beer-bottle brown in the lamplight. It demanded my attention and eventually I'd given in. I took the container in my left fist and held it there all night, quite definitely. It left the imprint of a rectangle in my palm. I slept with it close to my face, but not touching. Before falling asleep I'd entertained thoughts such as No one would find me for weeks, and What if someone finds me in time? I thought the despair would give me loud dreams, but I'd only dreamt of being asleep. The container lid slipped loose in the night, and in the morning white tablets were dotted all through my bedclothes. At first, because I'd been almost still dreaming, I thought they were teeth. I scooped up the tablets in my hands, as many as I could find, and flushed them down the en-suite toilet. It took three flushes and the time between for the water to gather.

I was glad I hadn't done it, whatever it was, with the tablets. I couldn't say it in words. I had the dropped-belly feeling of a fall only narrowly avoided.

'Things must change,' I'd decided that morning, and said this, out loud, to the reflection of myself, ghost-faced, in the bathroom mirror.

'You are still young,' I told myself, 'and you are reasonably good-looking. And it is not too late to make changes.'

That same morning the article had appeared in the *Belfast Telegraph*. It took some swallowing, coming as it did directly after the night before. I read it very many times and underlined sections. Eventually I was able to call it a kind of sign but I could not attribute it to God.

Belfast Is For Lovers, ran the headline. This initially caught my eye as a joke. It was not intended as a joke. I read on. The Northern Ireland Tourism Board wished to see the city pitched against the other great romantics: Paris, Venice, Berlin (before the Wall came down). Understanding that Belfast did not naturally scream passion (guns and drums aside), they'd decided to engineer their own romance. Singles were to be recruited and coupled off in believable pairs. Tall girls with tall boys. Bookish-looking souls together, all the better for seeing each other through their prescription lenses. Only girl on boy: nothing too modern. This was still Belfast, after all.

For a hundred and fifty pounds per day, these fabricated couples would spend a weekend hand in hand or kissing in the Botanic Gardens and by the Peace Walls, at thirty different locations frequented by tourists. The tourists, seeing lovers everywhere they turned, would soon believe Belfast to be a truly European city. They would forgive the rain and the shops for not opening till lunchtime on a Sunday. They might even take photographs for the purpose of convincing the sceptics back home. 'Look,' they would say, arranging their Kodak prints across rustic kitchen tables in France or Spain, 'Belfast is a very safe place to visit. It is a place of hope and love. Lots of love, like San Francisco in the sixties.' The Tourism Board was certain this would happen. They needed only a little help from the young, for they were mostly middle-aged men in suits and thin-striped shirts, too old for kissing in public.

I immediately knew this was for me. I drew a wide red circle around the entire article. The idea of it scared me immensely. I was fine as I was. I glanced at the empty pill container, waiting on the sideboard with the rest of the recycling. I was not fine as I was. Some large thing had to change and this would need to happen almost immediately. But surely I did not have to consider something so drastic. There were a hundred thousand safer options that could be tried first: dating agencies, walking groups, church or social drinking. I'd never seriously considered any of these before and I knew I would not consider them in the future. That morning a desperate kind of action was possible. Here was a bold chance presenting itself. If it was not taken there would be no such future chance. Ten years from now I would still be here in this quiet house, sleeping.

The decision was made.

There were contact details attached to the article. I wrote down the phone number on a Post-it note. Beneath this, I wrote the email address. Email would be easier. It would not require speaking. At first I didn't believe myself capable of contacting the Tourist Board and then, after I'd applied, was sure I would not go to the information session, and even then, in a room with dozens of other twenty- and thirty-somethings balanced on stackable chairs, could not picture myself in the Palm House, embracing Stephanie beneath the banana plants.

Then I was there, with her lips on my lips and her eyes staring into mine. I looked up and noticed the wide green leaves, like umbrellas, hanging over our heads. This is easy, I thought. Why have I never been in this situation before? The taste of Stephanie was like thin saline, swirling round my mouth. I was warm all over and melting. I couldn't remember how I'd arrived in that place, with the tourists taking photos and the menstrual stench of warm greenhouse, sweating into my pullover.

I began to think of spending Christmases and bank holidays with another human being, not necessarily Stephanie but some-one similar, or Stephanie would also do. This was no longer a ridiculous thing to imagine. I grew bold on the idea of it, push-ing my tongue into her mouth, though she'd not given me permission to do so. I held her hand before she reached for mine and was relieved to feel her fingers curling into mine. When we were scheduled to have short conversations while continuing to look lovestruck, we leant against the wall and talked. I dis-covered this was not such a difficult thing to do with a girl. Stephanie asked me questions and I answered and, in answer-ing, thought of questions I might like to ask her, and did.

The weekend went like a downhill sprint and suddenly it was Sunday afternoon. I hadn't seen this coming. I had an ache in my jaw from kissing but was otherwise inclined to continue for the rest of the week. At five o'clock on the dot a man from the Tourist Board arrived at the Palm House. He took an official picture of Stephanie and me for publicity purposes, and gave us three hundred pounds each in white envelopes.

'That's you, then,' said the man. 'Thanks for helping us out.'

'What about next weekend?' I asked. But Belfast Is For Lovers was a pilot scheme, funded for a single session and stagnant till further funding could be sourced.

The man left. He had the Ulster Museum to get to, the Tropical Ravine, then the quad at Queen's, and it was almost closing time.

'It was nice meeting you,' said Stephanie.

'You too,' I replied, 'thanks for everything,' and then, because I was still a little fluid from all that kissing, added, 'Would you like to go for dinner?'

'Now?'

'Now's great, or any time that suits, really.'

'I have a boyfriend, Jonathan. I don't think he'd like me going out for dinner with another fella.'

'You've been kissing another fella for the last two days. How does your boyfriend feel about that?'

'It was just acting, for the money. We're saving up for a holiday. He knows all about it.'

'Oh,' I said. I felt like a person who'd leant too far and couldn't stop himself falling. I would say the wrong thing to Stephanie now. The wrong thing was already in my mouth, preening itself for flight: 'It didn't feel like you were acting all weekend.'

'I was acting, Jonathan. For the money.' Her voice was knives.

'Did you not like it?' My voice was just as tight.

'It was OK.'

'Did I do something wrong?'

'No, you did nothing wrong, but this isn't a dating service. It's an acting job. It's only pretending.'

'Well,' I said, and later I would replay the conversation and cringe at my own desperation, which was like a small child's, wheedling for sweets, 'couldn't we just pretend a little more?'

'I have a boyfriend, Jonathan.'

'We wouldn't have to tell him. We could do this in secret or you could tell him that we got another job with the Tourism Board, in Bangor or some other town, doing the same thing.'

'Why would I do that? I don't even fancy you.'

'You don't have to. You can just pretend. That would be enough.'

'That's tragic. Why would you want to be with someone who doesn't really like you? Haven't you ever been in love with anyone, Jonathan?'

'No,' I said. 'I don't know if I can.' That was the most honest I'd ever been with another human being. Just saying it made my nose pinch. A tear started coming out of my left eye. Stephanie reached up and dabbed it with the cuff of her sleeve. She was a nice person. I could tell that from the way she was deliberately looking at me and not laughing. She slipped her arms round my middle like a belt and pulled me into her. I could feel her breasts, like soft fists, angled against my ribcage. It was very good to be me right then. I was not accustomed to being happy and began to cry in heaves.

'Oh, Jonathan,' she said, and let out a damp sigh, 'that's just about the saddest thing I've ever heard. You must be so lonely. Why don't you come round for dinner with us some night next week?'

'I don't want to have dinner with you and your boyfriend,' I mumbled into the top of her hair. From such a height I could see it was blonde with brown streaks at the top. It smelt like fresh Christmas tree. 'I want you to be in love with me.'

'I can't,' Stephanie replied, drawing back. 'I told you, I have a boyfriend.'

'I could pay you,' I said, 'same rate as today.'

This was when she slapped me. As her hand came towards my face I noticed that she no longer looked like a sympathetic person. Her mouth was a line and her eyebrows were angles and I could tell she was absolutely furious.

3

Burning Cars

SAMMY HAS BEEN walking round East Belfast for almost three hours. He keeps his head down and his hands in his pockets, following the laddered lines of the smaller streets, up one avenue and down the next. He zigzags his weary way towards the Castlereagh Hills, to his semi-detached house and his son, who lives in the attic, orchestrating Armageddon without ever leaving his room. It doesn't feel like home now he's seen the Fire Starter video. Now he's begun to see something familiar about the figure staring into the camera, spouting dark and dreadful sentiments. If Sammy's honest, it hasn't felt like home for years. The house seems smaller every time he walks through the door, as if the walls are inching inwards and the ceiling will soon be brushing against his head. He has no desire to go home today. He's letting the street take him where it wishes, like a river tide or a person falling from a decent height.

Commercial aeroplanes leaving and landing at the City Airport continue to pass overhead. They're unaware of Sammy and the shape he's spelling out as he walks. He's too small to be seen from the sky. He's a grain of sand, a dot, a pin, a misplaced punctuation mark. Even God would have to squint. However, if he could be seen from such a height, if, for example, you were peering through binoculars or some other magnifying lens, your eye would be drawn to him, dragging his heels from one street to the next, kicking an empty Coke bottle as he goes. You would know that Sammy did not belong on these streets, drifting.

Miles below the flight path Sammy's feet are firmly planted on the ground and he does not look up. His legs keep lifting and falling, right after left after right after left, like pistons nodding in an old-fashioned engine. He pauses for a moment on the corner of a larger street and searches his pockets for a cigarette. It's years since he last smoked but today he's bought himself a packet. Needs must. As the cigarette flares in his cupped hands he notices the trail of summer jets smoking away from Belfast to the mainland and those destinations beyond. He envies them their wings, their ability to up and leave. This requires a lightness he has long since lost. He keeps walking, dragging on his cigarette as he goes. Where the cars have mounted the pavement and there is no room to pass, he walks a midline down the road. No one stops him. No one smiles or lifts their chin to say, 'Nice day,' or 'Morning.' He has a face on him like a weekend funeral. Even the pigeons give him a wide berth.

Every couple of blocks the pavement rises in cupped craters, curling at the edges, like the burnt black crusts of an overdone pancake. These are the remains of old fires. Some are fresh and still steaming. Some have solidified and, in solidifying, formed tiny cities, lumps, lows and charred logs rising from the ash, like Hiroshima or Nagasaki in miniature. They are a very specific kind of beautiful. Some are as wide as the street is wide and cannot be avoided, only waded through. Strands of molten tar attach themselves to the soles of Sammy's shoes, stretching as he steps away, then letting go to snap silently back into themselves. He'll have to be careful not to tramp it into the hall carpet. He wouldn't want to get on the wrong side of his wife.

He walks past a burnt-out corner shop, several cars still

smouldering and a postbox that has caught only on the inside, like a cast-iron stove. Its shell is still a bullet but its red paint has peeled in the heat, forming blisters, making a mockery of the royal crest. Clearly the young ones haven't been listening to the rules. None of these fires are on the second storey. They're starting to lose the run of themselves already, burning anything they can get their hands on. The burnt trees sadden Sammy most so he doesn't look at them. He hopes that his son has seen these trees and the ugly way they're holding up their charred branches. They remind him of burns victims running from a fire, their arms held aloft, their faces open-mouthed and melting, like that Edvard Munch painting students still pin to their bedroom walls. Sammy hopes Mark's noticed the damage he's causing. He hopes the boy feels dreadful, but something in him suspects Mark incapable of regret of any kind. Sammy keeps his eyes on his feet falling and rising. He's all up in his head with the worry. He does not see the old man until he is almost standing on his toes.

The old man is sitting directly in front of his house on an upturned bucket. He has a dog beside him, a Jack Russell so elderly it has developed the same loose belly and whiskery beard as its owner. It is both fat-looking and simultaneously frail, as is the old man. Age has taken the dog's bark. When it opens its mouth to snap at Sammy, the noise that comes out is like the last arthritic gasp of a fish-tank pump. It is not the kind of dog you'd want to touch without gloves, but the old man is holding it as if it were a firstborn son.

'Jesus,' Sammy exclaims, bringing his feet to an abrupt halt. 'What are you doing down there? I nearly landed on top of you.'

'I'm just watching my wee house,' says the old man.

He keeps his seat so Sammy is towering over him, two foot taller at least. He can see the constellation of brown liver stains haloed round the old man's bald patch. He can smell his old-man smell. It's like burnt toast and paper, catching at the back of his nose. The dog lifts its head as if to snap. The effort is too much to sustain. It is a very elderly dog. The old man lays a hand on its head and it is almost instantly asleep.

Sammy looks at the house in front of them. It's a bog standard two-up, two-down with a hankie-sized lawn out front. There are thirty identical houses stuck end to end in this street alone. The only thing marking it out for attention is the fire. It's burning from the inside out. Through the downstairs windows Sammy can see the flames climbing up the curtains in long red licks. The chesterfield suite – a brown and orange polyester affair – is already engulfed, the fire complementing its lurid, seventies print. Even from the pavement Sammy can feel the heat flushing against his cheeks and arms.

'Your house is on fire, mate,' he says. 'Have you called the fire brigade?'

'Not yet,' the old man replies. 'I'm for giving it a few minutes, just to make sure it's properly caught.'

'Did you do this?'

'Course not. Some young lads done it.'

'Wee bastards. They don't know what to be at these days, starting fires all over the place. Are you all right yourself? You could have been killed. Them wee houses go up like petrol.'

'Uch, I'm grand. I was out here with Towsie when it started.'

'You could have been inside sleeping. They've no sense, these young ones, running around setting people's houses on fire.'

'Oh, no, son. You've the wrong end of the stick. I asked them to do it. I paid them a hundred quid to burn the place down.'

Sammy looks hard at the old man. There's a soft look off him, the sort of calmness you might catch on the surface of a puddle when there's no wind and the sky is beaming back up at the sky. He doesn't look at all upset about his house.

'Is it the insurance you're after?' he asks, though he's never heard of anyone going for the insurance on a two-up, two-down. It'd hardly be worth the bother.

'Naw, I couldn't give a toss about the insurance. I'm for moving in to one of them Folds tomorrow. I just don't want the government getting their hands on my wee house. When you go into a home they take all your assets to pay the fees. It's daylight robbery, so it is.'

Sammy neither agrees nor disagrees. He'd like to move on. His back is toasting and he's worried about the synthetic elements in his pullover. It won't be long before they begin to melt. He thinks the old man's lost it but he can't, with any decency, leave an elderly person sitting on a bucket while his house burns down.

'Are you sure you don't want me to call the fire brigade?' he asks.

The old man doesn't answer. Instead he says, 'I got one over them, did I not, son?' and starts laughing hysterically, rocking backwards and forwards on his upturned bucket, like some mad eejit out on day release. 'I got them bastards good.'

'You certainly did,' says Sammy. He feels tired all the way into his bones, the kind of tired that cannot be fixed with sleeping.

The noise of the old man laughing wakes the dog. It begins to howl like a thing possessed. Then, it raises itself off the pavement, danders round the back of its owner and pisses, in stops and gushing starts, against the bucket. Sammy feels like his head's on too tight. He steps behind a hedge to phone the fire brigade in private. He doesn't want to disrespect the old man but he's concerned about the houses on either side and the people, pets and various items of property currently contained within growing hotter by the moment.

The girl on the 999 switchboard has a muddy Fermanagh accent. It is difficult to translate the words containing multiple vowels. She's not particularly sharp on her consonants either but Sammy can still tell she's not that worried about the old man's

41

fire. 'Is anyone hurt?' she asks. 'Could you put it out yourself with a blanket? Is it, like, a famous building, or just an ordinary one? We're having to prioritize old and important buildings at the minute. Like the City Hall or castles.'

The waiting time for a fire engine (and, the girl has to be honest, with a fire of this size, it might just be a Transit van with extinguishers and buckets) is approximately twenty minutes, which, she continues, 'isn't too bad', and 'is way shorter than it will be tonight when the fire starters get going properly'.

Sammy hangs up and goes to advise the neighbours that, though their homes are not yet burning, they should probably phone the emergency services pre-emptively. Informing the fire brigade that their home will be on fire in around twenty-five minutes' time might be the difference between getting the blaze extinguished and watching it spread all the way down the row.

As he walks to the end of the street, in the naïve hope of spotting a fire engine come earlier than predicted, Sammy thinks about the fires of his youth: the bonfires, the burnt-out houses, the furniture store at the bottom of the Newtownards Road, which they'd doused with petrol after the owners failed to pay their protection money, the shops he'd done over for insurance, and all those cars set alight for the sheer godless rush of wreaking havoc.

They'd been wild keen on burning cars back in the day.

Sammy specifically remembers the night they'd driven out of the city to the sticks, thirty miles north to one of the wee farming villages on the outskirts of Ballymena. He'd a bunch of hard lads piled into the back of his Ford Cortina so it rode low on the country lanes, backside grating on every hump and muddy hollow. It was 1986 and every one of them was carrying a gun. Sammy kept his in the glove compartment. He'd seen this in an American movie, *Mean Streets* or *Dirty Harry*. It made him feel like a gangster just knowing the gun was in there. Sometimes at traffic lights he'd flick open the glove compartment and let his fingers run along the cold, grey metal. He'd think about shooting somebody pulled up next to him at the lights. He could if he wanted to. There was only glass between them. Sammy never shot anyone at the traffic lights, but the thought of it was enough to get his blood up. He could feel it, whiskey warm, running through his veins and lungs.

This one particular night had been in February or early March. In the country, without the interrupting grace of streetlamps, it was already pitch-black by five. He'd reversed the Cortina into the entrance of a field outside Cullybackey and left it there, its bonnet still steaming in the winter air. They'd purposely picked the sort of road you could get only one car down at a time. Cars went past slowly on these roads for fear of bends and loose cattle. When one came past, Sammy and his mates flagged it down with torches, held their guns against the driver's head and screamed, 'Sing "The Sash", or we'll pull the trigger and blow your brains out. You, and all them ones in the back seat.'

The point had been to put the fear of God into every Taig they came across. The point had quickly become confused in the head-rush high of screaming at strangers in the dark. They'd felt like gods when the women cried and the men begged and the guns began to sweat in their cold hands. They'd felt untouchable. You didn't need a Taig to get this feeling: any poor sod with a Skoda would do.

Sometimes there'd been children in the cars and they'd let them drive on, waving them past with the guns in their fists, clearly showing. They were not degenerates. They would not hurt children on purpose, though they'd not the same patience with old people. The old Fenians were nearly worse than the young ones, speaking their gobbledygook language and bringing the Pope into everything. They'd no fear of the old priests either. There was a clatter of them living in a monastery beside

Portglenone Forest, and all night they'd joked among themselves saying, 'Wouldn't it be deadly craic to go down there and burn the monastery, put the fear of proper God into them Holy Joes?' Nuns were a different matter entirely. Nuns had always scared the living shit out of them. They wouldn't have known what to do with one on an empty road so late at night. It would have been like coming across a ghost.

They put balaclavas on each time they flagged down a car, rolling them upwards, over their noses, to smoke freely when the road was empty. The balaclavas would probably have been enough without guns. People, round here, knew what a covered face stood for. But they'd held up their guns anyway and, from time to time, turned into the darkness and emptied a bullet or two into the fields. The bang of it, echoing into the blackness, was a ludicrous sound, like something belonging in a movie. It made people scream, then cup the scream back into their mouths, as if trying to stop the panic leaking out.

One young fella wet himself as soon as Sammy held up his gun. The stain, spreading out from his crotch and stretching down the length of his trousers, had been dark, like wine spilt on a sofa. He couldn't even make it through the first verse of 'The Sash', though he swore blind he was a Protestant. If they wanted they could have seen on his driving licence that his name was William and his second name, Rodgers. They'd laughed at him, all four of them with their guns, nodding at the wet patch on his trousers, and their heads tilting towards his girlfriend, crying quietly in the passenger seat, as if to say, 'Would you look at the cut of this one. What are you doing with a fella who pisses himself in the road?'

When they'd stopped a car with Catholics in it they burnt the car out, left the owners standing by the side of the road and drove two or three miles to another spot. Sammy liked to think of the car fires flaring across the dark countryside, like beacons from the Norman times. There'd been only three cars that night but each one had felt like it was meant specifically for them. It was easy to tell the Catholic drivers from the Protestants. They didn't know 'The Sash', couldn't even make a stab at the tune. They had rosary beads hanging from their rear-view mirrors: wee tiny silver Jesus, swinging on his wee tiny silver cross. They'd the look of Catholics off them too, the smell of Catholics, evidence of their two dozen children littering the back seat. They'd beat the men up – just a bit and only with fists – for something to do. It was expected. But it was the burning they'd really come for. The fire was something you couldn't do every day in Belfast, not without permission anyway. It was worth the drive just to see the cars catch and the drivers' faces glow demon red as the owners watched their shiny Fords and Peugeots reduced to blackened ash.

The third Catholic of the night had been different. After him, they'd lost interest in burning cars. They'd packed up the Cortina and driven back to the East, stopping in Antrim for a fish supper on the way.

The third man had been driving around by himself: Ballymena via Cullybackey to Garvagh where he had a Chinese takeaway and a young wife waiting for him in his brand-new bungalow. They'd got all this off him by pressing a gun to his head, but he'd probably have told them anyway. He was cool like that, barely sweating in his sheepskin jacket. He asked if anyone minded him smoking and when they'd said, 'Work away,' offered all of them one from his packet. He'd known 'The Sash' but refused to sing it on the grounds that he was a Catholic and this sort of nonsense was demeaning. Sammy had punched him three or four times in the ribs for saying that, but the man barely flinched.

'Are youse for burning the car, lads?' he'd asked, as soon as he got his breath back. When they informed him that, yes, they were for burning his brand-new BMW, right to the ground, and slashing the tyres, he'd replied, 'Well, I suppose there's not much I can do to stop youse.' Then he'd sat himself down on the grass verge and smoked the rest of his cigarettes, lighting one from the stub of the last. He'd not seemed at all bothered about losing his car, even when the petrol tank caught and the whole thing went up like Christmas.

'What the hell's wrong with you?' Sammy had asked, standing over him with his gun, tracing the line of the man's perfectly trimmed beard, down one side of his cheek, across his chin and up the other cheek, a gesture that started out a threat and, by the third stroke, felt painfully intimate, like something one man should not be doing to another.

'I've great insurance on the motor,' the man replied.

That was enough to provoke a kind of fireball inside Sammy. He'd gone at the man's face with the barrel of his gun, breaking his nose and blacking both eyes with the heel of his hand, causing those perfectly mown cheeks to cave in upon themselves, like underdone soufflé. His face, after Sammy had finished with him, was meat, with bits of bone and tooth whiting through the red. The others stood back, just watching: three black silhouettes burnt against the flames like those lads from the Bible in the fiery furnace.

They'd left the man in a ditch, not dead but very close. After this none of them had any stomach left for fires. They turned the car and went back to Belfast. Sammy drove. All the way home he felt sick inside and that was not because of the mess he'd made of the man's face. It was because the same man would get his insurance money. There was no way of ruining the bastard completely without killing him, and even then his Fenian of a wife would have the insurance, and by that stage it was too late to go back anyway. The peelers might have been there.

Sammy could not stand the feeling of being beaten, even just a little bit. It stuck in his teeth and seemed to swell daily for weeks afterwards. It was the only thing he'd been able to think about clearly. Every night he'd close his eyes and there was that smug eejit in the sheepskin coat with his brand-new BMW, smiling, smiling, smiling, as if to say, 'Who's won now, Sammy Agnew?'

He still thinks about this fella from Garvagh every time he sees a sheepskin jacket in the street or on TV. There are more of them out there than you'd think. Del Boy. Your man from Ballymena, who does the football results. Bloody David Beckham, posing with his missus in their matching coats. He's thought about that night at least once a week for the last thirty years. He's thinking about it more and more now that he's surrounded by fire.

Sammy doesn't wait for the fire brigade to arrive. He gets to the end of the road and keeps on walking. He has a bad taste in his mouth. He knows himself capable of ruining anything he wants to ruin. He should go home and ask Mark if the same dark thing is in his mouth, if it's the only thing that holds his interest now.

He knows it is.

He needs to tell his son that violence is a passed-down thing, like heart disease or cancer. It's a kind of disease. Mark has caught it from him. It's not his fault, none of it, not even the fires or the people who have been hurt.

'It's not your fault, son,' he will say, laying a hand heavily on Mark's shoulder. He will look the boy directly in the eye when he says this. He won't be able to mean it entirely but he's very good at lying.

He will say all this and other kindly fluff, though he knows the situation is too complicated to resolve with a shouldered hand. There are things a father can carry for his son and other things that must be borne alone. Mark is almost a man now. He votes. He owns a car. He has an undergraduate degree in something to do with computers, which Sammy doesn't quite understand. He is old enough to know that functional people do not start fires or incite others to start fires. He is old enough to deal with the repercussions.

Old enough to make himself stop.

Sammy thinks about his own hot anger. It hasn't gone anywhere. It is like ice inside him waiting to melt and, once liquid, boil. There are nights when he lies awake beside his wife, one hand pressed against his ribcage, and he can feel the febrile thump of it trying to climb back out. But he never lets the anger win. He never raises his fists or even his voice. He has made a wall between himself and the old way. It is a high wall with no possibility of doors and, while the larger part of him feels responsible for Mark, the other part, the part that whines and cannot help but compare himself to other men, even his own son, insists that Mark is weak. Mark is evil. Mark is to be blamed for giving in.

He wants to ruin the boy.

He wants to give him every good thing.

As Sammy walks towards the edge of the East, the road rises to meet the Castlereagh Hills. The houses expand. Terraced streets lead to semi-detached streets, then streets entirely populated by detached houses. The roads widen. There are more trees out here, more hedges, and lawns big enough to require a sit-on lawnmower.

Sammy owns one of these houses. He has a garden to the front and a garden to the back. He is miles from where he first started. Yet distance has not made the slightest difference. He is still the same man he has always been. His son will always be his son. He opens the front door of his house, steps over the Welcome mat and tramps black fire tar all over the good carpet. There is nothing he can do to lift the stain. Tar sticks to everything it touches.

The Girl Who Could Only Fall

*E*LLA STANDS BAREFOOT *on the branch. She never wears shoes when she's attempting to fly. Her mother insists that she strip right down to her knickers. Now she's older, and more self-conscious about the bumps and curves beginning to swell beneath her skin, Ella insists upon something more substantial: a bathing suit or leotard. Her mother agrees, so long as her legs and arms are bare. It is important not to add any extra weight, to preserve the impression of lightness. Not that it really matters. Ella could bind herself up with birthday balloons, suck helium straight from the canister, or pump her arms up and down, like a racing pigeon, and it would not make the smallest bit of difference. She'd still fall. Drop. Plummet to earth at a furious rate.*

Ella wraps her arms around the trunk. She can feel its damp bark grating against her fingertips. Her skin pressed against the tree's brown is so white it's almost glowing. There's a purple-blue smudge on her left hip from last week's fall, a pair of pink grazes beginning to crust across her kneecaps. Last week it was a wall. Today it's a tree. They've tried stepladders, climbing frames, even a bridge. Seemingly there is no end to the high things you can push your daughter off for her own good. Ella looks down and notes the springy green grass circling the tree's trunk. She's grateful for it. There's more give in lawn. Concrete is not so forgiving. A starling, rattled out of the tree's upper branches, goes sweeping past her face. Ella envies its easy flight.

As she edges forward she's careful to keep her elbows tucked in. She can't risk unfurling her wings. They're covered in a thin membrane, like skin but easier torn, and she must avoid loose splinters. She eases out towards the branch's tip, feeling it bow under her weight, curling her feet around its thin curve. Beneath her naked toes the branch teems with tiny creatures: woodlice, ants, microscopic mini-beasts. They're drawn to Ella and the power that leaks out of her every time she touches. She feels the tickle of them crushing against her skin. She could stay here for hours. She honestly could. But it's not what they want from her. It would be a waste of her wings.

'Ready?' shouts her father.

'Ready,' Ella replies.

Twelve feet below he removes the ladder and steps back for a better view. Her mother has the video camera out. Ella unfolds her arms, letting her wings unfurl like pink sails lolloping in the breeze. She bends her knees and pushes off. For the smallest second she moves upwards. It's only a second, but in this one small moment, Ella always believes. Then gravity grabs her by the ankles and drags her back to earth. She hits the ground rolling. She's taught herself how to lessen the impact. There's only so many times you can fall before you become an expert and Ella is only good for falling.

4

Siren

THIS IS HOW I meet Sophie's mother, how I remember it, anyway. It's easier to tell without hindsight. With hindsight I probably wouldn't tell it at all. I'd know the end right from the start. More than likely I'd call in sick and stay at home. There would be nothing to remember then. No Sophie. No crisis looming. Life would be much as before: simpler, slower, less unknown.

The first time I encounter her it is early June. Spring is still nipping at the summer's heels. I'm signing the evening's second death certificate when the call comes in.

'Sorry, Dr Murray,' the lady receptionist says. 'I can't understand what this woman's talking about.'

'Is she Polish?' I ask.

It's a fair question. There are thousands of displaced Poles calling this city home now. No one in Belfast speaks Polish. (In certain parts of the city they have not yet mastered English.) Very few are inclined to try. Polish is a particularly uncompromising language. It is like spitting words. Even the best-intentioned of social workers can only stumble, club-tongued, through the basics.

'Is she Polish?' I repeat. 'Or some sort of African?'

Lately there have been a fair few Nigerians and Kenyans appearing around the East, like exotic holiday souvenirs. The locals – far too Lagan-centric to mark the subtleties between one impoverished arid country and the next – deem anyone darker than goat's cheese more than likely African. They are not racists. They are simply under-travelled. They take all their learning from the television.

'No, I don't think she's Polish,' the lady receptionist replies. 'She's ranting in English. Not foreign, just sort of crazy.'

'We don't say "crazy",' I repeat automatically, my thirteenth repetition of the week. 'We say "mentally ill".' I make a note not to let this particular lady receptionist answer after-hours calls again. In the background I can hear the sound of a cheap electric kettle farting towards climax. I sigh and rest my forehead on the steering wheel. 'Can you pass the call on to my mobile, please?'

'Are you sure you want me to do that, Dr Murray? We usually ignore the crazy patients – you know, leave them for the day staff.'

'Mentally ill, Jean! The woman is mentally ill, not crazy!'

'Sorry, Dr Murray. I'll remember that for the next time I get a mad one on the phone. Will I pass her through to you?'

'Go on, then.'

I lift my forehead from the steering wheel. The lower part of a Renault diamond has left a fresh, furrowed frown between my eyebrows. I check my watch. It is seven minutes past three. This is the midpoint of the night shift and I'm only holding on by the hem of myself. If I'm not careful the idea of a drink will appear at the back of my head again. Then it will be at the front, and in the East, there are plenty of places you can go for drink, even at this time of night.

The phone starts bleating at me: thin, tinny music from a popular children's movie. This is not dignified, I think. We are an out-of-hours GP service. People could be calling about a death or a person who is dying. We should have classical music on hold, something like Wagner, not *The Lion King*. The lady receptionist is trying to transfer the call. She is not good with technology. It is surprising how many of the lady receptionists are thrown by the workings of a common telephone. The larger part of me hopes she will accidentally hang up. This is the best thing that could possibly happen. It wouldn't be my fault. Even if the patient dies I could still say it wasn't my fault and no one, not even Martyn, the eldest of my colleagues and something of a stickler for old-fashioned doctoring, could possibly expect me to shoulder the guilt.

I usually ignore these calls. It's considered quite acceptable to procrastinate past the cut-off point (which is approximately five a.m.), so there isn't time to do anything more than file the mad ones, and leave them in a folder for the day staff. I loathe nights. An average night on call will include strokes, asthma attacks and languid circuits of the local nursing homes where they'll be waiting on one or more patients to pass from age (specific diagnosis no longer necessary). I'll be presented with acid indigestion, gastroenteritis, gallstones, arthritic tumbles and at least one set of neurotic new parents fussing over a meningitis rash that will invariably turn out to be eczema. I cover the inner East, from the ring road all the way down to the Lagan, a section of the city roughly six miles squared. I have been blessed with a mere pair of hands, one head and a single, now-ageing Renault estate. In normal circumstances, it is beyond my means or wherewithal to tackle the crazy patients.

'I'm ready for her,' I say, and Elton John quits plonking in my right ear. There is a silence on the line. I can hear my own breathing.

I'm not ready for her. I'm always unprepared for the next patient. The possibility of what might come stumbling through the surgery door has kept me on nails for the last twelve years. I'm a good doctor, falling in the upper percentile of competency. In fairness, I'm not known for my bedside manner. Often the female patients will stop at Reception and say, 'Is it possible to see someone aside from Dr Murray? It's about women's problems.' It is not always about women's problems but they are prepared to sit up to half an hour longer in the waiting room simply to avoid me. I know this though none of the lady receptionists has ever said anything specific. I take small blue pills for my nerves and insomnia, which has afforded me a more respectable excuse to self-medicate. If my parents had not been so set on medicine, I think I might have become a librarian. There are risks with literature but it is rare for death to result from the improper handling of a book.

'I'm ready for her,' I repeat, as much to myself as the lady receptionist, who has fallen silent now, sliding back into the secretarial abyss of filing cabinets, instant coffee and Post-it-covered patient files.

'Hello,' says a voice on the phone.

'Hello,' I say. 'You've reached the on-call doctor. How can I help you?'

'What's your name?'

'Dr Murray.'

'What's your name for friends?'

'My first name?'

'Yes, your first name and your second name and whatever name your mammy called you when you were a wee lad.'

I take a long breath and, with my left hand, reach over myself for the handle on the driver's door. I lower the window by approximately one inch. The cold air catches at my face and pinches. In front of me the windscreen is stale with condensation. I can just about make out the sleazy Christmas blur of neon signs and stop lights blushing through the traffic spectrum: red and more red, orange, green, greener, greenest yet. I feel nauseous, my belly so light it's as if it has migrated upwards to meet my lungs. It's six hours since my last proper meal.

'How can I help?' I repeat, using the voice I keep for the elderly patients who are the bread and butter of my normal week, and for the occasional psychiatric patient, who will pass briefly through the health centre en route to a more specialized facility.

'You can help me out by telling me your name,' she replies obstinately. I picture her flirting with the telephone cord as she talks, twisting it into knotty kinks. I imagine her brown-haired. I have never seen much point in blondes.

'Dr Murray.'

'Not good enough! No first name, no information! I could be dying here and you'll never know.'

I think I hear her laugh, though it may well have been an overenthusiastic starling, pre-empting the sunrise by a good two hours. Earlier in the shift I'd have hung up at this point, filing her away for the morning staff. But the second death certificate of the evening has unsettled me and now I'm swimming through fog to find the right words and the right way to say them.

'Jonathan,' I say. 'Just Jonathan.'

'Jonathan,' she repeats. 'I'm going to call you Jonny.'

I wish she hadn't called me Jonny. The sound of it is tremendous on her tongue. She has caught at the very thinnest part of me and I don't know how to say stop.

'Jonny, I need you to come and help me. I'm dying here.'

That is the worst thing she could possibly have said. I'm hooked now from all sides. 'What are you dying of?'

'Oh, any number of things: claustrophobia, boredom, thirst, loneliness . . . I haven't seen the ocean for almost a week.'

She laughs again, an honest-to-God fountain of a laugh, twinkling down the telephone line, so I can picture the wires actually glowing with the warmth of it. Laughing in the face of death, I think, and claw this thought back. I'm romanticizing the situation. I don't feel at all like myself tonight. Just another junkie on a bender, I think, and this doesn't ring particularly true either. 'Have you taken something?' I ask.

'No, nothing at all,' she shoots back. 'I think that's part of the problem. I can't eat the food here. It gets stuck in my belly. It doesn't come out anywhere. I think I might be dying.'

'Be honest with me. If you've taken something just tell me. It makes everything easier if I know what you've taken.'

'You want to know what I've taken?' she hisses, suddenly serpentine, 'I'll tell you what I've taken. I've taken a wrong turn, a bloody great wrong turn somewhere shy of Iceland. Now I'm grounded here, four storeys up, with not so much as a duck pond to keep things homely.'

Common sense tells me to hang up. The old fears are pissing themselves: the fear of people and the fear of lacking people, the fear of being mocked by strangers. I should leave her for the day staff. Let them refer her to the psychiatric unit. Let them conquer the paperwork mountains and process the little blue pills and listen to her lunatic ravings. I sigh. My breath leaves a hoary circle on the window just above the dashboard. 'Where do you live?' I ask.

'I don't live anywhere,' she replies. 'But I'm crashing in this flat, fourth floor, top of the Castlereagh Road.'

'Hold on,' I hear myself say. It's not my voice making the words but my mouth is moving. 'I'm on my way.'

'Don't take the lift. It smells of cat piss.'

She hangs up. I turn the keys in the ignition, simultaneously fastening my seatbelt. The Renault coughs twice and splutters into action, jerking forwards with arthritic abandon. I pull a wide U-turn and head east.

*

Later, much later, I will try to piece this night together, stringing one half-remembered moment to the next, like a series of mismatched beads. I will never be able to come up with a reasonable explanation.

I park the car on the road, removing my doctor's badge from the dashboard for fear the Renault will once again fall victim to the local addicts, who seem to consider me a free delivery service. I lift my medical bag from the boot, slip into a grizzled tweed blazer – a gift from my mother some six Christmases ago – and, thus armed, contemplate her block of flats in all its blunted glory.

The grey concrete, the cubic red windows and crude lines make it look like a child's notion of a building. Everything is stacked, and there are no trees to break up the straightness. Only one window in the block is illuminated. It peers down at me judgementally: a great godless eye, butter blond and unblinking. I think about sliding back into the Renault and beating a tactical retreat to the safety of some petrol station forecourt. Over in Rosetta, a police siren stutters twice and shrieks into vicious, teeming life. I am startled by the scream of it.

I take the gravelled area in front of the building in five measured strides, draw breath and hold it against the stench of piss and stale cider, warm rubbish, aerosol, animal and weathered human. Remembering her advice, I avoid the lift and, with cautious deliberation, make my way up eight squat flights to the fourth floor. The medical bag, swinging like a pendulum against my thigh, counts the steps for me. As I climb I hold the horror tightly, imagining it as an actual lump inside my ribcage. 'She could be dead already,' I tell myself. 'She could have OD'd or slit her wrists with a safety razor. She could be blue and bloated, drowning in her own vomit.'

Any number of possible horrors may be hanging behind the

front door. If I had more time, I'd make a list of the very worst. I find lists tremendously helpful. But I don't need a list to help me realize that the thing I fear most is her presence: alive and staring at me, hungrily, with that voice.

The front door of her flat is wedged open with a battered tin of Campbell's chicken soup. I remove it as I enter, toe poking it into the hall. The door slams behind me, settling sharply into its frame.

'Hey,' she calls triumphantly. 'Jonny, I knew you'd come.' She is not dead, or even close to dying.

I can hear her clearly but I'm struggling to distinguish her in the dark. The room's features – furniture, wallpaper and occupants – are charcoal grey and furry, as if viewed through a sheet of tissue paper. I stand by the door, allowing my eyes to adjust. The space is a strange composite of living room, kitchen and – I'm guessing – bedroom. A single door, positioned to the right of the electric cooker, insinuates a second room, a bathroom most likely. I hold my ground by the front door, foot-anchored but leaning forwards, as if unsure whether to enter or run.

'How are you feeling?' I call into the darkness. 'Any better now?'

'I'm still dying,' she replies. 'You'd better come over here and examine me.'

Though I've been a doctor for almost twelve years now and examine dozens of patients daily, thousands per year, the word 'examine' has never before sounded so illicit. A thing pitches forwards inside me. It is like a magnet. No, this is not quite right. It is like something more dangerous, a cruise missile, perhaps.

'Um, no,' I say. I screw my heels deep into the ancient carpet. It is blue with faded fleur-de-lis swirls in turquoise. 'Why don't you describe your symptoms and I'll just diagnose you from here?'

'I'm dying,' she says. 'I don't have symptoms. I'm just dying.'

'And have you been dying for a long time?'

'Centuries.'

'Is it painful?'

'Excruciating.'

'Is there anything in particular which exacerbates your condition?'

'This bloody city for one thing.'

'Is there anything that helps?'

'Company,' she says, and though my heels hold their ground and my ribcage remains stoic to the last, it is impossible to stop my rebel spine sliding forwards. Reluctantly, the rest of me ventures into the darkness, chin first, frowning eyebrows, teeth and elbows, stomach muscles, knees, fingernails, and last – thick with reservations – my cotton-clad ankles.

'That's better,' she says, as I stand over her, still clutching my doctor's bag, like an excuse for what will come after. 'I wanted to see what you looked like.'

'I look like this,' I say, and for the first time in almost twenty years, I wonder what I actually look like. 'What do you look like?'

'I don't know,' she replies. 'I've never seen myself. Maybe you can tell me.'

I can't really see her. One arm is visible and also the porcelain arc of what might be a heel or could, just as easily, be an abandoned teacup. The better part of her is buried. Her voice, though instantly familiar, is struggling to surface from beneath a muffled mound of duvets and blankets, carpet tiles and old coats. Still as glass and barely lit, she gives the impression of a hastily wrapped corpse. I can't stop staring. I am only eyes and, behind the eyes, a mind like a camera, taking notes. Nothing good will come of staying here. Just the two of us, moving closer. I already know this. Just as I know myself incapable of leaving.

'Stop staring,' she says.

I stare harder. 'I'm looking for clues,' I say. 'Maybe I could stop you dying if I was able to see you properly. Can I turn the lights on?'

'No lights,' she snaps, and tunnels deeper. I can see the swell of her, swimming like a mountain range beneath the blankets.

'Come and find me,' she mumbles. Her words seem to float upwards in tiny handfuls, bursting on the surface, like a series of aquarium air pockets.

This is not something I'm capable of explaining, either in the moment or later, with several months of hindsight. Good sense leaves me every time she opens her mouth. I'm drawn to her, Medicine is no longer a decent excuse for what I'm doing here. This both shames and thrills me. I'm just as feeble, just as infectious and fading, as the people I call patients. I've always known this but now it is a comfort to me. The simplest explanation is desire, and granted, there are lusty little itches running the length of me every time she speaks. But even desire falls far short of the undulating contractions currently waging war on my brain. My tweed blazer shrinks, like a boa constrictor. My polyester underwear sweats disagreeably. My stethoscope threatens to strangle me for my own good. Even my short-back-and-sides appears to be rising rebelliously about my ears. I feel like a man standing over a woman. This is something I've only ever experienced on television.

I do not want to be a doctor in her presence. I set my medical bag at her feet. It falls open, spilling pills and potions and sterile bandages, like flat white rivers rolling across the filthy carpet. I prise my shoes off, one stiff heel at a time, remove my stethoscope and, attired as an average man, peel her, blanket by blanketty layer. As if she is an onion. When I finally arrive at cold cream flesh I am surprised to find her freckled and average, a little thicker in the thigh than I'd imagined. Her face is the pale face of a girl you'd see carrying eggs or milk in an old painting. She has very dark eyes. Not cold. Just dark. Hair as dark and swimming as her eyes. She laughs at my cold fingers and laughs at my cotton socks. I don't mind. I peel my own clothes off and stand before her naked, letting her look all over me. We don't dance but I know, with her, I could. She doesn't ask if I'm happy or having a good time or if I want to leave. It's as if she knows what I'm thinking or, perhaps, she's telling me what to think. I'm not bothered either way.

I'm having the only time of my life.

'I'm having the time of my life,' I say over and over again.

'Oh, I know,' she says.

She keeps me in her bed, starving, for three full days. Rising, on the third day, with an empty belly and seething static hair, I find her perched upon the kitchen bench observing me keenly. She's wearing the living-room curtains or, rather, one half of the pair. The remaining curtain hangs morosely from the window, a crushed velvet divorcee, humiliated by its inability to close. She is painting her toenails green.

'I should go,' I say. 'I have other patients. I've been here for hours.'

'Days,' she corrects. 'It's been three days.'

The enormity of this hits me. It's almost too big to believe.

'Shit,' I say. 'I've probably lost my job.'

'Probably,' she agrees.

'I need to go home right now. I need to eat something. Then I need to go home.'

'I'm coming too.'

'You can't come home with me.'

'Why not?'

'I hardly know you.'

'It's a matter of life and death, Jonny. If you don't take me home with you, I'll probably die here in this flat. Right here on the floor, wrapped up in this curtain. And you'll be to blame.'

While I consider my options, reminding myself that good sense should no longer be seen as a measuring stick for decision-making, she passes me a tin-opener and the long-forgotten chicken soup. I eat it straight from the tin, using the flattened metal arm of the opener as a makeshift spoon. It tastes like wallpaper paste.

'Besides,' she says, dropping the curtain to slip into a pair of royal-blue decorator's overalls, 'you're extremely lonely. You need something in your life aside from doctoring.'

'I probably don't even have the doctoring to fall back on any more,' I mutter, between glutinous mouthfuls.

'It's settled, then. You need me. You're taking me home.'

'I don't think I want to.'

'Yes, you do.'

Instantly I change my mind. I very much want to take her home with me. This is one of the best ideas I've ever had. She has no belongings, besides a second pair of overalls, which she retrieves from the cupboard beneath the sink.

'Toothbrush?' I ask.

'Never felt the need,' she replies, and grins to expose a set of baby teeth, perfectly capped and kept like pearly headstones.

'Underwear? Change of clothes?'

She shakes her head slowly, allowing waves of coal-black curls to flex and swoosh about her shoulders.

'Shoes? Surely you have shoes? Everyone has shoes.'

She has no shoes. I rifle round the flat and find nothing resembling footwear, not so much as a casual slipper. I turn her feet upside down and examine the soles. They are sausage pink and unlined, perfect as a newborn's. Though logic and eight flights of concrete stairs argue otherwise, though I've done my best to avoid podiatry, and I know there are reasonable scientific explanations for almost every bizarre occurrence, I suspect her feet are barely used. They are suspiciously unworn for a fully grown woman. I say nothing. Over the next nine months I'll find myself regularly saying next to nothing while an avalanche of questions threatens to tip me over some terrible edge.

'Right then,' I say. 'If you've got no shoes, I suppose I'll have to carry you.'

I have never lifted another human being before, even as a child playing with other children. I pick her up and fling her over one shoulder. I've seen this in a movie about firefighters, possibly *The Towering Inferno*. I pass her my bag. Obsolete as it is, I feel a strange attachment to its parchment leather, its stout belly, the chlorine and carbon smell it seems to emit. I can't leave it here in the empty flat. Thus balanced, we sashay downwards to the foyer. The weight of her is wonderful, a dull pain that burns louder with every flight of steps. By the time I arrive, panting, at the Renault's door I'm drenched with sweat. I feel capable of building brutish things: ships and houses, railway lines. I could probably kill a man with my bare hands. I set her carefully on the bonnet. Her backside leaves an indentation in the sheet metal, a gentle hollow that will pool with water every time it rains. This mark will last longer than our relationship.

'You've got three parking tickets,' she says, plucking the little plastic packets individually from beneath my windscreen wipers. 'It's your own fault. You left your car for three days in a one-hour spot.'

'I didn't mean to stay,' I reply.

'Oh, I think you did, Jonny. I think you had every intention of staying.'

And, I have to admit, she's absolutely right. I keep this to myself as I manhandle her into the passenger seat, forcibly buckling her in for she seems terrified of seatbelts, terrified of any kind of restraint. The dashboard clock reads 6:37. East Belfast is just beginning to wake. Straggles of sleep-deprived cleaners and factory workers huddle under the bus-stop hoods, smoking.

A solitary bin lorry beats up and down the Newtownards Road, purposefully ignoring the congregations of wheelie-bins, worshipping, open-mouthed on every corner. The church spires stretch maliciously, as if intent upon piercing the clouds, and the rain obliges, descending in gloopy streams, smearing like syrup across the Renault's windscreen.

Before turning the car I pause to look at her. She is silently folding herself into the passenger seat, her face barely visible above the peak of her knees. I like her best like this, quiet and compromised. While she holds her tongue I can order my thoughts, think in lines and strings rather than the cyclical swirls she stirs up inside my head.

'She doesn't belong to me,' I tell myself. 'I should leave her where I found her.'

I know this will not end well. In the silence I'm all for pitching her out on to the pavement.

'Here,' she says, lowering her knees to let her lungs unfold, 'do you have a bath or a shower in your house, Jonny?'

'Both,' I reply, and throw the Renault into second gear. The argument is over. My head is once more spaghetti. I'm already planning to make her sleep on the left side of the bed, as far as possible from the door.

'Perfect,' she says. 'Is it a large bath, big enough for me to be underwater if I fill it to the brim?'

'I suppose. I've never tried. I usually take showers.'

'Great. You can keep taking your showers and I'll take the bath. I'll feel much better once I'm underwater. You'll hardly notice me around the house. I'll just stay in the bath.'

And this is what she does for nine whole months, rising to the surface when the second trimester causes her belly to swell at an alarming rate. She is not happy. She wishes to be underwater, fully submerged, like an octopus or a submarine. At first it shocks me to see her pale face rippling beneath the bathwater, that thin line of bubbles rising from her nose and mouth. I sit on the closed toilet lid for hours, staring, waiting to haul her to the surface and perform mouth-to-mouth when her breath runs out. Her breath never runs out. She's built like a kind of fish. Like nothing I've ever seen before. Eventually I accept this. I never get used to it. But I come to accept that she isn't normal and I find a way to live with this.

Singing into my deepest sleep she demands a weightlifter's belt, a force with which to petition gravity, something to keep her head perpetually bobbing beneath the waterline. I order one off the internet, and when it arrives, I fasten it firmly about her expanding middle. It is the only thing she will consent to wear. The lust has long gone out of her nakedness. I see her now as I see my patients or pictures in a medical textbook. Except, of course, when she wishes to be seen with lust. This is all in the way she words herself, 'Come here, Jonny. I need you.' Then I cannot have enough of her nakedness. Then, I am in the bath with her or on the bathroom floor, dripping. Afterwards I regret what we have done and wish we could be normal together, in a bed.

'It's best if I'm underwater,' she explains, 'I feel better under-water, but this damn baby seems determined to drag me to the surface.'

I spend hours, while she's sleeping, riffling through medical textbooks. I google case studies and academic articles, searching for other human beings capable of flourishing on nothing but liquids, for adult men and women with skin as flawless as that of newborn children. I study hypnotism, mind tricks and ex-amples of ordinary people coerced into unusual behaviour, those subject to Stockholm syndrome or brainwashed by cults and charismatic individuals. I find myself typing 'Can human beings live underwater?' into the search bar and wonder what the point of medical school was, when everything lately has seemed to laugh in the face of science.

Of course I discover small snippets of her in many of these articles. Here, in the subsonic communication of bats and dolphins, is a possible explanation for the way her voice has a hook to it. The way it is impossible to hear fully, or resist with an ordinary ear. Here, in the smooth, unmarked heels of the South Pacific boat people, I find a precedent for her own flawless soles. Here are numerous freaks and addicts, mutated genetics and mental-health issues nodding towards her oddity. I collate them all in a hardback notebook, attempting to convince myself that there is a perfectly plausible reason for the way she isn't normal.

But science is not wide enough to contain her. She is not just happiest underwater, or unmarked, or capable of melding thought with the slightest inclination of her voice. She is so much more than a series of individual symptoms combined. She has, for many months, been a force of bloody reckoning occupying my en-suite bathroom. All my careful notes cannot scratch the surface of how it feels to stand under her voice, stripped of all resistance, fragile, floundering, hoping she will not choose to destroy me. And, though I can't admit it to myself, cannot even write the bad word down, I know exactly what she is, and there is no way to say this with science. Myth made flesh. Creature lifted from a story book. Siren she is. Wicked, matchless Siren, and I'll be lucky to survive her or the thing she's making in my bathtub.

I have fifty per cent shares in this child. I suspect it is caught in some sort of pre-natal wrestling match, a junior Jacob oscillating between the human and the divine. The human element, I reassure myself, seems hell-bent on making it to the surface. She costs me hundreds of pounds in hot water. The gas bill goes through the roof. Even in early April, while the city swelters beneath a pre-season heatwave, she demands piping hot bathwater.

'It's a luxury,' she admits, 'my only luxury, Jonny. It's not like I'm costing you much in food or clothes.'

This is true. Save the daily drum of Saxa added to her bath-water, and the gas bill and, of course, the loss of a stable income, she is a cheap date, a kind of overgrown goldfish. She only ever consumes liquids, water, juice, custard, tinned soup, continuing to insist that anything more solid will stick inside her and never come out. I've no idea if this is normal for her sort. It's not the kind of thing we covered in medical school. For months I live from hand to mouth, existing on Pot Noodle, cheap whiskey and the sound of her singing melodically in the upstairs bath-room. I read the Bible from cover to cover as a means of filling my time and find nothing, not a single line of helpful advice, on the subject of intoxicating sea creatures. I give up on the Bible and work my way through a box set of *The Chronicles of Narnia*. Even this seems a little too much like realism.

I watch her expand. Her hips and thighs swell against the bathtub sides. Her hair is like sea grass shuffling in the water. Her fingertips are prunes and raisins now. The dome of her stomach breaks the water's surface, belly button dilating, like the inverted funnel of an old-fashioned gramophone. When she sleeps, as she often does, head resting on the bathtub's bottom, her breath swims to the surface in glassy, marble burps and I whisper into her belly button, hoping the baby might have its ear inclined towards the outside world.

'What sort of a creature are you?' I ask the unborn thing inside her. It's my one and only question. No answer is forth-coming. Considering her mother's condition, the baby is remarkably quiet. I am a father now, no longer a doctor. I dread the advent of a tiny monster. A baby is almost as hard to imagine.

When the moment comes I am fast asleep, drooling over the living-room sofa. Behind me the television is chattering. It has once again become a thing I talk to as if it is another person in the room. Between the television and the sleeping I don't hear any of it. No screaming. No laboured breathing. No howls of dreadful pain. Nor do I hear her leave. Once she is gone, it is hard to believe in the strangeness of her. She is just another person who has upped and left me. She is gone but still stitched into me, smarting every time my mind catches on the thought of her.

I try to convince myself that she was just a regular woman. But I can't seem to skim over those unmarked heels or her always wanting to be underwater. The way I couldn't say no to her, would let her bite and claw me ragged even when my body yearned for softness. The magic of her. The way she could pinch my will and twist it, easy as a blink. How it hurt, real gut pangs, like being stabbed each time I tried to resist her. No, she wasn't normal. There was nothing ordinary about her. Siren she was. Irresistible, intoxicating Siren.

I know I can never speak of her in this way. How to say, 'I have been seduced by a mythical creature'? How to make the unbelievable true? It would help if she'd offered me a name, a back story, even the smallest sliver of information about her past. But she's left me nothing to prove her real. Nothing but the salt line crusting round my bathtub. Nothing but the memory of my whole body clenching, as if punched, every time I looked at her pale Ophelia face blooming through the bathwater.

I find the baby in the kitchen sink, half filled.

I read insecurity into the six inches of sink that remained unfulfilled. In the nine months of our mutual acquaintance I had never known her to hesitate. She must have hesitated then, leaning over the draining-board, scrutinizing her newborn daughter for the assurance that she was one hundred per cent hers, capable of all necessary aquatics. In the end she'd held back and filled the sink halfway. Perhaps she saw me in the cut of my daughter's shins, the way her second toes curled into the third, the frowning eyebrows, which, even in her earliest moments, threatened to avalanche her tiny face.

I want to think the child is clearly mine. I cannot see an ounce of myself in her. I wrap her in a wad of kitchen roll and a cautionary layer of tinfoil for I remember this will keep the heat in. I cannot, in the moment, remember anything useful learnt at university. A series of child-sized footprints in the flowerbeds beneath the kitchen window suggests her mother is long gone. My head is glacial. My lungs are on fire. I pour myself a glass of whiskey and, with no proper infant receptacle forthcoming, place the baby inside the largest of my saucepans. Her skin is the colour of sliced salami. Her hair, coal-toned and gleaming, is concentrated around her face in thick curls. Like question marks.

It is hard to call her beautiful but she belongs to me. I feel less the failure just watching her sleep. I have made a solid half of her – arms or legs, back or belly, fingers or toes. Fifty per cent of her is mine. I haven't abandoned her. I have found her floundering in the kitchen sink. And saved her. I fully intend to keep her for eighteen years at least. I wonder if this is something like being in love. It isn't as urgent as I'd imagined love would be. The closest thing I can compare it to is physics: a sense that one thing must naturally lead to the next. There is no feeling involved. It is as inevitable as gravity.

I can't think of a name for her. But there is plenty of time for that.

For one day I am the happiest man in East Belfast. Then I start wondering what will happen when she speaks.

5

The Difficult Son

PEEL BACK THE years. It is 2001, a month before September the eleventh. In East Belfast the children have two solid weeks of freedom left. They are acutely aware of the first day of term. It is like a small death looming on the horizon. They are sucking the marrow out of every remaining holiday moment. Up with the birds and down with the streetlamps. They're never inside. They're always filthy and knee-greened with grass stains. They're happy as children should be. Sammy has three children: Mark, who is eight years old, Lauren, who is seven, and Christopher, who is just five and still carries a comfort blanket.

It is not a particularly hot summer, but it is dry, and his children have no interest in television. They are, every waking moment, outside. Sammy watches them from the kitchen window kicking footballs and playing Wimbledon over the clothes line with ancient tennis racquets and balled-up socks. On those rare days when the temperature crawls close enough to twenty to approximate heat, Pamela gets him to blow up the paddling pool. The children run in and out of the lukewarm water tracking cut grass and mud behind them until they're bathing in liquid the colour of cold tea. By five they are goosebumped and shivering but still reluctant to come in for their dinner. When they eat they shovel the food into their mouths and barely give it time to hit their stomachs before they're speed-saying, 'Thank-you-for-my-dinner-please-may-I-leave-the-table.' Then they're up and out of the door with a choc ice in hand. That is what passes for pudding during the summer months.

Every afternoon the neighbourhood kids circulate through the Agnews' backyard, like downtown buses: wee Jonno and the twins, Mikey M and Mikey B, Lydia, Maureen (whose parents are older and dress her like a spinster aunt), and Stevie, from the top of the road, who has his right arm in a cast from playing cricket. Their bikes are abandoned in the Agnews' drive, wheels still spinning as they hit the ground, handlebars twisted awkwardly, like soldiers dropped dead on the battlefield. Sammy picks his way through the carnage to the garage. The bikes are a bloody nuisance but he cannot get the rage up.

This is everything he's ever wanted for his children: outdoors and innocence and friends from nice families, with parents who still live together, who don't believe in guns. His children are the most popular kids on the street. This has something to do with there being three of them. Boy, girl, boy, with only a year sandwiching one child to the next. A kind of condensed energy comes off them so they're like magnets for all the other kids. Sammy is happy when he sees his children being children. The roar inside him falls silent as he stands on his back doorstep, passing out plastic cups of orange squash, and ice pops. It settles down but doesn't ever go away.

He is worried about Mark. He is never really worried about Lauren or Christopher. They are good kids. They rarely warrant his concern, and when they do, it is an entirely normal kind of anxiety focused upon high fevers, wet beds and brief spates of biting. Mark is different. Mark has never bitten. Even as a very small child biting was beneath him. So much more damage could be done with a dinner fork pressed into another child's thigh. Aged three, he'd held another boy's arm against the radiator until it blistered. Afterwards he called it an accident and everyone, even the boy's mother, had believed him. There was a thing he could do to adults with his eyes, like a baby deer. Sammy hadn't believed him. He recognized the way his son's eyes could turn. Like marbles or cold milk. He knew the child was already considering what he might do next.

Mark reminds Sammy of himself as a boy. This is enough to keep him up at night, nipping whiskey from a coffee mug. Yet when he sees the child flying up and down the hill on his bike, standing soldier straight on the pedals and laughing as an eight-year-old should laugh – all open-mouthed and gap-toothed – Sammy can catch his concern by the throat and hope.

'Everything is going to be all right,' he tells himself.

There is more good in the boy than evil. He is five parts Pamela to every ounce of his da. He has his mother's looks, after all. Everyone says so, even strangers. All summer Sammy anchors himself to these cold hopes. He tries not to notice the rage when it comes flying out of Mark on the football pitch or at the dinner table. He looks sideways when other children fall off their bikes and there is Mark, laughing at their bloody knees and broken teeth, laughing with a cruel adult intonation. He takes pains to call it curiosity, natural scientific curiosity, when he stumbles upon wasps and other insects drowned in tumblers of cold water. He knows his son has done this, by himself, for badness. Sammy tries to see what he wants to see in the boy and lets his eye slide loosely over everything else. He can ignore anything, even the knives, but the incident with the chicken shed is like a mountain that won't let him pass by. It is so very calculated.

It starts innocently enough. Lauren is scared of the swans in Victoria Park. This is hardly surprising. She's always been a nervous child and the swans are a notoriously vicious breed, prone to chase small children and hiss, like hot kettles, when adults approach the water's edge. Lots of children are scared of swans and rightly so: a swan, when provoked, can snap a grown man's arm so it splinters like a bent toothpick. Neither Sammy nor Pamela is overly concerned about the swans.

Then Lauren develops a fear of ducks. Ducks are different. Children should love ducks. Ducks are printed on the side of Lauren's yellow welly boots and they are in her baby books, quack, quack, quacking, while the pigs on the opposite page go, 'Oink!' There is nothing threatening about a duck. They begin to grow a little more concerned. They play her videos of cartoon ducks, trying to lift the edge of her fear. They take her to the pond's edge and hold her in their arms while scattering bread-crumbs in wide circles around their own feet. 'Look,' they say, 'the wee ducks wouldn't hurt you. They're only after your bread.' Lauren howls, like a woman in labour. She claws her mother's neck in panic. When they get home, Sammy notices she has wet herself for the first time in more than two years.

The situation spirals. Three days before the start of term Lauren decides that she is terrified of all the birds in the world. 'Even penguins,' she says, though she is well aware that Belfast does not have wild penguins. She purges her bedroom of birds, chucking children's books, stuffed animals and plastic ephemera straight into the kitchen bin. The very act of engaging with pretend birds leaves her trembling. She is up five times through the night with nightmares.

Sammy wonders if they should take her to the doctor. Pamela says not to be so daft. There's nothing can be done with medicine. It's just a phase. The next evening he catches his wife praying the bird fear out of their sleeping daughter. Her hands rest gently on Lauren's forehead like a priest conferring bless-ing. They are not a religious family, though they were both brought up in the Church. Under pressure it is strange to see his wife default to prayer. He stands at Lauren's bedroom door and listens. Pamela is only saying the Lord's Prayer with a bit added on about birds. This is the only prayer she can remember entirely.

Prayer doesn't work. Lauren refuses to go outside for fear of the pigeons strung across the telephone wire. She is already testing out the idea of not going to school. 'There might be birds there,' she explains.

Pamela is firm with the child. 'Enough of your nonsense,' she says.

She lifts Lauren straight off the living-room sofa. This is some manoeuvre. The child is big for seven and as hefty as her dad. Pamela staggers under the weight as she carries her through the patio doors and into the back garden. Lauren is a limpet: arms and legs wrapped round her mother, like a baby koala, but she is outside and she is not screaming. Surely this is progress. Sammy, watching at the kitchen window, smiles and waves to them both. 'Good girl,' he shouts, through the open door. 'Do you want a wee dish of ice cream for supper?'

He hopes this will be the end of the phase. They've been calling it a phase rather than an actual problem. A phase, like the time Mark went off white bread, or when Christopher would wear only the one pair of trousers for two months straight. All is looking hopeful until Lauren spots a starling on next door's roof and, with a wail that has the neighbours raising their blinds, kicks her mother in the ribs and comes bolting back into the house. This sets a precedent for the next week. Lauren will go outside only if she can't see a bird. She enters and exits school with her anorak hood drawn tightly over her head. She refuses to go into the playground with the other children at break time. She keeps the entire family trapped inside the electric doors at Tesco for five minutes because there is a pigeon between her and the car. Eventually Mark goes at it, kicking. Mark has no patience with his sister. Mark has no patience with anyone. There is no weakness in him and he cannot tolerate weakness in others.

He is, by his own admission, trying to help Lauren when he locks her in next door's chicken shed. The neighbours believe him. He turns on the tears for their benefit, does his trick with the big doe eyes. Why wouldn't they believe him? They are used to ordinary children who are occasionally naughty but never, or only on television, actually cruel. Sammy does not believe Mark. It is Sammy who finds him leaning against the chicken shed, one ear pressed into its wooden frame, all the better to hear his sister howling, all the better to hear her fingernails bloodying themselves against the locked door and the chickens flustering round her head, like mad, feathered hurricanes.

For a brief moment, mere seconds, Sammy stands at the top of his neighbours' garden and watches his son. There is a look on the boy's face he has seen on the face of preachers, and football-ers, firing the ball into the back of the net. The name for this look is rapture. Sammy's seen it on his own face: once reflected in the window of a burning car, and once in the early days with Pamela, her face as loose and sex-soft as his own. As soon as Mark spots his father he steps away from the chicken shed and holds up his hands, like an innocent criminal. 'I was only trying to fix her, Dad,' he says. Then he lets the tears out. But they're only in the corner of his eyes, not the black parts, which are incapable of lying.

That night Sammy beats Mark with a wooden spoon. It has taken at least four hours to ease the hysteria out of Lauren. It has taken Calpol and hot chocolate and Pamela curled up next to her in bed with arms full of stuffed animals. He beats Mark with the bedroom door open so his wife can hear and intervene if he cannot stop himself. The boy doesn't scream or cry, but a dry gasp, like a stuck cough, comes scuttling out of him each time the spoon lands on his backside. Sammy never beats his son again. He is scared he might kill the child. There is something in him that wants hitting.

After the chicken shed Sammy is afraid for Mark in a way he has never feared for himself. The same rough blood runs through them both, but Mark is so much sharper than he has ever been. For the first time Sammy is glad of his own thick head, which could never see further than the next hard punch. He knows what it is to hurt people. He has felt bones splinter beneath his fists, and scrubbed strangers' blood from his hands and face. Violence has never been a concept for Sammy. It has always been a physical thing, heavy as a breeze block.

Mark is different. Mark has the ability to hurt people without actually touching them. It is the distance that thrills him, that makes him feel like God. This, Sammy knows, is a kind of greatness. He is sometimes jealous of his son who, even at eight, is quicker than his father and mother combined. This, Sammy also knows, is the worst kind of power: fists can be held down or even severed, but a mind like Mark's is impossible to contain. He is afraid of his son. There is no softness in him, not even with his mother.

Sammy tells Pamela that the chicken shed was an accident. He cannot look at her directly when he says this. He doesn't want to see her eyes swimming, trying hard to believe that everything is going to be OK. Everything is not going to be OK. They both know this. But Pamela is a kinder person than Sammy and inclined to see the good in everyone. Though they muddle through for the younger kids' sake, soon there will be little left between them but a thick cloud of disappointment. And guilt.

Then it is mid-September 2001. Lauren is still itchy around birds but she's seeing a counsellor now. The counsellor is confident she'll be fine by Christmas. Just in time for robin redbreasts and all the doves of peace. The end of the world has just happened in New York and they've decided not to let the children watch the news. This will be one of the last decisions Sammy and Pamela make together, like a proper couple. They discuss the matter over mugs of steaming tea when the children are in bed. The television in the living room is showing a constant loop of the first tower falling, then the second, the plane piercing the glassy wall over and over again, like a blip in the film reel.

'We can't shelter them for ever,' Pamela argues.

'Course we can't, love,' Sammy replies, 'but nobody should have to see this kind of thing, especially children.'

He is thinking of Lauren and Christopher, how Christopher has only just stopped having nightmares after accidentally watching a particularly bloody episode of *Taggart*. He is anxious to place a wall around their innocence. This is normal for fathers. However, when they decide that, in their house, September the eleventh has not happened, it is Mark he is mostly thinking of. Sammy is nearly always thinking of Mark now: his ghost eyes, his vicious tongue, his tiny white fingers, already adept at forming fists. The chicken shed is still fresh in his mind. Every time he looks at his daughter he sees her fear-shot face, pale and hanging, like a corpse, and the bile comes hurtling up his throat in waves. Mark has taken something of his daughter away from him.

Sammy isn't at all worried about traumatizing Mark. Nightmares might do the boy some good, put the fear of God back into him. He is strong as sheet metal. Everything glances off him, even physical pain. No, Sammy is afraid of how his son will react to all these vile images: the bodies fluttering from the sky, like wingless birds, the dead already ghosted in white concrete dust, the explosions, the glass screaming from its sockets as buildings evaporate, the sound of so many frightened people running.

Mark will be all eyes for this kind of misery. He'll try to see the footage again and again. He will, without any conscious effort, remember the details as other children hold tightly to the details of Christmas Day and Halloween. It will make him happy. Though he is shrewd enough at eight not to say this, Sammy knows that this kind of thing makes his son extremely happy. It is in the curl of his mouth and the questions he asks, numbers, distances, times and temperatures, as if he can see the logic in destruction, as if he is making plans inside his head.

They don't tell their children about the Twin Towers but they hear about it anyway, from friends with sloppy parents or sanctimonious parents, who believe that children should not be sheltered from the harsher side of life. Lauren cries and Christopher bolts into the house every time a plane passes overhead. Mark is different. Mark asks questions and lifts Sammy's newspapers from the recycling bin to clip out pictures. He keeps them in a biscuit tin underneath his bed. Pamela finds the tin tucked inside the toe end of a sleeping bag when she is lifting his laundry. There are other newspaper clippings and articles cut from library books: serial killers, motorway pile-ups, cruel things done to animals with knives. She sits on the bed for almost an hour, holding the tin against her chest. She feels as if she has been shot.

'We should take him to a psychiatrist,' Pamela says, when she tells Sammy about the photos. She is more upset than she was when her father died.

'It's just a phase he's going through,' he reassures her. 'Lots of wee boys go through this stage. He'll grow out of it.'

Pamela tries to believe him. This is what she wants to hear. But she can't bring herself to believe Sammy. She has always felt the coldness in Mark, even as a baby. She lets herself imagine what it would be like to lose him. The first and strongest feeling is relief. She knows that Sammy feels the same but they cannot ever admit this. There are certain things parents cannot say. Even to each other.

They buy football lessons for Mark, a computer of his own, books and videos, anything to keep his mind occupied. None of these distractions works. They do not take him to a psychiatrist. They do not ask their friends for help. They cannot bring themselves to talk about the situation directly. This is resignation on Sammy's part. For Pamela it is just pretending. They let Mark ruin himself up in his attic room, hardly ever speaking, on his computer, reading books he's ordered off the internet, out all hours with his friends, who are older or perhaps only hardened about the face. They let him go. He is still in the house but he is essentially gone. The weight of him bears slowly down on them. It is a kind of grief dripping from the attic, through the floorboards and ceiling, into their bedroom. It forces its way between them and they aren't strong enough to resist.

Fifteen years go by. A lifetime. Christopher and Lauren up and leave for university in Coleraine and Glasgow. They get into their second-hand cars and drive away. They do not look back. They return only for Christmas. Mark doesn't leave. He studies something with computers at Queen's and never moves out of the attic room. He pays his own fees. His parents do not ask where the money comes from. Neither do they ask for rent. They are afraid of what Mark might say.

Sammy and Pamela are not the same people they were twenty years ago. They do not even look the same. At night they lie in bed listening to the weight of their son creaking through the floorboards as he paces round his room. They want to blame him for everything. Instead they blame themselves – or, rather, Sammy blames himself and Pamela lets him.

The Boy with Wheels for Feet

MATTHEW COMES SLITHERING out arms first, his hands thrust far in front of his head, like Superman poised for flight. 'That's the head out,' says the midwife. 'The worst is over, Mrs Christie.' She doesn't know about the wheels. A woman's body is not cut for birthing wheels. Matthew almost rips his mother in two.

He's rolling before he walks. The slightest incline has him gliding from one side of the room to the next. As soon as he's on his feet, he's flying. Fastest boy in East Belfast. You should see him work the play area at Vicky Park. He takes the slide like a ski jump. Legs bent. Arms taut. Aiming to claim ten, then twelve and finally fifteen foot of clean air when his wheels lose contact with the slide's lip. By the age of eight he's done with baby slopes. Everyone says he's greased lightning on the hills. Cave Hill. Black Mountain. Any steep spot will do. It's a glorious thing to watch him hurtling from high to low. Like God himself, sweeping his holiness past at speed. His parents stand on the pavement admiring their boy grow closer and larger, until his quick rush passes by. So fast. It is more felt than seen. Their Matthew leaves burn marks in the road. Actual sparks electric off the asphalt. Holy. Holy. Holy smoke. They've no idea where such speed comes from. She's a dinner lady and he works nights on the line at Shorts. Neither has a fast bone in their body.

Now Matthew's ten and the speed is in him like the need to eat. He can't keep still. He thinks with his feet and every thought is quicker than the last. He is always on the internet looking up fast drops. Olympus. Everest. Kilimanjaro. He has his heart set on the world's steepest slopes. He only feels right when the floor is falling away from him at tremendous speed. 'If I can't be normal,' he tells his dad, 'I'll be really fast instead.' His parents know they're losing him. His browser history reads like a suicide note. Table Mountain. Matterhorn. Slieve Donard (which is at least close to home). They consider shackling Matthew to the radiator in his room. By the ankles. For his own good. His mother sits up at night winding individual strands of her own hair round the boy's feet. Anything to slow down his leaving. His father knows it's futile. Matthew's already gone. You can't be anything but moving when you've wheels where you should have feet.

6

The Naming

IT IS HIGH summer now and Sophie is four months old. She is the size of an indoor cat. I hold her like a cat, draping her over my shoulder as if she is a fancy scarf. She seems to enjoy this. Her legs hang loose against my chest. Her arms catch at my shoulder blades. I can't see her face for she is always looking away from me. This suits me just fine. It is easier not to believe in the back of her head.

I've called her Sophie because she required a name. Sophie was also the name of a medical student who shadowed me for six months last year. We weren't close, but it was easy to sit quietly in her company, like two people reading books in a library. When I began to consider names for my daughter, Sophie came almost instantly to mind and stuck. Perhaps I've come to associate this name with silence.

After acquiring a child you have one week in which to give it a permanent name. I know this because I'm a doctor. It's a sort of law parents are told when leaving the maternity ward. When she first arrived I stared at the baby's feet for seven days straight. They were the only part of her I could bear to focus on. 'What do you want to be called?' I asked the feet, and the feet didn't respond. For days all I was able to think of were very common nouns such as 'child', and 'person', and 'creature'. These wouldn't do for a baby. Sophie was the only proper name I could, under pressure, recall, and as it was quite an ordinary name – pretty even – I called her Sophie and this is her now. She will be Sophie for as long as she wishes to hold on to this name.

I've spoken her name just twice: once to the births-and-deaths lady at City Hall and once, on the telephone, to my mother in New Zealand. With my mother I practised before calling. I wanted to get the intonation right, like people I've observed in BBC dramas making important announcements. I wrote everything down in full sentences.

'Congratulations, Mother,' I said. 'You're a grandma now. Her name is Sophie. She's perfect.' I read this statement off a Post-it note. I expected a question to follow, such as, who is the child's mother? And where is the child's mother? And have you learnt nothing at all from our mistakes, Jonathan?

Instead, my mother said, 'No, thank you,' quite politely, as if turning down the offer of super-fast broadband. Then she hung up. I remained on the sofa, holding the phone against my ear for so long it left a red pressure mark on the side of my cheek. I waited for her to call back but she didn't. My mother's not the sort of woman who ever calls back. 'Am I angry?' I asked myself and, when I finally decided that this turned-stomach feeling was not anger but relief, I placed the phone back on the charger and determined that, when she is old enough, I will tell Sophie both her grandparents are dead. I'll say it was a car crash that killed them.

This was the first time I'd considered Sophie in the far-off future. It isn't so much of a stretch to picture her tomorrow: drinking milk and sleeping, sometimes turning over in the cot. From one day to the next there are changes in the child. But these changes are slight and incremental: an extra pinch of hair, longer fingernails, or the possibility of a tooth pushing through her gums, a little paler every day until one evening it is a solid sharpness biting into my finger. Most mornings when I lift her she is exactly the same baby I've laid down. Sophie at sixteen or seventeen is impossible to imagine. She'll have breasts by then and a face of her own. She will be a stranger to the child now draped over my shoulder.

I do my best not to speak in front of Sophie. I don't say her name or allow her to hear songs with lyrics. Classical music is fine because it is mostly just instruments. I wouldn't deprive her of music altogether. I'm not a monster. I only watch television when she's asleep or with headphones on. I don't want her to hear speaking of any kind, even from a distance or in a foreign language. I'm trying to keep her quiet for as long as possible. This is for her own good, I remind myself. But the fear of her wee voice rising is with me constantly.

I won't ever forget the stories her mother muttered in her sleep. Shipwrecks. Carnage. Cruel things done to men, just for the thrill of hearing them plead. Afterwards, awake, I'd try to question her and she'd neither admit nor deny the truth behind these mumblings. Maybe she did. Maybe she didn't. But I still knew she was capable. And that was the horror of her: the vile possibility.

For the last few weeks I have been too preoccupied to pay any attention to the news. Sophie eats all my energy: the washing and feeding and cleaning of her; the fretting over what should be done in the long term. When I'm not thinking about Sophie I'm asleep, dead with exhaustion, still dreaming of her. Later, when I begin to re-enter the world, one six o'clock news bulletin at a time, my ears will prick up at the mention of young men setting fires and flinging themselves into violent situations, ruining their futures for an ideal already failed. I'll wonder if her mother might be behind all this havoc, all the needless suffering. Could it be her voice singing the violence into these boys' ears, her sick words planted and beginning to sprout? I can picture her skinny arms raised above the city, like those of a wild conductor, orchestrating all manner of chaos. It's easy enough to imagine her implicated in the whole mess.

Maybe she's behind the madness. Maybe she isn't. I might never know for sure. Everything seemed fine and healing, until she came floating up the Lagan. People were 'hopeful about the future' and 'moving towards peace', slowly, slowly, but making progress. Now the city is like a raw wound, gaping. Now, they are all of them – politicians, Provos and public Joes alike – coming to pieces at a rate of knots. The whole situation stinks of her. So much hangs in the see-saw balance of this moment. The old trouble could kick up its heels and go in for another round. The place might slip twenty years backwards before Christmas. Into chaos, which is only a wordy way of saying war. I can't wash my hands and walk away. Not if she's the bad seed turning the whole city sour. Not if she's planted this darkness in my Sophie too.

I know I need to do something. I'm trying to formulate a plan.

It isn't easy. I have no friends for advice, no family worth considering. Beyond their basic anatomy I have a limited knowledge of babies. I don't know what to do with a faulty child. In work, Social Services is always the answer to children's problems that cannot be cured with medicine. Social Services takes messed-up families and fixes them or splits them up into slightly more functional units. I'm absolutely certain that Social Services won't believe me if I call up and say, 'I have accidentally produced a child with a Siren. Is there some sort of protocol for this kind of thing?' I'm struggling to think of another relevant authority: police, hospital, priest (I'm not a Catholic but wonder all the same if there is something to be done for Sophie with prayer or exorcism).

Occasionally I imagine myself as a patient presenting at my own surgery.

'I have an infant daughter who is not yet speaking but may, perhaps, be capable of hurting people with her voice,' the patient version of me explains to the doctor version.

In this scenario the doctor version immediately calls the psychiatric unit. The real me can't imagine an alternative outcome.

I don't even bother consulting his medical textbooks. I know there are no Sirens listed in their tables of contents. There is a section somewhere on mental health, and people who believe they are mythical beings, such as vampires, or Jesus Christ. There is nothing on how to deal with people who are actual mythical beings. There are thousands of pounds' worth of textbooks in my study and I don't trust any of them now. They are like monuments to a different time, a time when it was easy for me to believe things printed in books with diagrams. I am particularly keen to avoid those that concern themselves with ear, nose and throat surgery. I've pushed them to the back of the bookshelf, lest I be tempted to lift them down and fixate on the very many ways it is possible to silence a human being with kitchen scissors or a scalpel.

In the absence of other, more scientific, solutions I have watched hours and hours of *The X-Files* looking for answers. That isn't quite true. It's not answers I'm searching for. Sophie is not a question. She's a problem to be dealt with. I watch *The X-Files* for inspiration and affinity. When I try to draw a line between fact and fiction it isn't a straight line any more. One is truth and the other is also a kind of truth. They are not the neat opposites they once were, in university. There is some weird stuff in *The X-Files*, particularly the early seasons. I am not at all surprised by the vampires and werewolves, but the liver-eating man, who stretches, like pulled gum, through drains and

plugholes, gives me the creeps and I pause the episode, ten minutes in, to place a weight on my toilet lid. I have yet to come
across a Siren but there are at least three seasons left to watch.
The truth might still be out there. I fast-forward through the
credits to cram in more episodes per evening.

I'm not sure what I'll do if I find an *X-Files* episode about a
Siren. Aside from their aliens, Mulder and Scully have little
compassion for anything beyond the basic human. The other is
always the enemy, and I don't think I can stomach watching a
Siren killed or kept in a laboratory for experiments. There's still
an itch in me for Sophie's mother. My head can hold her coldly,
like a long-ago war, but my body remains sympathetic to her. I
feel the pull of her in my teeth and the tips of my hair every time
I shower. Sometimes I dream about her. She is always singing in
these dreams. This is an invention on my part, drawn from
mythology and, perhaps, a yearning for the sort of mother I
did not have. I remind myself that she never once sang to
me in all of our time together. This is a relief, also a kind of
disappointment.

I've looked up Sirens on Wikipedia. I don't, as a rule, trust
Wikipedia but there are few options left. The Sirens have their
own entry – Siren (Mythology), not to be confused with Siren
(Alarm) – though it seems likely they are both derived from the
same root. It is possible to add content to a Wikipedia page and,
for a while, I consider removing the parentheses and changing
'Mythology' to 'History'. Perhaps I'll even tag on a paragraph
about contemporary Sirens and the way they are now capable of
using telephones. I know these additions will be removed as
soon as they come to the censors' attention. Wikipedia doesn't
have a sense of humour. Still, I'm amused by the idea of instigating this small act of vandalism. The possibility of it is like
another, braver, person trying to climb out of my fingers.

The Siren page on Wikipedia is illustrated with heavy oil

paintings by Draper, Armitage and Waterhouse. Their work reflects a macabre obsession with Hellenism. It is rife with decapitated heads, alabaster nymphs and naked gods, the kind of art that demands a heavy gilt frame. I follow a cyber-trail of art, clicking from one page to the next, and eventually return to the original Wikipedia entry. I scroll past the introduction and a list of books referencing Sirens. These include Homer, Pliny, Kafka, and Borges' *Book of Imaginary Beings*. I have it in my study, a leftover from my parents' collection, which is, like my parents, angled towards the overbearing. Borges is, of course, wittier on the subject, though the Wikipedia article is far more extensive. It is this I return to several times during Sophie's first weeks. I'm quick to disregard the hyperbole. I've seen both Sophie and her mother naked; neither has a tail or feathers of any kind. The suspicion of cannibalism strikes me as a sort of joke. Sophie consumes nothing but milk and her mother survived on liquids, such as tinned soup and custard, as if anxious to surround herself with fluids both inside and out. I can't imagine either eating anything as solid as a human arm or thigh.

It is the talk of singing and the talk of speaking that grabs me and keeps me reading. The Siren's voice has always been pitched towards destruction: shipwrecks, madness and vicious death. I drag up the memory of Sophie's mother – her stranger's voice on the telephone and then, later, the way she cried out shrilly, like touched glass – during sex, and I understand her kind capable of calling all manner of calamities into being. With prior warning I might have been Odysseus, plugging my ears against temptation, or Orpheus, raising my own melody to resist, but I know myself too well for such comparisons. I'm not a brave man and I was far too hungry for her company. Even if all this happened again tomorrow I'd still press the telephone to my ear and listen. I'd still drive up the Castlereagh Road to her fourth-floor flat. I would destroy myself gladly for another hour in her bed.

All this is no longer relevant. She is long gone. She hasn't even left me a name to hold on to. I have a child now, and no idea what to do with it. I read the Wikipedia article over and over again, hoping it will rearrange itself into a kind of plan, a beginner's guide for parents of Sirens. I learn the Siren names off by rote: Aglaope, Leucosia, Ligeia, Parthenope, Peisinoe, Thelxiope and Molpe, who, with her squat name, I imagine as a dumpy Siren, a not-yet-woman, nothing to look at until she sings. I'm glad I've called my daughter Sophie. This name will call the ordinary out of her every time it is spoken.

I stumble upon a quote from Kafka's short essay 'The Silence of the Sirens': 'Now the Sirens have a still more fatal weapon than their song, namely their silence. And though admittedly such a thing never happened, it is still conceivable that someone might possibly have escaped their singing; but their silence certainly never.'

I've never been a big fan of Kafka. My parents loved his work and this association is enough to keep me sceptical. However, there is something in the quote that reads true. Sophie's silence is just as magnetic as her mother's voice. I'm ruined whichever way the next months go. For now I choose silence, and in the silence I can think of nothing but the fear of her speaking.

It is not just the speaking that worries me. I have other, more ordinary, concerns. It is almost a year since my last pay cheque. Now I'm dipping into my overdraft just to make the monthly mortgage payments. I can't ask my parents for money. They will not, for a moment, humour the idea of me as a stay-at-home dad. They'd consider it common, like signing on or going on a package holiday with strangers. I can already hear the click-hum sound of my mother hanging up every time I think about asking them for a loan. I could tell them I'm ill and cannot work on account of cancer or something equally long-term. They might send me money if I was properly ill. But my mother would still find a way of letting me know she was disappointed, that all this, even the cancer, is somehow my fault. I don't think I can have this conversation. I'm not brave enough.

I do my best to make the money stretch. I wash our clothes in the bath to save electricity. I eat yellow-label food, which is cheaper because it's just past the sell-by date, and buy Sophie imported nappies from Poundland. There is Polish writing on the back and sometimes they leak, but they are three pounds cheaper than the big-name brands. Thankfully, it's hot out, so I'm not spending anything on heating. Save the pennies and the pounds will look after themselves. But this only holds true when there are still pennies to save.

I put two dozen textbooks up for sale on the internet. They are expensive books, several of them worth more than a hundred pounds each. I think with fondness of the time when a hundred pounds was nothing to throw at a textbook, or a pair of shoes for work. The books will make enough to keep us in food, electricity and formula milk for another four weeks. After this, I'll have to start earning again. I don't want to go back to work. I'm not sure that I can. The memory of it has already left me. I wonder if being a doctor is a practice, like swimming, that cannot be entirely forgotten. If not I might kill someone accidentally with the wrong medicine. I add this to my list of fears.

On Friday morning I buy a lottery ticket in the little Tesco at the top of the road. I take it back to my car and hold it in my hand like a communion wafer. Right, I think. If I'm not meant to go back to work then this one's got to be a winner.

I smile at Sophie in the rear-view mirror. She's asleep in the car seat I bought online. Everything of hers is off the internet and has the same pale pink stripe running through it, like the seam ribboning through raspberry ripple ice cream. I want her to feel like a little princess. I've no idea where this desire has come from. I put the lottery ticket in my shirt pocket and drive home. Later that evening I watch the lottery on television with the sound turned off. I've picked one number correctly. It is the number seven. I'm not sure if this is worth anything and don't know if there is a place I can phone to check. This is the first and last time I'll do the lottery. Afterwards I pin the unlucky ticket to the fridge. This will remind me to get a job before we both starve.

I deliberate over my options for almost a week. I could be a postman. They're always looking for postmen in East Belfast. It is not a popular route. Parts of the East are so volatile that postmen require helmets and bulletproof vests. When the kids are rioting, anyone in a uniform is liable to be bricked. The possibility of this does not put me off. It would be nice to worry about something other than Sophie for a change, something less cerebral, like dodging fireworks or bottles. Plus, the anti-social hours might allow me to bring her along, tucked into the bike's basket or bound to my chest in one of those bandage slings. I could also deliver Chinese takeaways in my car, leaving Sophie buckled into her seat between deliveries. This could work well as she often falls asleep in the car. And there's always the option of telemarketing. With telemarketing I wouldn't even be required to leave home.

All these are perfectly feasible options but, ultimately, I'm too scared to try anything new. New involves meeting people I don't know, and there are already more people in my life than I can cope with. I decide to have another go at being a doctor because that is the only job I'm actually qualified to do. Even this feels like leaping over a dark cliff.

I have a stiff drink before calling work. I try to manage without the whiskey and can't. I phone up the health centre and speak to a lady receptionist. She doesn't recognize my voice. I ask to speak to Martin. He is the most senior doctor in the practice. I've never before called him Martin, and definitely wouldn't call him Marty, but I'm dreadfully nervous and this is the name that comes to me in the moment. When Martin/Marty/Dr Bell answers, I say, 'I'm sorry, there was a bereavement in the family, both my parents, in a car crash. The stress,' I say. 'We were very close. I fell apart. I should have called earlier. I just wasn't thinking.' I wonder if Dr Bell knows who he's talking to. I have forgotten to say my name. This happens to me sometimes when I'm on the telephone.

Dr Bell makes sympathetic noises as he speaks. He's using the special warm-water voice that all doctors keep for patients with mental-health issues. I suspect he's going to suggest a counsellor or ask if I'd like a prescription for some anti-depressants. I do not want to go on anti-depressants. I have, in the past, often prescribed anti-depressants for sad patients because it is a quick way to get rid of them without having to listen to the ins and outs of their sad lives. I'm not sure they work because the sad patients keep coming back, even after they've been on anti-depressants for a really long time. I certainly don't want to talk to a counsellor. As my parents aren't actually dead and I won't be able to mention Sophie, every single session would be an elaborate lie. Just thinking about this makes me even more anxious. I can't cope with anything else right now. I decide to stop Dr Bell before he has a chance to suggest anti-depressants or counselling. It's important that he believes I'm well enough to come back to work. Everything depends on this.

'Look,' I say, interrupting my own apology, 'I don't know if I ever mentioned this before but I have a child, a daughter. I need my job back so I can make enough money to look after her properly. I've had a tough time for the last few months but I'm better now and I'm a perfectly good doctor. I'm more than capable of returning to work. So, can I have my job back?'

I'm shocked by the strength of my own voice. It's like a series of perfectly placed punches. This is possibly the most forthright

I've ever been. I'm not sure I can keep it up for more than a few minutes.

'Well,' replies Dr Bell, 'technically your job's not here any more, Dr Murray. We waited three months, and when you didn't return any of our calls, we had to get someone else in. Susan – sorry, I mean Dr McAteer – is in your role now. I can't just turf her out because you've decided you want to come back.'

'I've not *just decided* I want to come back. I've been sick and now I'm better.'

'That may be the case, son, but we couldn't hold your job for ever. We have patients to consider.'

'Isn't there anything I could do? Locum work? Part-time? Anything at all?'

'Well, Dr Murray, you're a very lucky young man to have chosen today to call. Sarah – sorry, that's Dr McKeown – is expecting again. She's just about to go off on maternity leave and I'm literally sitting here at my desk, right now, filling in the paperwork to get someone in to cover her.'

'I could do that.'

'I know you could, Dr Murray, but I'd need some assurance that you're not going to go AWOL again. I've every sympathy for you. My mum died last year and it knocked me for six, but you can't just disappear every time something goes wrong.'

'It won't happen again,' I say. 'I haven't got any more parents to lose.'

So, I find myself employed again. I stop eating yellow-label food immediately. I suspect it was giving me bowel problems. The fear of money is for the moment replaced by a larger fear of what should be done with Sophie. I can't leave her alone but I can't leave her with another person either. Any day now she will begin making structured noises. There is no way of explaining how dangerous this might be to a stranger. There is no way of making 'Don't listen to anything my daughter says.

93

She's genetically wired to try to kill people with her voice' sound like something a nanny might believe.

I seriously contemplate the possibility of leaving Sophie by herself through the day: in a cupboard or locked room where she would be 'safe'. I could come home at lunchtime to change and feed her. I could wire up some kind of long-distance baby monitor, maybe using mobile phones. I actually consider this as a workable solution. I try to convince myself that isolation might be good for the child, might even go some way to fixing her. I read articles on the internet about children locked in cupboards or raised by wolves. Without words, they speak later. Often they do not speak at all, or they invent their own language: a guttural sort of speaking that sounds a little like ancient Hebrew. Scholars think this may be the language of God, the way the world sounded before Babel. They are fascinated by the noises coming out of these locked-up children. They are quick to condemn people who shut their children into cupboards but, all the same, it's easy to see they're grateful that someone else has carried out such experiments for them.

I begin telling myself that I'm going to leave Sophie locked in the nursery while I'm at work. This will not be a problem while she's still an infant. It is an acceptable practice in other developing countries. It might even be a kind of cure. I cannot bring myself to believe any of this. I can only picture the police breaking down my front door to find Sophie howling and soaked in her own piss or, worse still, suffocated. Eventually I admit that this will not work. I start again with a notebook, jotting down ideas and crossing them out with a biro. I think better in lists.

- I must work to earn money.
- Sophie cannot be left alone for her own safety.
- Sophie cannot be left with other people for their safety.

I work this list backwards and forwards like an algebra equation, drink several glasses of whiskey and amend it slightly. Sophie cannot be left with anyone who will hear her. This is progress. I have options now. I could hire a nanny and insist she wears headphones. This would be hard to explain. I could swathe Sophie's face and mouth in bandages, telling the nanny she has terrible infant eczema. This would not be practical for feeding. I could hire a nanny who cannot hear. I write this down a different way, just to be sure it still makes sense: hire a deaf nanny. This is what I decide to do. I'm a genius.

Of course, it isn't easy finding a trained childcare professional who cannot hear anything. I must be subtle. People can be very suspicious when it comes to children and I don't want Social Services involved. I think about ringing round a few agencies and asking if they have any deaf nannies on their books. This would require very little work on my part but I know the agency staff will ask why I'm specifically looking for someone who's deaf and I'll have no good answer for them. I will sound like some kind of deviant on the telephone. I need to find the perfect excuse. It's a sort of puzzle. I have both the problem and the solution in my sights but no clear idea how to link the two.

I'm in Connswater Tesco, picking up some proper nappies, when the answer slaps me in the face. The woman in front of me at the till has a child balanced on her hip. He's about two and struggling to open a banana. He holds it in front of his mother's face and shakes it violently to attract her attention. She is preoccupied with carrier bags and money-off coupons. The child shakes the banana harder and, when his mother continues to ignore him, throws it on the floor and begins to howl. The woman stops fiddling with her purse. She turns to glare at the boy. I assume she will speak sharply to him or even give him a clip around the legs. But she doesn't. Instead, she places the child in front of her feet, hunkers down and, with her raised hands, makes a series of tight little motions right under his nose. The child signs back – slips and pinches and neat fists, which clearly voice his frustration. It's like they are dancing, but only using their hands. The boy is deaf. Perhaps his mother is deaf too.

I'm standing in the line at Connswater Tesco with a bumper pack of nappies and a frozen pizza tucked under my arm, watching these people, when I have my epiphany. I will tell the people at the agency that I need a deaf nanny because my child is hearing-impaired and she will need to learn how to sign. I am once again a genius. I run back down the alcohol aisle and lift a bottle of good Merlot. Tonight I'm celebrating.

Less than a week later I have found Christine through a childcare agency. Christine is from Newtownards and is more than happy to drive into the city every morning to mind Sophie in her own home. Christine is one hundred per cent deaf. I've checked. She was born this way and has been signing since she was a very small child. She is around twenty-five, though she dresses like a teenage girl in slogan T-shirts and denim-look leggings. She has honest brown eyes and a smile that is too large for her face. She holds Sophie in the crook of her arm, jiggling her hip gently to reassure the baby when she fusses. She looks natural doing this, as if she has been doing it for ever. I don't look this natural with Sophie. I've watched myself holding her in the mirror and I look like I might drop her at any second. Watching Christine with my daughter makes me a little jealous, but also relieved.

In preparation for Christine's first day I learn the sign for 'welcome' and also the sign for 'thank you'. I figure 'goodbye' is probably just an ordinary wave. Aside from this, we will communicate with a notepad and pen. I leave instructions on the kitchen counter: sleep, feed and change schedules, emergency contacts and, at the bottom of the page, in bold, capital letters, the most important instruction of all: 'DO NOT TAKE SOPHIE OUT OF THE HOUSE.' I haven't given Christine a reason for this. I'm paying her more money than the agency suggested. I hope this will mean she doesn't ask questions. That's how it works in gangster movies. I've told the agency that my wife is dead. In childbirth, I explained, though as this sounds like something a Victorian would say I've added in an underlying heart condition to make the whole thing seem more believable.

'I'm a widower,' I've told them. I like the sound of this. 'And I must go back to work to support my daughter. It's important to me that she is well looked after, especially with her health problems.' I feel the need to reiterate that Sophie is hearing-impaired. I'm constructing an alibi for us both. I want to tell the agency that they must warn Christine not to expect any romance to develop. This is not a movie. I won't be looking for any comfort from the nanny, only professionalism. At the last minute I decide not to say anything about romance. It might sound creepy. I can't afford to lose her.

On the first morning of my return to work I kiss Sophie goodbye. She is still sleeping and her hair is swirled to the side with pillow sweat. I leave fancy biscuits in the cupboard for Christine and remind her to text if she needs anything. (Ordinary phoning won't work for us.) She smiles knowingly. I'm not her first anxious parent. At the front door we make the sign for goodbye. I get into my car and back it out of the drive, cruise through Orangefield and on to the Newtownards Road. At the traffic lights by the Holywood Arches, a carpet shop is still smouldering from the previous evening. There is a smell in the air like last night's campfire doused with water. I pass five more Tall Fires before I arrive at the health centre. I hardly notice. My mind is miles away.

My regular parking spot has been allocated to Dr McAteer,

so I leave the car in Dr McKeown's old space. The lady receptionists raise their heads and smile at me as I pass through the waiting rooms. 'Welcome back, Dr Murray,' they call out. I'm pleased to see my name is still up on the patients' information board, or perhaps it's been re-added in anticipation of my return. I take a deep breath as I open the door to my old room. The smell hits me before I step inside: iodine, coffee, furniture polish and the barely masked stench of old piss. Nothing has changed, but my spider plant is on its last legs.

I think about Sophie sleeping at home. It's only fifteen minutes since I saw her. This is already our longest separation and yet I'm quite calm, much calmer than I'd anticipated. A lady receptionist brings me coffee in my favourite Garfield mug. She's made it exactly the way I like it and I haven't even asked for coffee. Everything is going to be all right. I call Reception and tell them I'm ready for patients.

JULY

Sammy

YOU ARE YOUR father's son as I was my father's son and he the same, most likely. Definitely his father before him, who came back from the war and beat a fella dead with bricks for talking shite about the Queen. You've seen him in photos at your nan's. (He's the one with the beard and the soldier get-up.)

In our family we all have the same face on us. Intimidating's what they call it round here, which is a nice way of saying you wouldn't want to meet any of us on a dark street. It's not just me and your granda. Your uncles are cut from the same old sheet too: Matty's inside and Jim is just this month out. The other two are only marking time. They cannot hold their anger still. They're always looking to ruin something. Even your Aunty Kathleen has a mouth on her like hammers. She once broke a woman's finger for taking the last trolley at Tesco. When she was a wee lassie she done boxing. That wasn't normal for girls back then.

The rage runs through us all, as if we have two kinds of blood pumping side by side: red blood and blood that is much darker.

All the way back it goes, to the first brute eejit who raised his hand in anger and hit. That was Cain, was it not? Did you do him in Sunday school with the other lads, Noah and Moses and your man with the stripy coat? I did. I could see where Cain was coming from, killing Abel. You have to put the competition in its place. A fella like Cain would do well in the East.

Course, you're not just mine, are you? You've your mother's blood in you as well. Her side are country folk, the sort of people who lift their dinner straight from the field and properly believe in church. They're strong folk like us, but it's a strength for lifting and carrying, not for beating down. You've your mother to thank for your good looks and the way your hair turns straw in the sun. You're clean-whip smart. You didn't get this from either of us. You come at everything sideways, son. It's as if you're standing on a stepladder looking down. This is not to say you're better than me and it's not to say you're worse. You just have more options. You are sharp with your mind and sharp with your tongue. If you want to you can cut people. You do not need to use your fists.

When I was your age I had fists for every man who crossed me. This one was a Tout, the next a Taig, and the fella after, just your regular gobshite running his mouth off at the bar. I laid into every one the same. Up came the blood and the blood was a curled fist. You know it yourself, son: that kind of rage is a solid thing. You cannot swallow it or see your way through. I could never ease myself till there was blood on the floor or bones cracking, like split sticks. I had a sharp knife in one hand and a brick in the other. I liked to leave marks. I left marks all the way down the Castlereagh Road and up the Newtownards. You could see where I'd been. It felt as if I was leaking.

Later, the fists were not enough to keep me. I had guns. It was easy to find a gun in them days. Once you had one gun it attracted others. Your mother has probably told you about the guns and the way they left holes in us every time they went off. Your mother is a woman. Women do not understand guns. They do not like loudness of any kind. No doubt she's claimed the guns were the death of us, the end of all our smiling days. Probably she cried while telling you this, held your hand in hers, and asked you never to touch a gun, even for picking off rabbits. It's all true, son. Listen to your mother. Listen well. After the guns, we were not the same kind of together.

There's two sides to it, though. Your mother won't have told you that a gun is a kind of anchor, that it rests heavy in your hand. She's never known the way your head will slow and clear, like a pint settling, every time you pull the trigger. How you will be God in this second and afterwards wish to claw the moment back. Fully God and fully man, they said in the Bible of Jesus. You can get the same head-melt from firing a shotgun. No crucifixion required. There's nothing half as holy. Your mother doesn't understand that this was never about the politics – the flags and freedom, God and country of it all. They were only words I stood behind. I did it again and again with fists, and guns, and sometimes bombs, for the pure blood rush of being alive. Believe me, son, you'll always feel the bigger man when you're standing over someone else.

You were the end to this. You came down like a solid wall. I would not have stopped for your mother, or my mother, or even the cause calling me into line. But the first time I held you in the crook of my arm there was a weight to you, a heaviness, I'd never felt in a gun. You scared me shitless, with your wee face, and your fingers hooking on to mine. I hadn't been this feared in months. I hadn't ever felt this loud. 'This is it,' said I to your mother. 'I am fully God and fully man, right here on the living-room sofa' (or words to that effect).

'Away on with you, Sammy,' said your mother back. She didn't believe that everything could change so sharply, on a die.

She was like a ship going in the one direction for so long it couldn't turn without tipping.

Everything went forward from the moment of you. Job. House. Nice pullovers from Marks & Spencer's. Proper holidays in the sun. I couldn't leave the East completely but I moved us away from the river and over the ring road until we were so far east we were almost a different direction. I put you in a good school. Gave you a brother and sister to ground you. Forced a violin into your hands, and when it didn't take, I tried the trumpet. An instrument of some sort was essential, and a university degree. It would stand with you when folks asked where it was you'd grown up. I wanted you to take root here, to be a different breed of man.

I'm a different man, these days. It's been twenty years since I last raised my fists and hit. I do not feel like a different man. I feel like I'm a stranger. I'm carrying my own self around inside me, like a pregnant woman or one of them Russian dolls. When I look back I can still see where I've come from. I could close my eyes and drive them streets in my sleep, all those cars and little houses eyeing me from either side of the road. I could find the marks I've left there, in the street and on the people. They'll remember me, even now. You never forget that kind of rage. But I don't go there any more. I don't take you or your brother or sister. I don't even tell you about it.

I want everything to be golden for you, son. I want everything to move forwards.

But here we are with these Tall Fires and all the broken mess of you. The whole city's burning and you are at the centre of it, talking the bloody talk of my younger days. Flags and bonfires. Civil liberties and free speech. No point denying your involvement. Do you think a father can't tell his own son's hand raised in anger? Do you think your hand is redder than mine? I doubt it, son. Do you not know where your darkness comes from?

I would like to say I'm proud of you. I was almost proud of you once when you carried yourself like an ordinary boy, when you kicked footballs and rode bikes, thieved my drink when I wasn't looking. I'm not proud of you now. There is no sense in this thing you're doing. It's only moving backwards.

I would like to say I love you. Wanting to love someone is not the same as truly loving them, though sometimes it's a good start. Ask your mother about this. Say you're asking for a friend.

I am afraid of you now, son, as I am afraid of the violent man sleeping inside me, as I am afraid of my own fists and the way they clench without my thinking about it every time I stand still. You are your father's son. I can see it in your hands. I am afraid for you and how you are ruining yourself.

7

Tall Fires

I RETURN TO work in early July. I deal with my patients. I drive
home again. This is just about all I can cope with. This, and
the occasional glass of whiskey before bed. Everything in the
world is Sophie now and I'm determined not to screw her up.

On my first day back at the health centre my first patient is a
two-year-old boy who has wedged a raisin up his nose. 'There
might be a couple of them up there,' explains his mother. 'He
was in the larder for ages before I noticed. Sorry about this, Dr
Murray.'

I have forgotten that patients often apologize, as if they are
responsible for catching head lice or contracting leukaemia, as if
they might, with extra diligence, have warded off the early onset
of arthritis thereby saving valuable NHS resources. When a
patient apologizes I always try to smile, and say, 'Sure I'd be out
of a job if nobody got sick.' I learnt this from Marty, who is good
with people. I say this now and hook the offending raisin out
with tweezers. The child howls throughout the procedure. I
never once let my smile slip. I'm glad to have such an easy first
patient. It is months since I last felt so competent. I'm already
wearing my stethoscope. I've adjusted the chair to suit my posture and moved the stationery round my desk, leaving a clear

spot for my Garfield mug. It's all coming back to me with remarkable ease, like swimming or something more essential.

Once finished I fasten a 'Well Done' sticker to the boy's pullover and he immediately stops crying. I keep a roll in the top drawer of my desk. They're my only defence against children. The mothers I can handle, but the children terrify me. They're like cats at this age, entirely unpredictable.

Between morning coffee and lunch I see psoriasis, two throat infections, a nasty case of croup, three time-wasters, who could easily have stayed at home with a bottle of Benylin, angina, asthma, and an elderly gentleman named Ronnie, who cannot remember what year it is yet insists upon giving me a blow-by-blow account of last night's World Cup match. I refer Ronnie to the memory clinic where he will probably be diagnosed with Alzheimer's. When he leaves the surgery I shake his hand firmly. I know what the next few years will be like for him. I wish to send him off well, as if he is a soldier leaving for war.

At lunchtime I text Christine: 'HOW R U GETTING ON?' and she immediately texts back: 'ALL QUIET ON THE WESTERN FRONT,' which is a strange phrase for a deaf person to use. Still, I feel calm inside. I think about running across the road to the sandwich bar for a BLT. Seconds later, Christine texts again. This time it's a picture of Sophie sleeping peacefully in her raspberry-ripple cot. I take a mental snapshot of the exact moment when I look at this picture of my daughter, sleeping. This is the precise second I realize everything is beginning to get better.

I eat my sandwich in the staffroom. Usually I eat alone in my office but today I feel like starting a new routine. The lady receptionists pick up on this change straight away. They're all a-twitter when I appear in the staffroom. The new doctor, having no preconceptions, assumes my behaviour to be completely normal. No one tells her otherwise. I introduce myself as

Jonathan rather than as Dr Murray. She doesn't even wince. Instead she extends her hand towards me and says, 'Susan, lovely to meet you. I was so sorry to hear about your parents.' I dip my head in and out of her sympathy. The lady receptionists huddle round my chair, echoing her concern. They are like hens when hens are confined within a closed space.

'I hear you've a wee one we didn't know about,' says the lady receptionist with the particularly solid hair. It's a clumsy attempt to change the subject from dead parents to something more palatable and the rest of them take to it immediately, pecking at me for details.

'Aye, you're a dark one, Dr Murray. We'd no idea you were a daddy.'

'Is it a wee girl you have or a wee fella?'

'What's her name?'

'Have you any photos of her?'

'Sophie,' I say. 'Her name's Sophie.' This meets with a round of approving nods.

'Photo?' asks the one with the large chin, clapping her hands in front of her chest, like a sealion swiping at its own excitement.

'I've no photos with me, ladies,' I say, and then I remember the photo Christine has just sent me. I take out my phone and pass it round the circle. There seem to be more lady receptionists than there were when I left. It's possible they're multiplying behind the photocopier and the other doctors haven't noticed.

'The nanny took that this morning,' I say.

'Is her mammy back at work already?' asks the lady receptionist with the Ballymena accent.

'No, she doesn't have a mother.'

'What happened to her?' all of them ask at once. The lady receptionists are not known for their tact.

'She died,' I say.

'In the car accident with your parents?' asks the original lady receptionist. For a moment I don't understand what she's talking about and I'm confused. Then, I remember and realize I'll have to tell another lie.

'No,' I say, 'she died in childbirth,' and quickly add the bit about an underlying heart condition to make my lie sound a little more believable.

'Uch, you poor thing, Dr Murray,' says the original lady receptionist. 'You've been through the wars this past year. It's little wonder you went a bit mad.'

Then, all of them are trying to pat me at once as if I'm a kind of dog, a sad-faced dog, like a Golden Retriever. I enjoy this immensely. I lean into their pillowy concern. It is months since I've been purposely touched and the feel of them, pressing in with their breasts and their soft kindness, is the sort of thing that might leave bruises. When they draw back, returning to their phones and filing cabinets, they leave the lady scent of Estée Lauder and hair lacquer on my pullover. From time to time, between afternoon appointments, I sniff at my sleeve. It smells like nothing I've ever known before.

It is almost six when I get back. Standing on the Welcome mat, I'm caught by my own reflection, echoing back at me from the glass front door. I hardly recognize myself. The good day has run through me and left me a much stronger man. I turn the key and step into my house. 'I'm home,' I call out. Sophie's mother aside, it's years since I last came home to anyone. Even then, it was only the cleaner.

Christine is in the kitchen reading a book. She doesn't hear me approach. I make my feet fall heavily on the tiles and she doesn't even turn to look. It is a relief to know she has not been faking. I place a hand on her shoulder and she starts slightly. The book slips from her fingers and flutters to the floor, like a shot bird. I wish I knew the sign for 'sorry'. I'll look it up later.

It's likely to come in useful. I make my right hand into an 'OK' sign and she nods back, smiling with her too-big mouth. I reach for a notebook and pens and place them in front of her, indicating that she should pull up a chair. We begin a conversation.

'How was today?' I write.

'Really good,' she writes back. She is an extremely quick writer. This is probably because she's deaf. When a person loses one of their senses the others will rush to compensate.

'What did you do all day?' I write.

'Mostly slept. Sophie, I mean, not me.' She draws a smiley face on the notebook and we both laugh without sound. It's amazing how quickly I have slipped into her silence.

'LOL,' I write. I've seen this on the internet. It means 'laughing out loud'. Neither of us is laughing out loud. Christine can't. I don't know why I've written 'LOL'. Should I apologize? But I still don't know the sign for 'sorry' (maybe an upside-down thumbs-up, or a sad face, like a mime artist). I look at Christine to check if she's annoyed. She doesn't seem at all upset. Her face is folded in concentration as she fast-writes an account of Sophie's day: 'Sophie slept 2 hours. Bit strange when she woke. Then grand. She'd 4 wet nappies, 1 dirty one and 5 feeds. We looked at picture books and watched cartoons.'

I flinch as if I've been slapped. I can't help myself. It's involuntary, like sneezing. 'NO TV,' I scribble, and straight away notice that I've written it in block capitals as if my handwriting is screaming at Christine. I add a lower case 'please'.

Christine looks puzzled. She writes, 'Sorry. I didn't know. Sophie can't hear but she'll still enjoy looking at the pictures.'

'No TV, please,' I repeat. 'It's a religious thing.' In other cities this would make very little sense. Other cities do not have religion like a game where you make up the rules as you go along. Belfast does. Christine's grown up here too. She knows better than to push the issue any further.

'Got to go,' she writes. 'Same time tomorrow?'

I nod. I give her two thumbs-ups and a broad smile. I hope she'll translate this as 'thank you' and 'I'm very grateful' and 'Please don't ever leave us because you are the only good thing that's happened in months.' In my mind I'm making a list of sign-language words to google later. I should learn how to do her name so I can say, 'Hi, Christine,' every morning. I could learn Sophie's name too, and the sign for 'father'. I correct myself. I won't bother learning 'father'. Father is a solid word without arms or softness of any kind. I'll learn the sign for 'daddy' instead.

After Christine leaves I put a frozen pizza into the oven, empty the dishwasher and watch some TV. I feel like a very ordinary person. Normal, even. All over the world dads like me are doing exactly the same thing. This is the closest I've ever come to being part of a team. I could eat the feeling with a spoon.

Around nine Sophie begins to stir. I hear her on the baby monitor. She makes damp little noises with her mouth: clicks and kittenish mews, like two wet surfaces parting, coming together and parting again. I stand at the nursery door, listening to the sound of her not quite crying. I could stand like this for a very long time, just listening. When I lift Sophie she curls into the space between my collarbone and neck. The whole of her fits perfectly in this hollow, as if it has been carved out with just such a purpose in mind.

The day has been full. The day has also been easy. I can't remember the last time I felt so hopeful. I look hard at Sophie, even her mouth. I can't bring myself to be afraid. In this light, with the curtains not yet pulled, I'm almost certain her eyes are browner than they were this morning. They are the coffee-grounds colour of old soil. They are darkening down to mirror mine.

That's my girl, I think. Tonight it is easy to dismiss her mother's ears and the slick of dark hair curling over her head. The good day has coloured everything brighter. Outside it's still light. The moon is full-ish and already up. The sun sits opposite, like a petulant twin, refusing to descend. I carry Sophie over to the window and we stand for a minute, framed between the curtains.

'Look,' I say, pointing towards the pale face of the moon, 'there's the moon, Sophie.'

Such an innocent sentence, five words in total, the sort of thing hundreds of fathers are currently saying to their daughters, in different languages, all over the world. In other circumstances I might also be pointing out the stars beginning to prickle their way over the Castlereagh Hills. I could even be singing 'Twinkle, Twinkle, Little Star', making my hands flower in and out, like tiny cosmic explosions. Instead, I'm clamping a hand over my mouth, trying to suck the words back in. I'm sick in my belly, guts clenching and unclenching. This is how I felt every time her mother spoke. Pain. Nausea. Nervous twitching. I place Sophie back in her cot and steady myself. No harm done. She might not even have heard.

Despite this small setback, today has still been the best day in a very long time. I want to mark it in some significant way. I'd like to take Sophie out, have a small adventure together. It's not that we never go out. We've been to the little Tesco at the top of the road dozens of times, and every so often we visit the bigger Tesco at Connswater. But I always leave Sophie buckled into her car seat. Tonight I want to take my daughter out with me. I want to be seen with Sophie and allow myself to be proud of her.

I try to think of somewhere quiet and uncrowded. Coffee shops are out of the question and Sea Park will be full of people out walking, enjoying the late-evening sun. Then I remember the swings at Victoria Park. I could drive my car to the edge of the play area, wrap Sophie in my coat and walk sharply past any dog-walkers still on the prowl. There will be no children in the play area at this time. It's almost dark. The plan is foolproof. We'll go to the swings. I'll show Sophie the ducks and the loop-necked swans gliding across the pond. I'll take a few pictures on my phone to satisfy the lady receptionists next time they ask about her. If I take them under the streetlamp it might even look as if we're out in daylight, like an ordinary family, doing a completely ordinary thing.

That is not how the evening plays out.

I get Sophie buckled into her car seat and head for Victoria Park. On the way, we pass a group of ten- and twelve-year-olds gathered outside a Chinese takeaway. They are straddling their bikes, holding them balanced between pinched knees, as they watch the fire brigade work on a blaze in the butcher's shop opposite. They are staring at the flames with the same rapt attention I've seen on the faces of teenagers staring at phones.

At the park I drive as close to the swings as the car park will allow. Apart from my ancient Renault there are just three other cars scattered across the hundred or so available spots. Joggers, I presume, most likely fat joggers who prefer to run under cover of darkness. Aside from the ducks and swans we are all but alone in the park. This settles me. I lift Sophie out of her car seat, arrange her against my chest and, just to be on the safe side, zipper my hoodie over the tiny bump of her. In silhouette I must look like a pregnant woman. I follow the footpath alongside the pond, past the bowling green and the public toilets to the play area for children. The dry-bread stench of duck shit catches in my nose as I walk. It is worse tonight because of the heat. The pond has begun to evaporate. There's a half-metre line of exposed muck sandwiched between the water and the dry grass like the chocolatey layers of a tiramisu.

In the playground I pick a swing, sit on it and, after laying

Sophie carefully along the furrow of my lap, begin to drift backwards and forwards gently. I'm not sure whether she's enjoying this or not. It's impossible to tell. After a dozen or so undulations, I begin to wonder how long I should keep it up, if I'm doing it right, and what else you can do with a very small baby in a play park.

I'm just beginning to question the sense of bringing Sophie out when I hear footsteps approaching the play area. I stop swinging, hold my breath and wait for the footsteps to pass by. They don't. They stop at the gate of the play area. Something soft and heavy is thrown over the fence. It lands with a defeated swoosh on the rubbery tarmac. The gate grates open. The feet walk in. I can tell they're trainers, from the padded noise they make. There's more than one set. I try to count how many. All the action is taking place behind me so I can only guess that there are at least two other people in the park now, no more than three. They are trying to be stealthy. They are treading lightly on the ground, shushing each other as they walk towards me.

They are probably drug addicts. I've seen on television shows such as *Casualty* and *EastEnders* that drug addicts often congregate in children's play areas after dark. Perhaps they enjoy the stark juxtaposition of evil and innocence, shooting up under a primary-coloured climbing frame. More likely, they're just looking for a place to hide. I can't believe I've been so naïve. I'm a healthcare professional. I should be more aware of the East's drug culture. I brace Sophie against my chest, ready to run if the situation escalates. I think I may also be able to fight if they're young, or already under the influence of one of the downer drugs. This, if it happens, would be the first physical fight of my life. I'd be relying entirely upon moves learnt from moderately violent films. If they have syringes I will not engage with them at all. They could potentially give me AIDS or hepatitis B. I'm not sure how to tell if they have syringes or not. Perhaps I could ask before raising my fists.

I weigh up the odds and make a calculated decision to run as soon as the opportunity arises. I try to stand up, bracing my feet against the rubbery ground. My leg muscles refuse to move. I can't seem to stand or run. I remember this stuck feeling from dreams and begin to breathe quicker. Sophie, sensing my anxiety, starts to cry. The noise of her, which is like a siren going off in the quiet park, brings three young fellas beating round the corner of the climbing frame.

'Fuck!' shouts the first one to spot us. 'There's a man here and a baby.'

Automatically I drop my hands to my lap and cover Sophie's ears. The three young men line up in front of the swings. They seem confused. They are not at all angry-looking, or even threatening. I'm never very good at estimating how old young people are but these three look tiny to me. This is not to say they're still children. In the rougher parts of the East a constant diet of cigarettes and Pot Noodles has left many of the young men stunted, no bigger at eighteen or nineteen than the average American twelve-year-old. I'd guess these boys are about sixteen, possibly even a little older. They're dressed in identical outfits: blue jeans and tracksuit tops, the hoods drawn over their heads, framing their faces like tiny ninjas.

'Sorry, mister,' says the first, who is a half-head taller than the other two. 'I didn't mean to swear in front of your baby.'

I'm a little confused. I wasn't expecting an apology. The boy lifts his hands to cup his own ears, mimicking Sophie and me. He shrugs his shoulders and smiles as if to say, I see you there, looking out for your wee girl. I keep my hands firmly over her ears. It's not ideal. Sophie may still be able to hear them speaking, but there's little else I can do to protect her. The urgency has gone out of the moment. It would be ridiculous now to run.

'No worries,' I whisper. 'We were just leaving.'

'Why are you whispering?' asks the smallest of the three.

'The baby's probably sleeping,' replies the original one.

'It's not. I can see its eyes. It's totally looking at us.'

'It's not an it, Dean. It's either a wee girl or a wee boy.'

'Here, mister, is it a wee boy or a wee girl?'

I can tell these boys aren't drug addicts. They're too pleasant, too aware of other people. They're clearly interested in Sophie and trying to be polite. Maybe they have younger siblings at home.

'She's a wee girl,' I reply. 'Sophie.' I say this as quietly as possible, hoping the boys will match their voices against mine.

'That's a nice name,' says the tall one. 'There's a girl in our class called Sophie.'

'Pure minging she is too,' says his mate. 'No offence on your wee girl, mister.'

'None taken,' I say. I wonder what these three are doing in the play park after ten. I know we should leave right now but I can't seem to move. I've never once felt any Hippocratic responsibility outside the health centre, but since Sophie, it's inside me, like the bends, clenching and unclenching in anxious waves. I can't help feeling concerned. It's probably something to do with becoming a father. I keep my hands clamped against Sophie's ears, using my knees to balance her and, as a kind of excuse, mumble something about the child having an ear infection. I wish I was standing up. It would be easier to evoke authority if I wasn't sitting on a swing, but I'm wedged here now and it would be something of a palaver to stand.

'Are you lot here to take drugs?' I ask. I use my 'diagnosis terminal' voice. It is both empathetic and firm.

'Naw, mister, we're not druggies,' the tall one says defensively.

'Wee bit of weed sometimes,' adds the short one, winking at me, 'but nothing harder. Not ever. Not after what happened to your fella that used to run about with our Pete.'

'He's blind now, so he is. Can't see shite *and* he was in a coma for weeks. He near died three times. They done the paddles on him to bring him back, like on *ER*.'

'Bad ecstasy,' they say, all at once, as if this is the punchline to a joke they've told hundreds of times before.

I nod solemnly. I wish to appear sympathetic, but also older, a kind of youth worker. 'So, what are you doing here, then?' I ask.

'Nothing,' says the tall one.

'Nothing,' says the short one.

'Setting a Tall Fire on the climbing frame,' says the only one who hasn't spoken yet.

The other two turn to glare at him, 'Jesus, Sheepy, you've a mouth on you. We're not supposed to let people know who we are. That's in the rules.'

'Your man here's dead on. He's not going to say anything. You're not going to tell anyone you saw us, are you, mister?'

I've only really heard the part where the young lad called me 'dead on'. No one has ever called me 'dead on' before. I'm a little drunk on this and, without fully considering the implications, reply, 'Yeah, sure,' like a sitcom American. It's only a little bit of arson. There are no CCTV cameras around, nothing to link me to the boys or the incident. I'll leave now and take Sophie home. I won't even see them starting the fire. I'm a doctor, not a policeman. I'm not responsible for these young lads.

'See?' says the one they call Sheepy. 'Your man's a legend. He's not for telling anyone. He's probably on our side.'

'What side's that?' I ask, all of a sudden wondering exactly what I'm turning a blind eye to.

'You know, the Tall Fires and all.'

'What's a Tall Fire?' I ask. I've never heard these two words paired together before. I'm not entirely ignorant. I know something's going on in the city. I've caught snippets of the news, seen the smouldering remains of burnt-out buildings, but I've not really been paying attention. I've been preoccupied.

The three boys laugh as if I've made a hilarious joke. I don't laugh. All of a sudden I begin to feel as if the outside of the circle is sealing up against me again. I lift Sophie from my lap and zip her back inside my tracksuit top.

'What exactly is a Tall Fire?' I repeat.

When the boys realize that I'm in earnest, that I have very little idea what's been happening on my own doorstep, they tell me all about the Tall Fires. They are like prophets gathered round my feet, prophets who cannot keep their story straight and only deal in half-truths. It's difficult to pick the facts from their laddish swagger but, after ten minutes or so, I have the bones of it and I'm shocked.

'I don't understand,' I say. 'You seem like really nice lads. Why are you getting involved in this? You could end up getting yourselves thrown out of school. Or worse.'

'Them bastards are trying to restrict our civil liberties,' says the tallest one. Even as he wraps his tongue around this sentence I can hear the speech marks and the spot where it's been lifted from some older man's mouth.

I leave then, assuring the boys that I won't tell anyone they've been here. I wish I had something wiser to say but I'm not a philosopher and all I can think of is, 'You're nice lads, don't be getting involved in this nonsense,' which is the sort of thing their mothers might say or an old Sunday-school teacher. I know I have no clout with them, no means to change their minds. As I close the park gate behind me I see them hauling their duffel bag up the rungs of the climbing frame. My concern is tempered by curiosity. I wonder how on earth they're going to set solid metal bars on fire.

On the way home we drive over Connsbrook Avenue and past the Strand. There are sirens screaming in the street. Yellow police tape circles the entire block. People are standing behind it, staring and pointing as the old cinema burns. At the top of Pims Avenue I'm stopped by a policeman directing the traffic. I can see the Strand up close now. I've driven past it almost every day for decades but I've never been inside or taken the time to study it properly. I note the distinctive architecture, the aqua-blue walls, and the film listings board, its corners beginning to curl in the heat. Two films have burnt off already and the front doors have shattered, scattering tiny fragments of glass all across the pavement. The wall next to me is made of glass bricks stacked end to end in a kind of feature. Amplified by the flames, these iced cubes are casting an ungodly glow across the street and into the car. The whole building is a giant torch, beaming up Belmont Avenue. It burns like a pagan shrine, the sort of horror you might travel miles to see.

This is a Tall Fire.

I have a name for it now, and a muddled history. Something in me wishes to park the car and worship. Something stronger compels me to drive away quickly. The red light turns green. The policeman signals my car forward with both sweeping hands. As I drive off I glance in the rear-view mirror. Sophie is sleeping in the back. The light from the fire is drifting across her face in waves. She is flickering yellow, orange and demonic red. She does not look anything like me. I cannot take my eyes off her.

The Boy Who Sees the Future in Every Liquid Surface

CONNOR TALKS VAGUELY *of dark shapes and sadness. The world curling into itself like a piece of orange peel left too long in the sun. He sees strangers weeping in empty rooms. Children hurt for no reason. Many, many fires, burning brightly. When he looks at water he sees photographs of people he doesn't know, all muddled up together and moving quickly. It's like flicking through the TV channels at speed. He is eight when he says this. He has not yet learnt what a metaphor is. By the time he turns ten, Connor covers his eyes every time he leaves the house. It's easier not to see with a blindfold on. He reads widely, books borrowed from the Holywood Arches library and, thus armed, learns how to say precisely and exactly what is wrong with him. Connor sees the future in every liquid surface. Puddles. Toilet bowls. Tea paling in the cup. The rain, which is ever present in East Belfast. Sinks. Spilt drinks. His own piss and blood. His salty tears. He no longer limits himself to water. Any wet substance will do. Even a closed tap terrifies him. The future isn't something he wants to stumble upon first thing in the morning while brushing his teeth.*

Connor is fourteen now. He rarely leaves the house. He takes his drink in a child's sippy cup and bathes, twice a week, blindfolded in a darkened room. Even on dry days he keeps the blinds drawn and the curtains pulled for fear of condensation on the window. 'Sometimes a raindrop can be worse than the ocean,' he says. No one really knows what he means by this. How could they? They're blessed with ordinary temporal eyes. Occasionally Connor will ask to be taken to the sea. His father will drive him to Helen's Bay and sit beside him on the sea wall while Connor shudders, like a struck thing, yet nevertheless lifts his head to stare out across the Lough for as long as he can manage. He says he's trying to build up a resistance. He says he isn't unfortunate, just peculiarly blessed. His father doesn't believe him. He thinks his boy is looking for answers. Perhaps Connor wants to see the end of it all.

8

Eleventh, Twelfth, Thirteenth

THIS IS BELFAST in July. It's too hot for good sense, too hot to breed anything but further heat.

Tonight the city's heartbeat can be heard clearly without amplification of any kind. *Thadump, thadump, thadump*: the sound of drums thundering down the little streets. On and on and crisply on they go, until the entire city is catching its breath in time to their brisk snaps. The noise of them begins with the dinner dishes and stamps its thick beat into the wee small hours. It is a vague grumble, rising above the traffic hum, like the sound of distant gunfire, or biscuit tins stamped upon. It is not a sharp noise but it is persistent and racing, as a heart will race under pressure.

Thadump. Thadump. Thadump. With distance this noise becomes softer and more like wet thunder. It is the noise made by large drums, hung from the neck and balanced against the belly. These drums are hit with sticks, hit so quickly it's as if a stutter is trapped in the drummer's wrist, a devil thing defying speed. They are known as Lambegs. Lambeg is also the name of a small village between Lisburn and Belfast. There is a garden centre there, cottages and fields; it's the kind of place you might drive through without noticing. During parades the Lambeg swaggers about like a mouthy drunk. It can only be worn by men or, sometimes, a mannish woman. Such a thing could bend a girl in two.

Tonight it is too hot to bear a closed window. In the East the sound of drums comes tramping uninvited into the kitchens and living rooms of people who do not wish to hear them. Their children ask, 'What is that noise, Dad? Is it guns?'

And the fathers reply, 'No, son, it's only the drums.'

The children are relieved to hear this. They will fall asleep picturing the kind of formal drums played in American marching bands. They will fall asleep smiling, confident that a drum cannot be wicked, as a gun is wicked in the wrong hands. They will sleep like pinched nerves, flinching each time a drum crack floats through their open window. They have never seen a Lambeg for real, only on the television news.

Up close a Lambeg drum is a ludicrous thing, impossible to fear. The frames are painted with crude pictures: King Billy, soldiers at the Somme, red hands, Princess Di. 'Thou shalt not make unto thee any graven image,' the King James states quite clearly, but here, in painting-by-numbers simplicity, are all the icons of the Protestant faith, honoured, paraded, immortalized, like those awful Catholic saints.

The drummer waddles in front of the parade on legs reduced to tiny stumps. The look of a Lambeg, pinned to a man's belly so he leans away from the drum's weight, is like a woman fat with child. Walking any distance with such a burden requires brute strength and a short-sleeved shirt. Occasionally there will be blood on the drummer's wrists, deep pink grooves bitten into his neck and always, even on a cool evening, greased pools of sweat, like continents, spreading out beneath his armpits and up the line of his back. His mouth will be clamped grimly shut, his eyes pinned. All his energy is in his wrists flicking the drum, snapping, and flicking again, driving the blood and thunder out of its stretched skin.

Up close this is a sharper, more metallic sound. Tinna. Tinna. Tinna. Tinna, like a child going at an upturned saucepan. It is not music but neither is it noise. There's an art to handling a Lambeg as there is an art to managing any difficult thing. This cannot be understood from a distance.

There is nowhere to go from the drums tonight. Even the nicest parts of Belfast are thick with their death rattle.

Tonight is the tenth. Tomorrow will be the Eleventh and the following day the Twelfth. In other cities these are merely dates, numbers in the summer calendar. In this city the Twelfth is a holiday. It is pronounced with a capital letter, as is the Eleventh (though, like Christmas Eve, it is a date worth marking only after the lights go out). The Eleventh is for bonfires, the Twelfth for parades, piss-ups and commemorating proud Protestant victories of the past. King Billy. The Battle of the Boyne. All the truths, and well-learnt half-truths, which keep the Orange ordered. 'Remember 1690,' they say, the year it all kicked off, and three hundred years later they remain hell-bent on remembering, though the details have worn thin from passing one generation to the next. This year, like a three-for-the-price-of-two deal, the Thirteenth will be for the World Cup Final.

'Yeoooo,' they cry, like old-time revivalists every time the final is mentioned. You cannot pass a pub or drinking room for hearing this barbaric whoop come leaking through an open window. 'Yeoooo' is local-speak for overwhelming joy, or sometimes mortification, or simply not having anything coherent to add to a conversation but wishing to have your voice heard none the less. In this case, 'yeooo' is a small word – not so much a word as a guttural yelp – which speaks of anticipation, fraternity and three whole days of wild hedonism.

'Yeooo. How about this three-day weekend, mate?' they say, as they raise their pints to the football-themed adverts, now looped between every programme on TV. 'Sure, you can't be bad to that.'

They are happier in this moment than weddings, babies or honeymoon nights will ever make them. They would never say this to their wives and girlfriends. Women do not understand what football does inside a man. Speaking isn't even necessary when men are in a group, with other men, watching football. The ease of this is half the appeal. The same can be said of marching. They do not know what the women have as an equivalent, possibly drinking tea. The men of the East intend to suck every good second out of their weekend: the parades, the drums, the drink, the football, the smell of sweat, and other men pressing against them, like brothers or would-be lovers.

It's not even the weekend yet but most people have already started drinking. Beer and whiskey and wine from cardboard boxes with spouts. Vodka, gin and neon-coloured fruit drinks in glass bottles. These are more for the women but go down like greased ice in this heat. Shandy, neat bourbon and home-made sangria, tinned pineapple and orange slices islanding on the surface, like the stuff they serve in Benidorm. The wives have made gallons of sangria in washing-up basins. They are serving it with soup ladles, in plastic pint glasses from Poundland. These days, everything that can be bought from the pound shop is bought from the pound shop. It is a constant disappointment that Poundland doesn't sell drink of any kind.

The women let the children have a sup of sangria with their burgers. 'Sure it's only glorified fruit juice,' they say, and turn a blind eye when the same kids come back to swipe a tin or two from the ice bucket. They remember the taste of being nine and ten themselves: how you could claim drunkenness and go buck mad on a quarter tin of Harp, passed between friends. They open another box of wine and tell stories about being young and running the streets. When the wine is finished, there'll be beer, and after that a runner dispatched to the offie for more beer and cigarettes before closing. They'll drink anything that comes to hand this weekend, sopping up their drunkenness with tray after tray of lardy chips. They'll continue to drink for the next three days, only sobering up in time to make work on the fourteenth.

Between the sun and the football there is a general assumption that this year's Twelfth will be particularly glorious. Most hope the Tall Fires won't get in the way of their merrymaking. Others retain the old fondness for violence. They wouldn't say no to a good riot, if the opportunity presented itself. They watch the news each night, hoping it all comes to a head in time for the big day. The old people are stuck records on how the Twelfth used to be: sunshine, music and neat uniforms, properly worn, no trouble with the police, no trouble with the other side, and certainly no trouble with young lads getting plastered in the street. It is only the heat making them think like this. Sunshine has a sly way of bringing out the nostalgia. The past is almost always brighter than it actually was. The city would do well to remember this. It should be written with paint on the gable end of a few houses, one in the East, one on either side of the West. It'd make a change from Georgie Best and balaclavas.

It is stupid hot in the streets tonight. The neighbours' cats are sleeping on the roofs of parked cars, baking slowly against the warm metal. No one feels the need for a jumper. There are children, sitting scuff-kneed on the kerbs, sucking ice pops while they shove pennies and small stones into the molten asphalt. The sun is still hanging high behind the cranes, soft yellow on hard yellow, like raw egg running over a cooked one. There hasn't been a clean lick of rain in four weeks.

Hosepipes are banned entirely and the car wash on the corner of the Newtownards Road is shut. There's talk of drought in the country too, fields parched and crops ruined. The city folk don't care. Their world is made of brick and slate. They haven't been near a field in years. Seeing the stern-faced farmers on the news, standing outside Tandragee and Doagh in their wellington boots, is like seeing famine victims, bloat-bellied in some far-away country. These are not their people. This is not their country. They turn the TV to another channel and have, in a moment, forgotten all about the poor farmers and their ruined fields.

It is less than twenty-four hours till the bonfires are lit, and after this, the parades. The drums are loose from beating. They are ready for battle. Across the city thousands of white shirts have been ironed and uniforms laid to rest on spare beds and back-door hangers. The beer has been got in, and the value-pack crisps. The bowler hats have been dusted and the Sunday shoes polished mirror black. The sashes have yet to be lifted from their ornamental cases. This comes last, on the Twelfth morning, for fear of stains or unavoidable creases.

All over Belfast, but mostly in the East, the bonfires are being layered up, like enormous wedding cakes. Flags and stuffed effigies of the other side are bound to the pallets with rope. Chairs, borrowed from the community centre, have been looped around the fire's edge at a distance, accommodating those spectators too old to stand, or ill-inclined to dance, like savages, around the flames. Cranes and pulleys are being used to stack the top tiers. Miles below, at the foot of the pyre, young lads have gathered in bunches to suck energy drinks straight from the bottle and shout, through hands cupped, like megaphones, 'Wee bit to the left. Swing it to the right there, mate. It's grand where it is!'

They are their shipyard fathers and their grandfathers before them, standing with hands idly in pockets. They are waiting for a summer soon to come when they will be invited into the thick of the fire, to push the edges back with long-handled shovels, to work the crane, or empty handguns into the fire's flaming tongues. *Bang. Bang. Bang.* Like it's a beast to be slain. They must cover their faces when they hold a gun, not from shame, or fear exactly, but because a kind of horror comes off a hidden face.

Most of the bonfires are already lording it over the thirty-foot limit by twenty, thirty, forty extra feet, in one case fifty. They are daring the police to intervene. They are finger-flicking the politicians to stand over the stern words they've lately spoken. Politicians here are known for talking and counter-talking and folding, like seaside deckchairs, when required to take action. They are watching each other closely now, waiting to see who will be first to condemn the bonfires. No one wants to be the first stone-caster. No one wants to be last. The trick is to raise your voice at exactly the same moment as everyone else. In this, and other matters, the politicians are not unlike teenage children.

The local news has been and gone. They've captured the unlit bonfires from the ground and, once again, for perspective, from the top of a cherry-picker. They've been door to door around the East collecting interviews. Those people interviewed have spent every minute since on the telephone spreading the word; they might be on the six o'clock news if no better story breaks before then. The big BBC will only appear if there's trouble. There will be trouble. There always is. But the BBC proper has a scale for deciding how bad it needs to get before the mainland will be interested.

The police are here already. A trio of Land Rovers is parked within spitting distance of the highest bonfires. They've been there for a week now, pre-empting trouble and slicing a substantial chunk off the policing budget with each night spent twiddling their thumbs beneath the streetlights. Inside the Land

Rovers pairs of bored PSNI officers eat wine gums, text their other halves and read paperback copies of crime novels, one eye flitting across the dark streets. Each local child who passes a Land Rover knows well enough to kick the tyres squarely or run a stick along the vehicle's armoured flanks, rattling the officers inside.

Elsewhere in the city the Tall Fires continue to flame. The police are exhausted, endlessly trying to predict which building will burn next. It is not easy to be a member of the PSNI during parade season. On the Twelfth day people will want to walk down roads they are not allowed to walk down. The police will be told to stop them doing this (though many individual officers are not sure why). Nine times out of ten the act of stopping someone walking down a road will result in a riot. There are riots before the Twelfth and on the Twelfth and, sometimes, for up to a week on either side. These are to be expected and can be planned for in advance (annual leave suspended, extra officers drafted in from the more provincial towns, water cannons cleaned in preparation for picking off the worst offenders).

The Tall Fires are a different kind of trouble. They could not have been predicted so have not been planned for. They sit on top of the ordinary riots like another thing the PSNI is expected to carry. The police are already thin around the edges and there's still two days before the Twelfth. They wonder when it's all going to end, how long they'll be here, whether they can manage to get a holiday in before the kids go back to school. It's been four weeks now and the fires are only getting worse.

Each night they patrol the entire city in slow, languid loops, squinting into abandoned buildings and shops for anything that might be a flame. Often they mistake burglar alarms or the glow from a computer monitor for an actual fire and break into the wrong building. This costs time and money. It makes the PSNI look incompetent in the local press. Sometimes they arrest innocent people lighting barbecues in their own back gardens. Sometimes they're making these arrests while important civic buildings are going up in flames. This does not pass unnoticed.

The police are not winning. They've already lost the west wing of the City Hall and the central library, which burnt from the inside out: all those books and antique manuscripts flaring quickly and turning to dry ash before the fire brigade even arrived. They've been told they must try harder. They have received this message from their superiors, from the press, the public and, with quiet desperation, from the politicians on the hill, who wish to have the whole situation under control before the Eleventh Night. If the city is burning and rioting at the same time it will be impossible to keep it from the international press. 'God,' they mutter to each other, passing in the corridors of Stormont, 'as if we didn't have enough of a job selling this place to tourists. You'd think they could save their riots till after the summer. They wouldn't be half so hard to stomach, off-peak.'

In the last week the PSNI have pulled fifty of their undercover officers off regular duties and made them full-time fire-chasers. Some get paid extra money for this. Others are younger and just trying to make a name for themselves. They spend their days following leads and their evenings cruising the housing estates in unmarked Mondeos. Each car is equipped with a fire extinguisher, fire blankets and a first-aid kit specially designed for burns victims. This is a precautionary measure but it's only a matter of time before someone gets hurt. They've all been trained to drop and roll, drop and roll, to smother a colleague quickly with blankets should the situation ever arise.

They are like backyard cats: their eyes have grown accustomed to seeing in the dark. A streak of orange, a holy white flare, and they're out of the car and bolting across the road, fire extinguisher in hand, ready to coat everything in dry foam.

They are almost always too late. Rarely do they get to the scene of a Tall Fire before it's in full flame. Their uniforms stink of last night's barbecue, a smell they've come to associate with failure. It's not their fault. There are thousands of buildings in Belfast, each one capable of hosting a Tall Fire, and only so many police officers to go around.

They are no closer to catching the original Fire Starter than they were a month ago. There's been nothing new from him in weeks, just the same YouTube video endlessly re-posted on Facebook walls and Twitter feeds. There's nothing the police can do to stop this message. It's already gone viral in every English-speaking country. They've analysed the video for hours in the computer lab, magnifying each frame until it is nothing but a series of black, blue and flesh-coloured pixels. The Fire Starter is good. He (or could it be a she?) has left nothing for the police to catch on. It could be anyone, even one of them. So they continue to chase their tails all over the city, putting out one fire only to find two more have popped up in its place. It's like the game children play at amusement arcades, thumping moles with a padded mallet while others seem to multiply underground. It's hard not to feel mocked. Several of the younger officers have already gone off with the stress. They cannot sustain this for much longer.

Late in the evening of the tenth, the politicians reach a decision. They gather the local press on the steps of Stormont and make a brief announcement. The Tall Fires will not win. 'Anarchy,' they say, with uncharacteristic confidence, 'cannot be tolerated in any form.' They are all, even the women, wearing suit jackets to say this. It is the sort of serious pronouncement that requires a defined shoulder. First thing in the morning all those bonfires breaching the thirty-foot rule will come down.

The Nationalist side looks jubilant, the Unionists' weary. Those caught in the impotent space between glance from one side to the other, like creatures caught in the headlights, about to be run over. The decision will not be without repercussions. Everyone knows there will be trouble now, more trouble than the usual kerfuffle on the Twelfth.

The politicians are asked about the logistics of bringing down seventy-foot bonfires. Will they be dismantled entirely or simply reduced to the legal thirty-foot limit? Who will be responsible for this? Will a contractor be brought in or will PSNI officers be expected to do the job by hand? Is this kind of work included in a police officer's terms and conditions? Have the trade unions been consulted? Who is going to meet the costs for policing this mess? When the politicians open their mouths to answer, the noise that comes out is the spoken equivalent of a deep shrug. They don't know exactly. They are spent from having made this one hard decision and will require a week or more to think through its logistical implications. They do not have a week. In less than an hour it will be the Eleventh and twenty hours after this, the Eleventh Night. Something is going to happen now. It will not be good. The city holds its breath and waits.

Less than two hours later a new video begins appearing on the internet. By breakfast it has gone viral.

The format is familiar. A small room with a white sheet draped across an entire wall. A person, probably male, sitting in front of this sheet wearing a Guy Fawkes mask, blue jeans and a black hoodie drawn high over its head. It does not speak. It holds cardboard signs to the camera. 'They're not listening to us'; 'Burn the whole city down'; 'I'm the Fire Starter.' In the background, the music is the same thirty-second loop of the Prodigy's 'Firestarter'. Once all the cardboard signs have been revealed, a black screen appears, with seven words printed in white capital letters: 'YOU SHOULD HAVE LEFT OUR BONFIRES ALONE.'

The press are quick to pick up the story. With every subsequent news bulletin, it edges closer to the headline spot. The Fire Starter has decided it's time to escalate the violence. Who knows what will happen next? The police call for calm. The politicians echo this, issuing statements from their individual parties. Church leaders also make an appearance: a Catholic priest and a Presbyterian minister stand side by side on the Peace Line, asking people to pray and stay at home and think about how far we've come in the last few years.

The young men and women of Belfast have heard it all before. They don't want to stay at home and pray for peace. They don't want to follow rules or put the safety of others first. They are blood blind with anger: 'First the peace walls, and then the roads, the flags and now our bonfires,' they say. 'Soon we won't have anything left.' They are, at heart, terrified that once the last symbol has been stolen from them they will not know themselves different from the stranger in the street. They will be left without anything solid to lean upon. They wouldn't know how to say this to a news reporter even if a news reporter took the time to ask. Instead they talk of the loud violence their parents knew, as if it is a kind of birthright denied to them. They share their seething thoughts with each other, leaning against community-centre walls, on the phone, in vitriolic Facebook posts and tweets. They use the war-weary language of duty: 'It's up to us'; 'Now's the time'; 'Our civil liberties are at stake.' Over the course of a single sun-blessed morning, their anger sours until it spills on to the city's streets and they are burning buildings and cars and trees for the sheer blood rush of actually doing something.

Before the authorities can move in to dismantle the bonfires safely, every one of them is alight. Belfast bakes from the combined heat of sunshine and a hundred daytime fires. The tallest lose the run of themselves and swim down the streets, like molten rivers of lava. Unpatrolled, they claim everything in their path, setting cars and terraced houses on fire, turning the warm tarmac to treacle, scorching the double-glazing until it pops one layer at a time, making a noise like water laughing. The old people are evacuated from their houses and stand at the end of their streets watching the fires flame. Some are crying, even some of the men.

The fire brigade can't cope. Engines from the south are called upon. This hasn't happened since De Valera gave the word during the Blitz. Everywhere they go they are pelted by teenagers with bottles and bricks. It is hard enough to fight fire without adding children to the mix. The teenagers wear scarves wrapped round their faces to protect themselves from the television cameras. They stand spread-legged on the roofs of parked cars, and high walls, surveying the chaos they have caused. It is a kind of hell and they have only just started. They raise their fists in rage and triumph, sending their shrill, demonic 'Yeooo' echoing up and down the little streets. The noise harmonizes with the sirens and the drums, which are out again, thundering on the horizon, and the dogs howling in their hot backyards. This is the sound of war beginning and the young ones are proud to be doing their bit.

By midnight on the Eleventh the young fire starters have grown bored with the bonfires and moved on to other, less likely, sources. Hundreds of teenagers and youths in their early twenties have swarmed the streets of Belfast setting fire to anything that speaks of authority: churches, schools, Ulsterbuses idling by the side of the road, postboxes, post vans, police Land Rovers where they can peel the officers out from behind the wheel, shops, trees and pubs, which go up like Halloween night when the spirits catch. Anything that can be burnt has been burnt. In the early hours of the Twelfth an ice-cream van, already stocked for the parades, is driven on to the Albert Bridge and set alight. The tinkling sound of 'Show Me The Way To

Amarillo' shimmers loose as the flames catch hold, and masked children stand round the fire's edge passing out choc ices and Twisters lifted, just in time, from the van's freezer. This is the footage that the BBC run with on their breakfast show. It is like a snapshot of the world's end: masked children eating ice cream while the whole city glows hell red behind their backs.

By mid-morning they have replaced this clip with different footage. Before they show it, the newscaster lifts the papers stacked in front of her, shuffles them awkwardly and says, 'Some viewers may find the content distressing.' She looks as if something is lodged in her throat.

It is difficult to imagine a viewer who would not find this content distressing. The politicians in Stormont cannot look at it for shame. The police officers, drinking coffee in the staff-room between shifts, reach to switch the channels as a mark of respect, or possibly fear. Parents will not let their children watch the news this week, and in other countries, people who had almost forgotten the problems with Belfast watch this clip and suck air between their teeth slowly, making a noise that is both shock and sympathy, also something like an old memory resurrected.

In the attic room of a semi-detached house at the top of the Castlereagh Road, Mark Agnew cannot lift his eyes from the television screen. He is watching a group of young men wearing tracksuit bottoms, with football scarves bandaged across their faces. They are reaching across the barricades at the Short Strand to drag a female PSNI officer into the middle of the road.

He is still watching as they lift a litre can of tractor diesel and tip it over her head. He is watching the two who are holding out the police officer's arms, as if she is about to be crucified, the one waving a cigarette lighter over her head, and the one who is pouring the diesel. But mostly he is watching the girl, who is not moving, not even trying to escape.

Mark is watching in slow time as the lad whose job it is to start the fire lifts his hands, then doesn't flick the lighter open, or cannot, or perhaps realizes that a football scarf is not thick enough to hide behind. Then there are shots. *Snip. Snip. Snip.* Exactly the noise a gun will make in a movie. The one with the lighter is dead. The other three have fallen behind him. But the girl keeps standing there in the middle of the road, arms out, like Jesus waiting to be taken down from the cross.

Mark watches the clip and pauses it before the next news story starts, then watches it again and again. He thinks about the young PSNI officer as she stands in the shower tonight, smelling like a petrol station, trying to scrape it off herself with shower gel and shampoo, all the time knowing that it is not just in her nose. This smell is everywhere now. She will have six months off on the stress and talk about this moment till it doesn't seem real any more and, still, even after all the drugs and therapy, never progress beyond a desk job. He is thinking about all this as he rewinds and pauses and plays this clip, keeping his headphones on, lest his dad hear from downstairs.

Mark knows all this is his fault. He is absolutely sure of it. He feels like the king of the world but he cannot tell anyone.

9

The News

I AM FOLLOWING the news now. I have the television on in the kitchen while I fix Sophie's bottles and prepare my packed lunch. I keep the sound turned off and let the subtitles run across the bottom of the screen. I've only just thought to do this and it's already making evenings much more bearable. I've even started watching foreign movies on DVD. When you can't hear the words it doesn't matter which language they're spoken in. I like the idea of being a person who watches arthouse movies. Even romantic comedies are classier in French or Spanish.

Every day I'm finding new ways to adapt to Sophie. For the moment we're managing. We're more than managing. We may even be flourishing. I sleep better than I've slept in years and when I wake to Sophie, or the sun blushing through my bedroom curtains, I'm often smiling. This is the closest to happy I have ever been, even as a very small child. I still count my fears – this is a habit like brushing teeth or tugging an earlobe when nervous – but there's only one fear left and it's a brand-new fear: the fear of what will happen next.

Sophie is fussy this morning. She hasn't slept well these last few nights. I blame the heat and the drums rumbling around the city's edge. There's no way to explain the drums to a small child. They're like something awful circling and I don't entirely understand their significance myself. I lift my daughter from the cot and hold her against me as she fights tiredness. Her eyelids flutter against my neck, closing and opening, struggling against sleep, like a drunk playing sober. I enjoy the weight of her becoming heavier as she drifts off. My left arm has grown tighter than my right just from holding Sophie. The sweat from her head leaves a damp island on my shirt but I don't mind at all. I hum to her – old folk songs and television jingles, anything that comes to mind. I have a decent voice. My mother once told me this. It's the only compliment I can remember in a lifetime of subtle gibes. I sing and the drums keep time for me. I'm pleased with this arrangement.

Sophie sleeps better when I hold her, better still when I hum. I'm not humming now. I'm watching the news and trying to jiggle the fuss out of her. As I dance my daughter round the kitchen, the sound of her gurning is not quite human. It is more like the noise that comes off a domestic machine: a blender or vacuum cleaner. It's giving me a headache. She has woken early this morning. So have I. The heat rises during the night and is almost unbearable on the top floor of the house. I plan to buy an electric fan at the weekend. If the weather doesn't break first.

As I fix my sandwiches I keep one ear angled towards the front door, ready to turn off the television as soon as I hear Christine. Things are going well with the nanny. There have been no slip-ups since the first day with the cartoons. I don't want her to discover that, despite what I've said, I still let Sophie watch television. Life has been ten times easier since Christine arrived. I look forward to work and then look forward to coming home. I've begun to let myself imagine Sophie at one, two, and even four, heading off to school in buckle-up shoes. All this is because of Christine and the order she's brought. I can tell Sophie has taken to her too. There's a very specific way she lights up, like a memory surfacing, every time she focuses on Christine's face. She does the same with me, but this is to be expected. Looking into my face is like looking at her face in the mirror.

At night, after her bath, I hold my face beside Sophie's in the bathroom mirror and go at her like a spot-the-difference picture. Same eyes. Same nose. Same high cheekbones and teacup chin. I glance quickly past her mouth and ears. I can barely remember what her mother looked like. 'We are normal,' I tell my frowning reflection. 'We are a family.' I like to use the phrase 'single parent' when the opportunity comes up in conversation. It makes me feel normal. Lots of people are single parents, these days, even men. Lately I've been thinking a lot about what it means to be a man. This isn't something I've given much consideration to until now.

Last night was the World Cup Final. I watched a little of it half-heartedly, flicking backwards and forwards between an old Bruce Willis movie on Channel 4. I've never been much of a sports person but, now that I'm a father, I'm experimenting with different manly practices: drinking beer instead of wine, newspapers with breakfast, football, rugby, proper shaving with a blade and foam, ordering takeaway pizza. I had a go at watching porn but found this to be a strangely removed experience, like observing animals at the zoo through a sheet of protective glass. I didn't try it again. I'm probably the kind of man who enjoys golf more than pornography.

Watching the news is another of my man things. It's good to be informed. This morning the news is a game of two halves. Fifty per cent of air time is given to dissecting the World Cup Final. The rest of the footage is focused on the 'Belfast fires'. This is what the world's media have come to call the situation outside my front door. As a kind of courtesy, the newscaster flies briefly through the news in other places, then immediately returns to Belfast. The World Cup Final has only made things worse, he explains, for the benefit of all those unfamiliar with the city's partisan tendencies. The wrong team has won, which means that in certain parts of the city the right team has won. This has been interpreted as yet another good reason to riot. Things are becoming 'increasingly tense', which is newscaster-speak for complicated, for violent, for 'Damned if I know how they're going to sort this one out.'

There is weariness in the way the newscaster is reading the teleprompter feed, like an actor five weeks into a six-week run. He is one of the BBC's recognizable faces. He's been reading the news since the early seventies. It's not the first time he's spoken the words 'increasingly tense' and 'Belfast' in the same breath. It probably won't be the last. Nevertheless, it's reassuring to see him, suited and shuffling his notes, like God is still in his Heaven; the weather will shortly follow.

The last few days have been a kind of war. Stormont contin-ues to dally over what government involvement should look like. They might start another round of talks. No surprise there. The army marks time on the sidelines, neither fully committed nor permitted to retreat. The Orangemen decide to continue with their traditional parades. The Twelfth day storms angrily down the already flaming streets; all is fire, all is rage and chaos. There are stand-offs and riots, slanging matches, punishment beatings and, in an estate on the edge of Castlereagh, two young fellas are kneecapped, still wearing their pipe-band uniforms. It's unlikely that they'll march again.

The hospitals cannot cope. They are treating people on trol-leys in the car park. Thank goodness the weather is holding. They haven't got a back-up plan if it rains. The church folk are praying for rain. They're asking for a flood like Noah's, and while God has promised he won't be pulling that damp move again, they wonder if maybe he'll make an exception for them and their ongoing troubles. At the back of their minds they remember that the world will end with fire. 'No man knoweth the day nor the hour,' they repeat, as the smell of ash and brimstone drifts down the little streets and big. They are not as ready as they thought they would be.

The fire brigade cannot cope. There is talk of bringing in extra engines from Scotland on the passenger ferry. There is further talk of banning matches and firelighters of all kinds. Now the football fans are rioting with sticks and bricks and Molotov cocktails fashioned from empty milk bottles. It is mostly young people orchestrating this. A still from the Fire Starter video flashes up behind the newscaster, and a series of statistics about youth unemployment among the working class of Belfast.

The news desk disappears, seamlessly segueing into footage from an outside-broadcast unit on Cave Hill. The camera pans slowly across the Belfast skyline. The newscaster is saying something about lost revenue: tourism, retail, transport. He is mentioning a number significantly higher than a million. He looks like he's struggling not to roll his eyes in frustration.

I curl Sophie into the crook of my neck. I've spent so long making sure she doesn't hear things that could hurt her. Now there are things I don't want her to see.

On screen a sea of men and women is rushing the riot squad, pelting them with bottles and bricks as they run. Then, a small group of children, wearing children's clothes – Disney tops, white school gutties, tiny hearts and stars threaded through their pierced ears – appears. They are smashing the plate-glass front of a Chinese takeaway, raiding the fridges for fizzy drinks. Then there are cars on fire, ambulances on fire, a primary school on the Antrim Road charred inside, though it is still possible to distinguish the outline of the kids' artwork, giraffes, lions and crudely drawn elephants, pinned to the walls. None of this is more than a couple of miles from my front door. 'This is footage taken just an hour ago,' says the newscaster. I believe him. I can smell burnt petrol wafting through my open window.

I turn off the television, as much for myself as Sophie, and think about the three young lads setting fire to the climbing frame in Victoria Park. It's hard to believe they're involved in this madness. I remember their crisp tracksuits, the easy way they had of ribbing each other gently, as only good friends can. I can't seem to reconcile my memory of them with the crass violence on the news. I don't believe they're the kind of children who would ruin things on purpose. They were not without kindness, better than all of this or, if not above it, unfortunate heirs of someone else's spite.

The front door opens and closes sharply. Christine comes hurrying into the kitchen. She flings her handbag on to the table and reaches for Sophie. I pass the baby into her arms and am once again astounded by how natural they look together, leaning against the fridge-freezer. They could be mother and daughter. Maybe this could be said of any woman under fifty holding a child the right way up. Christine looks somewhat frazzled this morning. The corner of her eye make-up has slid downwards as if she's been crying or rubbing her eyes. Her normally pale face is flushed. She looks like a person who has recently been unhappy. I curl my thumb and finger into a circle, make comet tails of the other three fingers and raise my hand towards her. I arrange my face so it is also asking, 'OK?'

Christine nods. 'Yes.' She taps her wristwatch once, twice, three times. Then, balancing Sophie awkwardly in the crook of her elbow, she mimes holding a steering wheel, rotating it slowly left and right, all the time looking furious. I guess traffic. This is how we mostly communicate: snippets of sign language and a kind of charades. It works for us and when it doesn't work we use the notepad. I reach for it now and write, 'Tall Fires?' Christine nods. I write, 'It feels like the end of the world, doesn't it?'

142

She nods again. She lifts her right hand and slices it sharply against her forehead, perfectly in line with her nose. This, I remember, is the sign for 'idiot', or it could be something stronger. I've been teaching myself sign language online and there is a course at work I've asked to be sent on. Marty is pleased every time I mention it. He thinks I've come back with renewed enthusiasm for my job.

I place a hand lightly on Christine's shoulder. I still haven't learnt the sign for 'sorry'. I keep getting distracted by swear words. They are, for some reason, funnier gestures than the ordinary words. I like the idea of making them subtly when my colleagues or the lady receptionists annoy me. Christine shrugs off my hand. Have I been overly forward? Will she suspect me in love with her now? I'm definitely not in love with Christine but I don't know if I could cope without her. Once again I wonder if I should tell her there's no possibility of romance blossoming between us. No chance at all. But women are strange when it comes to this sort of thing. They hear the opposite of what men say. It might make everything more complicated.

Christine sighs and makes the sign for 'Go,' which is remarkably similar to the sign for shoving me face forwards towards the door. I grab my lunch on the way, return for my keys and, just before leaving the kitchen, turn to scribble, 'There's lasagne in the fridge. Help yourself.' I'll find this note later and allow myself the dry pleasure of pretending it has been left by an entirely believable wife, off to Pilates or working late. This is the kind of ordinary I crave in the same way that other people crave money or holiday homes in Spain.

As I back the Renault out of the drive I notice Christine's little Corsa parked under the streetlamp. It's missing a wing mirror. The passenger door is deeply dented as if it has been kicked or hit repeatedly with a blunt weapon such as a brick. I text her from the health centre: 'SAW UR CAR. WOT HAPPND?'

She replies immediately: 'RIOTERS GOT ME AT THE TRAFFIC LIGHTS. WEE BASTARDS.' Reading her text I instinctively raise my right hand like a vertical line, slicing into my face. I've remembered that is the sign for 'bastard'. 'Idiot' is a lot softer, like a wave.

The health centre is quieter than usual. People are staying at home if they can. There hasn't been a pre-dinner riot since the Twelfth and the fires only really get going at night. But people, especially the old, are cautious. They will stay in and quietly die of treatable illnesses, rather than risk getting caught in a blockade. Like back-to-front vampires they fear not being able to get home by dark. This is not just because of the fires. It is endemic here: something to do with the Troubles and the fear of those creatures, both mortal and magic, that creep around in the shadows. The old people practically hibernate during winter.

Neither of the two younger doctors has made it into work. They live further away, on the other side of the city, while Marty's house is just a block away and mine less than a mile. It is not safe crossing the bridges after five and, fearing they might be trapped here in the East, Marty has told them to stay at home till things calm down. He decides that we will divvy up the spare patients between us. That is how I come to meet Sammy.

The Girl Who Is Occasionally a Boat

*I*N A BACKYARD *on the edge of Castlereagh, Lucy Anderson is becoming a boat for the third time this week. She stands ankle deep in her sister's paddling pool and waits. Her father's let the hedge grow high so the neighbours can't see. Lucy prefers to be a boat on the river. She likes to glide with the loop-necked swans at Victoria Park. But sometimes the need to change comes on her quickly and there isn't time for anything but the backyard and the paddling pool, with its lurid pattern of tropical fish. Privacy's essential. Hence the hedge and the curtains drawn throughout the house. It wouldn't do for some passing stranger − a postman or politician canvassing − to peer through the front window and see her pale face straining from a boat bow, her arms and legs stretched to planks.*

Lucy waits in the tepid water. She waits patiently while the heaviness falls off her, like damp dripping from wet washing on a line. Her bones begin to ache in the familiar fashion. It isn't exactly painful. The stretching. The twisting. The coming together of separate parts. It isn't normal either. Lucy can't really say what her body's doing right now. Transforming. Turning. Taking the piss. She's come to call it 'changing' and afterwards feels like she's been crucified. She won't be able to bend for a week. In the moment it's glory, though. Her bones are made of air, her flesh feathers, and the breath in her lungs is not breath but some lighter substance, helium, perhaps, or pure white cloud. Then Lucy is not the dumpy girl she sees in the mirror. She is not hefty, big-boned or thick of thigh. She sits lightly on the water. She floats. She glides, which is how you'd describe an elegant girl's movements: a ballerina, for example, or a catwalk model.

Lucy's become a boat 149 times already. She can't remember her very first change. She was only two at the time, her small body discovering some new ability almost every day. Who's to say she hadn't taken it all in her stride, adding boats to walking, talking and all the other tricks she'd lately learnt to do? Her parents tell her she howled for hours afterwards. 'It was only a puddle,' they say, and tell her the noise she made was something shocking, like matchsticks splintering and rubber stretched to breaking point. Her father's never got over the shock. Lucy's body's grown used to becoming a boat now. She's almost sixteen and so accustomed to the bone-creaking, skin-yearning sensation of changing she's stopped keeping track of how many times she's done it. It's a curse she carries. It's a kind of blessing. She wouldn't know herself without it. She wouldn't know where to start. What's the point in being a boat? Lucy's not decided yet. She thinks it's something to do with the act of carrying: people, problems, large unwieldy things. She refuses to call herself unfortunate. But it would be nice to have a name for what she is, a word for being in between.

10

A Very Bad Man

SAMMY HAS BEEN a patient in this GP practice for the last six months. He's only ever seen Dr Owens before. He's the kind of man who would feel awkward exposing any part of his body to another man, even a doctor. He can't bear the thought of being naked and touched by anyone but a woman, though if it were a surgical procedure he'd insist upon a man. This would be a matter of competence.

Sammy is already waiting at the reception desk when Jonathan arrives at the health centre. The two men nod at each other as they pass. Sammy doesn't know that Jonathan is a doctor. He looks at the younger man, striding purposefully through the foyer in his suit and pressed shirt, and imagines him to be a lawyer or something equally well paid and accomplished. He wonders what he's in for. There's not even the slightest skiff of embarrassment off him, so Sammy diagnoses a throat infection or something similarly mundane; nothing sexual, nothing grim with bowels or flaky skin, certainly nothing mental.

Sammy is feeling a little mental.

It's taken him all night to get the nerve up to see the doctor. Now he is leaning his entire weight against the reception desk, as if leaning will make him less inclined to turn tail and march home. He asks for Melanie by name. The lady receptionist with the strong perfume wishes to clarify, does he mean Dr Owens, and Sammy nods. Dr Owens is a young GP, recently graduated. She lets her patients use her first name. Sammy can picture Dr Owens in his mind. She has a face like that of a kindly lamb. He has been up all night practising his confession and in every one of these dry runs it is this lamby woman who takes notes and prescribes pills. It is Melanie with her long, sloping nose and her teeth like the tiny smiling teeth of his late grandmother, who covers his hand with her own white one, and says, 'Don't be worrying now, Mr Agnew. It's not the end of the world.'

The lady receptionist is shaking her head apologetically. There are problems. Sammy is feeling increasingly uncomfortable. He can't be sure he won't throw up all over the counter. She says, 'I'm sorry, sir, Dr Owens isn't in today. Because of the fires, you know. I can give you Dr Murray or Dr Bell. Which would you like?'

'Is either of them a woman?' asks Sammy.

'Not the last time I looked,' replies the lady receptionist, and winks.

The wink is wasted on Sammy. He is a big man, but he looks like he might cry. Instinctively she reaches over and nudges the box of Kleenex closer to the edge of the counter, where Sammy's hands are curling into the wood, like a kind of knuckly vice.

'Which one's nicer?' he asks.

'Dr Bell,' she replies, then clamps a hand over her mouth. 'I mean, they're both great, but Dr Murray's just a wee bit more . . . serious.'

'I'll take him.'

'Are you sure?'

'I don't want nice, love,' he says. 'I want somebody who'll get me sorted out.'

Sammy doesn't know why he is saying this. He wants nice.

He has come here specifically to be treated nicely by the doctor with the lamby face. Now his mouth is telling him that he wants serious and blunt, possibly even cruel. His mouth knows that he does not deserve nice. He deserves somebody coming at him with a sawn-off shotgun.

'Right you be, sir. Dr Murray it is. Take a wee seat in the waiting room and he'll be right with you.'

Sammy unfastens himself from the reception desk and lumbers off in the direction of the waiting room. The lady receptionist watches him leave. He is like a sad gorilla, hanging over his own weariness. He takes a seat in the furthest corner of the waiting room, positioning himself between the wall and Barry, who comes in every day, with drink on him, just to get out of the weather. He lifts an out-of-date car magazine from the coffee-table and flicks through it, front to back, his eye never for a moment focusing on any page. When it is his turn to meet the doctor he remains in his seat for a further thirty seconds, staring at the toes of his shoes as if willing himself to stand up and walk down the long, carpeted corridor to Dr Murray's door.

He stops outside the doctor's room. He knocks on the door, though it's already partially open. He can see a slim slice of the young doctor sitting at his desk. Damn it, he thinks. It's the posh fella from Reception. He feels judged, and he hasn't even opened his mouth yet. He deserves to be judged for what he's done. He opens the door and slides into the room. Next to the doctor's desk there is a plastic chair of the variety often found in healthcare facilities. Sammy sinks into it. It is a relief to be finally sitting down.

He doesn't even take the time to introduce himself. 'I'm a bad man, Doctor,' he says, 'a very bad man.'

This strikes Jonathan as somewhat ludicrous, a phrase you'd hear in a movie and never actually say in real life. He stifles the urge to laugh as he looks up from the script he's filling in for yet

149

another course of antibiotics. (Antibiotics have replaced religion as the opiate of the East. Seemingly there's no illness, real or imagined, that cannot be cured by a prescription for penicillin or one of its sister drugs.) Jonathan pushes the script aside. He can finish it later. He gives the patient his full attention. The man in front of him is about fifty. He is wearing very white train-ers, blue jeans and a V-neck sweater of pale coral lambswool. He does not look like a very bad man. He looks like a retired geog-raphy teacher. Then again, Jonathan reminds himself, looks can be deceiving. Hitler's face on a different man might have been homely, reassuring even, like that of a retired butler.

Jonathan smiles at the very bad man. 'Dr Murray,' he says, extending his hand to the man. He glances down at his notes. 'And you're . . . Samuel Agnew. What can I do for you?'

'It's Sammy,' says the man. He looks furtively round the room. His eyes go left and right, all over the floor, like prison searchlights.

Jonathan takes him in, head to foot, the way his eyes are going. He decides to use his softly-softly mental-health voice. He smiles, careful not to show any tooth. Sammy shifts his weight in the chair. He lifts a leg and hooks it over his thigh so he's sitting there, like a right-angled triangle, all edge and sharp-ish nerves. He leans forwards. Jonathan leans forwards to meet him. He uncrosses his arms. He has learnt this from Melanie: open body language means you are open to your patient's needs. Jonathan is not open to his patient's needs. He is already else-where in his head, wondering what he will think about while this man tells him his own particular sob story. He can tell that Sammy's going to be a talker. Maybe the next ten minutes will give him an opportunity to think about Christine and how to nip their non-romance in the bud.

'You know that thing where you can't tell anyone what I say?' asks Sammy.

'Patient confidentiality,' replies Jonathan.

'Aye, patient confidentiality. Does it still work if I tell you something illegal?'

This is not the first time Jonathan has been asked this question. It is surprisingly common in doctors' surgeries. It usually prefaces an admission of drug use. He holds his smile by the edges. It's beginning to feel stiff on his face.

'Illegal how?' he asks. 'Like you've killed somebody or like you've taken drugs?'

This seems to throw the older man. 'Well, I've done both,' he replies. 'Not for years now and it's not like the peelers don't know. But that's not what I'm in for. It's something else. Something worse.'

In the East there is only one thing worse than killing someone.

'Did you touch a child?' Jonathan asks.

Sammy neither admits this nor denies it, so Jonathan assumes it must be child abuse. He is no longer miles away, thinking about Christine. He is sharp, like needles, running through the protocol in his head. He'll have to write a report and inform Marty, who is their designated child protection officer. He'll probably have to talk to the police. He is thinking, Shit, shit, shit, mostly because child abuse is a vile sort of thing to encounter on a Tuesday morning, but also because he is, at heart, a selfish man and there is an enormous amount of paperwork associated with processing this sort of allegation.

Sammy doesn't notice his consternation. 'Look,' he continues, leaning even further forwards, 'you need to tell me now. If I tell you something will you go to the police or not?'

Jonathan snaps back into the moment. 'If you tell me you've done something illegal and the police aren't aware of it, or I suspect that another person is at risk because of your behaviour, I'm duty-bound to inform the police.' This is a phrase he has learnt by heart and rarely had opportunity to use. It has been partially inspired by years of watching the BBC medical drama *Casualty*. Saying it now, Jonathan is not even sure it's factually accurate.

'Right,' Sammy says. 'There's little point in my being here, then.'

'I think a priest's what you're after, Mr Agnew.'

This does not go down well. Sammy leans back in his chair. Jonathan can see the ghost of an old paramilitary tattoo emerging from the cuff of his sweater. It's not the sort of tattoo you'd see in a chapel. It's the other sort.

'Look,' says Jonathan, trying to reel the conversation back in, 'is there anything I can do for you . . . medically?'

Sammy sits quietly for a moment, turning this offer over in his mind. His jaws circle slowly while he thinks, round and round in loose loops, as if he is sucking a boiled sweet. Twice he goes to stand up and Jonathan thinks he's going to leave, but he remains in his seat, breathing in, breathing out, struggling to keep each hoarse breath under control.

'I'm feeling a bit down, Doctor,' he says at last.

To Jonathan's great surprise, a little tear, no bigger than a lemon pip, sneaks out of the side of his eye and trails down his cheek. Without thinking he plucks a tissue from the box and hands it to the older man. Sammy stares at the tissue. At first he looks confused, then horrified, as if the doctor has placed a steaming lump of dog shit in his hand. He hasn't realized that he's crying. He's not the sort of man who ever cries in public. He reaches a hand to his cheek and it comes away wet. His cheeks immediately blood up. He is mortified. This crying business is almost as bad as letting a doctor see you naked.

'Sorry,' he says.

'Nothing to apologize for,' says Jonathan. 'You wouldn't believe how many people come in here for the same thing.'

'Even men?'

'Lots of men.'

'Pack of fruits,' says Sammy, his voice thick with self-deprecation.

Jonathan starts to run through the checklist for depression: loss of appetite, broken sleep, weight loss, weight gain, anxiety. Sammy nods after most of these symptoms, patting his ample belly and muttering, 'Does it look like I'm fading away?' when the doctor mentions weight loss.

He's been in the surgery for almost eight minutes already. Jonathan needs to keep the consultation moving or the next patient will be in on their heels. It's clearly depression. He's already thinking about prescribing anti-depressants. He could write a script for something that will take the edge off his sadness and have him out of the room in ninety seconds flat. He could say, 'Come back next week and talk to Dr Owens about counselling.' He could do both of these things and it wouldn't even be particularly bad practice. But he doesn't.

Something has shifted in Jonathan recently. Since Sophie. He has always kept to the rules – like a sort of recipe – one action naturally leading to the next. He has chosen the easiest route through every situation. He has thought, What would most people do when faced with this decision? and, regardless of desire or intent, always gone with the most popular option: general practice medicine instead of consultancy, carnivore not vegetarian, short-back-and-sides, blue jeans, brown brogues, four-door estate with a generous boot, Tesco instead of Sainsbury's, and U2 over other, more interesting, bands. This has nothing to do with laziness, though fear, as always, has been a factor. With Jonathan it is always about the desire to fit in or, perhaps more specifically, the fear – the loud, loud horror – of sticking out. Things are different now. He can't stop himself. He has opinions, tastes, likes and dislikes, which refuse to sit quietly below the surface of his reserve. He feels like a moving thing, a car or train, something capable of tremendous speed, something that could cause damage.

Jonathan does not say, 'Would you like a prescription for anti-depressants, Mr Agnew?'

He does not say, 'Come back next week and Dr Owens will get you sorted with a counsellor.'

He doesn't even say, 'Anything you tell me could be held against you, Sammy.'

Instead he opens his mouth and a thing like kindness comes rushing out of him: 'Is something making you feel down, Sammy?' he asks. 'Is it the thing you can't tell me about?'

'Aye,' he replies, and Jonathan can tell from the way his shoulders have risen a little, that a weight has lifted from him with the admission. He wonders what it must feel like to confess a thing, then leave it be and not return to it, over and over, like a picked scab. He thinks about Sophie and the secret she is every time he leaves the house. Maybe his own shoulders would go up like wings if he could – even for a minute – talk with another person about all the ways she makes him afraid.

'Oh, what the hell?' he says, which is a terribly unprofessional thing for a doctor to say. 'I won't tell anyone what you say. Your secrets won't leave this room.'

'Do I have your word on that, Doctor?' Sammy asks.

'You have my word. Go on now, tell me this terrible bad thing you've done. It'll help, getting it off your chest.'

Sammy straightens in his chair. He folds his arms, left over right, like a pair of coat-hangers catching on each other. 'I done bad things when I was younger, Doctor,' he starts. 'I'll not go into what I done but I'm sure you can use your imagination. It was during the Troubles. You know the sort of thing I'm talking about. I thought that was all behind me. I wanted to be different. I said I wasn't for hurting anyone ever again.'

'Did you hurt someone?'

Sammy nods. The tears start again. He rubs at his eyes roughly with the cuff of his pullover.

'Who did you hurt?'

'I hurt my son, Doctor.'

'Is he dead?'

'Naw, he's not dead. Might be better off if he was, though.'

'Did you touch him, Sammy?'

'Of course I didn't touch him, Doctor. I'm not a pervert.' His face curls up at the edges, like he's sucking hard on a bitter lemon.

'Did you hit him, then? Do you beat him? You have to tell me what you've done if you want me to help you, Samuel.'

'I never lifted a hand against the boy. But I've hurt him all the same.'

Jonathan is beginning to lose patience. He imagines the other patients piling up in the waiting room, like rush-hour traffic tailed around the Westlink. He tugs at the soft part of his ear, pinching it between thumb and finger till the pain pulls him back into the moment. He's starting to wonder if Agnew is one of those old men who just like moaning. If it's too late to stop his confession and prescribe a short run of Prozac instead. He reaches across the desk, drawing his prescription pad towards himself.

Sammy is still talking. 'I'm so worried about my son, Doctor,' he continues. 'He's turned into me. Not me now, me the way I was before. He's actually worse than me. He's going to hurt somebody properly. He's going to hurt a lot of people and it'll all be my fault.'

Jonathan's hand hovers over the prescription pad. 'What do you mean, he's going to hurt somebody?'

'It's all getting out of hand. The fires. There's so many of them now. I don't know where it's going to end,' replies Sammy, beginning to ramble. 'I have to do something, stop him before it gets worse. It's my fault he's like this.'

The softness goes suddenly out of his face. There is an urgency in him now, curling into the cut of his fists. Then he is up, out of the plastic chair, through the door and off down the corridor. He doesn't even say goodbye. Neither does Jonathan. He rises from his desk and shuts the door. He's not surprised by Agnew's behaviour. Most likely there are mental-health issues at play and it's impossible to predict how an appointment with a crazy person will proceed. Once, an elderly lady tried to kiss him on the lips, in the middle of having her blood-pressure check. He's also been slapped, shoved, sworn at and, on several occasions, spat upon. Leaving without saying goodbye seems almost normal in comparison.

Jonathan glances down at his hand and the prescription pad resting beneath it. He has, without thinking, doodled 'SORRY', in capital letters, as if regret is something that can be prescribed on the NHS. He wonders if he is sorry, or Sammy is sorry, or one of them is sorry for the other. All three options seem equally plausible.

He rips the top leaf off the pad, stuffs the paper into his pocket and tries to forget about Agnew. He moves on to the next patient and the next patient and the patient after that, who is a recently diagnosed diabetic. He can't forget about Samuel Agnew or the sorry he is now carrying inside his trouser pocket. His fingers catch on it every time he goes searching for a tissue or a piece of chewing gum. He carries it home with him after work. When he steps through the door into the hall, the old fears are waiting for him and some new ones besides: the fear of loving people and the fear of hurting the people he loves. He drops his bag by the telephone table, takes the stairs three at a time and lifts Sophie from sleep to hold her, screaming, against his chest.

11

Little Wings

ELLA PENNEY ARRIVES in the health centre at exactly the right moment. Two days earlier and I'd probably have missed her. Any later may have been too late.

I'm not known for my rapport with small children. Once, while taking a toddler's pulse, I made the mewing noise associated with attracting a cat. The mother was not amused. She lodged a formal complaint and moved her entire family to a different practice. There have been other incidents since: I can never remember to warm the stethoscope's ear before pressing it to a child's chest; I forget to let the magic cream take effect; and sometimes address my younger patients formally as Master or Miss, adopting the austere demeanour of a Victorian dentist. The lady receptionists know all this. They know everything that happens in the health centre. They are, in this and other matters, comparable to God. That which they are not told explicitly they discern from snippets of overheard conversation and the particularly furious way certain patients will enter or exit the building. They tend to direct small children and sensitive types away from me, towards the other doctors, who do not make children cry or mothers fume. Even Marty, who is a relatively old man with fierce glasses and a Communist's sunken face, is considered more child-friendly than I am. Maybe they will see me differently now I'm a father myself.

If the younger doctors hadn't been stuck at home with the fires and Marty at the dentist for a filling, Ella Penney would never have found her way into my surgery. Two days later, she would have been too late to make any difference.

Two days from today, I will arrive home from work early. I'll have a takeaway pizza with me: ham and pineapple with extra mushrooms on my side. Christine will meet me at the door, holding a hastily written sign that reads, 'Sorry, can't stay for pizza. I've got a date.' This so-called 'date' will come as both a shock and a relief to me. I will still be trying to let the girl down gently. For a moment I'll feel briefly, but utterly, mortified. I will stand on my own doorstep quickly flicking through all the occasions when I've been sure, absolutely certain, she was flirting with me: her hands lingering on my shoulder, her loose smiles, the red shirt she's worn three times now, its neckline riding low across her little breasts. Eventually I will conclude, as I've often concluded in the past, that women are not to be trusted and never to be understood with any certainty. Then I'll raise both thumbs and offer Christine the kind of blistering ear-to-ear grin that is our code for 'absolutely delighted'. On this occasion it will also mean 'No one deserves this more than you.' The sentiment will be entirely genuine. Sophie aside, I like Christine as much as anyone I've ever met.

I'll turn sideways in the doorway then, permitting Christine to squeeze past and get straight to her date, but she won't leave just yet. Instead, she'll raise a hand, beckon me into the kitchen and take her file pad from the odds-and-ends drawer, where it currently lives. 'Sophie was laughing a lot today,' she'll write. And, as seeing 'yawn' written down will often induce yawning, reading this sentence will make us both smile broadly. 'Next thing you know she'll be trying out words,' Christine will write next. 'You'll have to keep a record for when she starts doing speech therapy.' Then, she'll lift a slice of pizza from the mushroom-free side of the box, kiss me lightly on the cheek and jog down the drive to her date and the evening ahead.

I will remain in my kitchen for half an hour, holding the file pad in my hands as the untouched pizza cools and turns solid inside its box. I'll read her words over and over again, and wonder if 'next thing you know' is just a turn of phrase or something I should fear imminently. I'll tear the paper out of the pad and stuff it into my pocket, feeling it crumple against my thigh and the piece of paper I shoved in there on Tuesday. This will seem like centuries ago because I was happy on Tuesday and full of the future. I'll fish out the old note, unfold it and read 'SORRY' written in my own hand. It'll look like a fortune-cookie message all of a sudden coming true.

'Sorry.'

I'll know for certain then, without being specific, that everything good will eventually end. Something will have to be done about Sophie and I will have to do it. I'll take a drink for my nerves and follow it with a second. Neither glass will take the edge off my fear. I'll stop short of a third because I'm still a father and I take the responsibility seriously: there is Sophie to think about, sleeping upstairs. I will feel like a condemned man.

But all this is two days away. Today is Wednesday and Ella Penney is arriving in my surgery at just the right moment.

The child enters my consulting room first. Her mother is just two steps behind, holding her anorak draped over one arm like a waiter's towel. She lifts her daughter on to the treatment table, though she's old enough to climb up by herself. The woman scans the room and eventually perches uneasily on the plastic chair beside my desk. She has tired blonde hair hanging round her face in tails. It is the colour of nicotine-stained ceilings. Black roots are beginning to grease out of her scalp. She is

159

wearing a cheap pink coat, so bright it drains the last of the colour from her face. She could be anywhere between eighteen and forty. It's hard to tell sometimes with the women in the East, especially those who drink.

The child is not like her mother. She has copper-coloured hair hanging straight down the sides of her face, like the continuous pour of a waterfall. She has eyes the colour of deep seawater and rarely blinks. She's wearing wellington boots and a kind of cape, though it is not the weather for winter clothes. Her face is exactly the same shade as photocopier paper but it would be wrong to call her pale. Pale is a negative word, implying a lack of colour. Her whiteness is a luminous thing like porcelain, like unmarked snow, like Christ himself recently transfigured. She glows. It is hard for me to imagine this white-hot creature coming out of her mother. Perhaps she's one of those children who saps the life out of everyone she touches. I think of Midas. It is not exactly the right metaphor, but it sticks.

The child's name is Ella Penney. She is seven years old, almost eight. I know this because she's telling me. She's telling me many, many things without being asked: she's getting a dog for Christmas, not a puppy, an actual dog. She's the second tallest kid in her class. She can count to twenty in Spanish. She demonstrates this with great flourish: '*Uno, dos, tres, cuatro, cinco, seis . . .*' I have not yet had a chance to speak. '. . . *siete, ocho, nueve, diez . . .*'

I look directly at Mrs Penney and raise an eyebrow as if to say, 'Help me out here.'

Mrs Penney interrupts her daughter mid-flow: 'Quiet now, Ella. Let the doctor talk.'

Ella Penney stops talking. For a moment I forget that I am the doctor. This happens sometimes during a consultation. I must now ask questions about the child's health and what has brought her here today. I sit in my chair staring at her yellow wellington boots. The ceiling light is reflected once in each toe, like the sun in a puddle. I'd like to ask what her favourite colour is and whether she has picked a name for her future dog. The presence of this child has changed the atmosphere of my surgery. It's warmer in the room now. It's easier to breathe. It's all of a sudden a place I might want to linger in, like bed, first thing after waking.

'What can I do for you, Ella?' I ask. Even as I'm speaking I understand that I've got the situation the wrong way round. There's nothing I can do for a child so luminous. I should be asking what she can do for me and how long I've got with her.

Ella Penney smiles at me. She has a smile like a sonic boom. 'I broke my arm,' she says. 'I think they put the cast on too tight. My fingers are going blue.' She wiggles them to demonstrate.

'Oh, we can't have that,' I reply. 'Do you mind if I take a look?'

She reaches her right arm out towards me and I can see the tooth-white cuff of the cast emerging from beneath her cape. Her fingers are a little greyer than they should be. This is not a good sign.

'Can we take that cape off so I can see your arm better, Ella?' I ask.

'No,' exclaims Mrs Penney. She sits bolt upright in her plastic chair. The handbag tumbles from her lap, vomiting tissues, biros and loose change all across the surgery floor. She goes down on her knees to scoop everything back.

'Sure,' says Ella Penney.

She slips her cape upwards, over her head like a sweater, and she is naked from the waist up. She has not lost the soft round of her baby belly yet but I can tell the flesh around her nipples is already beginning to swell in anticipation of breasts. She is milk white all over, her chest as pure as her face.

It is impossible not to stare.

Spanning the gap between her arms and sides, like an infant pterodactyl, there is a pair of perfectly formed wings.

161

It is utterly impossible not to stare.

I find myself rising from my chair and striding across the surgery floor to take a closer look. I hadn't intended to do this. It is an involuntary reaction, like sneezing or crying over a cut onion. I am inches from her armpits with my eyes. I am staring with furious intent. Now, I am running my fingers across her left wing. Ella's mother makes like she's going to intervene, then seems to lose the inclination. She slumps back in her chair and watches. I should probably have asked permission first but I'm not functioning properly now. I am sucking the air in and out of my mouth through my teeth, my breath making a kind of soft whistling noise. I can't remember how to make words.

Ella Penney raises her arms for me. She's done this before. The folds in her wings concertina out and she is a bird in blue jeans and welly boots. I take her good wrist in my hand, stretch the arm out fully and eat her with my eyes. I forget that she is a child. She is only a patient to me in this moment, less than a patient, really, a specimen. I am taking careful notes in my head. I am writing a book.

There is a fretwork of tiny bones running through each wing at intervals. Between these bones a thin membrane of skin is stretched tight, almost transparent in places but fleshy and tough, like the loose fold between a thumb and forefinger. A fine blondish down covers each wing. I blow gently on the skin's surface and watch all the little hairs rise as one, like ears of corn, gently inclined. I can see where the wings join her arms. The flesh is thicker here and smooth as old scar tissue. I touch this place with the tip of my gloved finger and she trembles, possibly with pain or the shock of my hand, which I've often been told is much too cold for a doctor.

'I can't fly,' she says.

I haven't asked but of course I'm wondering. She pulls her hand away from me, folds the unbroken arm across her chest and lets the other hang limply by her side. I snap back into myself and retreat to my chair. The room is spinning slightly. I reach for my notebook hoping stationery might make me feel safe or, at the very least, grounded.

'You *can* fly, Ella,' says her mother, firmly. 'You just don't want to.'

'I can't fly, Mum. You know I've tried. The wings don't work. I can do other things, but I can't fly.'

Mrs Penney turns to me. 'I'm sorry, Doctor,' she says. 'I should have explained. I was hoping we'd be able to get that wrist sorted without having to go into the wings but, as you can probably tell, our Ella's the sort of wee girl who does whatever she wants to do, no thought for the consequences.'

I have a hundred thousand questions. I want to record our conversation. And take pictures. I want to gather all the lady receptionists inside my surgery to witness this miracle. I'm thinking about phoning the BBC. Instead I ask, 'Has she always had the wings?'

'She was born with them,' explains Mrs Penney.

'Incredible,' I gush. I sound like a cartoon doctor.

'She's not the first in our family. I'm from up round Cushendall originally and it's not like there's hundreds of flying children or anything, but out in the country it's not uncommon to have one or two born every generation. The farmers used to rely on them for flying over the glens, keeping a wee eye on their sheep when the weather forced them off the mountains. Course they don't do that any more. Most of them have four-by-fours and the like. But flying's bred into the country folk, and even now, it's not uncommon to hear of a flying wean. I wasn't that shocked when Ella came out with wings. I've a second cousin who has them. The husband nearly passed out, though. He's pure East Belfast. He'd never heard of a flying child. He thought she was some kind of mutant. It took him ages to see what a miracle she is.'

163

'And she can fly?' I ask.

'Of course she can fly,' says Mrs Penney. 'Can you not see the wings on her?'

'No,' says Ella Penney, talking over the top of her mother. 'I *can't* fly but they keep pushing me off ladders and things to try and get me started.'

'It's like birds, Doctor. Sometimes you have to give them a wee bit of incentive to get the wings going.'

'Is that how you broke your wrist, Ella?'

'Yeah. Dad pushed me out of the monkey puzzle on to the back lawn. I landed funny. My arm made a noise like when you stand on cornflakes. I knew it was broke straight away.'

'And who set it for you?'

Mrs Penney cuts in, 'There's a doctor in the Royal we always go to, Dr Kanuri. He's an Indian fella, but his English is not too bad. He looks after all the Unfortunate Children. Most doctors don't even know they exist. Dr Kanuri says it's better that way. People don't know how to deal with them. Other doctors would probably do experiments or put them on television or something. Dr Kanuri's more keen on looking after them. Course, there are way more Unfortunate Children in India than here but Dr Kanuri's been able to track down a fair few of them now. When Ella was born there was just one support group in Belfast. Now there's two, East and South, and they're thinking about starting another in the city centre. Obviously we go to the one in the East, for handiness' sake.'

I cross my arms. Then I cross my legs. It's good to feel the pressure of my own body pushing into itself. I don't feel real right now.

'Unfortunate Children?' I ask, and before Mrs Penney can begin another of her long, rambling explanations, Ella jumps in.

'Kids who aren't normal,' she explains.

'Like they have special needs?'

'More like special powers.'

'Like flying?'

'I told you. I can't fly. I've got other powers instead, better powers than flying. I can bring things back to life.'

'Like Jesus?'

'Naw, nothing as big as a whole person and nothing that's so old it should be dead anyway. I do a lot of insects and worms, a hamster once, tons of plants. I just have to touch things and they're not dead any more—'

'Stop talking rubbish, Ella,' Mrs Penney interrupts. 'You can't bring things back to life. You have wings. You're meant to fly. The rest of it's all in her head, Doctor.'

'So,' I say, allowing myself space to let the information swell, 'let me get this straight. There are lots of children with wings in Belfast.'

'Not really,' explains Mrs Penney, 'there's a handful of flying children, a couple that float, one that sort of hovers half a foot off the ground, not what you'd call loads. But there are quite a few children with different gifts.'

'So, there are lots of these children with special powers all over Belfast and Dr Kanuri looks after them.'

'He doesn't exactly look after them so much as get us together every couple of weeks, kind of like a support group. It's really more for the parents than the weans – it's not easy having an Unfortunate Child.'

'Why are they called Unfortunate Children?'

'Dr Kanuri just decided that's what they should be called. I think it's translated from what they're called in India. In India the Unfortunate Children get left to starve to death in ditches and bins. People think they're a kind of curse. Dr Kanuri prefers to call them miracles.'

'And there are Unfortunate Children in East Belfast?'

'There's about twenty of them all told. Some have better

165

powers than others. To be honest, Dr Murray, there's a couple of them I don't think should even qualify as Unfortunate Children, like the one who can hold her breath really long underwater.'

'I'd hardly call that a special power. She's probably just got larger-than-average lungs.'

'And there's that boy in the tree,' adds Ella.

'Exactly, pet. What's so special about sitting in a tree for five years? Anyway, Doctor, we meet every Thursday evening in the Portakabin behind Inverary community centre. Sometimes the children come. Sometimes it's just the parents. It's been a godsend having people to talk to, people who understand.'

I sit back in my chair. I look at Mrs Penney. She is deadly serious. She is used to not being believed, I can tell. She's holding her handbag like a kind of shield. I look at Ella Penney and the strange contraptions clinging to her armpits. The light from the surgery window is gleaming through her, making her wings translucent so I can see all the tiny blue veins spidering beneath her skin. She is the best thing that has happened since Christine. She's possibly even better than Christine.

'You think we're mad, don't you?' asks Mrs Penney. 'Every doctor we've ever talked to thinks we're mad, except Dr Kanuri.'

'No,' I say. 'I definitely don't think you're mad.' I stand up and turn towards Mrs Penney. Without being told she seems to understand that she should be standing too. She does so. We look hard at each other. Ella knows enough to hold her tongue. She watches from the treatment table. I am the first to move. I'm moving before I've even thought to move: it's that instinctual. I wrap my arms around Mrs Penney. At first she braces herself against the hug. She is a wall, a brick, an unyielding sort of thing. Then I feel her body loosen and she is embracing me back.

'I think I have an Unfortunate Child too,' I say. I whisper this into the cup of her ear, quietly so Ella won't be able to hear. The next breath is the deepest breath I have drawn in almost three months. When we pull apart Mrs Penney is crying. I hand her a tissue from the box on my desk and she reaches one to me. I'm also crying. I hadn't realized.

Later, as I'm loosening Ella's cast, while the child is preoccupied with pinched flesh and tight bandages, Mrs Penney leans in to whisper in my ear: 'It's not your fault,' she says. 'Just remember that it's not your fault.'

I try to remember this but it's hard to make it stick.

Mrs Penney writes down directions to the community centre where the Unfortunate Children of East Belfast meet. She offers to pick me up if I don't want to go alone. She says, 'Call me Kathleen,' and I do, twice, as she's on the way out of the door. She doesn't ask anything specific about Sophie. For this I am extremely grateful.

After the Penneys leave, I cancel my next patient. This is terribly unprofessional. I tell the lady receptionist I have a migraine and must lie down for an hour. I lie down on the examination table and cry and cry and cry. I try to make myself stop by digging my thumbs deep into my eye sockets and can't. I wonder if these are tears of relief. I'm not exactly sad, but neither am I happy. It is as if the fear has shifted to another part of my body and, for the moment, my lungs are better equipped for breathing.

Above my head, on the filing cabinet, the spider plant, which was previously dead, seems to be greening again. I know that Ella Penney touched it. Or perhaps she doesn't even need to touch. Looking might be enough for her, or thinking of good health, like Jesus and the man whose daughter was dead, miles away, and then, all of a sudden, wasn't. It feels as if a miracle has happened in my room and I need to sit for an hour or two in its glow.

Lois, the Daytime Vampire

*I*T'S MUCH EASIER *in the summer. Most nights it doesn't get dark till ten or after. Still, Lois has to be careful. Once dusk starts glooming over the rooftops the tingling begins. Her teeth sting. Her nails smart. The skin beneath her freckles starts to pink up. If she stays outside for too long, letting the night creep over her, her whole body feels like it's on fire. Lois's whole body might well be on fire if she let herself linger in the dark. She's never hung around long enough to find out. The movies seem to suggest a kind of rapid combustion takes place. Daylight. Screaming. A sort of pressurized crumbling and, afterwards, a small patch of ash, smoking on the ground. Common thought leans towards evaporation.*

Of course, in the movies, Lois's kind fears daylight. Lois is different. Everything about her is back to front. She can't manage without light. Sunlight. Spotlights. Even the cold blue light of an open fridge will do at a pinch. It's darkness she fears. In the daytime Lois is free to attend school and meet friends, hanging out beneath the luminous white lights of the shopping centre. She's permanently tanned, but what Belfast girl isn't? During the day, she can almost pass for normal.

At night, however, Lois is trapped in the house. The night is like a kind of wall, so high and low and all around: she wouldn't think of venturing out. Not even with a 60-watt searchlight shining in her face. She sits in her room, eating raw mince by the handful, for though the hunger's in her, she's learnt to sate it with dead blood and meat. She wouldn't lower herself to bite. The thought of it repulses her. Sucking strangers' necks. Not knowing where they've been, or whether they're even clean. During sleeping hours she sleeps in fitful starts and bursts. It's not easy to drop off with the big lights on and the desk lamp angled right into your face, but Lois is beginning to grow used to it. She spends every summer minute outside: cycling, running, sunbathing in the back garden with nothing on but a bikini. The winters here feel endless. They are. Belfast is not the best place for a daytime vampire. Sometimes Lois can go weeks without leaving the house.

12

Talks

IT'S EIGHT O'CLOCK on a Saturday evening. It's almost August. The Tall Fires are all over the news in every major country. The city smells like a crematorium. Everyone with any sense has gone elsewhere. Only those with nowhere to go remain, trying to preserve some level of normality. The politicians have almost lost hope. They can't see an end to it: the fires, the riots, the incessant heat. They are no closer to tracking down the Fire Starter.

Sammy is sitting on the top step of his stairs. There are two Penguin biscuits tucked into the breast pocket of his shirt: a blue one and an orange one. He can't even remember if Mark likes Penguins. Penguins might be Christopher's thing, or Lauren's. Now they're fully grown, the details of his children have blurred together and sometimes he confuses their interests with those of children on television soap operas. The biscuits are starting to melt in the damp heat rising off his chest. He thinks about leaving them on the stairs, coming back for them later, after it's all over. He wishes he'd brought a tray up from the kitchen. A tray would have been a comfort to him, something to hold on to at the start.

Sammy has two mugs of tea: one for himself, one for Mark.

He wants to make a solemn point of today so he's gone for the good mugs; mugs that match rather than the mugs that came free with last year's Easter eggs. These are what they drink from when they don't have visitors. Creme Egg. KitKat. Crunchie. Mars. They have an almost complete set. Today he's using the fancy mugs with the stripes. Sammy's tea is white with two sugars. Mark's is black. Pamela has warned him not to put milk or sugar in the boy's tea because he is a vegetarian, these days. This, Sammy knows, has no bearing on whether the boy takes sugar in his tea, or even milk, but he holds his tongue anyway. He has grown used to holding his tongue with Pamela.

She's never been book smart but she always had sense before. Now the worry seems to play on her constantly. Mostly it feels like she's miles away, not listening. It's not as if Sammy was ever particularly attracted to his wife's mind. He'd fallen for her face first. In the early nineties she was the spit of Princess Di. He liked the way she looked down at him with her eyes and her thin lips, as if she was too good for him or any of his sort. She'd been too good for him. Everyone said so. She wasn't from the East originally, or used to its grind. That was the main reason Sammy had married her. Also her long blonde hair, like a Barbie just out of the packet, and her backside, which was legend round the inner East.

The East has not been kind to Pamela. She'd started to disappear the day she left her daddy's farm. Now she is like an outline of herself without colour or force.

Sammy no longer feels the same pull off her. He tries. But it's just not there. The pair of them have very little left to talk about for all the big words are beyond them now. Children. Future. Sex. They speak different languages, and these languages are like a plate-glass wall rising up between them every time they sit down. They try. Even now, Sammy is not opposed to trying. Lips move. Brows crease. The anger goes up and slowly down.

Everything gets lost in translation. They only fall into sync on the basics. Money. Food. Television. These things don't matter. They are not nearly strong enough to hold on to.

He tries to work up an attraction to her, but it isn't easy. Pamela has put on weight, shitloads of weight. She looks nothing like she did at twenty. She tents herself in men's shirts and enormous jumpers every time she leaves the house. She calls herself a fat cow and he neither agrees nor audibly disagrees. He knows he should make more of an effort. He'll still compliment her when she comes back from the hairdresser, or she's dressed up for a wedding, but there's no power in his words. They don't seem to stick. Pamela diets and does her exercise DVDs, which she puts on the good-room TV, the whole house bouncing as she lifts and lowers her flabby thighs in time to the music. *Thump, thump, thump*, and the shrill bleat of Whitney Houston always wanting to dance with somebody. Sammy watches through a sliver in the door and wonders if they should have called it a day years ago, before things started to fall apart, when they were still youngish and might have found happiness elsewhere.

Pamela eats no meat, eats nothing but meat, cups of grapefruit and dry tuna fish, cottage cheese, wholemeal bread, only green things, no wine; fasts on Thursdays, binges at the weekends, weighs herself two nights a week in front of strangers at the leisure centre and pays five pounds for the privilege; sends off for recipes from women's magazines; tries Pilates, yoga and zumba at the community centre on weekday mornings, when it's cheap. She tries to get Sammy to join her, but he always has an excuse to hand. Never once does she stop to ask who she's shifting all this weight for. Sammy wants to say, 'Stop. Talk to me like you used to talk to me. Maybe there's something we could still salvage.'

He does not fantasize about other women. He fantasizes about having the old Pamela back. The slip of a girl he fell in

love with. On good days he'll catch the corner of her mouth lifting in the old familiar way, or they'll joke with each other easily
over the breakfast table, and he'll know he could never leave her.
Too much has passed between them and, besides, who is he to
hold Pamela's figure against her? He's no small god, these days.
He is a balloon on two pale sticks. There are fine paper-bag
crinkles where his skin is sagging round his arms and legs, pearly
stretch marks, like lightning bolts, zipping across his expanding
belly. Sometimes he thinks it's only laziness keeping them
together, laziness and guilt. At other times he remembers the
way they were once soft together, like children with secrets.
Then he cannot bear to be in the same room with her.

It is Pamela who's suggested talking to Mark. She's only done
this for badness. Sammy would have been quite content to spend
the evening side by side on the sofa, not really watching the
same television programmes. They've been watching a Jamie
Oliver cookery show. Her choice. Jamie Oliver's doing locally
sourced organic fish tonight. Pamela doesn't even eat fish fingers for fear of choking on the bones, but she is obsessed with
Jamie Oliver. She thinks he's good-looking in a Londony sort of
way. 'Like Michael Portillo,' she explains, and Sammy understands this is something to do with the way they are both fleshy
about the lip. She likes when Jamie Oliver rips lettuce with his
hands and the way he cried about the poor children having chips
for school dinners every day. Sammy thinks Jamie Oliver is a
gobshite. He has no interest in locally sourced fish. He'd have
been keen to watch the crime thing on ITV, but hasn't even had
the chance to argue his case. He'd barely had time to get comfortable before Pamela suggested he go upstairs and have a word
with Mark.

'You should go up and talk to him,' she'd said, out of nowhere,
like the thought of it had just popped into her mind.

Sammy had stared at Jamie Oliver's big, lardy face on the

television. He was peeling the skin off a bit of cod with his fingers. He couldn't understand why this would make Pamela think of Mark. (Jamie Oliver looks nothing like their son. Mark is a long white drip, with a skiff of white-blond hair, like a Brillo pad, perched on top of his head.)

'Why should I go and speak to Mark?' he'd asked, trying to sound disinterested.

'No reason, really. It's just that he never comes out of his room any more and I was watching this thing the other day on Channel Four – one of those chat shows with your woman that used to be on the BBC – and it was all about young lads killing themselves. There's hundreds of them doing it at the minute, all of them anti-social, like our Mark. They say it's an epidemic. It just got me thinking, Samuel. You should probably check he's not up there planning to kill himself or watching child pornography on his computer. They said on the programme that it's important these suicidal types know they're loved.'

Neither of them loved Mark. It was entirely possible that no one in the world loved Mark. They'd looked at each other across the sofa, not saying this exactly but admitting it with their eyes.

'Why don't you go up and tell him you love him?' Sammy suggests.

'Naw, I'm watching Jamie Oliver. I haven't seen this one before. You go . . . before it's too late!'

'Bloody hell, Pamela, we both know Mark's not up there killing himself.'

'How'd you know? When's the last time you actually saw him?'

Sammy had had to resist the temptation to reply, 'This morning, on the news, wreaking havoc.' Instead he'd said, 'I suppose it couldn't do any harm to have a wee chat with the lad, see if I can get him interested in doing some job applications.'

'On you go, then,' Pamela had replied, and cranked the volume three bars higher, hoping to irritate him out of the door and up the stairs. At first Sammy couldn't move. He'd tried to will his backside off the sofa but, like his head, and the rest of his posable parts, his muscles were ill-inclined to venture anywhere near Mark. Pamela had leant across the sofa towards him. He'd thought she was going throw an arm around his shoulders, like she used to do when they were in the car driving together. Instead, she'd made it into a scoop and tried to lever him off the sofa. 'Go and talk to Mark,' she'd said, 'take him up a cup of tea and a biscuit.'

The old anger had risen in Sammy, like hammers going up and down his throat. He wanted to hit his wife. He'd never hit Pamela before and was proud of this restraint. He'd sworn at her plenty, though, and she was always quick to swear back. They were like cats hissing at each other when they fought. He'd sworn then and thumped his mug down on the coffee-table. Cold tea went slurping over the latest copy of *Woman's Weekly*, forming damp crinkles across the cover star's face. Like waves in desert sand. Everything was ruined.

'Right,' he'd said. 'I'll go up and talk to Mark.' He'd tried to make it sound like this was his idea. But it was not his idea. Talking to their son was the absolute last thing he wanted to do with his evening.

Sammy has not made it any further than the top step of the stairs. He's been sitting there for almost five minutes now, holding two mugs, one in each hand. He can feel the tea cooling against his cupped palms. He stares at the mugs and catches a greasy reflection of his own face in the surface of Mark's, shadowed and frowning. He doesn't understand how anyone can take their tea black. The very thought of it makes his teeth shrink into his gums, like tin foil, accidentally bitten. There are so many things he doesn't understand about his son. Black tea is the last thing he should be worried about. Tiny ripples roll across the top of both mugs, moving from the centre outwards, like the first premonitions of an earthquake. His hands are struggling to hold themselves still. He sets both mugs carefully on the step and holds his palms flat against his thighs until they stop shaking. Then he climbs the last flight to Mark's bedroom and knocks on the door.

Mark doesn't open it. Instead he shouts, 'Hold on a minute!' and for two minutes, maybe three, Sammy stands on the landing, sweating, while the boy fustles round his bedroom hiding things he doesn't want seen. The door opens inwards. Mark is framed in the doorway. All the windows have been blacked out and the only light comes from a small, bendable lamp sitting on his desk. Sammy peers over his son's shoulder into the room. His bed is neatly made. His books are stacked in perpendicular towers on the floor. There are no posters on the walls, no photographs, nothing to mark ownership of the space. It might as well be a prison cell. Yet Mark has been living there for over twenty years, spending almost every moment inside these four walls.

'How are you keeping, son?' asks Sammy.

This is the way he would start a conversation with an old friend in the street. It seems strange to be talking like this to his son, who lives upstairs. But it's weeks since he last laid eyes on him. The boy eats only when they're asleep, scuttling up and down the stairs to fix bowls of cereal and frozen pizza. He uses the bathroom on the top floor. Sometimes the sound of the toilet flushing is the only way they know he's still alive.

'I'm fine,' says Mark.

'You look good,' says Sammy.

Mark does not look good. He looks ghastly pale, like a person who hasn't seen natural light in weeks. There is a luminous quality to his skin, like the smooth inside of an eggshell. His lips are almost bloodless.

'Are you up here to ask me about getting a job, Dad?'

'Yes ... no, not really. I just wanted to see if you were doing OK.'

'I'm fine,' says Mark. He is holding the edge of the door tightly so Sammy cannot even get a slippered foot inside the room. He is inching the door shut as he speaks, making it quite clear with his voice and his turned shoulder that he has no interest in talking to his father. Sammy can feel his fists curling inside his cardigan pockets. The blood begins to rise up the back of his ribcage. There is something about that pale ghost face that wants undoing.

'Listen,' says Sammy, and he is not even certain what he's going to say until he's actually saying it and he sees the way Mark's face goes stiff and smiling like a doll's face. 'I know everything.'

'Know what exactly, Dad?'

'I know about the video and the Tall Fires. I know it's you.'

'Do you indeed?' Mark laughs. It is not a natural sound. The noise is like something forced through a too-small hole. 'And how do you know that?'

'You have to stop, Mark. It's madness. Somebody's going to get killed.'

'Nothing to do with me, Dad. I haven't hurt anyone.'

'It's everything to do with you, Mark. You started it. I don't care whether you actually did it yourself or just told people to do it. You're responsible.'

'You've the wrong end of the stick there, Dad. It's nothing to do with me.'

'I know it's you,' says Sammy, 'and it needs to stop now.'

'Oh, it's not for stopping,' snaps Mark. 'Once a thing like this gets started, there's no way to stop it. It only gets worse from here. Nothing to do with me, like, but I'd put good money on it getting a hell of a lot messier.'

A thing like sheet ice slips across his face and just as suddenly melts so he's smiling again, smiling his horrible, leering smile. All the little hairs on Sammy's arms are prickling. He feels the cold draught of his son go running up his spine and down. He might cry. He can't cry in front of Mark. Evil bastard, he thinks. He can only see him as a stranger but there's a sickness in his gut, like the two of them are joined.

'I'll tell the police,' he says. His voice is a child's voice, whining.

'Tell them what exactly?'

'Everything,' he says, though he knows this is not the kind of thing he could say with words or ever prove.

'And while you're there telling the police everything, don't forget to tell them about yourself, Dad. You're hardly a saint, are you?'

Mark closes the door in his face. It doesn't exactly slam – the carpet is too thick to allow for a decent slam – but the intention is there. Sammy stands for a moment looking at the door, wondering if he should try again with a raised voice. He feels like a very old man. Even his eyes are tired. After a minute or so he turns and walks back downstairs. On the bottom step he pauses to retrieve the mugs of tea. Both are lukewarm now. He goes down to the kitchen to make a fresh cup and Pamela shouts from the living room to ask how Mark is. 'Fine!' he shouts back, because he can't bear the idea of making her any sadder than she already is. He makes himself another cup of tea and drinks it black with no sugar. He deserves this.

13

The Unfortunate Children of East Belfast

THE NIGHT OF the meeting I pay Christine double time to mind Sophie. I tell her I have a meeting with my accountant, implying it is something to do with my mortgage. The excuse sits easily with her and after we've eaten together – a quick vegetable stir-fry, and Swiss roll for dessert – I leave her on the sofa with a glass of wine and a paperback novel. Christine is a great one for reading. She has a different book on the go every time I see her. Perhaps reading is something you get better at if you can't speak.

'I'll text you if I'm going to be late,' I write on our notepad. 'You're welcome to stay over in the spare room.'

When I return four hours later I'll find Christine curled up like a pretzel inside Sophie's cot. This is something I've done myself when she's fussing and won't sleep. It isn't comfortable but I've found that, when sleep-deprived, it is possible to sleep anywhere horizontal, even in the bath. I'll consider waking Christine up and then decide not to, for the Unfortunate Children will have left me too exhausted to contemplate further conversation. I'll pull a blanket over them both and stretch out on the floor beside Sophie's cot. I will need to be close to my daughter tonight, close enough to see her little face, folding and opening as she dreams her soft baby dreams, close enough to remember that Sophie is a precious thing, not a burden, not a monster, definitely not a fear.

I decide to wear a suit and tie to my first meeting of the Unfortunate Children of East Belfast. I want to appear grown-up, like a person capable of looking after another person.

When I arrive at the Portakabin behind the community centre I immediately realize that this isn't a suit-and-tie kind of meeting. There are posters on the wall about breastfeeding and what to put in which recycling bin. The seats are the kind of plastic seats that can be stacked against a wall, up to twelve layers high. I take in my surroundings, then slip the tie, still in its noose, over my head and stuff it into my blazer pocket. I open the top two buttons of my shirt. I'm still overdressed. Most of the other parents are in jeans or tracksuits; one mother is wearing a dressing-gown. The pale peach glow of her satin pyjamas ghosts through the gap where the robe doesn't quite cover her belly. She's too tired to contemplate real clothes. This is perfectly acceptable here. Everyone with an Unfortunate Child is a little worn around the edges. No one is in any position to judge.

The man who sits next to me introduces himself as Mike. He spends the entire meeting pulling individual strands of hair from the scalp behind his ears. He is balding in at least four different places. He claims to have a child who glows in the dark and can only go out in public during sunlight hours. This, he tells me, isn't easy to manage in Belfast where the round-the-clock gloom begins on the first day of September and lasts all the way through to May.

'What have you got?' he asks me, as a tray full of coffee mugs and custard creams circulates round the room.

'A girl,' I reply, 'Sophie.'

'What's wrong with her?'

I'm not sure how to answer this. Most days she seems perfect to me. On other days I think she'd be better off dead. I've never had the opportunity to voice this fear. Under pressure I take a slurp of scalding coffee and burn the tip of my tongue. I can't catch my breath to formulate a response.

Then, at just the right moment, the meeting is called to order. Everyone introduces themselves. Some people are couples. The majority are here alone. I'm pleased about this, though really it means nothing. I am definitely single but everyone else could well have another half at home, minding the children. Dr Kanuri sends his apologies via an older man, Davy (whose teenage daughter is sometimes a boat and enjoys floating among the swans in Victoria Park). Davy is one of the founder members of the Unfortunate Children. He explains that Dr Kanuri is caught up in theatre and will not be attending tonight's meeting. A vague dissenting murmur goes mumbling round the circle. It is almost two months since Dr Kanuri last made an appearance. I'm a little disappointed. I was hoping to speak to the man, doctor to doctor, on the subject of Sirens.

When it's my turn to speak I introduce myself. The group says, 'Hi, Jonathan.' Some of them wave. For a moment it feels like America. Then I speak again. My accent is one hundred per cent Orangefield and the sound of it pins us all to this Portakabin off the Sydenham Bypass. I say, 'It's my first time here,' and, 'Thanks for inviting me,' and 'I have a little girl called Sophie.' I don't mention that I'm also a doctor. I don't say anything about Sophie's mother or what may happen when Sophie speaks. It is enough to have come tonight. Next time I will try to explain the fear of speaking and the fear of not speaking and all the other fears that came traipsing into the room behind me. No one presses me for anything more. The other parents smile and incline their heads towards me. They are pleased that I've come. They're always pleased to welcome a new member.

There is safety in numbers, and safety is probably the best they can hope for, for their children.

Everyone in the circle has a chance to speak. By the time the introductions are complete I've heard about two further flying children, a child who hears trees and a boy who lives in a tree, invisible twins and a little girl who was born with a bird's egg unhatched in each hand, a child who sees the future in every liquid surface, a baby who turns to cloud every time she falls asleep and, best of all, a boy, named Matthew, who has wheels soldered to the heels and balls of both feet.

'They're not metal,' explains his father, 'or rubber, like bicycle tyres. They're more like bone or whatever teeth are made of.'

The rest of the group have heard this before. 'He's like greased lightning on hills,' Mike mutters, under his breath, and plucks another hair nervously from behind his ear.

A split second later the man is telling us again that his son is like greased lightning on hills. I understand that the parents of Unfortunate Children repeat the same stories every time they meet. This is what they come for. It's a form of absolution, or perhaps confession. They are only here for the telling. The listening part is just a noise, which must be endured until the opportunity to speak arises. They aren't interested in the person sitting beside them or the various ways in which their child is unfortunate. They are only interested in their own children and their own problems. This is completely understandable. It isn't even selfishness. I'm interested, though. I'm all ears, all eyes. I'm a kind of camera catching every detail tonight.

Kathleen Penney keeps her seat as she tells the other parents about Ella's broken wrist. This is what passes for news among the Unfortunate Children. She is quick to skip over the details. She does her best to appear casual when she says 'broken in three different places' and 'reduced mobility'. She only half conceals a sob when she says 'possibility of further surgery'. She isn't to blame. Ella has not been pushed or coerced towards great height. The child has simply sustained a minor injury in the act of learning to fly. Such injuries are to be expected, and didn't the girl who is occasionally a boat once almost drown while learning to drift?

'Has she ever flown?' interrupts the mother of another flying child. 'Our Simon was clearing three-storey buildings by the time he was Ella's age.'

Simon, according to his mother, is hot shit in the flight department. Simon has been flying since before he could walk, possibly since conception. There is every likelihood he may one day orbit the moon. I do not like Simon on principle. He sounds like an overachiever. Or perhaps it is his mother's version of Simon that I have no patience with.

'Oh, yes,' exclaims Kathleen. 'Ella flies all the time. She's a great wee flier. She's just having a few problems perfecting her technique.'

I catch her eye. She gives me daggers across the circle, then blinks and looks suddenly away. Kathleen is lying. She knows I can expose her. I don't. Sometimes lies sit easier than the truth. My parents taught me this early on: don't upset the status quo. There is little point in calling Ella's mother out in front of the other parents. They're probably all leaning on their own sad little lies. I feel sorry for Kathleen and also for her husband, but I can't bring myself to feel sorry for Ella Penney. She is much too marvellous for sympathy. It would be like pitying the sun or something equally furious. I can't stop thinking about Ella and her redundant wings.

Even now I can picture her in old-fashioned flying goggles and hat, like a First World War pilot. She is about to jump from a very tall tree: a pine or a fir of some sort. She knows she will fall – she'll always fall – and yet she will never refuse to jump. She has enormous love for her parents. Another name for this

183

kind of love is patience or maybe long-suffering. The parents are fools. Ella is wise and kind and sometimes saintly. She will break every bone in her tiny body before she'll let them lose faith in her.

I can also picture her in a wooded place. Her feet are naked and she's up to the ankles in fallen leaves. It is autumn in this vision, or very early winter. Ella Penney has a face on her like Joan of Arc in the silent movie: old eyes on a young face; sure eyes, impossibly steadfast. While the sky remains temporarily unconquered, the damp forest ground is teeming with miracles: earthworms, centipedes, spiders and dung beetles, all recently resurrected and scrambling, like God's own messengers, for a place at Ella's white, white feet. I imagine all this and wonder if this is what it is like for the boy who sees the future in water glasses, in cold lakes and toilet bowls. If so, I'm jealous. This is a power worth believing in. I'm not at all sad for Ella Penney. I'm sad for her parents who do not understand what they've been given. Who may well miss the most glorious part of her.

A teenage girl is talking now. She is speaking from inside the curtain of her hair, softly, softly, like tissues crumpling into fists. She is wearing jeans, a hooded sweatshirt and, in lieu of ordinary gloves, oven mitts, taped firmly round her wrists. They are not a pair. One is shaped like a frog, with movable eyes and a pink tongue that lollops between her thumb and the blunt claw of her four conjoined fingers. The other is a gift from Tenerife. It is canary yellow with the entire island spread, like a birthmark, across the back of the hand. She rises to speak. An older man stands next to her. He has her chin, which is to say that neither has a chin so much as a softly sloping absence between jaw and neck. They look like gophers, or perhaps it's meerkats I'm thinking of, some kind of peering, upright creature.

'This is my daughter, Karen,' the man says. 'I'm really proud of her. She's going to share her story tonight.'

Everyone claps except Karen, partly because it's impolite to clap at your own achievement and partly because it's almost impossible to clap while wearing oven gloves.

'Hi,' she says, when the applause dies down, 'my name's Karen. I suppose I'm one of the Unfortunate Children. At least, Dr Kanuri says I am. Everything I touch turns to Christmas.' She holds up her oven-glove hands as a kind of illustration, and everyone in the circle nods knowingly. I have no idea what she's talking about. Perhaps she can impart some sort of vague festive feeling, or actually conjure up tinsel and sparklers; maybe the true meaning of Christmas – a holy baby-Jesus awe – is crouching in her, just below the skin. I have no clear notion what exactly Karen does and even after her testimony I'll be equally confused. I fold my arms, adopt a listening posture, and wonder how I might go about explaining my Sophie to the other parents of Unfortunate Children. It's not like she's done anything awful yet. But she could. The possibility is always there, like a small but definite storm cloud, looming overhead.

Karen tells her story. She is like Midas but with Christmas, not gold, in her fingertips. Karen would prefer not to have this 'gift', to enjoy Christmas within the accepted festive period and not have it leaking out all over the rest of her year. It's mortifying to be seventeen years old and have everything you touch turn festive. Karen had developed her gift at the age of thirteen. She'd managed to survive high school by wearing gloves and keeping her distance; she'd left at sixteen with nothing but a GCSE in PE. Long-distance running had been her chosen sport. It didn't require touch of any kind. Other subjects eluded Karen. She couldn't be trusted to contain herself in group work. Scientific experiments were risky and computers went hysterical every time her naked fingers brushed against their keys. After high school she'd taken a job on the checkout at Connswater Tesco. Though she'd have preferred hairdressing or

childcare, she'd gone for Tesco because it didn't require qualifi-
cations or touching people directly with her hands.

Karen wore oven gloves to keep from accidentally touching
the customers or leaving a Christmassy sheen on the produce,
which tumbled past her like a circus parade. She lasted two
weeks and three days. That was a kind of miracle. She hadn't
even expected to manage a full day. Things began to go wrong
during her second week. On the Wednesday she arrived to find
the next cash register over occupied by a middle-aged lady with
a 'Doreen' badge.

'Hello, love!' Doreen yelled, exploiting a brief break in the
grocery parade to introduce herself. 'What's your name? I'm
Doreen.'

Karen said nothing. Most of her existence was focused on
avoiding unnecessary attention. She elbowed a watermelon from
one end of the checkout to the other, using the tip of her nose to
operate the buttons on the electronic scales. Doreen stared.

'Ugh, I'm sorry, love,' Doreen mouthed, a little quieter on
account of the customers approaching her till. 'I didn't realize
you were *handicapped*. Do you need a wee hand?'

Karen pretended she hadn't heard. She continued nudging
onions and red peppers across the grocery scales. Doreen, unper-
turbed by the silence, turned to the lady on the next register and,
with an accent thick as buttered bread, asked, 'Is that wee girl all
there?'

'Aye,' replied Margaret from the next till over. 'She's as canny
as you or me. She's just up herself. Wouldn't bother with the
likes of us.'

'I dunno, love. She looks a bit special-needs. She's a pair of
oven gloves on her. She's doing the register with her chin.'

Karen heard this entire conversation from behind a mam-
moth box of washing powder. She wanted to hide, but short of
ducking beneath the till, there was nowhere to go.

'I'm just going to check on her!' shouted Doreen. 'Would you take my customers for a wee minute?'

The next sentence was lost in a scurry of panicked squeaks and scratches as Karen abandoned the washing powder, the customers and all hopes of holding on to her job, and attempted to tunnel her way under the cash register. After a few seconds she peeped out. Doreen's moonish face, huge and haloed in the strip lighting, was peering over the credit-card machine.

'Hello, sweetie,' she said slowly, her entire mouth caving over each syllable. 'Nothing to be scared of, nothing I haven't seen before. Sure, hasn't my youngest got a wee touch of autism, goes pure hyper on the Smarties, so he does.'

She smiled. Karen glared.

'There's a silly girl, working the till with a pair of oven gloves on. Sure, you won't be able to do the buttons.'

Before Karen could brace herself to bite, to kick, stab and defend the older woman against the onslaught to come, Doreen had reached behind the register and whipped both gloves off. Right first, then left. Christmas came rushing out of Karen, all of a sudden, like a vomiting bug. Though the phenomenon is never quite explained in detail, I imagine it to be something like an outpouring of the Holy Spirit. The sort of thing you read about happening in charismatic churches. Not unpleasant, but somewhat overwhelming. Karen couldn't help herself. She stood up behind the till. She had the sensation of simultaneous losing and gaining something important. The sensation was strongest in her fingertips where they were touching Doreen's wrists. Everyone stopped packing and passing groceries to stare in her direction. She could feel their stares poking through her polo shirt like toothpicks.

Doreen did not stare. Otherwise preoccupied, her mouth fell open, like a castle drawbridge. Karen could clearly make out the fillings in her bottom teeth. A strange noise came dribbling out of the older lady, something similar to the sound created by a slow puncture. People stopped staring at Karen and stared at Doreen. It was pleasant to be on the periphery for a change. Doreen sat down, then lay down, forming a stranded snow angel on the linoleum floor. Her hair – grey, gold, speckled – came loose around her head, flaming upwards in the direction of the trolley store. Her hands were starfish, swimming easy at the end of each arm. She looked drowned and lovely. It was on her like sunburn. Karen could not even be angry with her when the Christmas was this thick.

'Oh,' said Doreen and her smile was funny, all up and down at the sides, all into her eyes and cheeks. 'Oh, that was so lovely. Can you do it again?'

'Yes,' Karen said, 'I suppose so.' Then she unleashed Christmas, liberally, outrageously, without reservation, up and down the aisles until even the frozen food section melted out of sheer rosy good cheer. When the management began to notice strange things appearing on their CCTV monitors they came rushing down to the shop floor and fired Karen in full view of the tinned vegetables.

'Don't you know where you are?' they screamed. 'This is Connswater Tesco, no place for miracles!'

They gave her extra money, an entire month's wages, to leave immediately, to say nothing of this to the local newspapers and promise she would shop elsewhere from now on. They were careful in their dismissal, fearing litigation and the tabloid press, to state that Karen was not a bad person, that Christmas was a good thing, far too good for Connswater Tesco, better perhaps for an upmarket place: Marks & Spencer, they suggested, or House of Fraser.

'You give these kinds of people a good thing free,' her supervisor explained, 'and they'll always be wanting more.'

Then they escorted Karen from the premises under the

watchful eyes of three security guards. They prodded her out with a three-metre roll of birthday gift-wrap lest the littlest part of them make contact with the littlest part of her and bloom. Though they could not bear her in public, the staff were waiting in the car park, loitering by the bins, awkward and hungry, hands wide open, asking for a touch, just a small touch: the slimmest slice of Christmas.

'The chance,' they explained anxiously, 'might never come again.'

They couldn't look each other in the eye. They wouldn't even raise their heads when she touched them. They wouldn't say her name. The next day they'd deny it all. The following day, feign ignorance. Only in the moment when the Christmas came rushing over them, and they felt, for the first time in years, like tiny expectant children, did they smile and allow themselves the enormous pleasure of possibility. Karen knew she wouldn't be back there again.

All that had taken place in March. Karen has hardly left the house since. She's working as a telesales person now, holding the telephone with a tea-towel so she doesn't leak down the line as she pushes double-glazing and payment-protection insurance to elderly people on the mainland. Sometimes she has doubts. She wonders if she'll ever be able to love another person in the ordinary way. She knows that none of this is fair, but what good is knowing the difference between fair and unfair when nothing can be done about it?

This is a common enough theme among the Unfortunate Children and their parents. I've only known them for a single evening but I've already heard 'What will become of them?' repeated half a dozen times at least. The future lingers in the room, like last night's dinner, souring the air. It colours everything the parents say, the things they don't say too. There's a grand unknown looming on the edge of all their horizons.

Perhaps Karen will become a radio DJ, her voice touching people in a way her fingers aren't allowed to, or maybe she'll learn to love those same errant fingers and find a job in a nursing home or hospice, laying hands on hopeless souls, bringing joy and respite in the darkest places. Maybe the girl who is occasionally a boat will grow into her land legs and no longer feel the need to float alone among the geese and beaky swans, or she will acquire a summer job, transporting holidaymakers round the boating lake at Pickie Pool and come to understand her calling is to carry strangers, to be present, but hardly noticed, in their good-day photos. Perhaps, that one boy will stop seeing the future in every liquid surface, or that other boy will come down from his tree and take a job in the civil service, wearing Next office clothing to work like an ordinary man.

Maybe the Unfortunate Children will grow out of themselves, or into themselves, and in the end, sit easily in their own odd skins. Perhaps they won't become unfortunate adults. Every parent in the room hopes for this. I hope for it, too. I hold tightly to the knowledge – medical, social, psychological – that children are fluid, not-yet-formed creatures. That they are not, at six months or even six years, set in their ways. That some children, even those who have never known a single unfortunate day, will often grow into adults so far removed from their early selves it is impossible to recognize them in old photographs and anecdotes. All this is possible. Every parent in the room, myself included, is hoping for their own peculiar version of happy ever after. But from this side of their stories there's no way of knowing how any of them will end.

Karen looks as if she's going to cry, but she won't let herself. When she's finished telling her story everyone claps. 'You must be very proud of her,' says Davy, and her father says he is. I can understand why he's proud. Yes, Karen is an Unfortunate Child. I can see it in the way she draws her hair across her face and never lifts her eyes from her feet. But she doesn't hurt people. She's blessed with a variety of goodness too great for her to control. I glance around the circle. The invisible twins do not hurt people, and neither does the boy who sees the future in liquid surfaces. The girl who is sometimes a boat is odd, but not destructively so, and Ella Penney couldn't harm another person if she tried. These are the sort of children who are hurt rather than harmful. They are unfortunate.

Sophie is different. Sophie has the potential to be a terrible kind of creature. She doesn't belong here with these children. She belongs with the dark beasts – the devils and vampires and soulless haunting things – who cannot keep both feet in the underworld. I do not belong with the parents of the Unfortunate Children. I have brought a shameful thing into their midst.

I make my excuses, lift my jacket from the back of the seat and slip out before the second round of coffee begins. All the way home I think about how close I have come to belonging. This nearness, followed by distance, is somehow worse than always being alone. I remember this feeling from childhood, from university, from every day I've ever spent in the health centre. I am always, always on my own. Of course, there is Sophie now, but she is not the kind of company I'd hoped for.

AUGUST

Jonathan

I CUT MYSELF last night, deep enough to require stitches.
I did it to see what it would be like for you. I pressed the
blade against my thigh and watched the blood line, then form
bubbles, and finally a solid red gush, rushing down my leg and on
to the bathroom floor. The blood made a dark pool on the lino, a
stain like red wine left too long in the glass. I should have put
newspaper down before I started, or towels. I should have been
ready with the bleach.

I thought cutting myself would hurt more than it did, that it
would sting like an accidental burn. I thought my hand would
refuse me. But it didn't. My hand was just as curious as the rest
of my body, eyes, nose, muscles, skin, testicles retreating as the
blade dug in. I felt every named part of myself a separate unit,
tensing and easing and tensing again, like a labouring woman.
I could feel myself dividing. Once started, I hadn't the sense
to stop.

Cutting was a new experience.

I've had broken bones and stitches before but never an injury,
on purpose. You are also a new experience for me, as was your

mother and almost everything that's happened since I first picked up the telephone and heard her, like a magnet, speaking or possibly singing. No, let's be honest here: she was definitely only speaking, though the books would suggest she sang. Speaking, singing, it doesn't really matter what she did. I couldn't help myself around her. Your mother was a new experience for me, a kind of accident. She was not the sort of thing that bears repeating.

Cutting myself was different. I was all intention. I felt compelled to do it properly, like a surgeon on TV. I brought a suture kit and scalpel home from work. No one noticed these items missing. I take things from work all the time: painkillers, thermometers, plasters, the nicer pens advertising prescription drugs. All doctors steal things. Most don't use the stolen items on themselves. But I did. I've been planning to cut myself for more than a week. I'd memorized all the details so they became a kind of music running through my head every time I wasn't speaking.

All my other sadnesses have felt like falling over. But this one felt just like dancing: one learnt step after another until there were no steps left to follow. I can pace these steps even now. It's important not to forget. I may have to do this again.

I chose the leg because legs are fleshy and because a leg can be easily covered with trousers. I chose the left over the right because I'm right-handed. This made everything less awkward when it came to angling the blade. I used a disposable razor to shave four square inches of leg. My pale grey flesh appeared beneath, like a freshly stubbled field. I poured antiseptic on the leg, poured antiseptic on the scalpel, drew the scalpel lightly from one side of the square to the other so it formed a faint line, a guide line no thicker than an eyelash. I drew the blade along this line using a heavier hand. I dug in, avoided the artery, avoided the bone: such things could not be dealt with alone in an en-suite bathroom. I held the edge of the toilet seat with one hand, as if it was the hand of a woman who wished to offer me genuine support. Not my mother. Not your mother. A perfect kind of mother, with hair drawn back in a soft bun, and a smell off her like just-baked cake.

I sweated a little. This was the hardest part.

The hardest part was still to come. I poured antiseptic on the wound. It screamed. I did not look at it directly. It was the world ending in fire, the sacred heart of Christ bleeding, a woman spread open like sliced meat, too pure a thing to be looked at directly. I thought I might fall over from the lightness in my head. It was a kind of rapture.

I pulled myself together and did not fall.

I was already sitting down. I took my own raw edges and sewed myself together, one tight black knot at a time. It took six, maybe seven stitches. I do not remember the details. I was doing this in my head to another man. This was how I managed without anaesthetic. I poured more antiseptic over my leg. It ran off me, like lies. I would have drunk the antiseptic if I'd thought it would soothe me.

This was actually the hardest part.

When the stitches were finally in they were 'xxx', like a series of neat black kisses ending a letter. The rest was window-dressing: antiseptic, gauze, clean white bandages collaring my thigh like a turtle-neck sweater, two ibuprofen for the pain, which would begin rawing through my leg as soon as the shock wore off, a pair of clean pyjama bottoms settling against my hot flesh, gently, gently, gentle as soft-brushed air. I mopped up the blood with old towels, put the towels in the washing-machine and made sure it was a hot wash so there would not be stains. Then I nipped whiskey for the pain; nipped a second glass to chase the first; might possibly have returned for a third. By this stage the painkillers were beginning to sing. I took myself to bed with a pillow lumping beneath my thigh.

I did not sleep and did not sleep and still do not sleep for thinking about you.

I'm thinking about your mouth again.

I thought I was over your mouth. I'm not. I'm constantly thinking about your tongue, and your lips, the two knuckly walls of your gums. They are spit smooth and yet to tooth. I check them every morning, running a finger from one side to the other, bracing myself for the grit nip of a cresting tooth. You suck at my finger. Your mouth muscles draw it in and out so I feel my blood pulsing upwards, root to tip. You are powerful with your mouth, like a much larger machine. Even without a mother you are pre-conditioned to go for the nipple. You have not been taught this. Some skills do not require learning.

Every time I close my eyes I see your mouth smiling at me. Sometimes you have a face. Sometimes you are just a mouth floating up and down the stairs or hovering over the kitchen table. You are the Cheshire Cat without teeth. Your mouth is so many different shades of pink, and red, and pinkish red. It is like a butcher's window. The mouth is where the inside comes climbing out of a person. This is why I'm afraid and cannot look at you straight or even sideways. This is why I'm still not sleeping, even with the tablets.

It would be so much easier to seal you up.

To take a needle and sew one plump lip to the other, or possibly use glue, the strong stuff, which is recommended for holding furniture together. This would keep you quiet. This would surely keep you safe. But I have always known it would be necessary to cut you. Your tongue should suffice. I have no desire to disfigure you further. If you keep your mouth closed and do not try to speak no one will know. Who am I kidding? Of course they'll know, but by then it will be too late to undo it.

You won't understand this now but your tongue is a root, like a potato eye running long beneath the surface. Your tongue is connected to your throat, to your lungs, to your heart, which clutches and releases all the very essence of you, sixty-five times per minute. If your tongue is rotten, all of you is ruined: heart, lungs, throat, head and eyes. A rotten tongue must be cut out with knives. You cannot seal the wrong into a person and expect them to heal. This is a lesson I have personally learnt. I have used doors and neck ties and tightly folded arms to hold my rotten self in until I'm all shot through with the sadness of it. I have spent thirty years perfecting this operation. Wood glue would have been much more convenient.

I do not want you to be always holding yourself in. I want a clean start for you. I want every good thing. I can give you this with a knife. I promise I will do this properly, once and never again.

I cut myself last night, deep enough to require stitches.

I told myself I was doing it for you. 'Now I'll know how she feels,' I told myself. 'Now I'll be able to look at her with empathy when she bleeds.'

What a coward I am. What a fearful man. This had nothing to do with empathy. This was all about absolution: my little hurt for your grand hurt, which will not hold water in comparison.

Here will be a red gash on my thigh and there, the bloody stump of your severed tongue.

Here a smooth pink scar, barely noticeable with time, and there, your mouth at twenty and thirty, incapable of solid thought.

Here will be the memory of a quick blade digging in, and there, the emptiness of all your silent years, screaming and screaming, and only catching on your own teeth.

What a coward I am. What a fearful child.

Will you forgive me when you're old enough to understand forgiveness? Will you have the words for it?

I'm hoping that it will not come to this, little one. I'm

watching your mouth like a clock. This is where the world will begin and end for us. I'm wondering if my hand will refuse me in the moment. I suspect it may. I'm practising the first cut in my head. It's so much harder to call this kindness now, now you've grown into me, like a stubborn root.

Like a thing that other people would call love.

14

The Rains

FOR DAYS THERE'S been a heaviness in the air that will not sub-
side or come to thunder. Then a cloud appears behind Cave
Hill, a single cloud, no bigger than a child's fist and no more
threatening. It is remarkably white against the emptiness of the
sky, like a sheep lost at sea. People stare at it. They come out of
their houses to stare. They point out the cloud to their children.
They take pictures on their mobile phones, texting them to relatives in Portrush and Enniskillen. It is months since they last
saw a cloud. They're so very thankful to see one now, casting its
cottony shadow over Cave Hill.

The older folk are happiest. Having exhausted all but the
most obvious things to say about heat they've been waiting anxiously for some variation in the weather. They have all manner
of damp sentiments ready to drop into conversation – drizzle,
fog and biting winds – but they need a little rain for lubrication.
'Looks like it might rain,' they say eagerly, their eyes never for a
moment falling from the little cloud.

The cloud takes several days to swell. It makes the weather
report on Friday, and by Saturday evening is featured on the
actual news. People allow themselves to believe a little. Some are
praying for rain. Some do not want to force the hand of God.

They ask for his will to be done, even if this means more heat. No one wants the heat to continue. The northern constitution can take only so much sun.

While the city is sleeping the cloud gives birth to other, larger, clouds. This has everything to do with pressure fronts and cold currents sweeping in from the Atlantic, but the local churches still call it answered prayer. In the morning the sky is a thick beard of a blanket descending upon the city. The weathermen speculate. 'Maybe, possibly, hopefully,' they say. They don't want to disappoint their viewers. They don't want anyone switching to the other channel. People start to carry a light coat every time they leave the house. 'Just to be on the safe side,' they say, as if they require an excuse for their own hopefulness. Some even keep pocket-sized umbrellas tucked inside their handbags.

When the rain finally arrives, the sky is an ocean. Everything is upside down and gushing. The world appears to be ending with water and, in the downpour, all thought of fire is washed away. In the East they are taken by surprise. They have forgotten what it is to be damp. What a relief the rain is. What a way to start again.

The rain starts on Monday morning. Monday is as good a day as any for a new start. Most of the city's residents are still asleep when it begins. They wake to the shrill patter of raindrops tickling their windows and skylights. They wake smiling. The air is good today. It smells of nothing but air.

The first fat drop of rain lands on the hand of a postman as he reaches to stuff envelopes through a letterbox on the Beersbridge Road. Instinctively he looks up, wondering what has hit him. The second drop makes contact with his forehead and, within seconds, he's drenched to the skin, not cold for the rain is lukewarm, like the rain in Mallorca or Tenerife, but drenched none the less, all the way through his uniform, right down to his underwear and socks. The letters go soggy in his hand. Ink runs. Paper disintegrates. He finds himself holding a wad of brown mush. All over the city other up-early-and-outside types experience the same sudden baptism. Dog-walkers, joggers, bin men and shift workers waiting for the bus find themselves soaked and squelching onwards. They are smiling this first morning. What a laugh it is to be wet after all that dry. They are seeing the rain as a definite blessing. They have no idea how long it will last.

By Saturday most people have had more than enough of the rain. Gutters have overrun and sewage is swimming down the street in thick, meaty chunks. The worst parts of the city reek of damp animal, potato peelings and raw human shit. The West-link is three feet underwater. It is nothing but the memory of a road now. In the south of the city, near Cutter's Wharf, the Lagan splits its banks and parked cars go gliding down the street, their windscreens peeping above the waterline, like submarines coming up for air. The university rowing team burst open their boat shed and paddle round the roundabouts in luminous orange canoes. They are featured on the news at six, grinning for the cameras, holding their paddles aloft, like happy-birthday banners. It is a holiday for them, a break from the everyday dull. It is not a holiday for those unfortunate residents whose houses border the river on either side. It is a reckoning. There's only so much that can be saved with a mop and bucket.

In the city centre the pavements are the same gunmetal grey as the sky, as the shop windows, as the lake quickly forming outside the markets. Everywhere is grey and sliding. People are pale pink thumbprints smudging behind the rain. Most stay indoors, only leaving the house when strictly necessary: work, groceries, elderly relatives, who may require anchoring down. Walking, even a short distance, feels just like swimming tastes deep inside the lungs. The smell of the rain is painfully clean after so much smoke. Some people go out and stand in it with their hands and mouths open, drinking it and grinning like actors in romantic movies. Many of these people are not even in love. They're just relieved to have their weather back. Umbrellas are all but useless against the torrent. They exist only to indicate which way is up. Everything is damp. Everything is sleek as spit and softly lined.

It has been raining for six days now. Monday to Saturday, without so much as an hour's reprieve. It is still coming down in sheets, bouncing off the pavements, as if anxious to be back up in the clouds, beginning the cycle again. It is impossible to light an outside fire. The rain has no patience with heat. Even a cigarette requires careful manoeuvring with umbrellas and cupped hands. Water kills fire, over and over and over again, like some grand game of Rock, Scissors, Paper. Belfast swims.

The Tall Fires are over. The rain has drawn a line under the summer and all its nonsense. Now the city is gearing up for another season. It is possible to hear the murmur of it rumbling round the downtown buses: 'The nights are drawing in,' they say, 'and there's a quare nip in the air.' They rub their hands together when they speak, though it's hardly cold enough for a coat. The schools are back in a few weeks' time and the leaves will soon be turning. Christmas is only four months away. It isn't summer any more. The Tall Fires are already history. If you look them up on Wikipedia you will find the article is past tense. There are dates, like bookends, birthing and deathing this particular chapter in the city's story.

Nothing has been resolved or achieved but this is not considered failing. This is how it has been in Belfast every summer since the Agreement. The same hot anger rises at the end of June and goes stamping up and down the little streets. Stamping and shouting and raising Cain all the way through July until, by August's end, the energy's gone right out of it. The spite leaves gradually, like a pendulum losing swing. There are fewer angry people on the streets, fewer and fewer with each end-of-summer evening, until only a handful stand on the corners, talking football and last night's telly to keep their boredom still. These people are not as loud as they once were. They no longer have the numbers for a decent riot, or the inclination to set fires or shout about their civil liberties. They are younger and younger with each passing night, some no bigger than babies. Round here, protesting is just another way to pass a dull weekend, something to do before the football starts in earnest.

The remnant begin to wonder why they are still there making half-hearted plans to burn shit or protest about how they've been treated. Where has the rest of the rabble gone? 'Nice for some,' they mutter, 'staying in, watching their soaps, getting the weans ready for school. We're the bigger fools for keeping on with this.' Every day they are fewer and fewer until one evening no one is standing on the corner muttering or holding a banner. There's no way of predicting this day precisely. It happens when it happens and goes almost unnoticed, like the last neat sneeze of a head cold. The angry time is over for another year. The people of East Belfast roll up their rebel souls and return to normal. They are relieved to have their nights back. Any evening now *The X Factor* will be starting on ITV, and *Strictly* on the other side. They wouldn't want to miss them. 'What a summer it's been,' they say, and pack their rage, like holiday clothes, ready and waiting for next June when the rising will start all over again.

This is how it's always been in the East. Though the Tall Fires have made this summer hotter than most, it is widely understood that it's August now and time for settling down. Even the young ones have no interest left in setting fires or screaming at the police. The need for it has left their system.

They walk past the places where the Tall Fires have been and cannot, in the moment, picture themselves angry enough to burn anything. The rain has washed the memory of fire right out of them. They stare at the marks on the ground, the charred black stains that are no longer shops or houses. They poke the damp ash with sticks and clean white trainer toes, leaving slight indentations in the tar. 'Did we do this one?' they ask each other. 'Or was it the one down the road we done?' They can't remember a single definite second of the summer.

The politicians say nothing. They are particularly gifted in this arena and can often talk for hours at a time without saying anything at all. Passing each other in the corridors of Stormont, they shrug their shoulders and smile knowingly. They cannot believe the situation has washed itself out. When they speak they speak quietly, behind closed doors and raised hands. Their mouths are full of platitudes. Sleeping dogs must be allowed to lie and there is no point looking a gift horse in the mouth, especially when the horse in question has rained on exactly the right kind of parade. Some even go so far as to say, 'We've got away with murder this time, lads,' but this is a dangerous sentiment to voice round here. The older contingent knows better. They throw their entire weight at the rain, ordering sandbags, water pumps, flood provision and, where necessary, evacuations.

Everyone agrees that the rain must be stopped.

Everyone wants to get involved.

What a relief to be on the same side for a change.

The politicians are on the television together, talking about the floods, loudly, loudly, in casual jumpers, sleeves rolled to the elbow, as if ready to spring into action. They are shoulder to shoulder with politicians from the other side. This is called a united front. The like is rarely seen in Belfast. They are reasonably certain that no one has noticed their failure with the fires. Just to be sure, they're all front and bluster. Politics is sleight-of-hand in this city, pain here lessened by pain there; an endless game of quick distraction. All is quiet on every front: West, East, city centre and the posh bits on either side.

The tourist season is also over. It has not been a success – first the fires and now the rain. The uncharacteristically fine weather has not been draw enough to distract from Belfast's more obvious problems. All but the bravest souls have stayed away. Some have come and kept to the north's peripheries: Enniskillen, Donegal, Bushmills' whiskey and the Giant's Causeway, which never seems to lose its appeal. Even the Tourist Board, whose job it is to spin the city sideways, are calling this summer a wash-out. They are counting up the cost in millions: more than ten, but less than a hundred. What a mess. What a bloody waste of decent weather. There might not be another decent summer for a decade.

There have been no more videos from the Fire Starter. It's been almost a month since the last, and even this is no longer trending on social media. The proper BBC have packed up their cameras and returned to the mainland. There is nothing in Belfast worth pushing to the London set, nothing to compete with real terrorism: hijacked planes, bearded radicals and suicide bombs. The local news is once again weather and car accidents, occasionally drugs and, every week or so, a racist attack. Nothing like the old days, nothing to keep the old folk indoors.

Confident that the Summer of the Tall Fires is finally over, the PSNI disband their specialist unit. Off go the brave fire-chasers to Florida and Lanzarote on last-minute package deals. They are glad to get a fortnight in the sun before the kids head back to school, gladder still to wash the smoke stink from their clothes. The extra fire engines return to Scotland. Back they go, with grateful thanks and the ill-defined promise of help from Belfast, if this sort of help is ever required. The *Newsletter* runs a picture of the six Scottish fire engines edging their way up the ramp and on to the Larne–Cairnryan ferry. They are Christmas red against the grey of boat and sky, almost pornographically cheery.

Elsewhere in the city the builders have moved in. One man's loss is another's opportunity, and there has never been a better time for building in the East. Watching the builders congregate outside the trade section of B&Q, it is hard to believe in the recession. The insurance money is beginning to trickle in and everyone is flush. The builders are battling the elements to get their concrete mixed and their foundations down, to get the roof on before winter sets in. They are cutting corners and Building Control is keeping a soft distance. It is in everyone's interest to get the city rebuilt.

Up go the walls. Up go the shops and houses. All the builders are saying, 'Sure, you'll be in and settled by Christmas.' It is a kind of mantra. The whole city takes to believing it. Wee terraced houses are rising from the rubble, schools and cafés and community centres springing up from the ashes of their former selves. Surely they'll all be in and settled by Christmas. It'll be as if the Tall Fires never happened. Belfast will be good as new. She won't be knowing herself for all these fancy buildings.

15

Anarchy

A T THE TOP of the Castlereagh Road Sammy Agnew does not know himself for sheer, dodged-the-bullet relief. The Summer of the Tall Fires is over. It won't stretch to ruin another season. It will not claim a single life. For this, he is particularly thankful, and for his son, who has failed, and in failing left himself open to other, more innocent, summers to come. The boy might yet be turned. He's not killed anyone, not directly – at least, there's been nothing mentioned in the papers. This is more than Sammy can say for himself.

He allows his imagination to run loose over his son's future. Gracious he is with the boy, picturing him at thirty or thirty-five, a different man with a desk job and a solid name around town. Somebody you could count on/lean on/bet your bottom dollar on; all the clichés flying now. Mark will be something big in computers. Sammy's too ignorant for specifics, but definitely something big with an office of his own. Maybe he'll even have children and a wife, a nice house with a garden in Holywood or Bangor. He won't have a criminal record, oh, no, for certain sure, not so much as a speeding point on the boy's licence. He tells himself that Mark will turn out fine. This isn't the world's biggest leap. Sure, aren't there always reformed characters telling

209

their stories on breakfast TV, lads who've done much worse things than Mark?

Sometimes they hear the boy creaking around upstairs and Pamela will ask with her eyes, 'What's ever going to come of our Mark?'

Sammy tells his wife exactly the same thing he tells himself: 'Wait till you see, love. The lad'll turn out grand. It's just a wee phase he's going through.' He curls his fists into hammers when he says this, as if hope is something that can be grabbed and held on to. He actually believes himself. There are nail marks pinked into the palms of his hands, proving just how hard he believes. All Mark's violence will turn out to be a passing phase, like online gaming, or that summer he ran with the Goth kids, shoplifting and loitering outside City Hall.

If Sammy manages to avoid the actual Mark it is easy enough to imagine his son with a decent future. He can even picture them doing Christmas together, some time soon, like a family in a sitcom. Christopher and Lauren will come home; Pamela will have shifted a bit of weight and be happy again. They'll all be laughing, laughing, laughing and playing board games round the dining-room table. They'll watch Christmas movies together: *Home Alone* and *Mary Poppins*, *Die Hard* for the boys. They'll eat Quality Street straight from the tin and wee nibbly things from Marks & Spencer, heated up in the microwave. They'll take photos like a normal family.

What crap. What utter self-indulgence. Five seconds in Mark's company, even a glimpse of him glooming along the upstairs landing, is enough to remind Sammy that the boy's just the same as he's always been. 'Troubled,' his teacher once called him, but troubled is much too passive a sentiment for Mark. Mark *is* trouble.

For the moment, Sammy shoves his son to the back of his thoughts. He needs to rest his nerves. He does his best to avoid the boy around the house. It isn't hard. Mark keeps ghost hours. Every so often he'll hear the floorboards creak and remember that his son is still up there, plotting. He can feel him, like a kind of weariness, seeping through the ceiling. But there's nothing to show for Mark's schemes now, not so much as a newspaper cutting. The Tall Fires are over. The air inside the house is thinner and better for breathing. When Sammy sleeps, he sleeps with both ears closed, confident that the PSNI aren't about to come stampeding through his house with guns. He sits in his living room, coffee mug in hand, and watches the rain slugging down the windows. He feels like a cancer patient in remission. He can't stop watching the rain. It is the answer to a prayer he hadn't even thought to pray. Of course, there's still a mean itch lingering behind all this contentment, but Sammy chooses to ignore it. It's good to sleep his nerves. They are thin as piano wire, these days. There is always a headache just starting on him, always a tightness in his chest.

He keeps his days light and his evenings ever so slightly inebriated: three beers to chase dinner and a whiskey before bed. He likes the feeling of a slurred tongue. He talks to Pamela about the box sets they're watching, what to order from the Chinese, whether they can afford a new kitchen this year or next. They only do the surface chat, nothing like a siren going off. It's important to keep the conversation going, though; doesn't much matter what they're saying, so long as they're talking. Talking's like a muscle. If you don't keep at it, eventually it'll seize up. They can't run the risk of this. Sammy only has Pamela and Pamela only has Sammy and neither could manage on their own.

They are kinder than they've been in ages. They tiptoe round each other's nerves, fixing endless cups of tea and saying, 'Are you warm enough, love? Should I fire the heating on for an hour?' You'd think there'd been a death in the house, they're that gentle with each other. It's not like they've fallen in love again, nothing so bold, it's more like they're remembering how to be together, every day, in the same place. It takes a crisis to remind you of what you've got, thinks Sammy, and never once considers telling Pamela just how close they've come to losing everything. He keeps things nice and quiet, normal, relying on the television to fill in all the awkward gaps. He turns up the volume when Mark starts to move around upstairs. He does this to protect Pamela. He knows they're just pretending. He knows this well enough for both of them. Best to keep their heads in the sand. Best to avoid a scene. He doesn't have the balls to go upstairs again. Secretly he hopes that Mark will never come down.

It is almost September now and still raining. Sammy is off into the city centre for a new pair of slippers. Other men's wives buy their clothes for them but Pamela's never been that kind of wife. He's glad of this. He's not the sort who'd take easily to being hen-pecked. The soles of his slippers are gaping at the toe, making mouths every time he walks, but she hasn't even noticed. He's buying his own slippers as he has bought his own jeans and jumpers and button-up pyjamas for the last thirty years or so.

It's Saturday and hell to find a parking spot so he's taking the bus. On he gets at the top of the Castlereagh Road. He's still several years shy of a bus pass so it costs him the better part of two quid to travel the four miles into town. 'It'd be cheaper flying,' he mutters at the driver and, just to spite him, the cheeky bastard starts off at a clip before he's managed to sit down. Down he drops, stumbling like a Friday-night drunk, into the first available seat. Two young lads are sitting behind him. He notes their pale faces, smells the second-day sweat crawling off them. They are wearing beanie hats, like builders once wore in the seventies, or fellas from the shipyards. They are every second word cursing, all harsh consonants and phlegm. Click and cluck and gutter spit, like a pair of angry chickens. The sound of it catches at Sammy's ear so he cannot help but listen.

Aside from the three of them, and an old one with a zimmer frame, the bus is empty. If he turns his head sideways Sammy can see the two lads reflected in the opposite window. They are watching something on a mobile phone, holding it away from their chests so both can watch at the same time. Sammy has the most basic phone. It does calls and texts. It costs him a tenner a month and half the time is out of battery. This young fella has the same iPhone Sammy bought Christopher for Christmas last year. The price of it had almost killed him. 'You could have a car for that,' he'd moaned to Pamela, but handed over his credit card anyway. He can't afford to ruin things with Christopher too. He only has the one decent son left.

The bus passes a pizza place and, for a moment, captures all three of them in the plate-glass window: Sammy, in his summer anorak, the two tracksuit lads behind, heads inclined towards each other as they hunch over the phone. They have big, chunky bastards of watches on, gold straps flaring against the glass, and smaller devices for music hanging on wires from their ears. They spend most of their lives plugged in. Life support, thinks Sammy. He wonders where the young ones get the money for all their toys. Probably drugs.

'Have you seen this one yet?' the lad directly behind him is asking. The other lad hasn't.

'It's your man that done the Fire Starter videos,' says the first lad. 'He put a new one up last night.'

Sammy is suddenly electric. The shock runs up the back of his neck and shoulders. He is struck glass. His stomach swims. His head clenches. He feels as if he might be sick and has nowhere to put it, not even a carrier bag. He wants to turn and whip the phone away from the boys. He doesn't. He can't. Instead he looks straight ahead, focusing on the bus's windscreen, the wipers waving, the back of the driver's baldy head. He holds himself like a telegraph pole, stiff and straight and thickly present. He must not turn round. It wouldn't do to draw attention to himself, to seem more than averagely interested.

He isn't afraid of the young lads. He could have both of them on the floor, even now with his gammy knee and the old-man gut ballooning round his middle. No, he isn't particularly afraid of anyone. He is only afraid of the angry knot lodged behind his ribcage and the way it is already clawing up his throat. He knows there will be no end to it, once started. He clamps his teeth. He fists his hands. He wants to ruin everything: these two lads with their mobile phones, Mark, himself, the whole bloody city. There's no sense in him, only rage. He holds it tightly down. He has taught himself how to do this with breathing and certain key muscles, mostly his head. He sits perfectly still and listens. He listens like he is nothing but ears.

'What's he saying now?' asks the second one. 'Sure, the Tall Fires is all over since the rain started.'

'Not according to your man, here. He says it's only getting started. Look, till you see for yourself.'

In the window sideways, Sammy can see the second lad in profile. He can't be more than fifteen. His voice is still girlish on the vowels.

'Give us a look,' he says. He takes his mate's phone in his own hand and holds it up to his face, plugs the earphones into his own ears so Sammy can't hear what's being said. He has to imagine the threatening thump of the Prodigy bookending either side of the clip and the papered flinch of cardboard signs passing through his son's hand, like Bob Dylan feeding lyrics to the camera. He has to imagine it all. It isn't difficult. He dreams about those videos.

The lad watches the video all the way through. It takes less than a minute. It feels like a month to Sammy but the bus is still idling at the same red light when he yanks the headphones out of his ears and passes the phone back to his friend.

'Deadly,' he says.

'I know,' replies the second. 'That lad's a psycho, isn't he?'

'Complete mentalist.'

'Some balls on him having another punt at the whole thing. You'd think he'd have given up by now.'

'Naw, my da says lunatics like that never change. He went to school with this fella that was deep into torturing and stuff during the Troubles. Dad says you'd always have known there was something odd about him. He'd no fear nor nothing. No sympathy for other people. He was just unhinged. Your lad in the Fire Starter video's the same.'

'Do you think so?'

'Aye, my da says he's no more interest in the politics. He's only doing it to cause chaos.'

'Like the Joker.'

'Aye, Darren, exactly like the Joker.'

'Cool.'

'Very cool. I wouldn't want to be on the wrong side of that bastard, though. You never know what a psycho like that's capable of.'

The lads fall briefly silent as the bus pulls away from the stop lights and goes lumbering down the Castlereagh Road, wavering between the rows of parked cars.

'I'd be up for it, so I would,' says the first lad, breaking the damp silence.

'Up for what?' asks the second.

'Whatever your man's after.'

'More fires?'

'Whatever – fires, beatings, bricking the police. Sure, wasn't it good to have something to be at for a change?'

215

'Aye, it was great craic.'

'Best summer ever.'

'No reason why it has to end.'

'No reason at all.'

'Wee bit of rain shouldn't stop us defending our civil liberties.'

'Dead right. Psycho or not, your man's no pussy. He's not lying down and letting the other side march all over him. I'm in. Whatever it is he's wanting us to do, I'm totally in.'

'Chaos. Anarchy. No surrender,' they chant together.

Boom. Boom. Boom. Like lyrics from an old punk tune. Sammy can only imagine this is part of the Fire Starter's call to arms. He pictures each word individually, printed on a single sheet of card. He can almost hear the thundering bass line. It's not the most original, but Mark knows exactly what he's doing, wheeling out the mother tongue, provoking nostalgia.

No surrender, indeed.

The vomit comes sliding up Sammy's throat. He forces himself to choke it down, placing a hand over his mouth to keep the bile in. It isn't my fault, he thinks. I did everything I could to keep him straight. Sins of the fathers, he thinks, dredging up all the old Sunday-school guff. He knows his hand is in this, heavy as a dropped hammer. He might as well be posting these videos himself. Part of him wishes he was. The smallest, ugliest part of him is proud of Mark. Jealous, even. He feels a headache coming on, a tightening in his heart, which might be angina or just anxiety. Maybe, if he's lucky, the bus will drive itself off the Albert Bridge, put him out of his misery.

'What's anarchy?' asks the lad behind him. The other one isn't quite sure but thinks it definitely involves guns. 'Deadly,' says the first lad. The other claims he's heard from a mate of his brother that the Fire Starter's going to do a bomb next.

'Is it still anarchy if you use a bomb instead of guns?' asks his mate, and the other lad reassures him that it's totally still anarchy so long as there's some kind of explosion. This seems to satisfy them both. They return to their individual phones, googling football results and texting their friends.

They get off the bus two stops before the bridge. Sammy sits on, all the way to the depot. He means to get off at the markets and can't. He tries again at Rosemary Street but his muscles won't move and he doesn't trust his legs for standing. When he finally manages to make it down the three steps at the front of the bus he feels as if he's aged ten years in the course of the journey. He holds tightly to the door to keep himself from toppling over.

Sammy walks round the town for an hour. He does not buy slippers. He doesn't buy anything at all. He moves from one bench to another, sitting down to watch the Saturday-afternoon shoppers cart their carrier bags and children round the shops. In and out they go, buying birthday presents and books, school shoes for the weans and wee tasty things from Marks & Spencer, a jumper they fancied in H&M, make-up remover from Boots, cappuccinos in Starbucks: a hundred thousand ordinary exchanges, which Sammy usually doesn't take the time to notice. He notices now. He wonders where they are all coming from, these people he doesn't know; where they will be in three hours' time; who they matter to; who will feel the gap they leave behind. They are so ordinary to him, unremarkable as ants. This is how God must feel with all the power in his hands.

He imagines the afternoon in pieces. It isn't hard. There are photos from before: news reports from the seventies and eighties come quickly to mind. Those pictures are not easily forgotten. Shattered windows. Shopping bags shredded, like wedding confetti, tins of beans and other groceries rolling down the street. Dust settling. The grainy hint of something no one really needs to see: an arm, a head, a shoeless leg kicking at thin air. A child's stuffed animal, sooty now from the blast. Blood. Cars and rubbish bins turned wrong side up. Flashing lights. Sirens. The dead, ghostly silence before the screaming begins. Sammy sees it all: the way it has been; the way it could be again. He sits for fifteen minutes outside Build-A-Bear watching the children queue to spend their pocket money. Families with buggies and little babies strapped to their parents' chests. Grandparents. Tourists. Teenagers chirruping away, like angry starlings. Shop girls on their breaks. No one is bracing themselves for an explosion. No one is suspicious or afraid.

These people are like children, trusting implicitly. They should know better. How could they have forgotten so quickly? Sammy's anger rises against them. Stupid they are, like sheep moving in the one direction, never looking back. He wants to scream at their ignorance, spit judgement like an old-time street preacher. Then the pity comes in waves. He might cry. He can't, not in public, but the sobs are going through him, regular as contractions. He wishes to place himself as a barrier between them and the things his son might do. He can do this right now with his mobile phone. He can call for help. Police. Ambulance. Fire brigade. All of the above, and the Coast Guard too. This is my son. He's going to ruin everything. Abraham he will then be, or maybe God, offering his son up as a sacrifice. No, this won't be anything close to true. Sacrifice only works with good sons. The bad ones are dispensable. Still he can't bring himself to dial the number.

His chest is turning itself inside out. He can't breathe. This must be a heart attack, he thinks. He hopes it is: an easy way out; a decision lifted out of his hands. It isn't a heart attack. After twenty minutes his breathing evens. He can walk so long as he doesn't think too much about the step after the next. He gets a taxi home, through the East, over the ring road to his house. And Mark.

Police. Ambulance. Fire brigade. Sammy knows what should be done. He doesn't know if he can do it. Not today, he tells himself. It's not that urgent. He decides to sleep on it. He doesn't sleep. The next morning he feels like death. Pamela puts him into the car and drives him to the doctor's. She doesn't ask him what's wrong. She knows better.

16

The Flood

THE RAIN IS coming down in torrents now. The city is swimming in its own piss and everyone is worried about the rising waterline. It hasn't rained like this in decades. I am at work when Christine texts to say downstairs has flooded. The water's seeped under the door. It's half a foot deep in the living room. Lighter items of furniture are beginning to float.

I can't leave immediately. Marty still has me on a kind of probation. He's keeping a tight eye on everything I do and I want to look as professional as possible. There are two patients before lunch. Then I can escape for an hour, maybe more if the flooding turns out to be an actual emergency. I could ask one of the women to cover for me. They have small children themselves. They have partners to share the burden and are soft when it comes to my situation with Sophie. Sometimes they bring me home-baked cakes and buns, or a portion of lasagne in a disposable plastic tub, the kind Chinese takeaway comes in. 'Just bin the tub when you're done,' they say, and explain how long it'll need in the microwave. They wouldn't be doing this if I was a woman. They certainly wouldn't be doing it if I had a wife. I'm not complaining. It's great that they're so willing to cover my shifts.

My phone keeps flashing. I can feel it vibrating in my pocket all the way through my first appointment. I check it surreptitiously while the patient is undressing. I am careful not to look suspicious. It's best not to be messing around with mobiles when you've a half-naked patient with you. Christine wants to know what she should do. She has texted three times now. The third is just a series of question marks: two dozen or more in a block. I stare at this line of tiny hooks and feel dizzy. Damned if I know what you should do, I think. I don't write this. I don't know what I should write. In this sort of situation I never feel like a grown-up or even a proper man. I'm equally useless with car problems and anything to do with electrics.

'HOLD TIGHT,' I type. 'WITH U IN A MIN.' Christine is using sad face emoticons now, one with actual moving tears and another like a little man waving his hands wildly above two squiggly lines. Not waving but drowning, I am meant to think. Not funny, Christine. Not funny at all. I begin to panic. The panic gets thicker when she asks if she should call someone: a plumber, a handyman or her father, who is very good in such emergencies.

'NO,' I text back. No one must be called to the house until I get home. Even in an emergency I can't risk strangers around Sophie. 'STAY UPSTAIRS. KEEP SOPHIE WARM. DONT PANIC. I'LL B HOME IN AN HOUR.'

I am home in forty-five minutes. I'm not proud of myself but I'm hardly even present with my last two patients. I write prescriptions for painkillers and anti-depressants before they've even finished describing their symptoms. I have them in and out in under five minutes. This is record-breaking speed, even for me – I don't, as a rule, do chit-chat. I can think about nothing but getting back to Sophie. I have an image lodged in my head: my daughter in an old-fashioned life-ring, bobbing around her flooded nursery, screaming hysterically. It's not rational. The water hasn't even made it up the first stair but I can't seem to shift the thought of her wee face, curled up in panic. I try to concentrate on my patients but all I can think about is Sophie.

On the way home the rain is spit-thick sliding across my windscreen. The wipers can't shift it. It moves from side to side, like spilt grease, leaving track marks on the glass. Outside, the water is bouncing off the pavements, coming down heavy as a drive-through car wash. I'm drenched while dashing from the health centre to my car and about to be drenched again between the car and my front door. I've sorted it with Susan. She's covering for me so I don't have to come back after lunch. I make a mental note to buy her a bottle of wine and a thank-you card: something with animals on the front. I'll sign the card from Sophie and myself, fake a scrawly signature for the baby. Susan is a sucker for that kind of crap.

I park my car in the drive. A river is running through my garden, sweeping the shrubs out of their beds and across the lawn. A bigger river is the road. I can barely see through the sheets of rain. It's like being in a room where all the walls are running. I tent my hands above my head – they make a useless umbrella – and sprint from the car to the house, not even bothering to lock the doors.

I can smell the water before I even step through the front door. It is not the same as tap water or even river water. It has a stale nip to it, like stagnant puddles or laundry left wet inside the washing-machine. It is the colour of weak tea, seeping across the hall carpet and pooling on the kitchen tiles, staining everything it touches. I stand for a moment on the doorstep, sheltered by the roof's pitch, and survey the chaos. The coffee-table is doing its best to float. There is a dark tideline creeping up the curtains' hem and the electricity is out. At least we don't have to worry about electrocution. I hesitate on the edge of my home. It's a horror show. I could easily turn tail, run away from it all and come back later when the insurance has dealt with the mess. Old me probably would have done that. I've never been good in a crisis. But now there is Sophie. She's like an anchor lodged inside me. I can't help but think about her. It isn't in me to leave her behind.

Up the stairs I slop, two at a time, dragging the wetness with me. I haven't got the right shoes for this. I was soaked to the knee just puddling through the hall. I find Christine in the spare bedroom holed up with a paperback novel. I stand on the landing, dripping sediment all over the carpet, and wait for her to notice me. I still haven't worked out how to approach her and often appear abruptly at her side, making her jump or drop whatever's in her hand. Thankfully, never Sophie. When she finally looks up she smiles and makes the sign for OK when 'OK' is a question rather than a statement. I give her a thumbs-up. I'm OK. She indicates with her hands and her head that Sophie is fine, fast asleep in the cot next door. There's nothing to write with up here. In the panic Christine has left her note-pad on the kitchen table. The table is an island now, marooned in a sea of brown sludge water. We use our phones to talk, typing out messages and passing them backwards and forwards across the bed.

'SORRY,' I type. 'I DIDNT THINK THIS WOULD HAPPEN.'

'NOT UR FAULT,' Christine replies. 'UR NOT GOD.' She adds a winking smiley face.

Just thinking about smiling is enough to make her smile. She's a sunny sort of person by default, the opposite of me, and though she isn't exactly beautiful, when she smiles she's decidedly less odd-looking. Later, when we're not in the midst of an actual emergency, I must find a way to tell her so without sounding creepy. Christine isn't good with compliments: even the smallest accolade seems to fluster her. She still blushes every time I tell her how good she is with Sophie, or what a tremendous help she is to me.

'HOWS SOPHIE?'

'ALL GOOD. V HAPPY. TOTALLY LOVES WATER. ITS WEIRD. U SHOULD TAKE HER SWIMMING SOMETIME.'

This is not what I want to hear. I'm keen to keep her land-locked. If anything, I'd prefer the child to be terrified of water. I certainly don't want her drawn to it as her mother was. But Sophie is not afraid of water. She's happiest in the bath, half submerged, and wriggling around the tub, like a slick pink salmon. Her skin seems to hold wetness like a cloud. Even hours after a bath her hair is sleek and cold to the touch, as if permanently damp. She will watch a running tap with the same rapt attention other children give to moving pictures on a television screen. Now, here she is, a little mermaid baby, riding high and happy on the surface of a flood. This means nothing, I tell myself. All little kids like water, something to do with being in the womb so long. This means nothing at all.

'THANKS,' I type, '4 EVERYTHING 2DAY. I REALLY APPRECIATE IT. U CAN HEAD HOME IF U WANT 2.'

'WHAT RU GOING 2 DO ABOUT DOWNSTAIRS?'

'BUCKET AND MOP?'

'Smiley face. NO REALLY J. WHAT RU GOING 2 DO?'

'CALL A PLUMBER.'

'WELL IF U THINK U CAN MANAGE WITHOUT ME I MIGHT HEAD HOME BEFORE IT GETS DARK.'

'GO AHEAD. WELL B FINE.'

Christine reaches across the bed and pats my hand, once, twice, three times. If she was the sort of girl who could speak, she'd be saying, 'I have every confidence in you,' or 'You've got this one covered, mate.' But she can only use her hands to drum these feelings into me. This works almost as well as words. Each time her hand meets mine I feel entirely capable. Like a man. Like a man who is also a father. Perhaps I should ask Christine to stay. It's so much easier when she's around. Two can bear a lot more than one. I think this is a saying from the Bible, or possibly Shakespeare. But I can't ask her to stay. She might get the wrong idea. She might panic and leave us for ever.

I find a torch in the bathroom and help her downstairs. As she wades through the floodwater she holds her handbag high above her head like a jungle explorer. This is hardly necessary. The water is only ankle-deep and it makes me smile. She's not a subtle girl, not the sort to practise restraint. Even this is an adventure to her, a fuss to break the silence. I'm jealous of the way she sinks her teeth into everything. I envy her joy. I've never had the gall for it.

After Christine leaves, I feed and change Sophie. She is particularly content tonight. She curls into the corner of my neck to doze. I hope it isn't the water that's soothed her. She hasn't been so limpet-like in weeks, not since she first learnt how to roll. We sit on the edge of my bed for a few minutes, enjoying the closeness of each other as the room begins to darken. It is only when the hall clock chimes six that I remember the plumber. I flick through the *Yellow Pages* and choose one from the very end of the list. Mr Young, with a Y: I think I'm being clever, avoiding the beginning of the alphabet. Plumbers will be in hot demand tonight. People will call the first name they come to. Not me. I'm smarter than that.

Mr Young turns out to be older than I'd expected. He arrives in a white van with a pair of thigh-high fisherman's boots and a young lad, Mickey, who's doing his work experience. 'What a week to pick,' says Mr Young. 'At least he's getting his money's worth.' Mickey shrugs. I can tell he's heard this line several times already and will hear it again, numerous times, before the end of the week.

'Work away,' I say, 'but if you can be quiet it'd be much appreciated. I've just got the baby down upstairs. She's all over the place today, with the floods and everything. It was a nightmare getting her over.'

'Understood,' replies Mr Young. 'I've three of my own. The youngest one was up a dozen times every night until he started nursery. You'll not hear a peep out of us, not a single peep.'

This is hardly true. The pair of them make a tremendous racket splashing around downstairs, pumping water out the kitchen window and tinning their various wrenches off the pipes. I don't mind. They can knock the walls down and set the burglar alarm off, yawp and yowl like savage beasts for all I care, so long as they don't speak in front of Sophie. She's upstairs in her cot, sleeping deeply through the whole fiasco. The plumbers are downstairs, making the mess go away. Everything is almost under control. Everything is not the end of the world it was a few hours earlier. I lie down on my bed for half an hour. What else is there to do in a house with no electricity? I think about reading. I lift a novel from the stack on my bedside table, and wake up to find Mr Young standing in the doorframe, cap in one hand, wrench in the other, like a caricature of a plumber.

'All sorted, Mr Murray,' the older man says. 'It's a bit of a mess downstairs but the water's gone and we've put some sandbags round your doors so it shouldn't come in again. If you call an electrician first thing they'll get the lights back on for you.'

I draw myself up into a sitting position and rub the sleep out of my eyes. I wonder how long the older man has been standing outside my room, watching me sleep. 'Thanks,' I say, trying to sound coherent. 'How much do I owe you?'

'I'll get the invoice out to you at the end of the week, son. No panic. I'm heading straight on to another job now. Half of Belfast's drowning.'

'Thanks again, Mr Young.' I make as if to stand up. I should show the plumbers out of my house. This is what you do with tradesmen.

'Trevor,' the older man insists. 'It's just Trevor, for the next time, and don't be worrying about showing us out. I'm all packed up. Mickey's already in the van. Go and see to that wee lassie of yours. She's been up for ages, babbling away to herself in the cot. I hope you don't mind, she was already awake, and when I heard her giggling, sure I just couldn't keep from having a peek. She's a wee dote so she is, looks like she's going to be a right talker when the words start coming properly. You'll have your hands full with that one, son.'

I go from sitting to standing in one fluid movement.

'She's not talking yet,' I say. 'She's ages to go before that.'

'Sounds like she's already trying, mate. It won't be long. Trust me, I know from my own three. Best feeling in the world, the first time one of your own calls you "Dad". There's nothing like it.'

Mr Young leaves. I sit there for ages, frozen to the bed. I can hear Sophie beginning to cry in the other room. I don't want to go in to her. I'm loath to admit this but, for the first time in weeks, I'm properly afraid of my own daughter. I try to move but my muscles stick. I attempt to reassure myself. The plumber could've been all talk. He's not to know that Sophie mustn't be allowed to speak. Most parents want their children to talk and walk and hit all the milestones of development early. He might well have been trying to be nice, just saying the first thing that came to mind. The alternative is terrifying. What if the plumber is right and she's going to start talking soon? My hand would be forced. Things would have to be done and done quickly.

When I finally go into the nursery to lift Sophie I'm wearing headphones: big buckets of ear defenders, left over from my student days. I lift her from the cot and change her nappy by candlelight. The flames cast wild lava shadows across her belly. She looks like a savage in the warm glow. a little hell baby. She's all smiles tonight. She swipes at my head playfully, intrigued by the big red growths bugging over my ears. She dimples. She laughs. She might well be making other sounds but, with my headphones on, I can't hear anything. I carry her into my own room and place her carefully on the bed. She crabs her legs and arms around, rolling from tummy to back and back to tummy, enjoying the spring in the mattress. She is eggshell white in the flickering dark. She weighs less than a bag of potatoes. It is hard to believe her capable of destroying anything. Yet the fear is in me now, like a little bit of grit lodged between my teeth. It catches on everything.

I take Sophie's jaw in my left hand, ever so gently. It is no bigger than a grapefruit. I can pinch it easily between finger and thumb. I make my right hand into a point and trace my first finger lightly across her neck. She smiles up at me. This is a game to her, like tickling or blowing raspberries on her naked belly. She trusts me. Perhaps, in some deep-down part of her, she already knows I'm her dad. I draw my finger across her neck, slowly, deliberately, like a needle pulling thread. This is where I will go in with the blade. This is how I'll save Sophie. This is how I'll save myself. It is my job to do this, no one else's. I am her father, or, as my long-gone father liked to remind me, I am responsible for all of my own mistakes.

'Could I hurt her?' I ask myself. 'If it was for her own good?'

Other parents hurt their children every day. I know this. I'm a doctor after all. They stick their children with needles and feed them sick-making medicine. They thump them hard between the shoulder blades until all their phlegm comes choking up. They strap them down and hoist them up, poke, prod and hoke the illness out of them. They say, 'Trust us. It's for the best,' and do their crying in bathrooms and hospital corridors where the children won't see. They make themselves deliberately cruel. They have to.

These people aren't like me. They are brave and selfless. Their children need saving from cancer, or diabetes, or lungs that have forgotten how to breathe. They are not to blame. They are to be carried by sisters and brothers and other parents whose children are without fault. No one should feel compelled to carry me. My child is not a victim. My child requires saving from herself. The fault runs through Sophie, like a blood-borne disease. I've done this to her, passed on my weakness. What a pair we are. What a cruel mess.

I don't think I could hurt her. Or, to see the problem from another angle, I don't think I can help her. Not with scalpels. Not with blood. Even with a stranger I'd struggle to break the skin. With Sophie I could barely keep my hand still. Which is why I phone the Royal and ask for Dr Kunari, why the anger comes galloping out of me when the secretary won't put me through: 'Not without an appointment, sir. Not even if you're a doctor yourself.' It's why I put Sophie in the car and drive her through the floods to sit in the car park outside the Portakabin where the Unfortunate Children meet, waiting for Dr Kunari to come out. Why I'm weeping over my steering wheel, misting up the car windows, when Mrs Penney finds me, still waiting, almost two hours later.

'I need someone to help me,' I confess. 'I can't do it myself.'

Mrs Penney understands. She has been here herself, and not so long ago. Eventually everyone needs help with an Unfortunate Child. She probably has a vision of me sitting at her kitchen table, drinking tea, crying if I need to cry, driving home later with an extra portion of shepherd's pie for tomorrow night's dinner. This is how she would help me. This is how she has been helped. I'm imagining something entirely different when I say I can no longer continue on my own. I'm picturing myself on the sidelines while Dr Kunari slices the tongue right out of my daughter's mouth. This is how I want to be helped. I don't want to hurt her myself. It might be more bearable if I'm only watching. Like Judas, hovering on the sidelines.

'Is that your little girl?' asks Mrs Penney, peering through the condensation at Sophie in her car seat. We're talking through a tiny sliver of empty window. Even this is a risk with Sophie. I get out of the car and close the door gently behind me. It's raining. Mrs Penney has an umbrella. I step under the roof of it and notice Ella, hiding behind her mother's legs.

'Yes,' I say, 'that's Sophie. But she's sleeping.'

'She's lovely,' replies Mrs Penney. I don't know how she can tell through the sweaty glass. She's probably just saying this to make me feel better.

'Where's Dr Kunari? I came to see him.'

'He's not here tonight. He's hardly ever here. Between you and me, I think he favours the children in south Belfast. Their parents can afford to go private.'

'Oh,' I say. I turn towards the car, as if to leave.

Mrs Penney reaches for my elbow and steers me back under her umbrella. 'Can I help?' she asks, and I wonder if she wants to kiss me. If this was a movie and a lady was standing in the rain, asking if she could help a man, it would definitely mean kissing. But she is a married woman and this is not a movie, and Ella is peeping round her mother's waist, grinning out from under the hood of her anorak.

'The group's here to help, Jonathan,' Mrs Penney says. 'I know it's hard work being the parent of an Unfortunate Child but we're here for you . . . if you want us to be. You have to want the help, though.'

'I need help,' I say.

Mrs Penney leans towards me. Her arms go up at the side as if she's about to embrace me. I step back.

'You can't help me,' I say firmly. 'None of you can. Your children aren't unfortunate. They're just challenging or a bit odd . . . or really gifted.' I look directly at Ella when I say this. 'Sophie is actually unfortunate. She's probably going to hurt people, I mean really hurt people. She won't be able to stop herself. You can't help me with her. It'd be too much of a risk.'

'Look, Jonathan,' says Mrs Penney, 'I could take you into that room right now and ask each of those parents to tell you how awful their children are and it wouldn't take very much to get the stories out of them. The tantrums. The violent rages. It's not easy being an Unfortunate Child. That little girl who turns into a boat, well, her parents don't talk about it very often, but when she was five she got so mad about not being normal, she tried to drown her baby brother in the paddling pool. And the one who sees the future in liquid surfaces, he used to be so mean, he'd go around telling old people they were going to die soon, told them he'd seen it in a puddle or some such crap. Completely made up. He was just a vindictive wee bastard—'

I interrupt her mid-flow: 'Yes,' I say, 'I hear you, but those kids aren't wired to be evil. They're just good kids stuck in weird situations, trying to work out who they are. Sophie's actually, well, maybe dangerous.'

'Oh, you think there aren't dangerous Unfortunate Children?' she says, her voice getting high and twitchetty. 'You think this is just a little club for parents of kids who are a bit odd? I wish. You just turned up on a good night. You missed the parents of the teenager who sets things on fire every time he gets horny. Unfortunately for you, they were preoccupied with their other son. He's in the burns unit at the minute. As is their next-door neighbour's daughter and their son's geography teacher. Oh, and Lois the daytime vampire. She can't be left alone at night, so her parents weren't there either. And, of course, we don't even talk about Simon any more, not since they locked him up for sneezing acid on the school bus. All those beautiful little baby faces marked for life. There's not much they can do for an acid burn even now, with all the advances in plastic surgery. No, Jonathan, we have no truly "unfortunate" children here. Nobody's as badly off as you.'

'Oh,' I say. 'I didn't know. I honestly thought Sophie was the only one who could really hurt people.'

'All children hurt people, Jonathan,' says Mrs Penney. Her voice has lost the spiteful edge. She just sounds defeated now. 'Mostly they hurt their parents. You can't protect Sophie for ever. None of us can.'

'I know. But I have to try.'

'Look, you know where we are if you want our help, but we can't force you. You're always welcome here.' She sounds weary, as if this is a conversation she's had before, many times, in this same car park. I wonder if there have been other parents too scared to hang around, parents with children as messed up as Sophie. People who might be even worse off than we are.

'Thanks,' I say. 'I really appreciate that.'

She turns away from me, taking the umbrella with her as she steps into the darkness. The rain is drumming on my head. It seeps through my pullover and down the back of my collar. I have never, in all my empty life, felt quite so lonely. I want to say something to her and can only manage a strangled 'Goodbye.' She doesn't hear me through the rain, or perhaps she hears and chooses not to respond. The thing I want to say is 'Pray for us,' but I don't know if I believe in prayer or the point of it when nothing can be fixed.

Ella doesn't follow her mother immediately. She stands on the puddling tarmac smiling up at me. Her face is a kind of moon, glowing beneath the shadow of her anorak hood. She is such a thing to look at. It's impossible not to stare. She holds her hand out. The rain collects in the cup of her palm. I stretch my own hand to meet hers. Our hands clasp. Hers is so much warmer than mine, so much smaller.

'It'll be all right,' Ella says, and almost immediately she's gone.

The place where she touched me is now warm. I feel the life of her go shooting up my arms and over my chest, into my mouth and lungs, like hot whiskey heat. It enters my heart. It enters my head. It will be all right, I think. I wonder if this is how a prayer is answered. 'It will be all right,' I tell myself, as I drive home and put Sophie to bed and later go to bed myself and rise for work the next morning to sit at my desk, knowing something must soon be done about the child.

A decision must be made. In some strange way, it has made everything both better and worse to know Sophie is not the only one. It is comforting to think of other children capable of instigating evil. Comforting in the sickest sense. It also makes my daughter more real. This is not my imagination ticking into overdrive. Not some latent neurosis kicking in late. Other parents, right here in Belfast, are dealing with their Unfortunate Children, decisively, brutally, with cold objectivity, for the sake of protecting others. I must take my situation in hand. I must be cold, stiff-lipped, equally objective. I can't delay for much longer.

At the surgery, my first patient of the day is Samuel Agnew. I'm not expecting this. I'm not prepared for the questions he has come to ask.

17

Confession

THE DOOR IS knocked.

'Come in,' says Jonathan.

The door does not open. The door is knocked again. *Tat.*
Tat. Tat.

'Come in,' says Jonathan, louder this time. He stops writing
and lays his pen on top of his notepad. The door remains closed.
The door is knocked a third time and then, in quick succession,
a fourth and fifth.

It is probably an elderly patient, most likely an old man with
an improperly fitted hearing aid. They are the worst when it
comes to knocking. Behold, I stand at the door and knock and
knock and never bloody well come in, thinks Jonathan, and
smiles a little at his own wit. He reminds himself, as he does
every time the not-opening-the-door thing happens, that he
must ask the lady receptionists to make a sign. 'Please enter' or
'The doctor is in' or 'STOP HAMMERING ON MY DOOR
AND BLOODY WELL OPEN IT YOURSELF.' He will ask
for the sign to be entirely written in bold-as-bullet capital letters
so the short-sighted ones can't cite blindness as an excuse. He's
reasonably sure it won't make any difference: the old people will

still stand there knocking cautiously. But making a sign will give the lady receptionists something to do.

They are always on at him for fresh pictures of Sophie. At first he'd enjoyed the attention. Now they make him feel inadequate with their questions.

'Isn't she a bit small for her age?'

'Is she not sleeping through the night yet?'

'You'd need to be giving her supplements, seeing as she's not getting the breast.'

He tries to avoid the lady receptionists. but there are so many of them, it's like attempting to avoid air. They keep demanding to see Sophie, as if they have some kind of right to her.

'Why don't you bring her in to the surgery, Dr Murray?'

'Jesus, the child'll be married before we've clapped eyes on her.'

'Do you think we're going to eat her or something?'

'Yes,' he wants to say, 'yes, I think you will eat my daughter alive, you harpy bitches. That is, if Sophie doesn't go for you first.'

They don't know what they're asking of him. They can't possibly understand the implications.

The door is knocked again, so violently that Jonathan's coat, hanging on its hook, slips off and crumples on the floor. He can't ignore the pounding any longer. As he crosses the floor and reaches for the door handle, he is cheered by the realization that talk of a sign will give him something to say to the lady receptionists. Today they will discuss colours, fonts and paper choices. Sophie won't even come into their conversation. The relief of this is mighty. He will insist that the sign is laminated. The lady receptionists are particularly fond of laminating things.

Jonathan opens his door. He braces himself for an elderly man. They have their own particular smell and way of entering a quiet space. He already has his old-people's voice on. It is louder and sharper: more like a hammer than a spade. He opens the door away from himself and steps back to accommodate his visitor.

'Please come in,' he says, with a grand sweep of his hand. Once again, he feels like a character in a BBC period drama: an elderly vicar from Austen or Dickens. The patient doesn't move. He must be older than Jonathan has imagined. Perhaps he's deaf or blind or muddled with dementia. Any number of illnesses will make a statue of a human being. The man in the corridor is younger than Jonathan has expected. He knows this man. His name is either William or Samuel, something dry and of the East. Samuel. Sammy Agnew. The sight of him makes Jonathan's stomach drop, not like nausea, more like fear.

'Oh, it's you,' he says, no need for the old-people's voice now. 'You'd better come in.'

Sammy Agnew is standing in the corridor. His fist is raised, ready to begin another assault on the door. He pockets his hand quickly. It is less than a month since Jonathan last saw him but the change is profound. Sammy has aged a decade in a matter of weeks. There are lines around his eyes and mouth now: deep, well-etched folds, like the wrinkles in a paper bag. His pullover is crumpled, his trainers filthy. His chin is frosted with a three-day stubble, white and grey to match the unkempt thatch of his hair. He is slouching, shoulders hunched above his neck, like a man who is bracing himself against the cold. He enters Jonathan's room and wilts into the nearest chair.

'You look like I feel, Doctor,' he says.

This is hardly a compliment. Sammy looks like shit stirred. Instinctively Jonathan raises a hand to his collar, straightens his tie and slicks the fly-away ends of his hair back into place. He knows he's not looking his best today – he's hardly slept all week – but he hadn't thought the patients would notice. They rarely ask after him, and even when they do it's out of politeness, in passing, a kind of introduction to their own ill-health. They say, 'How's yourself, Dr Murray?' and he says, 'Not too bad. What brings you in today?' and off they go with their aches and ulcers, their fungal foot infections and croup. They are not interested in the doctor. They probably wouldn't notice if his arms fell off, as long as it didn't impact his ability to write prescriptions for antibiotics and hydrocortisone cream. It is rare for a patient to look him in the eye. But here's Sammy, giving him nothing but the big beady eye and a running commentary on how he's looking less than A-star.

'I'm fine, Mr Agnew,' Jonathan snaps. 'I take it you're not feeling so good yourself.'

'No, Doctor. I'm feeling rough as.'

'Is it the same thing as before?'

'Yes. It's worse now, though. It's all the time now. I feel like death when I get up in the morning and I feel like death warmed up when I go to bed. It's playing on me constantly.'

'The anxiety?'

'Anxiety, worry, fear, call it whatever you want, Dr Murray. Half the time I feel like there's no point going on.'

'Would you say you were depressed, Sammy?'

'Well, I'm not sitting round the house crying and getting on, if that's what you mean.'

'There's other symptoms you might have. People with depression don't necessarily cry at all. Are you more tired than usual? Anxious? Off your sleep or your food? Lost your libido?'

'Libido?'

'Sex, Sammy. Are you not as interested in sex as you used to be?'

'Aye, Doctor, I'm not. But that's more to do with my wife putting on the weight than anything else. I'd say yes, definitely yes, to all them other things, though, the not sleeping or eating and such. I'm not feeling myself at the minute. Not at all.'

'Would you say you ever have suicidal thoughts?'

'Jesus, no, Doctor. That's a thing to be asking anyone.'

'Sorry, it's not meant to be offensive. I just have to ask. It helps me to understand how bad your depression is.'

'It's not that bad. I'd never seriously think about doing myself in.'

'Do you never feel really down, Sammy, or wonder how you'll make it to the end of the day?'

'Well, when you put it like that, sometimes I do feel a wee bit desperate. Like the walls are coming in.'

'Is there anything that triggers these feelings?'

'Uch, it's usually when I'm thinking about my oldest lad and the mess he's got himself into, and all the stuff I done when I was his age. Well, I know it's my fault that our Mark's the way he is. That's some weight to be carrying round with you. If I let myself dwell on it for too long I sometimes get to thinking it'd be easier if I wasn't around any more.'

'Easier for who, Sammy?'

'The wife, the weans, myself, half the East. Most everybody in Belfast would be better off without Sammy Agnew.'

Once again, Jonathan is struck by how obvious this statement is, like a line lifted from a blockbuster movie. He can picture Tom Hanks or one of those other sad-sack A-listers looking straight down the camera as they question whether the world wouldn't be better off without them. There's a Christmas movie, a classic black-and-white number, entirely built around this premise. Jonathan struggles to surface the name of it and can't, and wonders for the hundredth time this year why these people talk the way they do, in cheap slang and clichés, phrases they've lifted from the television. It's as if they've lost their own language. Or grown lazy with it. He doesn't think he can stomach another season of patients talking like LA hustlers or extras from *EastEnders*.

'Of course your family would miss you,' Jonathan says. 'Their world wouldn't be the same without you.' Almost instantly he regrets this, starts replaying his own words. He is just as bad as Sammy. He sounds like the poetry part of a greetings card, the sort of thing women stick on their fridge doors.

The older man is touched, though. He looks as if he might start up the weeping again. Jonathan does a quick desk check for tissues and, yes, there is a box of Kleenex, unopened beside his pen holder. He sees this as a sort of safety net, to be avoided if possible. He isn't good with crying patients. Especially men. He clears his throat and allows his voice to settle into the calm teacher voice he keeps for slightly hysterical patients. When speaking in this voice, he delivers each sentence like a set of operating instructions. Here's how it's going to be. Here's what you're going to do. Everything will be fine.

'Listen, Sammy,' he says, sliding effortlessly into the realm of familiarity, 'you're going to take a deep breath and tell me all about it. Then we're going to work out a plan. Together. So you feel better.'

'It's getting worse, Doctor. I don't think I can ignore it any longer.'

'Well, if the situation's getting worse, we should definitely try to do something about it sooner rather than later. We have some options here.'

'What sort of options?'

'Well, I know you're reluctant to go on the anti-depressants, Sammy. A lot of people are. But it would be a short-term solution, something to get you back on your feet, help you sleep and keep the anxiety at bay. That's one option. Or I can arrange for you to talk to someone professional, a counsellor. Or we can do both. I'd recommend both, to be honest. It wouldn't hurt to talk to somebody about your issues, even if you were already on the tablets.'

'I don't want to see a shrink.'

'Not a shrink, Samuel, a counsellor. Somebody who'd help you work through the things that are bothering you so much.'

'I don't want to talk to a stranger.'

'So, I'll just write you a prescription, then?'

'Naw, I don't want drugs either. I came here to talk to you.'

'I'm not a counsellor, Sammy. I'm just a GP. You'd be better off talking to someone who's actually trained in that kind of thing. I can arrange it for you.'

'No, Dr Murray. I only want to talk to you.'

'Why me?' asks Jonathan. He doesn't know why he's asking this. He doesn't particularly want to hear the answer. He knows it will be ugly. But his mouth is raising the question before his head has the sense to stop it.

'Because you're in the same boat as me,' says Sammy. 'I could tell the first time I clapped eyes on you. You're just as shit-scared as I am. Just as down.'

'Don't be ridiculous,' replies Jonathan. But there's very little point in trying to argue with the older man. His hands are stuttering all over his desk, straining to hold their itch still. He picks up a pen. Puts it down. Picks up his notepad and turns it sideways. He is sweating. He can feel the wet of it pooling at the base of his spine, gathering in great greasy slicks across his forehead. He is sweating like a stuck pig. He is just as messed up as Sammy Agnew, just as down.

He thinks about disappearing all the time. In his head he calls it disappearing but he could just as easily be saying, 'The world would be much better off without me.' It's only snobbery that has him baulking at the cliché. He pushes his chair away from his desk. There is a foot or more of empty space between his knees and the edge of the desk now. He crosses his legs at the knee, rests his elbows on his thighs and cradles his entire head in the cup of his hands. Like a small boy trying to fold into himself. Out of the corner of his eye he can see the unopened box of Kleenex. It's good to know it's still there, if needed.

'You're right,' he says. 'I'm not fine either.'

Sammy gets up from his chair, crosses the room in two clumpy strides, and locks the door. He locks them both in. Locks everyone else out. Jonathan isn't supposed to lock doors when he's with a patient. For his own safety. For their protection. He can see the situation from both sides but the door is locked now and there's not much he can do about it without causing a scene. Sammy drags his chair across the room so they will be looking directly at each other, like two people sitting in a café, if they didn't have a table between them. He sits down heavily.

'Talk,' he says. 'I'm listening.'

'You first,' says Jonathan. He feels he must insist upon this. He is the professional, after all. Technically he is still sitting behind a desk.

Sammy tells his story. Before beginning, he decides not to hold back any part, even the ugliest bits and those that may not be relevant to the telling: the way he sometimes has to think about your woman who does the TV weather when he's giving it to his wife. The bitter relief of putting two children on the P&O ferry, floating them off to the mainland and knowing they wouldn't be coming back. The time wee Mark caught him in the garage, angering his fists against an old tyre, pretending it was that young lad from the Falls, the one who got the promotion over him. And how, when the boy had asked, 'What are you doing to that tyre, Dad?' he'd replied, 'Stopping myself hurting someone, son.' He'd thought the child was too young to remember the way his face went like an animal's when the rage was on him. But maybe the boy had remembered. Maybe something in that exact moment had turned him. Or maybe the change could not be placed so precisely: point of conversion timed and dated like a born-again Christian. Maybe there was no way of knowing exactly when a good thing went bad.

Sammy Agnew's story begins: 'There's this thing inside me that wants to ruin people.' Jonathan has heard the same story before, with variations. There are dozens of men in East Belfast who do not know what to do with their anger. They are red in the face with it and often drunk. They are occasionally hysterical. Sometimes he suggests counselling or some sort of talking group. Mostly he knows that rage so deep cannot be rooted out with words. 'Try running,' he says. 'Lift weights. Join a boxing club.' Anger can't be exorcized, but sometimes you can wear out the force of it.

Then Sammy is telling him about Mark: his son, the Fire Starter. Jonathan hasn't heard this version of the old story before. Most of the men he listens to are doubled over with guilt and sore regret. They're looking for anti-depressants or pills to knock them out at night. They still have dreams about the vile things they did back in the seventies and eighties. They know they're not exactly victims. But you try telling that to a night terror. You try reasoning with a panic attack. They're only after an opportunity to confess, to shove the guilt up their throat and into somebody else's ears. This is what passes for relief in the East.

They won't talk to priests, they can't trust the police, and they wouldn't, for a minute, consider burdening their women. So, the doctor it is, because there's that promise all doctors have to make, where everything a patient says is between the pair of you and the four white walls. Before they start talking they always ask, 'You can't tell no one what I say, sure you can't?' Afterwards they feel less heavy, less monstrous, but only for an hour or two. Only till the next time they catch sight of themselves reflected in a shop window and remember that they are still, despite all their confessing, the same men with the same filthy hands.

Jonathan knows these men. He sees at least one a week. He listens to their ugly stories. They follow a kind of pattern. Guns. Bombs. Beatings. Fear. Long 'holidays' inside, or over on the mainland. The air in his surgery grows thicker each time one enters and, when they leave, he has a desire to wash his hands hard with surgical soap, like you would after touching something rotten.

Sammy Agnew's story is different. He skims over the guns, the bombs and the beatings with sticks. He isn't here to talk about the distant past. He's here to offload his son. To try to talk himself into a happy ending. Maybe, if Mark plays his cards right, if this is the end of the fires, and there's no more trouble out of him, maybe, just maybe, the boy will be OK. Jonathan wants to stop him mid-sentence. He wants to say, 'Wise up, mate. Your son's a psychopath. He wants locking up. This story will not have a happy ending,' but he holds his thoughts close and lets him finish. It's important not to interrupt. They teach you that in Clinical Skills. Sammy Agnew's story does not end so much as fade out. 'I don't know what to do now,' he says, and he's done. He sits back in his chair, hands clasped behind his neck so his elbows make wings. He takes a deep breath and slows it out. He looks exhausted.

Jonathan doesn't know what Sammy should do either. He knows he should. He should be lifting the phone and dialling 999 for this is nothing if not a proper emergency. As a doctor he has made promises to protect the general public from harm. Illness. Infection. Lunatic elements with bomb-making capacities. He is a responsible man. Answers are supposed to come easily to him. But since Sophie they haven't. He can't see past the end of his own problems. He doesn't care as much as he should, and at other times he cares far too much. If anything, it is comforting to hear someone whose life is even more impossible than his own. He is inclined to keep Sammy Agnew's story at the back of his mind, something to revisit every time he looks at Sophie and thinks, Things couldn't get any worse.

'You should probably go to the police,' he says. But he doesn't force the point. He says it like he could just as easily be saying, 'You should probably bring a jacket for later.' His voice is without edge or any kind of authority. He's in no position to advocate hard and set rules. Not when he's already considered locking his daughter into a cupboard, not when he's planning the most efficient way to slice her up. Rules are for simple men, not for the fathers of Unfortunate Children.

'You're right,' says Sammy Agnew. 'I *should* probably go to the police.'

'Sooner, rather than later.'

'Give me a week, Doctor. To get everything sorted out.'

'Tomorrow, Sammy. Before anyone gets hurt.'

'Two days,' says Agnew, splitting the difference, like they're haggling over a used car.

'Two days, absolute max. If you've not done it by then, I'll be phoning the police myself.'

'I have to be the one who makes the call. You understand that, don't you? I'm his da.'

Jonathan understands. It's different for fathers. He agrees not to go to the police. He makes Sammy Agnew promise to phone him as soon as he's made the call. He has no intention of calling the authorities himself, even if his patient never does. When he tries to imagine Mark planting bombs and shooting people in the street it isn't real to him. It's a montage lifted from old action movies and television dramas. Dead people. Blood. Shattered glass and smoke rising, like dry-ice clouds. The image of it engenders no sense of urgency, no gut tug of responsibility. His sympathy has grown blunt worrying about Sophie. He can't see any situation as sharply as his own. He isn't fit to be a doctor right now, but no one else seems to have noticed.

The phone on his desk flashes red and begins to ring. It's one of the lady receptionists. The patients are backing up in the waiting room. They're wondering how long he's going to be. He's already been twenty minutes with Sammy and he can't see himself finished before lunchtime.

'I have a migraine,' he says, to the lady receptionist (Ciara? Claire? Cathy? Definitely something beginning with a C, though it could just as easily be an L).

She sighs. 'Another, Dr Murray? That's three in the last two weeks. Maybe you should see a doctor.'

She's trying to be funny or, perhaps, cheeky. He can never tell when the lady receptionists are insulting him. He needs to take a firm line with this one. She's far too brassy with the doctors and she doesn't wear the uniform correctly. He uses his no-nonsense voice: the voice he keeps for telesales marketers and taxi drivers.

'Tell the patients I'm taken ill and reschedule them for tomorrow, Cathy,' he says.

She doesn't correct him so Jonathan assumes she's either Cathy or too cowed by the sharp edge in his voice to admit she's actually Claire or Ciara. He puts the phone down before she has a chance to take the conversation any further. He turns back to Sammy, apologizing for the interruption.

'Your turn, Doc,' says the older man, folding his arms and nodding ever so slightly, like you would with a hesitant child.

Jonathan tells his story then. He keeps all the details in, but censors the part where he's seduced by Sophie's mother. He is not comfortable talking about sex in the first person. 'One thing led to another and then she was pregnant,' he says. He can't believe how easy it is to skate across such complex truths.

Words are elastic. He tells the whole sorry mess from his

never-there parents right through to the recent floods, but he doesn't mention that he's planning to cut out the child's tongue with a scalpel. That's not happened yet. No need to include something that may never take place, he tells himself, excusing his own censorship. He doesn't want Sammy Agnew to think him a beast. It's one thing admitting to a psychopathic child, another thing entirely confessing your own cruel intentions. He is too ashamed to say this thing he's already decided to do.

When he's finished there is a loud silence in the room. The air is funeral heavy. Both men sit back in their chairs and eyeball each other.

'That's some story,' says Sammy Agnew.

'It's a hundred per cent true,' says Jonathan.

'I believe you.'

'You don't have to humour me, Sammy. I know it sounds ridiculous. Nobody believes in all that supernatural crap nowadays. Most people don't even believe in God.'

'There's plenty of people in the East believe in your so-called supernatural crap: ghosts and God and weans with powers nobody really understands. I've never heard them called Unfortunate Children before but, I guarantee you, if you go down any of them wee streets off the Albertbridge Road, or round Orangefield direction, and stop the auld ones and ask, "Did you ever hear tell of wee ones with special powers?" they'd all have a story for you. Every single one of them.'

'You're joking.'

'Swear to God. Sure, wasn't there a wee lad in the year above me that could make people fall asleep just by looking at them hard? Sort of staring and squinting at the same time. And my ma used to tell us about a friend of hers who'd a baby come out already speaking German. Fluent it was, before it was even two hours old, and, by the time it was walking, it could make a fair stab at French and Spanish too, though there wasn't a one on the

Cregagh Road could tell if it was pronouncing the words right. Oh, and there was a wee girl – a real bad egg – in the year above my sister, who used to make a weird noise, rubbing her hands together like a cricket does with its knees, and if you didn't get the hands over your ears quick sharp, you'd not be able to catch your breath. It was like suffocating. I swear she actually killed a wee lad with asthma. She done her hand-rubbing thing on him so much he had a massive asthma attack and died in the back of an ambulance. Of course, they never proved nothing, but all of us knew about her and what she could do with her wee bony hands. Naw, Dr Murray, you haven't shocked me at all with your talk of Unfortunate Children. Though, I have to say, I've not heard of Sirens in the East before.'

'And why did I never hear about any of this before Sophie?' asks Jonathan.

'Cos – no harm intended – Doctor, you're too posh to have known what was going on at the other end of the road.'

Jonathan feels as if he should apologize for his own ignorance. If Sammy Agnew's to be believed, the Unfortunate Children are no new phenomenon in East Belfast. He fully understands the upper-class horror of scandal. Any Unfortunate Child blessed with a home on the Upper Newtownards Road would have been closeted away like a pregnant teenager: denied, disowned, kept like a dirty little secret in the back bedroom. What Jonathan can't understand is how anybody living in a terraced house could keep such a thing from their neighbours. Surely the word of it would spread up the little streets and down, quick as summer flu.

'Why did the papers never get the hold of this?' he asks, but he could just as easily be asking, 'What else do I not know about?'

'Ah, now, if there's one thing the people of the East are good at, it's holding a secret close. All them wee houses jammed together arse to elbow, you can't so much as turn in bed for letting your neighbours know it. Everybody knows everything. But the ranks are tight and they're good at keeping their business to themselves. If the people of the East don't want you to know what's going on, there's no way in hell you're ever going to know. It's hard work and secrets keep this place together.'

'I suppose it's good to share your problems with your neighbours,' Jonathan says. He has a brief mental image of introducing Sophie to the two old bitches across the road. He sees himself holding the child under their noses, like a kind of sacrificial lamb. He can't imagine them particularly pleased to meet her. He can't see how they could do anything but make matters worse.

'They do say a problem shared is a problem halved,' says Sammy Agnew.

'That may be true when your baby speaks German or comes out with wings, but it's not the same when she's an actual threat. I don't think I could tell anyone about Sophie. It wouldn't help. She's different from all those other children. She could actually hurt people.'

'Or she might be completely fine, Doctor. It's fifty–fifty, isn't it? She could take after you just as easily as her mammy.'

Fifty–fifty, thinks Jonathan, and thinks of all the parents he's encountered on ICU wards and special-care baby units: the sort of people who are encouraged to take their bad news sitting down. 'Fifty–fifty chance of survival, or recovery, or making it through the next few hours.' He's said the words himself many, many times. Also 'thirty per cent chance' and 'ten per cent' and, at least a handful of times, 'no chance at all', which is a sentence you have to practise saying over and over, before you get it right. You cannot hesitate with 'no chance at all'. Neither can you cry. You must be a brick. 'Fifty–fifty' is almost positive. It's so far from 'no chance at all', Jonathan's known parents who'd cut their own arms off to be offered odds so high. He is, in a sense, lucky. He should be seeing his glass half full. He should be hoping for the best.

'You're right,' he says. 'She's fifty per cent mine. She might be entirely human . . . or she might not.'

'No telling at this stage. So, there's no point worrying about something that may never happen.'

'I just wish there was something I could do to influence the odds.'

'Uch now, son. Maybe you already have: nature versus nurture and all that. I'm a big believer in training a child up, leading them down the right path.'

Jonathan resists the urge to say, 'And how's that gone with your Mark? Did you always want a balaclava-wearing lunatic for a son, or was it more of a recent aspiration?' Instead he says, 'I don't really go in for that nurture thing myself, Sammy. You are the way you are, regardless of what anybody does to you.'

'So, Mark would have turned out bad no matter how we brought him up?'

'I think so, Sammy. I've no scientific proof of it but I've seen it over and over again. Good people sometimes raise bad kids. There's nothing much you can do if you've got an evil child on your hands. Not that I'm implying your son is evil.'

'Imply away, mate. You've got to have something of the dark side about you to plan the kind of stuff he's dreamt up this summer.'

'It works the other way too, Sammy. I've seen kids turn out decent even though they've been treated really badly. Take myself, for example. My parents didn't love me. They made it quite clear they didn't even want me and yet here I am, a fully functional human being, a doctor, a father, a reasonably decent man.'

Every word of this is a lie. Jonathan knows he is not a fully functional human being. He is a poor doctor, a conflicted father: a reasonably pathetic specimen of manhood. He has always believed himself to be half a person: the poor product of bad parenting and upper-class neglect. But he can't admit this in front of Sammy Agnew. It's not what the older man needs to hear. He wants Agnew to believe that he's not to blame for the badness in his son. No heavy hand or lack of discipline could have made any difference to how the boy has turned out. Jonathan wants him to feel as if he's not responsible for Mark or, at the very least, less responsible.

'It's scientifically proven,' he says. 'I could show you an article in the *BMJ* if you don't believe me, tests they've done on monkeys and dolphins to show it's the same in animals as humans. People don't change, no matter how much you try to influence them. If you're born evil, you'll always be like that. Born nice, you'll basically always be a decent human being, no matter what life throws at you.'

'Really?' asks Sammy. 'Are you sure?'

'Don't take my word for it. It's in the *British Medical Journal*. Brand-new case study, completed last year. No matter how much you try to lead a person, at the end of the day they can only ever be who they actually are.'

'Nature, rather than nurture.'

'Exactly, Sammy.'

'So, I'm not to blame for how our Mark's turned out?'

'I don't believe you are.'

'I still feel guilty, though.'

'I understand completely, but you've to try to let it go. Guilt like that'll eat you up. You'll be no help to the boy in this state.'

'I'll try. No guarantees, though. And what about you? If your nature-over-nurture thing's true, you're in deep shit with that wee lassie of yours. You could be sitting on a time-bomb.'

'I know, Sammy.'

'What are you for doing with her, Doctor?'

'I have absolutely no idea.'

Of course this is another of Jonathan's lies. Each lie is easier to tell than the last. But this is the biggest and boldest one of all. Jonathan knows exactly what he's going to do about Sophie. He's not prepared to take any chances with her. He has already brought home everything he needs from the surgery: scalpels, gauze, anaesthetic, sterile needles, sewing thread. He has stored it all at the back of his underwear drawer where Christine shouldn't be looking. He is making plans for the weekend. He is going to cut her tongue out.

He isn't about to tell Sammy this. He's not even admitting it to himself.

18

The Last Supper

I T IS EARLY evening in the East. The sky is sliding down in sheets.

Ballyhackamore is a river banked by coffee shops and restaurants, Chinese takeaways, chippies and pizza places. At one end of the street the restaurants are fancy-name pricey. At the other, giant slices of pepperoni dance the Macarena while burgers with wide-mouthed grins haunt the restaurant windows, like effigies of obscure saints. People come here to eat and to be seen eating. They call it 'Ballysnackamore' and park their cars two deep at weekends. They do not give a moment's damn for the residents who also have cars in need of parking. They come all the way from Dundonald, and even Newtownards, for breakfast with the in-laws, brunch and afternoon coffee, for overpriced cocktails in retro glasses, late dinners, long nights, and drinking themselves sideways with the lads from the rugby club.

They have a tendency to overdress. The women are fleshy and frocked in the kind of clothes you'd wear to a wedding if only invited to the evening do. They are highly heeled and, for the most part, orange in both hue and political outlook. The men wear sports jackets and tieless shirts, unbuttoned to reveal small triangles of tongue-coloured flesh tucked just beneath the chin. They hope the women will notice this brief flash of naked-ness and wish to investigate further. The women don't. Unless they've been drinking. They have often been drinking: wine on week nights, spirits at the weekend. When they speak they are shrill as morning birds. The sound of them all together in a room is enough to set your teeth on edge or force you outside with the smokers. Even if you don't smoke, even if you never have, it is a relief to be outdoors in the cold just-beginning rain, finally capable of hearing where one sentence ends and the next begins.

No one is standing outside today. Even the smokers are abstaining. The rain is coming down in tides. People dash from their cars to the coffee shops and back, dragging their partners and children behind them. They group beneath golf umbrellas and slouch down the street like hunchbacked turtles. One foot, one arm or straggling child always escapes the brolly's edge and brings the wetness inside, leaving sad little perspiration marks on the floors and seats. Afterwards the shape of their left-behind dampness is a loose figure eight from where their buttocks have pressed softly in. Drowned umbrellas wilt beside every door, like tiny defeated trees. Every other window is sweated up: body heat frosting against cold glass. The waitresses are even more strained than usual.

Sammy doesn't care about the rain this afternoon. He's hardly even aware of it sleeking against his windscreen. The traffic is murder, though. He can't help but notice it huffing to front and rear. He drives halfway through Ballyhack before he finds a free spot outside the fruit shop, three minutes' walk from his favour-ite Chinese. Three minutes' walk through the pissing rain.

Sammy isn't wearing a coat today. He's stopped thinking about practicalities or how he must look to other people. He's wearing tracksuit bottoms and a church pullover, sandals with gym socks whiting between the straps. Pamela would be mortified if she could see the cut of him in his sandals. She wouldn't stand beside him in the street. But Pamela isn't here. Sammy knows he has to face this day alone. As he fumbles with the car locks the rain creeps down the collar of his shirt, plastering the fabric to his back. He is uncomfortable in his dampness. The rain is leaking into his sandals. It's sweating between his toes. The wool of his jumper is beginning to itch. It is already autumn-cold in Belfast, colder still in this rain. But Sammy doesn't complain.

Sammy has recently come to accept even the smallest irritations – hiccups, paper cuts, constipation and such – as a form of penance. In light of past and current sins he sees himself deserving of no good thing. No ease or get-out-of-jail-free card. No avoiding whatever discomfort might come his way. Be it life inside, a quick bullet through the kneecap, or just a soggy V-neck, he must endure the annoyance for it's nothing more than he deserves. He won't allow himself the luxury of complaint. He will not even sigh. He drags the cuffs of his now-damp sweater over his shivering hands and steps into the traffic.

This is to be his last decent meal. It might even be his final time in the rain for a good long while. He doesn't know if they'll allow him outside. In the movies they do. They walk the prisoners round and round sun-drenched yards in orange boiler suits. They sometimes let them play basketball. But the movies are all set in America. It's probably different here. Here, there is rarely any sun and not much interest in basketball, and they couldn't be dressing prisoners in head-to-toe orange. The other side would quickly cry, 'Human-rights violation,' and ask for their own boiler suits in jolly racing green. Sammy has no idea how it will be inside. He's heard rumours, of course, but he's long since stopped believing in things he hasn't seen himself.

A bell tinkles above the door as he walks into the Chinese restaurant. The rain comes in with him, leaving a scummy puddle on the lino. Mr Chang pops up from behind the till as if he's been hunkering on the floor, beneath the counter, just waiting for a customer to arrive. He is always down there, waiting, except on Saturday nights when the door can hardly close for swinging open.

'Sammy, my friend, how are you keeping?' he asks, his accent pure East Belfast, with inflection in all the wrong places.

'I'm fine, Mr Chang,' he says, 'and yourself?'

'Grand so.'

Sammy has decided to have a last meal. He's not particularly hungry. He hasn't been able to work up a good hunger in weeks. He nibbles at toast and biscuits, leaving cups of cold tea half drunk and skinning on the coffee-table. He is only ever ravenous in the middle of the night when the weight of everything keeps him from sleeping. Then, he sneaks down to the kitchen and eats dry crackers or bran flakes by the handful. It all tastes like cardboard but he won't allow himself to enjoy his food, even when he's bingeing. Today is different. Today's dinner will be the meal Sammy remembers every time he sits down to stodgy porridge or over-boiled potatoes. He'll hold the memory of it against the tasteless days to come for months, years, maybe even decades. He has no idea how long he'll get.

'You will be having the usual, Sammy?' asks Mr Chang.

'Yes. Maybe. Actually, I'm not sure. Let me have a wee look before I decide.' He leans over the counter and scrutinizes the laminated menu, which is Sellotaped next to the till. Chow mein. Sweet and sour. Kung Po chicken. Satay beef. Honey chilli prawns. Which will he miss most when he's reduced to prison stodge and wee parcels from home?

'I'll have beef chow mein, please, sweet and sour chicken Cantonese style, a portion of spring rolls, them duck pancakes you gave us last weekend, and a beef with mushrooms.'

'Fried rice or boiled?'

'Sure, go for the fried rice, Mr Chang, and don't be telling the wife. She has me on the Slimming World these days.'

Mr Chang winks conspiratorially across the counter. Sammy has never seen a Mrs Chang but she is, occasionally, implied.

'Wee portion of prawn crackers, my friend? Little secret not to tell the wife.'

'Aye, why not?'

'Tin of Coke?'

'Bottle, please.'

'You are having party with your friends, Sammy?'

'Naw,' says Sammy, then, glancing down at the enormous list of food scribbled on Mr Chang's notepad, decides it's best to lie. 'Yes,' he says. 'I've the lads coming round to watch the match. The wife's away up to her sister's for the day.'

'When the cat's away, the rats will play.'

'Mice,' says Sammy. 'It's mice, not rats.'

But Mr Chang has already turned away from the counter and is shouting orders to his brother, the younger one, who is never allowed out of the kitchen. Sammy takes a seat in the window and begins flicking through an old car magazine. He keeps turning pages one after another. Their corners are frail and greasy from dozens of similar flickings. Here is a red car. Here is a blue. Here is a car with a roof that comes off, and one that does nought to ninety almost as fast as a jump jet. This is the sort of stuff that interests people, the crap people go mad for. Cars. Money. Drink. Women.

What nonsense. What utter shite it all seems to Sammy today.

Tomorrow he won't have a car. He won't have money or beer or any woman touching him with lust or even fondness. He won't have anything but dry memories and, if he's lucky, the occasional phone call. This should give him some clarity, should sharpen the edge of his thinking. He's not after a moment of epiphany or anything. He'd just like to think that, faced with losing everything, he might have some idea of what's actually important. He's definitely not doing this for love. And it's not guilt propelling him, or even hope. It's some odd notion of duty. I must do this, he thinks. I must try to put things right. This, then, he decides, as he waits for his sweet and sour chicken to cook, is the most important thing. He calls it making amends. It could just as easily be called absolution, but that sounds a bit too papal for Sammy Agnew.

'There you go, Sammy-boy,' says Mr Chang, depositing two carrier bags full of individually boxed meals on the counter.

'Cheers,' says Sammy. 'You look after yourself, Mr Chang.' He presses an extra twenty into the man's hand, just in case this is a never-again scenario. He hopes he hasn't embarrassed him or lorded it over him in some sort of racist way. Jesus, he thinks, as he reaches for his food, your man'll be thinking I'm dying or something, giving him a twenty-quid tip, and it not even Christmas.

He lifts the bags from the counter without looking at Mr Chang directly. They are slippy with hot-food sweat, the prawn crackers already ghosting inside their translucent plastic sack. He balances the bags, one in each hand. They lump awkwardly against his legs so he has to swagger like an old-fashioned gun-slinger. Mr Chang laughs, just a little, not unkindly. Sammy keeps his eyes on the floor, on his sandals, on the pale inch of skin cuffing between his socks and tracksuit bottoms. He is just a hair's breadth from tears, the first dull throb of them already gathering at the base of his nose. He tips his forehead towards the counter, mumbles something that could be 'Night' or 'Thanks for everything' or 'Maybe I'll never see you again' and backs out the door into the rain.

'Enjoy!' shouts Mr Chang, as the door settles behind Sammy. Sammy knows he isn't going to enjoy a single mouthful of his

257

food but he'll drive it all the way home. He sets it on the floor of the passenger side and adjusts the air-conditioning so it is blasting hot, hot heat directly at his ankles. He learnt this trick from Pamela, who learnt it from a girl in college. Perhaps she got it from an older brother or cousin. Nothing is actually learnt in this place, only inherited. He does the hot air on all his takeaways now: everything except pizzas, which are too big to fit on the floor. It is the sort of habit that doesn't break even in a crisis. After a mile or so his wet socks start steaming. Then his feet grow uncomfortably warm. By the time he reaches the ring road his toes have begun to roast, curling instinctively away from the heat. This, too, he bears, although it would be easy enough to adjust the air-conditioning. It is like a little needle poking away at the wrong in him. Never letting him be. There is more of this to come.

At the end of his street the steering wheel tries to turn against him. His head says home but his arms are drawn south: to Lisburn, to Dublin, then the ocean, which could easily swallow him whole. His hands, gripping the wheel, are all knuckles, white-capped with the pressure. His eyes itch. His throat is dry. No part of him wishes to go home. Sammy's body is bracing itself for something painful, something like a punch. He can already feel the stiffness of it running up his spine and across his shoulders. If he raises a hand to his neck he can touch it. It is tight and coiled like muscle that has lumped into bone. The thought of stepping through his own front door makes him feel sick, but he goes home anyway. His head wins. His head is thumping with guilt, with the migraine-sharp need to make amends. It's a kind of magnet drawing him off the ring road, up the hill and home to certain ruin.

Mark isn't in tonight. Thursday is the only evening he leaves the house. Sammy has no idea where he goes. Pamela has even less notion. Every Thursday, for the last two years, the boy's come thundering down the stairs at six fifteen and left the house without so much as a 'See you later' for his parents sitting, like a pair of stuffed pigeons, on the living-room sofa.

'Where's Mark off to?' Pamela used to ask, as if Sammy might actually know, might be party to the odd chit-chat with his son on the landing.

'Pilates,' he used to say. 'Book group. Prayer meeting. Weight Watchers,' and they'd laugh at the idea of Mark doing normal things with normal people in a community centre or church hall.

'Zumba,' Pamela had once suggested, making Sammy choke on the image of their spade-faced son shaking his booty to a Latin beat. Lukewarm tea had come chortling down his nose, spraying the TV magazines piled on the coffee-table. They'd laughed all the way through the weather forecast and into the ads. Now Sammy doesn't make jokes and Pamela doesn't ask where their son is off to. They barely lift their eyes from the television screen to acknowledge the door closing behind him. Terrorist cell. Brothel. Drug den, Sammy thinks, every time Mark leaves the house. He wonders if Pamela is having similar thoughts. Or worse.

Of course they could try to stop him. They could stand in the doorway, blocking the boy's exit route, to ask and continue asking until Mark gives them some sort of answer. They never do. The truth is, the whole house feels lighter without him. Sometimes they even chance conversation on a Thursday night. Nothing too heavy: news and weather, funny things they've seen on the internet. Memories. There's more room for them when Mark isn't in the house. Sammy is glad he can count on Thursday evenings. None of his plan would be possible with the boy holed up in the attic, listening.

Pamela isn't at home either. Sammy's made sure of it. He's given her his credit card and permission to take the girls out for the night. Drinks. Dinner. More drinks in a different place. 'No special reason, love,' he said, pre-empting her suspicion. 'You just deserve a wee treat.' Pamela hasn't believed him. He isn't the sort of man who does 'no special reason'. He can barely remember to pick up a card on their anniversary and sometimes mixes her birthday up with the children's. He knows she hasn't believed him. There is a particular way her mouth twitches when she's suspicious. He felt the flicker of it, like a moth pressed against his cheek, as she kissed him on the doorstep. Does she think I'm bringing another woman round here tonight? he wonders. Does she think I'm trying to get rid of her? And the answer to this is, maybe she does, which makes Sammy feel dreadful. He wishes he knew how to make things right with Pamela, how to draw a line and start again.

Sammy turns the car into his own street. He's done this a hundred thousand times before but maybe never again. It's a cul-de-sac with all the little houses spun out around an island of carefully mown lawn. When they were younger all three of his children learnt to ride their bikes on this particular patch of grass. Removing the stabilizer wheels he'd watched each of them wobble and sometimes topple over, safe in the knowledge that grass was much more forgiving than the tarmac roads they'd soon be speeding along. Only Mark had not required his assistance, had kicked out at him with trainered feet when he offered a steadying hand. Only Mark had flown on the first attempt, never faltering, never looking back as he sped from the grass to the road and the other streets beyond.

The rain's let up for a bit and the neighbours are out on the grass getting the good of it: Tom, who lives three doors down, and his oldest lad, Caleb. Sammy knows them from coming in and out of the house and sometimes keeping their post when they're not at home. The boy is a tall lick of a kid, seven or possibly eight years old. He is California blond to his father's grey-greased crop. Sammy can see how handsome Caleb will be once he's grown into himself. For now, he carries his arms awkwardly, like he's holding them for a much older boy. He is sometimes shy and at other times driven by that peculiar friendliness found in much-loved children.

The pair of them are playing cricket in matching Liverpool shirts: the boy's kit is bang on season, the older man's a throwback from his student days, sponsor's logo faded from one too many runs through the washing-machine. They're using a proper cricket bat, but the ball is a tennis ball and the stumps an upturned mop bucket. They are laughing like they don't know how lucky they are, how normal, how easy, how everything Sammy has never been with Mark.

He stares at them through the windscreen. He can imagine the boy twenty years from now, married or not married, maybe even bringing his own son home for show-and-tell. He will leave home and do things and come back occasionally, just to visit. His father will always be glad to see him. He can see all this in the way the boy is looking at his father, all eyes and pitched ears, like the older man is something worth learning. Mark has never once looked at Sammy like that. Not even when he gave the child expensive toys.

He slows the car almost to a stop. He's in two minds. He hates his neighbours. He hates their bold joy and their matching shirts, their bloody upturned mop bucket. The future belongs to people like them, people who already have their hands all over it. His foot hovers over the accelerator pedal. He could easily mount the pavement and run them over. Rush. Crush. Crunch. It wouldn't take much effort to destroy them. Only a slight tipping of the ankle. This is how it must be for God every day, he thinks. Every act an act of restraint. Afterwards they wouldn't be laughing. They wouldn't be easy with each other again. It would be a relief of sorts not to have their happiness thrust upon him every time he backs his car out of the drive.

Tom sees him and raises a hand to wave. His own hand is too heavy to return the gesture. It is only good for fists and hitting now. Up comes the old blood, hot and jealous. Up comes the rage. There is a particular way it tastes at the back of his mouth, like last night's wine in a morning throat. Up comes the need to break things crisply, to ruin. Stop, says he to himself, to his hands at the wheel, and his feet on the pedal, to all the thinking bits between. Stop, says he, because in that moment he understands his own son and the feel of this is vile. He turns the wheel away from them, skirts the edge of the grass and pulls up the car outside his own house.

'Hey!' he shouts across the cul-de-sac. 'Hey, Tom! Hey, Caleb!' He even raises a hand to wave.

'Hi!' they shout back, and Sammy feels a certain kind of tenderness towards them. He knows how breakable they are.

He carries his dinner into the kitchen and places it, still steaming, in the fridge. He knows he's not going to eat any of it tonight. The nausea is like a solid wall sitting at the bottom of his throat. He chances a couple of prawn crackers and they come sliding back up on a tide of sick. He shoves them into the bin, gagging at the fried ocean smell as it slicks across his fingers. Tomorrow, after he's gone, Pamela will find his dinner in the fridge. Maybe she'll reheat a portion of the chow mein and wonder why he never touched any of it. She might even see the provision of food as a small act of kindness on his part. Sammy likes to think of himself looking out for her, even after he's gone. He opens the Coke, lets the fizz of it sizzle out, and takes a swig straight from the bottle. The sugar goes screaming to his head. He pops two headache tablets and downs them with a second swig of Coke. He needs to have a clear head. He needs to be sharp. There is so much to do before Mark gets back.

Up the stairs he goes, past his own room, its door lolling open to reveal this morning's bed, yet to be made, the laundry avalanching out of its hamper and the cat curled up, like a tiny Buddha, atop a mountain of mismatched pyjamas and damp towels. He pulls the door to. He can't bear the ordinariness of it: the cat hair, the smell of Pamela's good shampoo wafting out of the en-suite, last night's paperback splayed open and rising, like a tiny tent, from his bedside table.

He stops in the main bathroom to lift bin liners and Marigolds from the cleaning cupboard. He's watched enough *CSI* repeats to know about fingerprints and DNA, not leaving any damp trace of himself at the crime scene. As he eases his hands into the yellow rubber gloves he tries to think of his own house as a crime scene, to imagine how it will look tomorrow morning with police tape running round the drive. The neighbours staring from a distance. He can't. His head keeps catching on the stillness. There isn't a noise in the house tonight. He pauses for a moment on the landing, allows the breath to stick and swell inside his lungs. Now there is no movement at all, not so much as a dry shudder in the entire house. Without Mark, there's no urgency to the place. No pressure.

Sammy keeps climbing, up the back stairs, to the extension where Mark lives. There is a creak on the third and sixth step. He already knows this. Sometimes the sound of ancient floorboards groaning is the only way they know the boy is still alive up there. Mark's bedroom door is closed tightly and, for a moment, Sammy wonders if it might be locked. He hasn't a plan for this. Perhaps he could do something with a hairgrip or a credit card, like they do in the movies. This isn't necessary. The handle turns freely. The door opens and here he is, standing in the middle of his son's bedroom. It's hard to breathe. There's not enough air up here.

Everything is white: the walls, the carpet, the cheap IKEA wardrobe and matching drawers, the sheets on the bed, drawn into neat right angles at every corner, as if freshly made by a

263

hotel chambermaid, the single desk lamp, bowing its tulipy head over the white desk and chair. Sammy has not expected so much whiteness. He looks at his arms, with their yolk-yellow gloves bursting from either end, and his filthy sandals, and he feels awkward in this white, white space. Exposed. Like a coloured creature in the snow.

He begins opening drawers. It isn't difficult to find the things he's looking for: in the wardrobe, carefully hung next to shirts and sweaters, the hoodie from the videos. A plastic mask in the bottom drawer of the desk. Cardboard signs underneath the bed, laid flat beneath a duffel bag, which contains a video camera and tripod. Markers, standing upright in a jam jar, like a huddle of helmeted soldiers awaiting orders. And Mark's laptop, which is sitting right in the middle of his desk, its edges squared against the desk's edges. Two biros are laid neatly on either side of the keyboard, like cutlery cupping the rim of a plate. Sammy throws everything into a bin liner. He doesn't care if things break or bleed into each other. Everything's for the fire anyway.

He begins riffling through drawers and cupboards. He doesn't know what he's looking for: diaries, letters, bomb-making equipment, anything that might hang over Mark when the police arrive. He finds nothing of real interest but tosses every third or fourth item into his bin liner anyway. Just so he feels like he's achieving something. There's no sign of anything that could be a bomb. But, then again, bombs don't look like they used to look in Sammy's day. Clocks. Pipes. Bottles. Nails. Petrol. Actual flames. Nowadays bombs are more like computers. He throws Mark's alarm clock into the bag, fires in his phone charger and computer plug after it. Best to be on the safe side, he thinks. He feels like a blind man, groping around for the way out.

Once finished, he closes the wardrobe door, slides all the

drawers shut and smooths the creases from Mark's bedspread. The room looks untouched. He stands for a final moment in the middle of the floor, surveying the space for left-behind things, like he always does before leaving a holiday rental. After he leaves this room he won't be back. It will be the end of one time and the beginning of another. He tries to summon up the ghost of his rage, but it's gone. His fists refuse to curl. His blood has no heat left in it. Up comes nothing but the need to cry. He pulls the door behind him, drags his bin liner all the way down the stairs and into the backyard.

It's more difficult than he thought to get a fire going. Everything is sodden after a month's worth of rain and the electronics refuse to catch. He piles all Mark's stuff into the barbecue and douses it with lighter fuel. The papers burn off quickly, the fabric and plastics melt and re-form under the heat, but the laptop refuses to burn. It just sits there, singeing around the edges, emitting an acrid grey smoke, which catches at the back of Sammy's throat, like breathed-in hairspray. He pulls the collar of his sweater up over his mouth and, breathing through a woolly filter, goes back in with a canister of petrol.

All of a sudden the barbecue is engulfed in an explosion of hot red flames. The heat causes him to step back, catching his heel on the edge of a planter so he is, for a moment, shocked back into his own skin by the sting of concrete on raw flesh. He sits down on the back doorstep, cradling his heel in his hand until it stops throbbing. The blood has soaked through his sock and on to his fingers. Absent-mindedly he raises his hand to his mouth and sucks the blood off before it has a chance to crust. It tastes like salt and money. Something he shouldn't be putting in his mouth.

At five to ten he rises and calls the police from the hall phone. Mark will be back any second. He's never out later than ten on a Thursday. Sammy has to time his phone call just right. Too early and the police will have him away before he gets a chance to speak to the boy. Too late, and Mark will try to stop him. It's almost dark outside and the fire is down to its last embers, the glow of it a brief orange smudge reflected in the greenhouse windows. As he dials the numbers Sammy can see through the hall to the kitchen, where the sky is like a pint settling in black and golden layers above the garden fence.

It'll be a nice day tomorrow, he thinks, knowing the weather will have little relevance to him now.

'Police,' he says, when the lady asks which emergency service he's after. Then he gives his address and phone number.

'I'd like to hand myself in,' he says, all the time wondering why he doesn't sound like himself, why he's fallen into a filmy way of speaking. 'I'm the man who done those videos, the Fire Starter ones. I want to turn myself in.'

They tell him to stay where he is.

He tries to make a joke of it, says, 'Sure, I'll just put the kettle on and wait till you get here.'

They don't laugh.

They try to keep him talking on the telephone. 'Is there any-one with you? Do you have a weapon? Is there a dog in the house?'

So many questions. They have to keep him on the telephone. It's the closest thing they have to actual handcuffs. If Sammy's here, shooting the breeze with some nice lady telephonist, he can't be making a break for the border. He answers their questions. Why wouldn't he? He's the one handing himself in. It's important that he's seen to be compliant. 'Yes,' and 'No,' and 'I'm not really sure,' and 'Isn't it grand the rain's finally stopped?' until he hears the front door fidget on its hinges and knows Mark's back for the night.

'I have to go,' he says, and hangs up on the operator before she can ask any more inane questions.

He stops the boy in the hall, stands between him and the staircase. He's standing one step up and so, for the first time in years, finds himself looking down on his son. He notices the patch of baldness beginning to bloom in the middle of Mark's hair and, without thinking, reaches a hand to trace the smooth slide of his own crown, naked now, across most of his head. He lets his arm drop. He wants to place a hand on his son's shoulder but he hasn't the energy left for kindness.

'I've sorted it out, son,' he says. 'I've told them it was me. They'll believe me. I've got history. They never sent me away before. I was part of the deal. You know that, don't you?'

Mark doesn't say anything. He just stands there, hands in his pockets, staring up at Sammy like he doesn't speak the same language, like he can't be bothered trying.

'The police are on their way, Mark. They'll be here any second. You need to go along with this. Make them see you weren't involved. You've your whole life ahead of you, son. Plenty of time to turn things round and start again. Please. If not for me, then for your mother.'

Mark shifts his weight from one foot to the other, takes his hand from his pocket and looks at his watch, ever so casually, as if checking the time for a television programme about to start.

'You don't need to worry about getting caught up in this. They don't have anything on you. I've burnt it all on the barbecue and cleaned out your room so there's no evidence. I'll say it was all me, Mark. I don't mind doing it. I'm your dad. It's what I'm meant to do.'

Mark looks Sammy straight in the eye. His face is like a concrete block. There is no warmth in it. It's hard to tell if he's even listening. 'Jesus, Dad,' he finally says. 'It's not the seventies any more. People don't burn things in their back gardens. The police'll take one look at the place and know it was me, not you. You haven't the intelligence to do what I've done. Did you really think you could swan in here like Christ on a cross and take the blame? You're an even bigger idiot than I thought you were.'

The clock in the lounge starts calling out the hour. One. Two. Three. Four. Five. Six. Seven. Eight. Nine. Ten metallic thuds, the sound of each hour muffled as it makes its way from the back of the house to the front, through such thick, thick air.

'Sorry,' Sammy says.

It comes sneaking out of his mouth before he can stop it.

'Sorry,' he says, a second time and louder.

Up come the sadness and the strong regret. But he isn't sorry for Mark. He will not apologize to him. He's only sorry for himself now and for all the years he's spent lugging his guilt round, like a dead leg. Making amends. Holding himself responsible. Looking at the boy and seeing only his own ugly reflection. Mark is nothing to do with him. He can see that now. No chip off his block. No bad seed. No second coming. Mark is his own monster.

Sammy steps away from the boy, climbs another stair so he's towering over him. Up comes the rage and the old blood thumping. Up comes the clean white anger. Up come the fists. First the right. Then the left. He draws back his arm and drives the weight of himself hard into his son's face. He hears the crunch of bones snapping, the wet slap of tongue against cheek and, in the distance, drawing closer, a host of holy sirens screaming through the night. He keeps hitting and kicking and clawing until he can no longer feel the hot blood thundering round his head. The breath goes first, for he's not as fit as he once was. Shortly afterwards the rage has passed and he can hardly remember how he got there, broken-knuckled, dripping with his own son's blood.

Mark is still standing. He sways in front of Sammy, left then slowly right and left again, like a twelfth-round boxer trying to find his feet. Behind him, blossoming through the front door's frosted glass, Sammy can see the neon blue flare of police cars announcing their urgent presence. He has hardly any time left with his son. All the air is coming out of Mark, in gasps and throaty wheezes. He is the colour of dirty paper. His head droops. His legs buckle and Sammy only just catches him before he hits the floor. They sink together, backs braced against the hall radiator, Sammy cradling his son in the crook of his arms. He holds the boy tightly against his chest. Like Christ just off the cross in medieval paintings. He has so much to say to him. All the needy questions. All the very-sorries. All the things he might do differently if such a thing as start again could ever be. There's no time for any of it. The police are at the door now, yelling through a megaphone, waking the neighbours, surrounding the house with dogs and guns.

There is so little time. No space left for fixing. Nothing that can be done with words.

Sammy looks at Mark and he cannot see a bad man, only a little boy lost and broken, only a thing he has lifted his fists to and ruined. The red of blood is smeared across his face, dripping down his chin, pooling in dark smears across his shirtfront. He goes fishing up his sleeve for a tissue. He hokes it out, wets it with his own mouth juice, and tries to bring the whiteness back into the boy's face. His hand dabbing gently at Mark's split lip remembers this gesture from years ago: so many cut knees tenderly plastered, faces washed, cowlicks dampened down with Daddy's spit. His hands know how to work this fragile moment. His arms are strong enough to hold it. He feels closer to his son than he has for decades. He knows him, surface skin to devil core. And this feeling is not love but something more essential, like the knowing of his own bastard head. And he would do anything to keep him here, safe and docile, held within his arms. Close. Closer. Close as a just-born infant.

Sammy is still holding his son when the police break down

the door and cart Mark, unconscious, into the street. His shoes come off as they drag him across the front lawn. His naked heels leave track marks in the flowerbeds. Sammy watches from the doorstep, horrified. He cannot turn away. He cannot bear the sight of strange men holding his boy all wrong, not even caring about his poor face grazing against the gravel. He knows without reason or regret that he will still be feeling the heavy burn of Mark years later, still carrying the dead weight of him in his blood and bones. For this is what it is to be a father and he cannot give back the privilege.

19

Cut

IT IS THE day of Sophie's 'operation'. I've marked the date on our kitchen calendar, making a little X beside the day I've chosen: a Friday, the last of the month. I can't risk writing the word 'operation'. It feels too explicit. Besides, Christine might see and ask questions. I'd have no good answer for her. No believable excuse. It's harder to evade a question, to mumble half-truths or change the subject, when every conversation is written down in solid, indefensible ink.

I've walked past the calendar five or six times each day for almost a week. Every time my eye catches on that sharp little X, as if it is a barb on a steel wire fence. It hurts just to look at it sideways. Eventually I take a marker and change it from an X to a tiny star, which is less threatening, less like a crossing-out of something precious. I still know what the mark means, though. My eye still strays towards it every time I fill the kettle or empty the dishwasher. I want to throw the calendar out, but I can't – can't even push it temporarily to the back of a drawer. I need that little star, twinkling, twinkling through the everyday muddle of electricity bills and grocery reminders, to keep me pinned to Friday. The last Friday of summer. The end of one time and the beginning of another.

I have asked for a few days' leave. I've told Marty I want to make the most of the bank-holiday weekend. 'I'd like to spend some time with my daughter,' I say. 'She's growing up so quickly. I feel like I'm missing all the good bits.'

The other doctors understand. They have children too. They've noticed the way time goes swimming past, blurring baby steps into first teeth and school starts, until there you are, depositing your almost adult child at the university gates with no sharp memory of the moments between.

'You're just right, Jonathan,' they say, 'enjoy every second of her while she's still little.'

They're relieved to see that I'm softer round the edges since Sophie. I laugh easier now. I take more time with my patients and occasionally remember to ask what other people are doing with their weekends. When I say the word 'daughter' there's a kind of shyness in my voice, like the way a religious person sounds when saying 'God'.

The lady receptionists are all chat today. Their enthusiasm expands to fit whatever space is available. This afternoon they're standing on the edge of a long weekend, the chitter of them rising and rising as the clock twitches closer to five.

'And how is the wee pet keeping?' they ask, trapping me against the staffroom wall with their hot coffee mugs and their false-nailed fingers.

'Any teeth yet?'

'Do the pair of youse have plans for the long weekend?'

'Yes,' I say. 'We have plans.'

I don't elaborate. Less is more when you're dealing in lies. I smile at the lady receptionists. I'm careful not to focus on anyone in particular. They can be dreadfully territorial in their affection.

'Have a lovely weekend, ladies,' I say. 'Don't do anything I wouldn't do.'

And I'm off, past the reception desk, across the car park and into the safety of my own car. I lock the door behind me. Click. Clunk. It's not even dark out but I feel the need to place an extra wall between myself and anything that may try to interfere with the plan. Car-jackers. Crazy patients. Lady receptionists knocking politely on the passenger window, wondering if they might beg a lift to the other side of the East. Damn them all. Tonight my door is locked. Tonight nothing is going to come between me and Sophie.

In my medical bag I have local anaesthetic, sterile needles and antibiotics, just in case the child picks up an infection. I've also lifted the photograph of Sophie from my desk. If something goes wrong, I'll never darken the health centre again and I wouldn't want her photo, still there without me, possibly binned with my left-behind biros. I'm not clear exactly what constitutes being 'struck off' and don't want to raise suspicions by asking Marty for clarification. I imagine it's a process comparable to excommunication. I have specific questions. If struck off, would I still be able to administer basic first-aid assistance if I happened to stumble into an accident? Would I be able to give Sophie Calpol or cough syrup if she were ill? Would a plaster, applied to a cut knee, be too much like actual doctoring?

I know that being struck off is a very real possibility. Also prison. Or possibly lynching if the paramilitary elements get wind of what I've done. The lads in the East don't take kindly to grown men fiddling with children, and it's not as if I can explain the why of what I'm planning to do. Most ordinary people would struggle to understand the necessity of cutting out your own child's tongue. Most people don't have a child like Sophie and I suspect that those who do – the unfortunate parents of Unfortunate Children and those Unfortunate Children old enough to speak up for themselves – value their anonymity too highly to advocate in my defence. I know I'm on my own if anything goes wrong tonight. Even if it goes right, I'm going to have to come up with the mother of all stories to cover myself. I've thought about this. We'll probably have to move to a place where no one knows us, where people will think Sophie was born deformed.

I take a last long look at the health centre's front door before pulling out of the car park. My head is like bottled water, cold and still. I am my former distant self, not caring if I never see Marty again, or the lady receptionist with the pleasant smile, not giving a second thought to the possibility of my spider plant, binned, and my office passed on to a recently graduated doctor. I'm not even bothered about losing my patients. But the Garfield mug is different. I have a real attachment to that mug. So, I've thieved it from the staffroom, my first actual crime of the evening, a practice run for all the misdemeanours to come. I test my conscience over the mug. There isn't a single twist of guilt in me, even though it actually belongs to Marty. It will be different with Sophie. The thought of her, cut and stuck with needles, is already weighing on me. I toss my bag into the back seat, where I can't see it and feel any worse than I already do.

On the way home I stop at Connswater Tesco to pick up a fancy pizza and a bottle of wine. Christine will still be there when I get in and I don't want to make her suspicious. On Friday night I almost always have pizza, or chips from the chipper on the Newtownards Road. Weekend food, the sort of thing almost everyone in the East consumes on a Friday evening. I like to stand in line beside the other shoppers, holding my wine and pizza proudly, tucking a garlic-bread baton under my arm, like a rolled umbrella, as I wait for a self-service checkout to come free. Better still, if I'm juggling a box of Sophie's nappies or formula milk. This is when I feel closest to normal, like a spy who's managed to go unnoticed among the locals. I've not yet chanced conversation with my fellow shoppers, but I've practised in my head: 'What about that rain?'; 'Thank God it's Friday'; 'The wee one's had me up all night.' It doesn't sound forced when I talk about Sophie. It sounds like I'm actually speaking the native tongue.

I've no intention of consuming any pizza tonight but, still, here I am, standing in the pizza aisle, deliberating between goats' cheese and buffalo mozzarella. I hold one box in each hand and feel the refrigerated cardboard sag beneath the weight of uncooked dough. I feel vaguely nauseous. Which of these two pizzas do I want? I feel the sweat begin to slime around the collar of my shirt. This hasn't happened in months. A full-blown panic attack is imminent. Yes, it's only a four pounds seventy-nine sort of decision, but I know that if I don't choose one pizza or the other, I'll be similarly stuck between Merlot and Shiraz, incapable of deciding which side of the drive to park on, and then, after all the little choices slip past, I'll be frozen when it comes to the biggest decision of all: to cut or not to cut, and just how deep to go.

Breathe, I tell myself, and try to hear the pulse ticking in my ears. Breathe and breathe, and now there are little dents in the cardboard from where my fingers have held the pizza boxes too tightly. I'll have to shove the one I'm not buying to the back of the fridge so no one notices. I want to fling the damn pizzas, like damp Frisbees, all the way down the aisle and into the fresh-fruit section. But I don't. I force my shuttering tongue still and, turning to the Tesco lady, who's stacking individual tubs of marinara sauce in the next refrigerator down, ask, 'Which of these pizzas would you recommend?'

'Chorizo,' she says, pronouncing the word like there is an eye in the middle of it. Even though I'm all in bits with the stress, I still notice and imagine the chorizo an actual saucy eye winking up from its mozzarella bed. The buck is passed. I feel relieved and also ashamed. What sort of full-grown adult cannot decide between one pizza and another? Still, I've calmed down a bit. The wine is much easier to pick. And the journey home is without incident. I don't even have to choose which side of the drive to park on because Christine's car is already taking up the space closest to the door. By the time I'm stepping over the Welcome mat, I'm hardly sweating at all.

Before I can even get my key out, Christine opens the door. She has Sophie hipped against her left side, an empty bottle in her right hand. She smiles – no hands free for signing hello – and passes the baby to me. I hold her awkwardly. My hands are full of medical bag, coat and groceries shoved carelessly into a Tesco carrier. For ease of transport, I have stuffed the wine precariously into my blazer pocket. It leans away from my side, like a man about to leap from a hotel window. I feel the tipping weight of it starting to gain momentum. Sophie is just another thing for me to hold but somehow I find the arms for her and curl her into the crook of my elbow, like a little anchor.

Every other part of my day is just a preamble to this moment. The evening reunion with my little girl. She smells of milk, baby urine and Calvin Klein perfume because Christine has been holding her all day against herself. I drop my bags and parcels on to the floor, lift my daughter to my face and kiss the dark swirl of her hair and the back of her curled fist, the precise spot where her cheek begins to pucker into her mouth. She is milk-drunk, her lips still dreaming about the suck and thrust of the teat.

I look at her lips. The quiet pink colour of them, the caving wideness of their yawn, the deep wrinkles folded into both upper and lower lip where the flesh has yet to fully inflate. I touch her lips with the tip of my smallest finger and think about the man in the Bible – Old Testament most likely – whose lips were burnt by an angel with hot coal. Holiness was the point of this story, or maybe not talking too much in front of God, or perhaps a little of both. I touch Sophie's lips again and wonder how something so small, no bigger than a beach shell, could possibly ruin everything.

Christine returns with a notepad and cocks her head towards the kitchen as if to say, 'Follow me.' We lean over the breakfast bar as she scribbles down their day. It has been an inconsequential sort of day: regular feeds, regular naps, nothing too startling in the nappy department. I draw a little smiley face with my left hand. The smiley face looks like a stroke victim's, not smiling so much as grimacing intently. I switch Sophie to my left arm so I can write properly.

'Anything else?' I write.

'Did you see they got the Fire Starter?' Christine writes. 'It was on the news at lunchtime.'

'No,' I write. I've been so preoccupied with Sophie I haven't listened to the news today, haven't even let myself eavesdrop on the usual staffroom discussion of it.

'Who was it?'

I'm all of a sudden right back inside myself, sharply present, recalling Sammy, in his mismatched tracksuit, slouched against my desk, incapable of holding his sadness in.

'Some young lad called Mark something or other.'

'Agnew?'

'Aye, Agnew! That's his name. How did you know?'

I think quickly. Lying comes so easily to me, these days. 'I must have heard it on the radio and not realized.'

'That's always happening to me,' writes Christine. 'But with watching TV . . .' and she starts scribbling down some anecdote about how she always has the subtitled news running in the background, how she knows stuff without knowing she knows it, like the fact that Angela Merkel is the chancellor of Germany, all the different palaces the Queen owns and other irrelevant stuff. The way she only realizes she knows this stuff when she's out with her friends at the pub quiz and, hey presto, all the answers come to her. 'It's like I'm getting smart by osmosis,' she finishes.

I'm only half reading what she's written. I'm miles away, wondering if Sammy slept easy last night. If the weight lifts once the worst has happened. I wonder if he still feels responsible now the damage has been taken out of his son.

'You have to go now,' I write.

It's hard not to be blunt when you're scribbling everything on a notepad. I know Christine won't take offence at this. Our conversations are often reduced to the barest bones of meaning. I add another smiley face just to be sure, and to let her know I've enjoyed her anecdote. She gives me a thumbs-up and kisses Sophie on the forehead. I wonder if this kind of ordinary kitchen moment will ever happen again. I start moving round the room quickly, tidying away the groceries, placing my bag on the counter, rinsing out Sophie's bottle in preparation for the sterilizer. I'm keeping myself occupied so the sadness has less chance of sinking its teeth in. I return to the notepad. 'I'm off next week,' I write, 'so we won't need you.'

Sad-face emoticon from Christine.

'I'll still pay you.'

She smiles: a real-life smile, with her actual face. 'It's not the money. I'll miss Sophie.'

Our conversation has reached the end of the paper. There's a brief pause while I rip off the sheet, bin it and begin again at the top of the notepad. If I was speaking this conversation I'd say something along the lines of 'Listen, Christine, I don't know how to explain this, it's very complicated, but the chances are Sophie's going to be sick for quite a while, and I'll need to look after her myself. Thank goodness I'm a doctor. It's nothing to worry about, and of course I'll make sure you're reimbursed fully while we don't need your services, but I can't tell you much more than that. You've been an amazing help . . . No, more than a help, a great friend to Sophie and me, and we really appreciate all your support. I wish I could give you a more definite idea of the time frame, but I don't know myself. It could be a week. It could be six months. It all depends on Sophie. I hope you understand and that you'll come back and look after her as soon as she's recovered, but I'll understand if you want to find something else.'

If Christine was crying then, or even looking like tears might be imminent, I'd probably hug her in a fatherly kind of way, carefully avoiding too much contact with her breasts, making sure to break the embrace first so I could not afterwards be accused of enjoying it too much. But I can't talk to Christine. I am, at the basest level, a snivelling coward. So, I don't mention any illness, any deviation from the usual plan. Instead I write, 'See you Monday week,' all the time knowing this is highly unlikely.

'No probs,' writes Christine. Then she grabs her coat from the banister, lifts her books and bag, and flies out of the door before I can make any sort of occasion of it. I feel as if I have, in some unspecified way, robbed her.

I carry Sophie to the front window and flail my free arm wildly until I catch Christine's attention. Then I make the sign for goodbye and the sign for each of the nine letters in her name. This is something I've learnt off the internet. I was saving it for a special occasion: a birthday or some sort of argument. I use it now like a kind of compensation. Christine might never see either of us again but, hey-ho, isn't it lovely that I've learnt how to sign her name properly? She smiles through the windscreen of her car, through the front window and right into my living room. She signs 'Goodbye, Sophie, goodbye, Jonathan.' I feel the need to sit down quickly. It isn't dizziness that has overcome me so much as sadness, the weight of everything being finally wonderful and probably ruined.

I prop Sophie at the far end of the sofa and wedge her in with a rolled-up blanket. She looks directly at me, then turns her fat little head to look over my shoulder, her eye catching on something just behind the lamp. I turn. There isn't anything obvious there. Only a framed IKEA print. I hump my shoulders and raise my hands, making my face say, 'What are you looking at?' without using any words. Sophie says nothing. She never does.

This isn't the first time I've caught her staring at something I can't see. I wonder if this is normal for babies. Perhaps their not-quite-focused eyes are more sensitive to light waves and shadows. Or perhaps she isn't built like other babies. Maybe she'll always be susceptible to the unseen side of things. Ghosts. Visions. Holy Spirit prophecies. It's the not knowing I can't bear, the will-she-won't-she side of Sophie, which has me watching every inch of her progress for clues.

- Today she cries in the bath. She won't tolerate water on her head for washing the shampoo out. Surely this is a good thing. A point on the side of humanity.
- Today her hair seems twice as long as yesterday and swirls down her back in a long, dark river, more like a tail than hair. More like something you'd see in a fairytale book. Not good. Not good at all.
- Today she has an appetite for liquids unrivalled in any child I've ever doctored. This seems problematic. It's milk she goes for rather than water, and even the youngest school child knows mammals drink milk, not sea creatures. Unless of course you count whales. I choose not to.
- Today she looks exactly like my mother when my mother is perturbed. A victory for the human case, but a somewhat Pyrrhic one.

I can't hold out any longer. It's not the waiting that's wearing me thin. I've spent my entire life waiting for some unspecified thing to happen. Another year or two won't kill me. It's the watching I can no longer bear.

I carry Sophie into the kitchen and hold her up in front of the calendar. I point out the little star in the box marked Friday, 29 August, and, though I know she can't possibly understand what it means, the whole plan feels definite now, like a show we are already holding tickets for. Not till later. Not till it's dark outside. This isn't procrastination so much as shame. I can't picture myself hurting her in the full light of day. In the shadows, with the curtains pulled, the cutting and sewing and bloody mess of it all seem much more believable, like a thing you might actually do to another person in the dark.

I want whiskey. To steady my head. To sweat out the fear. I can't have whiskey. My hand must be iron tonight. My muscles must be perfectly tight. I put the kettle on instead, make myself tea in the stolen Garfield mug and wait for the darkness to descend. The fear is particularly loud now. Old fears and brand-new versions of the same tight pain. The breath rush. The sweats. The sheer stomach-turning sickness of it. The fear of failing and the fear of succeeding. The fear of ruining a good, true thing. The fear of people and the fear of lacking people. The fear of cutting too soon, too deep, not deep enough. Loudest of all, the fear of losing my little girl.

Last night I dreamt about Sophie's mother. I haven't had this dream in months. I thought I was shot of it. I'm still not sure it was a dream but the idea of her here in our house again is a hideous thing to consider. If she's capable of coming and going as she likes, through locked doors and double-glazed windows, up the water pipes for all I know, she is also capable of snatching Sophie. I haven't the hope left to deal with this possibility tonight. All my will is presently focused on the cut and afterwards the cleaning up. I choose to call it a dream and press on. After the operation, Sophie will be one hundred per cent mine. Her mother and her mother's shrill kind won't want anything to do with a tongueless child. It's for her own good, I tell myself, another excuse to add to my slim list.

I try to drag my thoughts away from the dream but the memory of it won't leave me be. It started with a phone call to work. The familiar voice saying, 'I'm dying, you'll have to come and save me.'

The urge in me rising up, incapable of doing the sensible thing. Hearing myself say, 'I'm on my way. Where are you?'

And that unearthly laugh of hers, like crystal chandeliers, shivering. 'Oh, you don't need directions,' she says. 'Just follow the river.'

Then I'm in my car, or is it some kind of boat? The sides of it blur in and out of focus, as if it is made of clouds or a sort of cloudy material. I am driving/swimming/flying up the Lagan towards her.

I can't separate her voice from the sound of the city clamouring round me: the sirens, the chatter, the engines thundering up and down the ring road. It all bleeds into one diaphanous melody, and I wonder if this is the sound of her finally raising her voice to sing. Up the Lagan I go. And all around, on either side of its filthy banks, Belfast is burning. Tall flames lick the night sky. People, silhouetted against the red, hurl themselves off the Albert Bridge, their arms and legs forming crosses as they drop into the river below. The heat is unbearable, and the sound of people crying. It is a very particular kind of hell and she is at the centre of it all, sitting pale-skin-naked on the riverbank. Bold Siren of a woman, with her hair come loose, snaking down her back.

'I did all this,' she says, with not a note of shame. 'I raised my voice and ruined everything.' Dream me knows she isn't lying.

In the pit of my belly I feel the same tight knot of lust and fear coil and uncoil, like clenching fists. I remember this feeling from every second I have ever spent in her presence. The darkness of it; the unspeakable lightness. I hate her as I have never hated a person or creature in my entire life, yet still lie down beside her, right there in the mud. The taste of her mouth is saltwater brine and beneath it something sour, like the smell that rises off a corpse on the third or fourth day.

'What do you want me to do?' I ask. I hope she will not answer for I won't be able to hold myself back. I will do vile and terrible things if she asks me to. I don't know myself every time she opens her mouth.

I wake then with the fur of her baulking on my tongue, the vomit already climbing up my throat. I make a mad dash down the corridor to the bathroom, lift the toilet seat and empty myself into it. Chunks of carrot and boiled potato bob around the bowl, swimming jauntily through my unflushed piss. I don't turn the light on for fear of waking fully, and not being able to get back to sleep. I swill my mouth out with cold water and spit. I towel the sweat off my face and turn to leave the bathroom.

This is when I notice the bath, full to the brim and dripping down the sides. This is when I see her hair, swimming darkly through the water, her features blurred as if viewed through a wedding veil. I step back sharply, clipping my foot on the radiator's edge. No blood, but a good chunk of skin comes cleanly away. She sits up suddenly. The water rushes off her head and over her breasts, dripping on to the bathmat and the floor. A whole row of shampoo bottles, upset by her sudden appearance, topple off the bath's rim and go bobbing drunkenly round the tub.

'What do you want?' I ask. (It's hard to stop myself getting into the tub beside her.)

'Not you, that's for sure,' she says, and looks me up and down scathingly, as you would a second-hand car. I feel the insult of this run down my spine and into my groin. I wish I didn't care.

'I wanted a bath,' she says.

'Mission accomplished. Now get out of my house.'

'I left something behind,' she says. 'Did you keep it for me?'

'Your clothes?' I ask, playing for time. 'You didn't have anything but the clothes on your back.'

'Maybe that's it,' she says. 'It's hard to remember details when you're constantly dying. But I feel like I left something else here, something much more precious.'

'No,' I say, 'you're mistaken.' It takes all my head-set strength to lie to her. My blood is already up, rushing to my face. I'm flushed with the effort of holding it all in. I make myself think of Sophie. The way she is mine now for the rest of our living time. For birthdays and Christmases. Beach holidays to come. Also for everyday ordinary being. Tesco trips and homework. Head colds and temper tantrums. The way I can no longer imagine any kind of existence without her. The thought of Sophie is both a shield and a distraction. I feel her dragging at me, tugging me insistently by the hand/arm/hope-thick place, so I'm caught between wrong and right, like a tug of war.

'She's not yours to keep,' she says. 'She's one of us.'

'No,' I say, voice wobbling slightly. 'She's not like you. She's just a little girl, no badness in her.'

'Wait till she starts talking. There's not a man in this city that girl couldn't destroy if she wanted to.'

'You're wrong,' I say. But there's no certainty in the way I say it. No way of talking her down.

I turn away from the bathtub. Avert my eyes. Cover my ears. Thing she is. Vile thing. Siren. Beast. I can no longer see her as Sophie's mother. She is a creature to me, nothing more. Nothing like my little girl. And yet I cannot trust myself in her presence. Not if she rises naked from the bathtub. Not if she stands in front of me, milk white, wet and maybe singing. I'm not strong enough. No man is.

I force myself to walk away. My feet are dead weights shuffling. The draw of her is all the way into my bone marrow. Tugging. Sucking. Dragging at my goodwill. My whole body is ripping in two but I press on. Out of the bathroom. Down the hall. Past the nursery where Sophie is sleeping quietly on her back. When I turn around the bathroom is empty. She has left me again. My next breath is thin with relief, the breath that follows it something like a howl.

'You're still dreaming,' I tell myself, and go back to bed. I don't sleep until just before daybreak, and wake at five thirty to the sound of Sophie fussing in the next room. The bathmat is still damp, but isn't that always the case with bathmats, unless you hang them over a radiator? The shampoos are back where they belong, soldiered along the rim of the tub. But she could have done this herself, just to confuse me. I sniff my way round the bathroom, trying to nose out the presence of salt. I smell it on the towels, or maybe it's just my senses playing tricks. I think about checking my heel for a cut but don't. It's easier to believe it all a mind trick. Especially today. With every part of me wanting to run away.

Now it is dark. I rise and draw the curtains. I am already wearing a clean white T-shirt and tracksuit bottoms lifted straight from the laundry. I smell of detergent and, beneath this, sweat. I unplug the phone at the wall and turn my mobile to silent. I feel as if I'm in a movie, a thriller of some sort with police and gangsters hovering round the edge. This is a good feeling: it drags me outside reality to a place where I can wield a scalpel, cut out my daughter's tongue and afterwards comfort myself with the knowledge that all this, even the pain, was a kind of fiction.

I fetch all my medical equipment from the places where I've stashed it round the house. Gauze bandages. Anaesthetic. Scalpels. Sterile needles and stitches. One of those little mouth masks that keep the surgeon's breath off a patient. A surgical bandanna for holding my hair back. I arrange everything on a card table in the spare room. Slipping each item out of its plastic sheath, I place it in a kidney dish. I've bought a brand-new Tupperware box for Sophie's tongue. It is the smallest of all the Tupperware options on sale at Tesco. According to the packaging, it can be used for storing condiments, small portions of dried fruit or spices. It is perfectly adequate for holding an infant-sized human tongue. Afterwards I plan to toss it into the sea. There's a certain symmetry to this action.

Sophie is asleep in her cot. She's been dopy since Christine left. I've dosed her up on Calpol and Nurofen. She's not yet ill or in any pain but the medicine will keep her docile while I administer the anaesthetic. I lift my daughter out of her sleep and jiggle her gently in my arms until she is fully awake. She is a good baby and wakes happy from even the longest nap. Within seconds she's grinning and playing with the tips of her fingers, curling her toes up into her mouth, making contented-baby noises. I can't keep my eyes off her. She is the most perfect thing I've ever seen and I'm about to steal this perfection from her. To permanently flaw her and give her a scar she will carry for the rest of her life. She smiles up at me, reaches for my face. It would almost be easier if she screamed.

I strip her and place her in the baby bath. I keep a hand behind her neck, supporting her head and begin to soap her slowly all over, running a soft flannel over the mound of her belly, round her back and legs. It's important that she's clean tonight. Sterile. The operation itself isn't that dangerous but afterwards there's a terrible risk from infection and I don't have the means to deal with this at home. Any outside intervention means losing Sophie. They won't give her back after they've seen what I've done. Why would they? There's no way I could pass this off as an accident: the neatness of the incision, the stitches – practised to perfection on a cold pork joint – the anaesthetic floating round her system, evidence of premeditation. I understand that everything must go perfectly tonight. I don't have a back-up plan.

I lift Sophie from the bath, towel her dry and fasten her into a clean nappy. She curls into the space between my neck and shoulder, like a cat nuzzling my heat. This is when I almost stop myself. This is when my will begins to sap. I hold her out at arms' length, fully lit beneath the bathroom light, and force myself to see the Siren in her.

The glossy black hair, dry now, but never without the look of wetness.

The unbroken skin on her heels and palms, smooth as a sea-buffed pebble.

The love of water.

The closeness of her eyes. The way they dance around beneath their lids, never for a moment resting, as her mother's eyes once danced up at me from the bathtub.

The beauty of her, which is like a fire I cannot look away from.

I wish for the false courage of prayer. I wish once again for whiskey. There is nothing for me to lean upon but the over-played notion that this, even this, is in the child's best interest. I carry her into the spare room where everything is sterile and covered with freshly laundered white towels. I've rigged a series of desk lamps to hang over my operating space, illuminating every inch of Sophie's head. There is so much light in the room it feels like the future.

I place my daughter on the bed, directly beneath the lamps. She begins to squirm away from their brightness. Her eyes are furious and blinking. I block her in with pillows so there's no place for her to roll. When she is fully under, I will pin her head down with surgical tape so she's perfectly still throughout. I turn away from her to prepare the anaesthetic, pausing at the mirror to fix my bandanna and mouth mask. Only my eyes are visible now. I don't recognize myself in the mirror and this is a kind of comfort. Another man will do this horrible thing to Sophie, and when she sees me next there will be no association. Nothing to link me to the pain and the taste of blood pooling at the back of her throat. Nothing she can hold against me when she's fully grown.

I lift the first needle of the evening. I hold it to the light and ease the plunger upwards until a tiny bead of liquid appears on the nib. I flick it twice with my fingernail, allowing myself to hide behind the routine of it all. How many injections have I given in the last twelve years? How many times have I said, 'Sharp scratch, that's all,' and watched the patient wince their shoulders away from me? Dozens. Hundreds. Thousands. But none of those injections have mattered like this injection. None of them cost me anything at all.

I turn back to the bed. I stand over my beautiful daughter as she blinks up at me, almost naked and terrified. I reach for her wrist and the place where the needle will go sliding into her tiny vein. She looks up and she does not see me. She sees a monster man in my place. A hooded, half-masked creature with his arm raised over her. She opens her mouth and roars. The sound that comes out almost kills me with its intensity.

One syllable.

'Da.'

The possibility of an infinite number of syllables to come.

For now, just one syllable, like a snub-nosed bullet piercing my ribcage and moving upwards. Lungs. Heart. Head. Every part of me succumbs. I feel the same familiar knot of thrill and fear coil and uncoil, like clenching fists inside my belly. This is exactly the same way her mother made me smart and soar. This is the way I will be ruined. And it is godawful raw to know myself so helpless. And it is also glorious. It's impossible to stop it now. Like holding back the Lagan with one hand. I should have covered my ears but it's too late. I've already heard her and nothing now can ever be simple again. Everything will be on Sophie's terms. There isn't anything I won't do for her. No reasonable limit to what she can ask. I drop the needle. It rolls away from me and comes to rest beneath the bed. I pull the mask away from my left ear so it hangs like a hinged door from one side of my face. Every part of me is liquid and rushing towards my child.

'Sophie,' I say, lifting her from the bed, pressing her close to my face, 'talk to me, Sophie. Daddy's here.'

I know she will destroy me. I wouldn't have it any other way.

Acknowledgements

It is a very fortunate thing to find yourself with far too many people to thank.

Thank you to everyone who made this book possible in little ways and big. Thank you to the trio of wonderful women who saw its potential and encouraged me every step along the way: Fiona Murphy at Doubleday, Alice Youell (the world's kindest editor), and my amazing agent, Kate Johnson, who has been an absolute joy to know and work with since the very first day our paths crossed. Thank you also to Brian Langan for early encouragement and kind words.

Thank you to those incredible individuals who have offered friendship, encouragement and support for years now: Sinead Morrissey, Damian Smyth, Peggy Hughes, Michael Nolan, Paul Maddern, Jean Bleakney, Bernie McGill, Nate Grubbs, David Torrans, Andrew Eaton, Emma Wright and many others. Every wise word has been thoroughly appreciated.

Thank you to all the hundreds of artists and arts organizations who make Belfast the absolute best place to practise art in community. It's always a comfort to know I have good people to come home to. I am particularly grateful for the ongoing friendship and support of Eastside Arts, No Alibis, the Lifeboat, the

Queen's Film Theatre, the Crescent Arts Centre and the John Hewitt Society.

A huge thank-you to the power women who keep me sane on a daily basis: Emma Must, Hilary Copeland, Orla McAdam, Emily DeDakis, Cailin Lynn, Kelly McCaughrain, Hannah McPhillimy, Kristen Kernaghan, Olwyn Dowling. This place would fall apart without you.

Thank you to the Arts Council NI and Seedbed NI for financial support and guidance over the last number of years.

Thank you to my family for putting up with an awful lot and always coming back for more.

And a final heartfelt thank-you to the two unnamed baristas in Costa, Waverley Station, Edinburgh, who found the laptop containing this manuscript three days after it went missing. This book, quite literally, wouldn't have happened without you.

Photo © Jonathan Ryder

JAN CARSON is a writer and community arts facilitator based in Belfast. Her first novel, *Malcolm Orange Disappears*, was published in 2014 to critical acclaim, followed by a short story collection, *Children's Children* (2016), and a flash fiction anthology, *Postcard Stories* (2017). Her work has appeared in numerous journals and on BBC Radio 3 and 4. In 2016 she won the *Harper's Bazaar* short story competition and was shortlisted for the Seán Ó Faoláin Short Story Prize. She specializes in running arts projects and events with older people, especially those living with dementia. *The Fire Starters* is her second novel.